Cruel Designs

Cruel Designs

Cherry Wilder

PIATKUS

Copyright © 1988 by Cherry Wilder

First published in Great Britain in 1988 by
Judy Piatkus (Publishers) Ltd of
5 Windmill Street, London W1

British Library Cataloguing in Publication Data

Wilder, Cherry
 Cruel designs.
 I. Title
 823 [F]

ISBN 0-86188-764-6

Phototypeset in Times Compugraphic by
Action Typesetting Gloucester
Printed and bound in Great Britain by
Mackays of Chatham PLC, Chatham, Kent

PART ONE

Summer

Chapter 1

Without Warning

It was a hot summer evening; the clock on the Lutherplatz showed six o'clock, eighteen hundred hours. Kate finished her shopping and headed for the car park. The warm streets, some with decorative new cobblestones, were full of tanned, lightly dressed people. Germans loved the sun and soaked up as much as they could.

Kate stopped outside a florists's shop and gazed at the massed roses, the tiger lilies, the tender green of the indoor plants. She picked out an Alpine Violet, in pink, not too big or too showy, just the thing to take as a present to a new neighbour. She saw a row of pottery containers, used to hide the homely plastic flower-pots. They were creamy white, ranging from small to very large, all bearing the motif of a tree swirling round the vessel, its branches forming the handles on either side. Yes, the potter was paying homage to Art Nouveau, the *Jugendstil,* the spirit that infused the whole of Europe, from the tea-rooms of Glasgow to the lamps of the Paris Métro, more than seventy years ago.

The smallest *cachepot,* not much larger than a coffee mug, was just six marks. Very suitable. Her new neighbours were only there for the summer. This would give Mary Limbard something to take home to America as a memento of her German summer in the Villa Florian.

As she emerged from the florist's carrying the pink Alpine violet, a hearty American voice assailed her: 'Hello there, Kate!'

She slipped the wrapped pot-plant into her cloth satchel, juggling the plastic bag from the supermarket.

'Hi, there!'

They loomed up with the sun at their backs. Cindy Saxon was nearly as tall as Kate herself, and the Major, in civvies, towered genially over both women. They stepped into the mouth of an alley, out of the way of the shoppers.

'My word, aren't you the lucky one,' said Cindy, 'to have our dear Jason Limbard right over the road.'

'I'm a great fan of his,' said Kate. 'I thought I might go over and ask Mary Limbard to coffee.'

'Well, honey, I wish you luck,' said Cindy.

She was well-preserved, every inch an officer's wife, a little too WASP-y for Kate's liking but the Major was a nice man. He sent his regards to Frau Kramer, Kate's aunt by marriage.

'When *we* were renting the Villa Florian,' he said, 'she was the soul of kindness.'

'Always popping over with German plum cake,' said Cindy. 'Does she still have that black cat?'

'Yes.'

Kate tried to picture Tante Adelheid as a witch and failed.

'Must go,' she said. 'I want to get out of that car park before six-thirty.'

'Don't tell me you're driving the old van!' said Cindy.

Kate drove out of Breitbach, past the ruined walls and the watchtower, then through green fields tangled with wild flowers. She passed small garden plots and garden houses then turned up a tree-lined street at the base of the Steinberg. Tomorrow she would march over the road with her Alpine violet and accost Mary Limbard at her kitchen sink. Were the kitchen cupboards still decorated with vineleaves?

Kate knew the Villa Florian well, knew it from books; she understood how it had been – a temple of Art Nouveau, a jewel of the *Jugendstil*. The desks, chairs, clocks, porcelain, the precious glassware, the lamps, were a matter of record, displayed in museums or cherished in private collections. She had been taken round the empty villa once at Christmas time by Tante Adelheid. It was cold and strange but still beautiful; the glass cupola, the two hexagons in the east, the snowy expanse of the north lawn with one lone blue *tannen*. All the rooms were of moderate size, none of them uncomfortably grand, and on the stairs there was a breaking wave of wrought iron, curling higher at every step. . . .

Kate saw the boy at the roadside with his broken bike and drew up the van before she recognised him. He was a big boy carrying too much weight, a fat kid, clutching a plastic bag from the supermarket. Wasn't he a little too old to be red-faced, almost in tears, with a bent front wheel and the knee out of his jeans?

'Hello there!' said Kate. 'Can I help you?'

He said something that might have been: 'Hit a rock. . . .'

Kate stopped the motor and got out.

'I'm Kate Reimann,' she said. 'And you're Buddy Limbard, right? Did you hurt yourself? Are you okay?'

'Yes, Ma'am,' he said. 'I'm fine. But the wheel is kinda bent.'

'I'm sure it can be fixed,' she said. 'There's a good bike shop in the town. Let's get it in the van now and I'll take you home.'

He hesitated, red-faced with embarrassment.

'I don't know. . . .'

'It's no trouble,' said Kate. 'I'm staying with Frau Kramer, the lady across from your place. In the Forsthaus, you know?'

'Yes, Ma'am.'

He wiped his hands on his jeans and they loaded the bike into the back of Tante Adelheid's *kombivan*. It was still going strong from the time when Onkel Ernst had been the estate manager for the convent. Kate tried to explain all this to Buddy but it was heavy weather.

'You know,' she said, 'the place at the top of the Steinberg, this hill we're on. The ladies up there are not exactly nuns, although people still call them the Sisters. They just have a commune now.'

She baulked at the term 'lay sisters'. It made most Americans giggle, might make this lump of a boy blush again.

'Do you swim in the lake?' she asked.

'It's kind of cold.'

'Cold and deep,' she said. 'And there's supposed to be a sunken treasure and a water nixie, a kind of mermaid. How about that?'

But Buddy did not react. They passed the crossroads then drove on up the gentle slope of the Steinberg. There were only two houses in this region, each thickly surrounded by trees.

Kate parked outside the Forsthaus; they both stared in silence at the Villa Florian. The double gates of wrought iron had smaller gates to left and right and altogether four massive stone pillars painted in weatherfast white paint. Kate found the gates too pretentious for the house and had noticed that they were imperfectly joined to the old fence among the trees.

The double gates stood open; they bore an asymetrical design of a nymph scattering flowers. There was a carriage sweep before the house and the garage was tastefully screened from view behind the lilac trees. The square bulk of the villa was set off by its undulating roof, the glass cupola, the pillared porch and swirling balconies.

'My Dad isn't home yet,' said Buddy with evident relief. 'He drove to Frankfurt.'

Kate thought this was a pity even if it meant that Buddy would postpone a bawling out about the bike. She wanted to meet Jason Limbard... he was the big draw not only for her but for Andreas. Now she helped Buddy lift the bike out of the van and they carried it in through the double gates, then took a side path to the garage. Kate found that she knew her way a little. She left Buddy with his ruined bike in the garage doorway and went on down the path, staring at the north wall.

The balconies showed stars and snowflakes. The solitary *tannen* on the lawn was balanced by a tall conifer sculpted in relief upon the wall of the house, together with a hooded figure, almost life-size. A shepherd? Santa Claus? It was a Christmas scene at any rate, almost but not quite kitsch.

The north lawn was cool and shadowed; the night was coming at last after the long, hot summer day. She could see the glint of the lake, the Waldsee, at the foot of the hill. It might have been a thrilling and mysterious picture, in keeping with the sunken treasure and the water nixie, except for the sound effects. Summer visitors and the local inhabitants were shouting, splashing, laughing as they bathed in the lake; it sounded like any old swimming pool.

Buddy, coming up behind her, made a sound between a laugh and a sob.

'They sure make a row... swimming,' he choked out.

'At Christmas it must be very quiet,' said Kate. 'Just that big *tannen* there on the lawn.'

'Could put lights on it,' said Buddy.
A lighted tree in the grounds of the Villa Florian. Why not?
'Does the lake freeze over?' asked the boy.
'Not every year.'
There was something there that she stumbled over mentally, a story about the frozen lake, something hinted at by Tante Adelheid and pooh-poohed by Andreas. Gossip. Superstition. Old Wive's Tales. She pressed on round the corner of the house and saw the western aspect. The back porch had a hood of small dark slates and steps down from a small porch. At the far corner, where west met south, where the autumn aspect of the villa met the summer, there was a small 'area' like a London house's, with steps heading down to the souterrain, the basement apartment. The balconies, up above, were twined with vines and fruit; below them were two new windows, the kitchen and a second bathroom. Across the west wall was another large relief, a garland of fruit and leaves; from the kitchen or the back bedroom one could look out into the orchard with its apple trees, cherries, apricots.

Mary Limbard came out on the the stone porch.
'Buddy?'
'Hello there!' said Kate. 'Mrs Limbard? I'm Kate Reimann, Frau Kramer's niece. Buddy had a little accident with his bike and I brought him up the hill.'
'*Buddy!*' said Mary Limbard in alarm.
'I'm fine,' said the boy. 'The front wheel is bent, though.'
'Did you get the cream?' asked Mary anxiously.
'Sure!'
He held up the plastic bag from the supermarket. Kate walked up the steps of the porch and stood back so that Buddy could go past her. He ran into the house. It crossed her mind that he had wanted to go to the toilet and had been too shy to cut away into the bushes. Germans were more shameless about the calls of nature, the young men stood at the edge of the picnic areas in full view...

'Well, thank you,' said Mary Limbard faintly. 'I'm afraid I didn't catch...?'
'Kate Reimann.'
'You speak very good English.'
'I come from Pennsylvania,' said Kate patiently. 'We're

neighbours. I'm staying with Frau Kramer in the Forsthaus.'

'Oh.'

It was flat, almost shocked. Kate pressed on.

'I was planning to visit you and say "Welcome to Germany."'

'Thank you,' said Mary Limbard. 'My husband did mention...'

She was short and slight, a little older than she looked from a distance, maybe as much as ten years older than Kate. She was a pretty woman with honey-coloured hair that curled naturally round her head.

'Do come inside,' she said. 'We could have a cool drink. It has been such a day...'

Kate felt as if she had stormed the citadel. The kitchen was roomy and cool but so dark that an awful round neon tube was already alight overhead. The vineleaf cupboards were long gone, replaced by a built-in kitchen unit in walnut veneer. The back door, which was old, protested with a loud haunted-house creaking as Mary shut it behind them. The family noise inside the house stopped. A child, the little sister, stopped crying; the television was turned down; the older boy said 'Quiet!'

'It's Kate, the American lady who brought Buddy home,' called Mary Limbard.

Kate looked into the corridor and saw a huge flower shape, all of light, upon the dark nondescript carpet of the round central hallway. It was the light from the dome overhead, which was of multi-coloured glass. She turned back reluctantly, wishing that Mary was just a little more forthcoming. A touch of good old Amurrican enthusiasm after all the German restraint. She saw now that Mary was cooking an elaborate meal. In spite of the heat of the day she wore a dressy little cotton number protected by an apron, nylons, earrings.

Kate said: 'Oh, I'm sorry, I'm interrupting you. You're having guests.'

'No, I'll fix us that cool drink. The children have eaten.'

'How do you like this house? It is quite famous.'

'Yes,' said Mary. 'Yes, we heard about it from Major Jeff Saxon, my husband's air force buddy.'

'We know the Saxons,' said Kate. 'Small world. I just spoke to them down in Breitbach.'

'Cindy Saxon gave us a book about this house,' said Mary. 'It used to be full of queer-shaped furniture. Jason says that some of the spoons...'

'I have to admit that I'm quite a fan of Jason Limbard and his column,' said kate. 'Is he doing anything like a book-signing on this trip'

'Yes,' said Mary. 'Just a little at the officers' clubs, you know, at some of the bases.'

Kate looked into the corridor again.

'Would you mind if I looked at the south side of the house?' she asked. 'That's the summer aspect, with the terrace.'

'No, sure,' said Mary. 'Go ahead. You can use this door or the one in the passage. The terrace room is on the right.'

Kate went towards the flower of light from the dome; just beyond it the staircase swept upward. She looked up, following the breaking waves, and saw Buddy sitting in the shadows at the top of the stairs.

The room that opened on to the terrace was one of the largest in the house and it looked rather bare. The queer-shaped furniture had been replaced with a couple of armchairs and a small couch, all oldish and brownish, the kind you let the cat scratch. There was no cupboard or bookcase, only a plain coffee-table and a stand for the old flickery black and white television. It was showing the German version of Sesame Street: minus a bunch of black and Puerto Rican children and plus hard-working actors, talky puppets and a guy in a kind of Abominable Snowman suit.

Kate beamed at the boy and girl in the room and said 'Hi there!' She knew their names... in fact quite a lot of people knew their names, thanks to Jason Limbard. All a bit Christopher Robinish and probably a drag when they went to school. Roddy, the older boy or 'Number One Son', was sixteen years old, thin, bespectacled. Melissa, the exquisite girl-child, was five years old, with golden curls and a fussy cotton dress printed with bumble bees. The boy stood up politely and mumbled a greeting. Melissa stared and then smiled, a slow unconvincing smile. She stared at Kate with this pasted-on smile and deliberately drew a battered teddy-bear from under a cushion and hugged it.

'Your bear has been in the wars!' said Kate.

Melissa hid her face against a brown armchair.

'She's shy,' croaked Roddy.

'Oh, you shouldn't be shy of *me,*' said Kate. 'I live just over the way. We have a black cat over there called Frau Moor. You could come over and play with her.'

The two kids laughed, not because of her talk about the cat but because their mother had come in. Mary Limbard was carrying a bowl of popcorn on a tray with a glass jug of lemonade and a set of glasses.

'A cool drink,' she said.

She was shy too, decided Kate. They were a shy family in the shadow of a near-famous father. Mary called: 'Okay, Buddy!'

The staircase gave off a distinct resonance as Buddy came down. Mary poured the drinks and Kate remembered the Alpine violet. She quickly stripped off its paper into her cloth satchel and set the small pot on the coffee table next to the tray.

'For me?' said Mary Limbard. 'Oh, you shouldn't have... really you shouldn't...'

'German custom!' said Kate firmly.

The Limbard children stared in silence. The pot of pink flowers fairly glowed in the shabby room. Kate sighed inwardly for past glories. She looked out through the glass doors and saw another table on the terrace. It was of smooth brown wood, marvellously bent and curved under the table top into leaves and dragon-flies. There were chairs of rattan, just as old.

'Oh, Mary, I must just see...'

She walked out on to the terrace, ravished by the summer aspect of the Villa Florian. She went quickly down the shallow steps and walked backwards across the lawn, staring up at the house. There was a single balcony above the terrace with two sets of french windows which bore thorny crowns of iron roses. The plastered surface of the balcony had not been well kept up, it was peeling in places. Kate could not remember seeing it illustrated, could not recall if the moulding had been coloured or not. Yet the summer aspect was familiar to her. She realised that the few 'exotic shrubs' in the old photographs had grown into a thick grove of trees at the corner of the house. Kate turned her head this way and that, trying to make out the design that filled the oblong space on the balcony. Long swirling shapes, in low relief. Was it full of leaves? Was there an animal shape, a lion or a greyhound? Was it a man lying full-length with his hands before his face?

Kate experienced at that moment... what could it be called? A false alarm? A fleeting impression? Something very slight and unimportant that might happen to anyone. She looked to her left, starting slightly because she felt that something, a dog perhaps, had come out of the bushes at the edge of the lawn. She might have turned like that, indoors or out, to speak to someone she believed had come up behind her and found no-one, or found that her companions were further away than she had imagined.

It was a little cooler now. The sun had not set but it hung low in the western sky, hidden behind the evergreen trees and bushes that ringed the south lawn. Inside the living room the kids were in a party mood, digging into the popcorn. Kate went back inside and sat next to Mary Limbard on the couch. What she had taken for lemonade turned out to be home-made ginger beer.

'Hey,' she said, 'I haven't tasted it since I was a kid!'

'We make it every summer, wherever we go,' said Mary.

'You must all come over for a barbecue... what they call a grill-party,' said Kate. 'Please let's make a date. Andy has built a new outdoor grill for his aunt. He's very proud of it.'

'Yes,' said Mary, 'Yes, perhaps we... Is your husband German?'

'Yes,' said Kate. 'We met when I was doing a post-graduate course in Art History. We live in München...Munich. Andreas works for a publishing firm, Lorbeer Verlag.'

'Oh well yes, maybe we...' said Mary.

The kitchen door gave off the wail of a damned soul. Steps sounded on the tiled kitchen floor. Buddy made as if to spring up but his mother gave him a warning glance. Roddy switched off the television. The whole family smiled. Melissa smiled and hid away her old bear under a cushion. Jason Limbard strode into the room.

He was in his middle forties and he looked a little younger

than he did on television: younger and more heavily built. He was dark-haired, almost too handsome; the neat grey slacks and navy-blue blazer had something to do with it... he could have used a more rugged image. He saw Kate at once and gave her one of his smiles all to herself. He came toward her with his hands out-stretched, welcoming, just as he did on his regional talk show.

What was Jason Limbard? It was hard to say. Not a doctor of medicine at any rate, and not quite a crank or a quack. He was a psychologist and a dietitian. He was a moderate health nut. He had written two diet books and a syndicated column called *Here's Health*. His family: Mary, Roddy, Buddy and Baby Liss, featured peripherally in the column. Kate had been pleased when she heard that he was on their doorstep because Jason Limbard was essentially a local hero, a New Englander. He wasn't Johnny Carson or Dr Atkins and maybe he didn't want to be. The visit to Europe suited him. Kate could imagine columns and holiday film clips about castles and home-cooked food.

'Ah, our neighbour from the Forsthaus,' he said in passable German. 'Frau Reimann?'

'Kate Reimann!' she said. 'A fan of yours from Lessing, Pennsylvania!'

'What's that?' he cried heartily. 'Hear that, Mary? A long-stemmed American beauty right next door. No wonder she has such a fine jogging style. Up the Steinberg every morning!'

'That hill does me in every time,' said Kate, blushing.

She was long-stemmed all right, one metre eighty, but did not find herself beautiful.

'Kate was just asking...' began Mary.

She stopped as Jason turned his attention to the Alpine violet.

'Now where did that come from?' he said, twirling the little *cachepot* between finger and thumb. 'Who's been shopping?'

'I thought Mary might like it,' said Kate.

'That's right neighbourly of you, Ma'am,' he said, putting on an exaggerated Southern accent. The children all grinned at his act.

Mary said eagerly: 'Kate was just asking us all to a barbecue. Her husband is with a publisher in Munich.'

'Aha, a grill-party!' said Jason. 'Are you sure you want the whole tribe? The kids too?'

'Of course,' said Kate. 'Every last one of you!'

'Very kind. I was speaking to Frau Kramer...your husband's aunt, right? What a marvellous old lady! Knows all about herbs and spices.'

'We'll have a Limbard salad,' said Kate, 'and I'll get you to sign a book.'

He grinned, waving away the flattery.

'What are you chomping, Roddy? Popcorn? Reminds me how hungry I am!'

Mary sprang up, smiling, and Kate took her cue.

'I must go,' she said, 'but please let me pin you down. Today is Monday, how about Wednesday?'

'That could be,' said Jason.

He pressed her shoulder with harmless gallantry and steered her into the corridor; Mary followed. They walked into the circle of light under the glass dome. As they passed the staircase Jason struck the bannister gently with the flat of his hand so that it gave off a thrumming note.

'This is some house,' said Kate.

'Haunted too,' said Jason cheerfully.

'I've never heard that,' she laughed.

'The Saxon family discovered this place,' he said. 'You know Cindy and Jeff? I always think of them as the perfect American family, eh Mary?'

'Oh, yes!'

'Cynthia Saxon and the boy, Jeff junior, caught a glimpse of someone when they were trimming their Christmas tree,' said Jason, 'Over in that other large room we don't use.'

'Well, Christmas is the time for ghosts!' said Kate.

'I'm collecting evidence,' said Jason. 'I heard some more from a guy down by the lake...a forester.'

The room on the right of the front door was a dining room, the table elaborately set for two people, with flowers and unlit lilac-coloured candles. Kate wondered if it was an anniversary or a birthday. When she had pinned the Limbards down to Wednesday, eight o'clock, she stepped out through the pillars of the porch and said to Mary: 'I'm so glad we met at last. I hope you all have a great summer!'

'Yes,' said Mary.

Her thin smile got on Kate's nerves; she wanted to get a reaction out of the woman.

'And you won't be afraid of the ghosts!' she said.

'I don't believe in ghosts,' said Mary flatly. 'I don't believe in anything like that.'

With her smile gone she looked sad and wan, a ghost herself.

Kate took the right hand path and let herself out of a side gate. When she looked back, Jason and Mary had gone indoors. It was just beginning to get dark. She stood in the twilight and looked at the Forsthaus, in the shade of an enormous spreading poplar tree. It was no villa but a tall white house with grey shutters. This was the place for her, she thought, with a twinge of resignation. Andy and Tante Adelheid and Frau Moor had become her family. She thought suddenly and surprisingly of her mother who was dead and who had never had a decent house. *You see, Mom, things haven't worked out so badly...*

The nightmare began at this point. She had climbed into the van, ready to drive it into the garage, when she found that her cloth satchel was gone. She had left it behind in the family room, on the couch or under the coffee table. Her wallet and car keys were in the pockets of her jeans but the blue cloth satchel was gone. It contained nothing but Tante Adelheid's prescription from the *Apotheke* and the crumpled paper from the Alpine violet. Kate sat there, cursing. She had made a fair beginning with the Limbards but she did not want to go crashing back into the preparations for that special dinner. Then she had an idea.

She went quietly over the road again and tried the side gate that she had just used, at the summer corner of the house. It was locked...she guessed that all the gates were locked and could only be opened by pressing buttons inside the house. But there was that idiotic gap between the gates and the old fence that ran across the front of the grounds, hidden most of the way by trees. A post had been bent aside and a thin, long-legged person could just step in, as Kate did now. She would go back to the terrace, tap on the doors, and Roddy could hand out the bag. With any luck she wouldn't have to disturb Mary and Jason at all.

It was darker in the garden of the Villa Florian; the trees that ringed the south lawn grew thickly across the path. She pushed through and strolled into the deep shade of the exotic trees at the edge of the terrace. The doors were opened abruptly. A terrible voice, flat and hard, said: *'This time it will be burnt!'*

Something went hurtling through the air and landed in the bushes on the other side of the lawn.

The voice continued: 'You are all to blame! You can't be trusted! You let that fucking pushy bitch into the house. Eh? Eh?'

There was a small shriek and the crash of breaking china. Kate found that she could see right into the lighted room. She saw Jason Limbard catch Melissa by her golden hair and fling her to the ground as she ran for the open doors. Mary came into the picture, seemed to come up off her knees, and the boy Roddy bent over his sister. Jason caught his wife and his elder son each by an arm, held them to right and left in a strong grip, and shook them. The boy grimaced but did not speak or cry out. Mary was repeating words over and over, in a low voice. It might have been: 'Please...please Jay, please Jay...' He changed his grip and began to bend their arms up behind their backs until the boy gave an eerie cry of pain.

'Not yet,' said Jason Limbard. 'That arm is not quite gone yet, Roddy-boy. But it could go, that arm. And that arm could go, eh Mary?'

He stood firm, easing himself fully upright, spreading his legs. He relaxed his hold, then put on the lock again. He had taken off his blazer and loosened his tie. His face had changed crudely into a mask of hatred, nostrils flared, cheeks folded and flattened. His neck muscles stood out, his thighs strained at his trousers; his crotch bulged as if he wore a cod-piece.

'Where's Buddy?' he panted. 'Where's my good-buddy? Where's my good Buddy-boy who trashed his bike and let that stranger put it in the van?'

Kate felt sick and terrified. She could not look away; she did not dare to run. She shut her eyes and opened them at the sound of a thump. Jason had flung aside his elder son who sat whimpering and nursing his arm. He held his wife very close now, in front of his body.

'Dinner ready?' he panted. 'Dinner ready, honey? I just

have to finish this little lecture on discipline.'

He had an arm across his wife's throat. Buddy came along on his hands and knees.

'Get up!' ordered his father. 'What's that I see? Snivelling, cowardly, disobedient yellow-dog Buddy. Wet yourself... you wet yourself! Get to the stairs, that is the punishment seat in this house. Go on all of you! Get that baby girl thing out before I tread on her, squash her like a bug!'

There was a dreadful scrambling and crawling.

'*Now*...' said Jason Limbard. 'Now, honey...'

He thrust his body against his wife's, holding her by the throat still, his other hand tangled among her skirts. He swung her round to face him and began to unbutton her dress.

'No, Jay,' said Mary Limbard in a small cold voice. 'No, Jay, please not. No Jay. ...'

'Shut the doors,' he said. 'Shut the doors and then do exactly what I say and maybe we'll have dinner.'

The doors were shut. Kate felt faint. She leaned against a tree, feeling a warm wave of nausea and faintness wash over her. She knew that she must get away; she came out of the shadow of the trees beside the terrace and sprinted for the next cover, by the path. There was a rending crash; she never knew exactly what caused the sound. She dived into shadow, flattening herself in thick leaf mould. Had *she* caused the sound, tripped over a wire, pulled something down in her flight? She saw the table and the rattan chairs falling about on the empty windless terrace.

Jason Limbard opened the doors again, then stepped out and picked up a chair. He tucked his shirt into his trousers and said briskly: 'Anyone there? Is that you, Frau Reimann?'

He brushed back his hair, yet he was not quite the same handsome fellow who had welcomed Kate with out-stretched hands a short time ago. He had not changed back, she thought. And for her he would never change back again. She was shivering in the sultry garden, alternately shivering with cold, then burning. Jason came down the steps from the terrace on to the path. He would find her, she would die of fear.

'Who's there?' asked Jason in a louder voice.

Kate turned her head, where she lay, and saw that there was another person in the garden. At the farthest edge of the lawn, opposite the house, a young girl stood watching; she was beside a tall bush with pale flowers. Kate could see her pale face and long dark hair; the girl wore a whitish dress under a dark jacket or cardigan. She was standing very still. Now something flashed in the darkness under the trees on the west side. There was a little sparkling as if light had caught a piece of metal. A dog... there was a dog. She saw it clearly as if the animal were outlined in light. Perhaps the sparkling had come from its collar. Jason Limbard saw the dog too and turned off the path on to the lawn.

'Get away!' he cried. 'Get the hell out of here, you filthy mutt.'

Kate gathered herself together to make a try for the gate. The noise began; she saw nothing and did not look... though she was certain that the girl had gone, had stepped back into the shadow of her flowery bush. The noise was as horrible as anything she had ever heard: the dog... or dogs... were worrying at their living prey. Growling, slavering, making grunts of effort as they tore and crunched at flesh and bone. Jason went back to the terrace.

'Hey,' he said, pleased. 'Take a look, Mary. The dog has got something.'

He watched, Kate could still see him. Then he turned and went inside the villa; the doors were shut again.

Kate went through the space beside the white gatepost. No-one was about. It was still not quite dark; the Steinberg dreamed in the shade of its old trees; a lone street lamp shone at the intersection further down the hill. The convent on the hilltop had one low tower that rose above the high wall of ancient, rose-coloured stone. Warm yellow light shone out from Tante Adelheid's kitchen behind the poplar tree. Kate leaned against the van for a moment, catching her breath. She retrieved her bag of groceries from the back of the van but was too shakey to drive into the garage. She went through the unlocked side gate of the Forsthaus and crept up the steps into the kitchen.

She stood shaking for a long time, simply holding on to the sink and shaking, her eyes seeing but hardly registering the little vases of fresh parsley and chives on the back ledge of the sink. Tante Adelheid was resting before dinner; it was hot in the kitchen because there was a casserole in the oven. Kate ran cold water on to her scratched and earth-stained hands. She took paper towels and cleaned her face and tried to get a little of the dirt off her clothes. In the mirror beside the inner door she saw a stranger, a fugitive, wild-eyed and tousled. She dragged her fingers through her hair.

'Hallo?' called Andreas softly from the landing.

Hà-llo with the accent on the first syllable; it sounded like a hunting call. When she did not reply he came down a few steps and said: 'How are your Americans? How is Diet Jason?'

Kate stared at him as if the sight of Andreas Reimann, 32, M.A. and Diplom Kaufmann, could restore her sanity. There he was in black bathing trunks and a heavy tan. In the handsome stakes he could give anyone a run for their money. Her friend Ruth had said: 'Kate, you sure can pick 'em.' He was one metre ninety with a well-muscled chest and good biceps for which he did absolutely nothing; he had golden hair on his chest, his belly and his head. His clipped beard was golden too but his eyes were brown and weak from all that reading of German tomes and English best-sellers. On the beach he peered charmingly through prescription sunglasses. Now he put on his reading glasses which he had been carrying along with a copy of *Publishers Weekly* and stared owlishly at his wife.

'Katie, what's the matter?'

'Come in here.'

They were almost whispering because Tante Adelheid napped in her bedroom opposite the kitchen. They went into the front room, still quite small, dominated by the poplar tree and its quivering leaf shadows.

'Andy, promise you will believe me. Promise you will believe every word.'

'Of course. Was there some accident? I saw you come back in the van. Did *you* hit the Limbard boy and break his bike?'

'Nothing like that. Andy, promise you will believe...'

'I promise, I swear! Here, sit down. What is so unbelievable, *Kätchen?*'

She told everything from the beginning, when she had come upon Buddy at the foot of the hill. Andreas squirmed at her side and put a few questions.

'Yes,' he said. 'Yes. That is pretty hard to believe.'

He got up, poured half an inch of their best Armagnac into a glass and gave it to her.

'And he wasn't drunk?'

'He was sober,' said Kate. 'Hadn't touched a drop. Andreas, that is how they live. He does it all the time.'

'He was angry because you had been in the house,' said Andreas. 'He has a thing about privacy. His home is his castle.'

'I mean it was some crazy *ritual*... all that kneeling and crawling.'

'They are all taking part,' he said. 'Mary, the wife, goes along. Who knows how other people...?'

'Here we go,' said Kate. 'Blame the victim! It was more than just rough sex. I saw him deck the little kid, the five-year-old girl, and nearly break the boy's arm!'

'He must take many risks!'

'Wait,' she said. 'Someone else was watching. I told you about the dog. I thought I saw a girl as well, at the edge of the lawn.'

She held out her glass for another Armagnac and he raised an eyebrow.

'You are beginning to strain my belief just a little,' he said. 'A girl as well as a dog? Why didn't you mention her before?'

'I don't know... it was just a glimpse.'

'Wait,' said Andreas. 'It's cooler in here. I'll get some clothes.'

She heard him go softly up the stairs. Through the leaves of the poplar tree outside the window she could see the gates of the Villa Florian. She sipped her brandy and considered the girl. Maybe she had just imagined her, the girl had been an illusion. Or a different sort of experience.

The door opened and Tante Adelheid came in quietly. She was a tall, lean old woman with a long, downy face and thick white hair, decently waved at the hairdressers in Breitbach.

'*Aber Kind!*' said Tante Adelheid. '*Was ist geschehen?*'

'Oh, Tante Adelheid,' said Kate. 'It is the most dreadful thing...'

For the first time her eyes filled with tears. Tante Adelheid sat beside her on the handsome old leather couch and held her hands while she told the story all over again, with girl and dog.

In talking to people that she liked and trusted her German, which was pretty workable these days, became even more fluent.

Andreas came padding in halfway through and said angrily in English: 'You're telling this horrible story to Tante Adelheid!'

He was too embarrassed to wait for his aunt's reaction and went away to the kitchen. Tante Adelheid asked certain questions which showed that she understood very well. Then she said, 'Oh God, did it have to be in summer? In summer at the Villa Florian!'

Then, seeing the shocked, questioning look on Kate's face, she continued: 'It is a bad time. This wicked house-tyrant has come in summer, so he will be difficult to defeat.'

'The girl that I saw...was she...?'

Tante Adelheid sighed and looked down.

'I must telephone,' she said.

She took her spectacles from the pocket of her flowered overall and polished them with her handkerchief.

'The story of the girl and of summer at the Villa Florian should come from Sister Florentine.'

Andreas burst back into the room holding an open bottle of beer. He began to make a speech, striding up and down before the two women.

'Kate, I know this is very close to your heart...womens' rights and all that, and I have always supported you, you know that. Personally I don't doubt that Jason Limbard made some outburst, which you saw from some distance away behind the trees, through a window, a glass door. You must remember that he is a summer visitor...here today and gone tomorrow. We have this word in German: a house-tyrant. It shows that there are plenty of them about. It just so happens that he is American, he and his family are all Ammies, which makes it even more difficult. I mean...what about the consulate? Does the wife have any family? Many other people must know of his proclivities.'

'Andy,' said Kate, 'what are you trying to say?'

He stood still, panting a little.

'That we can't do a thing about it.'

'No,' whispered Kate. 'No, I don't suppose we can.'

'Not in summer,' said Tante Adelheid. 'But we can keep watch.'

'They are all coming over for a grill-party,' said Kate. 'On Wednesday. The day after tomorrow.'

II

'Someone watching?'

Watching from the edge of the patio. Bet she got an eyeful!'

'This is just your bullshit. How could you see?'

'I carried up Liss, straight up to her room, and put on the lamp and laid her on the bed. She was crying pretty bad so I said I would go and look.'

'What for?'

'For the fucking *bear,* for chrissakes, where he threw it. I thought if I could see it on the edge of the lawn, I could get it back.'

'Okay,' said Buddy, 'I believe you. I heard you fooling around from where I was sitting on the stairs. Where did you look from?'

'I went through *their* room,' said Roddy, 'on to the long balcony over the terrace. . . . '

'Whew!'

'And just as I looked down I saw her streak out of the trees there below and head for the gates. It was that bitch Kate, that stupid Kate who got us all into trouble.'

Buddy knew that his brother was just a little crazier, more psycho than he was himself. He couldn't make a judgement about Mom: sometimes she was right around the twist, sometimes not. But Roddy was going slowly but surely to a place where he could hardly be reached, and one of the signs was that he couldn't recognise ordinary things any more.

'Kate is just an ordinary neighbour,' said Buddy. 'It was what anyone back home would have done. . . brought me up the hill with the bike, then said hello to Mom.'

'She came in the house.'

'Mom was taking a calculated risk. She would have had to be pretty rude not to ask her inside.'

'What was this Kate doing spying on us?' panted Roddy.

'I bet she came back for some perfectly ordinary reason,'

said Buddy. 'Like she wanted to change the day of their cook-out.'

'Anyway she near as hell got caught. There was some kinda noise on the terrace, chairs and tables crashing about, and then *he* came out!'

'Shit!'

'You shoulda seen her dive. She dived right into the trees by the path. She hit the dirt like she was stealing a base.'

'What did he do?'

'Called out. Said her name. But she just lay there.'

'She must have seen something. Seen him in action.'

'Do you recall Miz Hart at Pelican Bay?'

Buddy recalled Miz Hart and was afraid with a tearing crescendo of fear, quite different from the fear he lived with every day. This was the almost pleasurable fear of Everything Coming Out. Everything: the ordinary believable cruelty, and the unbelievable cruelty, and the lies, the hospitals, the false names, the attempted divorce, the suicide attempt and things that could only be guessed at like what happened to Miz Hart. For a long time, he knew, Roddy had kept a newspaper clipping about Miz Hart with the headline: RAPE SLAYING. HOUSEWIFE FOUND IN THE DUNES!

Miz Hart had come into the kitchen of the holiday cottage and seen him, seen the Old Man set down the frying pan, and had gone to the sink and got a wet cloth and quickly wiped the hot fat from Mom's arm and the few drops from Liss's baby face. She was a lot older than this Kate, and fat and common, not just a bitch but a Piece of White Trash, the Old Man called her. There was nothing much said, Mom made an excuse saying he spilt the fat, but Miz Hart knew. He couldn't remember how many days later she was found in the dunes. Mom said what a terrible thing and the Old Man had said Miz Hart was a fat whore who was asking for it, no wonder someone gave it to her. Mom had a second degree burn and it was treated again when they left Florida, and Liss had a little scar like one tear drop that stayed on her cheek. And now here they were years later in fucking Germany and still everything had not come out.

'Kate is different,' he said. 'He doesn't know about her.'

'He would want to know,' said Roddy softly.

So Buddy knew that his brother would use this as something to trade with; he would tell the Old Man in exchange for some favour.

'Aw, you're crazy!' he said. 'It wasn't her. Either it was someone else, a real prowler, one of those Kraut terrorists — you know, with long hair — or you imagined it. You were seeing things.'

'No,' said Roddy solemnly, 'it was her all right. And I'm not seeing things but I know who is... the Old Man. He came right out on the lawn, looking for spies, you know, and then he saw a dog. He yelled out "Get away you dirty mutt!" and then he went back on the patio and called Mom to see because "the dog had caught something".'

'Plenty of dogs around,' said Buddy. 'That forester Dad and I were talking to by the lake had this really *huge* brown critter, a real neat dog, and it was called a d-o-g-g-e, pronounced dogguh... a Deutscher Dogge.'

'Uh-uh,' said Roddy. 'He was seeing things. There was no dog. It was just starting to get dark but I could see everything there was, I could see the lawn and I could see into the bushes as far as the garden shed. There wasn't any dog at all.'

'It was a ghost dog,' said Buddy.

'Bullshit!' said Roddy, who was afraid of ghosts.

'No, wait,' said Buddy, 'remember how old Cindy Saxon and Junior Saxon thought they saw a guy standing on the lawn by the big Christmas tree, and then when they looked there weren't even any footprints in the snow?'

'Junior and his old lady are a pair of prize creeps!' said Roddy.

Buddy guessed that his brother shared his feeling about the Saxon family... a mixture of exasperation and dull envy. They had a father who never lifted a hand to them; they were not crazy, they were just, well, ordinary.

'Maybe they are creeps,' said Buddy, 'but that forester guy is not and he told the Old Man this place was haunted too. They were talking German so I didn't get too much.'

'It's a bunch of lies!' said Roddy, squirming. 'This is a kind of fancy house but it isn't a castle or Norman Bates's house or anything.'

'If this place is spooked, maybe we can...'

Roddy gripped his arm and they both fell silent. Buddy was ready to dash back to his own folding bed in case it was the Old Man making a night raid. They were in a crazy six-sided room a hexagon, at the very front of the house, and Melissa had the other one across the corridor. The rooms were painted all white with brown wooden strips at the corners like tree-trunks that grew up into swirling branches just under the ceiling. Liss slept with the shutters closed on the two windows that opened on to her balcony but the boys kept theirs open and the room was almost too light to sleep in...there were no curtains or blinds. Now there came a sound that was peculiar to the Villa Florian, a soft resonance of wrought iron, from the staircase or one of the balconies. It was as if the house uttered a single low note and then was still. The boys listened; Buddy was impressed. *Could be!* he told himself. *There could be something...*

He whispered to Roddy: 'I had this idea.'

But Roddy turned over, ready to bury his head under the featherbed.

'Fuck off!' he whispered. 'Get back to your own bed. You want him to wake up?'

Buddy climbed slowly and quietly out of his brother's bed. He knew he was as expert in moving silently, just as he was an expert in fear. He moved silently across the white room to the window and stared out, testing his own fear. He looked down at the drive and the back of the iron gates with the girl, the iron girl scattering spring flowers. Nothing there.

Across the street the old lady's house rose up tall and white behind the tree, the roof shaped a little like a Dutch barn. They had an attic, a big spooky attic, he bet. The Real Estate Agent had apologised because the Villa Florian had only two small attics, suitable for storage...on account of the crazy glass dome. But it had extra fine roomy cellars, suitable for sleeping if required.

So the Old man had said to him and Roddy, very cheery: 'All the better to lock you in, eh boys?'

And they had laughed and grinned and nudged eath other as if their Dad was a great little kidder. As if he was a Dad like any other...like Jefferson Saxon, for instance. This was one of the Old Man's little ways: he purposely made kidding remarks like this to test their reactions and to make the rest of the people look stupid.

How many dear old ladies had said: 'I guess you boys have the best father in the world!'

'Yes, Ma'am!'

Then the other idiot bit: 'I guess you are mighty proud of these two fine boys, Mr Limbard!' The answer to that was a frown from the Old Man and a phoney gruff voice.

'What, these two sorry rascals? They need a bit of licking into shape, don't you boys?'

'Ha-ha, sure, Dad!'

Buddy's heart thumped. Something had moved. A flicker of movement in the attic window of the Forsthaus. Jesus. A ghost? Someone watching the villa? No, goddamn, it must be a reflection, the reflection of a branch or part of the villa. He stared, testing his fear, and was certain that something inside the attic had moved. He looked away and moved silently towards his bed. There was a familiar sound... Melissa began to grizzle and fret. Would someone have to go to her and see that she settled down? Perhaps she was just crying in her sleep. The noise had stopped.

Buddy lay down under his feather-padded quilt that would be too hot after a while... stupid Kraut bed! He was tired, all his limbs were heavy. He tried to gather strength inside himself, to feel his power, the power of his thought reaching out and summoning help and sustenance. Not from God, exactly, he had given up on God long ago, but from Invisible Forces. Let them all come.

Come, please come and end our pain. Lightning, laser beams, cosmic rays, monsters, spirits, ghosts... if you're here you won't scare me. Come get him. Save Mom and Liss and Roddy and me but get him, get him before he kills us...

Every night a miracle occurred. He went from his angry prayers, his summoning, into sleep, without ever remembering that he fell asleep. Buddy went deep down and dreamed a heart-breaking sweet dream of the time at Miscogan Lake in Canada, where they escaped for six months, two years ago. Grandpa Hale was alive and the divorce was under way and they were saved. It would never happen again. They spent summer and fall in a cabin on the lake with a boat and colour

TV. They even had a dog and a cat, Blackie and poor Samantha.

Back he went in his dream and knew that all the bad years before and after, they were the dream, and this alone was real. The dream place was not quite like Lake Miscogan, it had overtones of the Villa Florian. They were safe; there was nothing of the Old Man in the dream, no fear, no violence, no hatred. They were busy in the dream, eating, drinking, getting together some party, talking, playing. Then the dog, Blackie, ran on down the hill through the tall pines to the very edge of the lake and he followed.

He looked back at the cabin among the trees and behind it was a dark cloud. A pillar of black cloud rose up into the sky above the trees and became solid, like a huge metal construction, a crane or an oil rig. This was the sign: it was the Old Man coming. He felt terror rising in him and it was a hopeless, selfish terror that left no way out. Blackie, the dog, was already splashing about in the lake and Buddy did the only thing possible for him to do. He plunged into the cold water and went deep, deep down and knew that he would never come up again. He was too far gone.

When the light woke him this was the only dream he could remember. Buddy came awake on the instant, registered that he hadn't wet the bed, got up and went quietly to take a leak at the very end of the upper floor. The corridor divided around the central well with the dome and the stairs; he crept along the northern branch, past the rooms they weren't using. The villa had this old bathroom upstairs, with blue and green tiles and taps like dolphins, and another newer bathroom underneath, opposite the kitchen. It was still hot and going to be hotter, another cloudless, perfect summer day in central Germany, like the guy said on the Armed Forces Network. He didn't wash yet, he went back and lay on his bed until the Old Man came bouncing into their bedroom in his tracksuit.

'Rise and shine!' he said. 'Hup, two, three, four! Under the shower, you two stinkers! You know what happened last night, don't you? We had an uninvited guest...so today we have work to do!'

The Old Man was in a good mood. As the two boys made for the bathroom a whiff of coffee and bacon came up from the kitchen. Mom had fed the Old Man. Now they heard him look in on Melissa.

'Time to get up, baby!'

'Daddy!'

Buddy's heart sank whenever she said the word. She really believed there were two people, and the good one, the one not shouting at her or hitting her, was called Daddy. Buddy knew better; there was only the Old man.

III

Kate set out jogging at eight o'clock: up the hill towards the convent, then to the left. In the back lane a big orange dustcart turned the corner ahead of her; she passed the back gate of the Villa Florian, stooped down, then ran on into a patch of sunlight. She was holding a fragment of glazed pottery: a swirling tree branch, brown on white, one of the handles of the little *Cachepot*. She zipped it into the pocket of her tracksuit and ran down towards the bakery.

When she arrived back at the Forsthaus her cloth satchel was hanging on the front gate. At the Villa Florian there were signs that everyone was up and about. Kate went into the kitchen and delivered the warm bag of breadrolls to Tante Adelheid. Andreas was drinking coffee and reading *Der Spiegel*. The radio was tuned to the AFN. 'Another hot day,' murmured the announcer. 'Another perfect summer day in central Germany...'

Chapter 2
Seeing Things

A trestle table from the days when great feasts were celebrated in the courtyard of the Forsthaus had been set up on the back lawn near the new grill. Rough-hewn garden furniture was grouped under the nut tree for the grown ups. From a certain branch of the old apricot to a hook embedded in the house wall there ran a length of nylon clothesline holding six large Chinese lanterns: turquoise, orange, yellow, pink, scarlet and gold, their dependent tassels wafting in the lightest evening breeze. The salads waited on the flowered runner that covered the long table; Andreas, in his apron printed with amusing vegetables, was busy at the worktable beside the grill. Frau Moor, the black cat, a small compact animal with amber eyes, sat on the path.

Kate kept herself busy in the kitchen. The bell at the front gate rang very promptly at eight o'clock. When she came into the garden Tante Adelheid and Andreas were greeting the Limbard family as they came down the path. The children came first; Roddy kept taking his hand away from Melissa who tried to hold it. He urged her forward and she stumbled. She fell down almost at Tante Adelheid's feet, then scrambled up and presented a bouquet wrapped in silver foil. Jason Limbard gave a rich peal of laughter and Mary joined in after a second with a high, gasping laugh.

'Botched that entry, Melissa!' said Jason. 'I'll deal with you later, baby! *Guten Abend,* Frau Kramer...Frau Reimann, *Kate*...Herr Reimann: my wife Mary. Well, you see what a tribe of savages we've brought!'

'The flowers are beautiful,' said Tante Adelheid. 'Roses from the Villa Florian.'

While Kate and Andreas greeted and smiled she reached down almost absently to Melissa who took the big, white, lined hand with perfect trust and was led to her place at the trestle.

'See,' said Tante Adelheid. 'There is Frau Moor.'

The black cat picked her way across the grass. The two brothers sat down at their places then leaped up again when Andreas called them to the grill to choose their chops and sausages. Jason stood in the midst of the back lawn, more handsome than ever in his striped green polo shirt.

'Fabulous!' he said. 'Now I begin to believe in *Gemütlichkeit,* eh Kate? All's right with the world. Mary...'

Mary had slipped away to consult with Tante Adelheid as they dished up Melissa's food.

'Fever?' said the old woman.

She clapped a hand to Melissa's forehead.

'Mary, honey,' said Jason, 'don't let me catch you fussing.'

'I just have to see...' said Mary.

'We'll sit here,' said Kate, 'under the nut tree. Perhaps you could open the wine, Jason.'

'Needs a strong right hand, does it?'

He operated the automatic corkscrew with grave concentration.

'Mary,' he said, putting on a gruff voice, 'come sit down. Don't fuss over your bratty brood. Don't ever have kids, Kate, it takes too long to get them house-trained. Isn't that so, honey? We really have to regiment those little devils, mmmm? Bread and water and down to the cellar.'

Mary's laughter was so violent that she nearly choked and had to be patted on the back by Jason.

'Oh sure!' she said. 'Oh sure! Hup, two, three, four!'

Kate was hot and cold. She looked at Mary Limbard and saw a madwoman. A pretty, discreetly made up woman of perhaps thirty-eight, in a sleeveless blouse of yellow synthetic and blue linen trousers, who was, nevertheless, insane. Her large blue eyes were staring and sleepless with huge pupils, her neck muscles stood out with strain, her lips were strained over her teeth in the mockery of a perpetual smile. Kate felt the signs of this madness begin to creep over her, straining her eyes open, pulling at all her muscles, making the sweat soak into her hair.

Jason had been praising the cold Riesling; at last Andreas

came to sit down. The two men talked companionably about Germany.

'I'm impressed by the order and lack of aggression,' said Jason seriously. 'I keep seeing beautiful quiet places: the corners of old towns, little villages seen through the trees... even the city parks. And München has this real ambience... those beautiful women, just strolling or drinking coffee. I have to go there for a few days on business, before the end of the summer.'

'Will you be taking the family?' asked Andreas.

'Haven't made up my mind,' said Jason. 'Never does any harm to keep the beggars guessing, eh Andreas?'

Kate felt a small satisfaction when Andy's smile became fixed.

'No, it depends how they behave, doesn't it, honey?' continued Jason.

'Oh, Jay,' said Mary, turning to Andreas and to Kate. 'The kids are very good, really. Anyone would think the kids are troublesome.'

'They are! They are!' said Jason happily. 'And not only the kids. This woman leads me a terrible dance. Can you believe that, Kate?'

'No,' said Kate.

'He's a great little kidder,' said Mary.

'Yes,' smiled Jason. 'Mary's right for once.'

He slipped an arm around his wife's shoulders and squeezed.

'I was wondering,' said Andreas boldly, 'if you are planning a new book with continental recipes?'

'Just collecting material,' said Jason. 'I need a holiday. We all need a holiday. I think we were very lucky to catch you two, Kate and Andreas, on our doorstep. Why aren't you off in Spain or Sardinia like half the other inhabitants of this land?'

'Easy,' grinned Andreas. 'We are too poor this year. We might take a week or ten days in winter. A friend of ours, Nicholas Lenz, is taking a house in the mountains.'

Kate suddenly wished with all her heart that she was actually in that house right at that very moment, sitting by the fire telling Nicki all about summer and the Villa Florian.

Jason was saying: 'Winter is one of my favorite seasons,

back home. We batten down the hatches, light the lamps, cook the seasonal dishes. Those big louts of boys that you see there feeding their faces are still kids at heart when it comes to Christmas. I swear we went ten miles there and back last year, finding the right tree.'

Kate forced herself to look Mary Limbard in the eye.

'Do you have a family Christmas?' she asked. 'I mean with parents and aunts and cousins?'

'We used to,' said Mary.

'Ssh,' soothed Jason. 'Mary's father passed away last year. Now she's left to my tender mercies. Just me and the kids.'

At that moment the Limbard children and Tante Adelheid all broke out in delighted laughter. Frau Moor had been persuaded to leap up for a scrap of meat; now, excited by the children's laughter, the little black cat went skipping away to the steps and then to the kitchen window sill.

'Oh, this is too bad,' said Jason, springing up. 'My dear lady, Frau Kramer, please come and have your wine. Let me see to those rowdies!'

He held his chair and Tante Adelheid allowed herself to be persuaded. A silence fell. Kate was watching Mary who was rigid, her elbow braced on the table, her wine glass held so tightly that the stem might break, watching her husband. Andreas and Tante Adelheid could not help but watch too.

Jason went to his sons and playfully cuffed them on the backs of their heads. He laid his hand on Melissa's curls. He bent down and whispered to his children. They stopped eating. The boys did not look at their father but Melissa stared first at him and then, turning her head, at the cat on the window sill. Buddy contrived not to eat another bite. When Andreas returned to the grill and prepared the adults' round of marinated pork steaks and shish-kebabs, the boy hung around the fire, helping.

Presently Jason strolled back to the three women and said, 'I was just saying, Mary, that the cat looks like your Samantha, poor old Samantha who came from Canada.'

'No,' said Mary. 'Yes, well, Samantha was black too. Please, Jay, we are just going to have dinner.'

'What happened to your cat?' asked Kate.

She felt like an accomplice to Jason; she was feeding him his lines.

'She took a bait,' he said sadly. 'Just at Thanksgiving. Terrible sad thing with a family pet. And it was nicely timed too... sitting at dinner and the cat dies of a dose of strychnine.'

'A cat?' asked Tante Adelheid.

Kate translated briefly.

'Who would do such a thing?' murmured Tante Adelheid rhetorically.

'*Ein grausamer Mensch,*' said Kate. 'A very cruel person.'

'Yes,' said Jason, also in German, turning all his attention to Tante Adelheid. 'It was an object lesson, dear lady, for those children. Afterwards, I am sure, they understood what cruelty was abroad in the world.'

'Of course we never found out!' said Mary, her voice rising, almost out of control. 'We never found out who gave Samantha the poison!'

'No,' said Jason, still addressing Tante Adelheid and Kate, 'but it could have been any one of the people round about. Respectable citizens... successful young professionals... people one would never suspect of cruel practices.'

Tante Adelheid put her head on one side; her expression was serious and pained. She lifted a hand to the small silver locket that she wore inside the neckline of her summer dress of blue and white crêpe.

'Ah, Herr Limbard,' she said, 'here in Germany we have known a great many respectable citizens who turned out to be monsters. Mere respectability would offer less protection.'

For an instant Jason was caught and held by this pronouncement. His expression of eager concern was frozen on his handsome face; he looked at Mary who tried to get out of her chair. Kate thought: *He will beat them all when they get home.* Out of the corner of her eye she saw the black cat, Frau Moor, slip down from the window sill and retire into the house. Kate glanced at the sky, which was cloudless. Frau Moor often withdrew ten minutes or so ahead of a thunderstorm.

Melissa began to scream. She scrambled up on to her chair and screamed a thin, high, tearing scream that it seemed would never stop.

Roddy, trying to get to her, overturned his chair. He was crying out: 'Shut up! Shut up, Liss!'

Down the path from the front gate trotted an enormous dog, the size and colour of a calf, with a big mastiff head. Kate, who had not seen the beast for some time, flinched at its size.

'*Aber Kind!*' said Tante Adelheid, making good time across the grass to Melissa in the general melée. '*Es ist Bodo!*'

Bodo, the Deutsche Dogge, who was extremely gentle and sweet-natured, stood still and hung his great head apologetically. No doubt he had set off this kind of reaction before. His master, Herr Walther, the forester, was a stocky dark man of about fifty, who took off his hat now, shyly, and nodded to the company. As far as Kate was concerned he always wore fancy dress: in winter, in full loden green with silver buttons, he seemed to have stepped straight out of *Der Freischutz*. Now in summer he wore his loden green knee breeches with long fawn socks, heavy boots and a short-sleeved khaki shirt.

He said a word to Bodo who sat down on the grass, head erect, paws outstretched, like the Sphinx. Buddy went and sat beside him but Roddy kept his distance; Tante Adelheid held Melissa silenced in her arms. The forester excused himself for interrupting. Andreas and Tante Adelheid both urged him to join the party, to have a drink and something to eat from the grill. Herr Walther placed his hat on the trestle table gratefully and proceeded to shake hands with everyone present. With Tante Adelheid and with Melissa, whom he told not to be afraid of Bodo, with Roddy, to whom he said his name '*Walther!*', with Buddy, with Andreas, with Kate and with Mary, bowing a little, and finally with Jason. He uttered a few words in his soft bass voice.

Jason said, 'Fountains?' He took a few steps down the path. 'It's the darndest thing – fountains playing outside our house!'

Mary followed her husband timidly and Kate went after her. Tante Adelheid followed and handed Melissa to her mother.

'Look, honey,' said Mary softly, 'see the fountains.'

They were all watching now. In the evening light the Villa Florian, behind the massive gateposts and the tracery of the wrought iron gates, was barely three-dimensional. Kate saw it as a theatrical façade, with the balconies and mouldings, the pillared porch, suggested by skilful scene painting or simply glued on. The strange effect was caused by the extreme squareness of the villa. It had no projecting wings, the observer saw only one aspect of the house at a time. On the lawn, on either side of the driveway, two spreading columns of water rose and fell.

'Who could have turned them on?' asked Andreas.

'I don't even know where the faucets are,' said Jason.

Kate had some memory of the fountains marked upon a ground plan of the villa and described in the text as 'rising from small cups of stone on the east and south lawns'. Tante Adelheid and Herr Walther both knew the location of the faucets and pointed them out: at the south-east corner of the house behind the cypress tree.

'There are fountains on the south lawn too,' said Kate, 'I wonder if they...'

'Okay, you wise guys,' said Jason jovially. 'Roddy? Buddy? You've had your little joke!'

'No!' said Roddy in a choking voice. 'No, sir! We never touched anything. At least I never did!'

'Me neither,' said Buddy. 'Honest, Dad!'

'Honest, Dad!' mimicked Jason.

Herr Walther rumbled away a little and Kate seized on his suggestion.

'The fountains could have been in the on position for months, all through the winter and the spring. Then the water level in the system alters or a blockage is removed...'

'Yes,' said Mary, 'Oh yes, I'm sure that's it!'

'You forgot poltergeist activity,' said Jason drily. 'Roddy, it's time you ruffians took the brat over to bed anyway. Turn off the water.'

'I'll just go,' whispered Mary, 'and settle Liss down, Jay. She has a little cold.'

'You'll do nothing of the sort, sweetheart,' said Jason. 'Your dinner's ready. Go to Roddy, baby.'

Melissa held out her arms obediently to her elder brother. Kate saw that the child looked sleepy and sick. Buddy, the spokesman, said an awkward *'Danke Schön'* in the direction of Tante Adelheid; since they were not German children they had not been programmed to shake the hand of every guest before departing. They trailed across the road to the Villa Florian and let themselves in at the left hand gate.

Jason took his wife by the elbow and steered her towards the back lawn. Kate sensed that all the other adults wished to remain at the gate, see how the kids got on, see whether or not they could turn off the fountains. But they followed Jason. Herr Walther wanted his drink, Andreas was ready with his food and Tante Adelheid had to settle the guests down to table.

Kate stood her ground. She saw Roddy set down Melissa and lead her along the path, through the trees on to the south lawn. Buddy broke away from the others and stumped over to the cypress tree, across the grass, holding a hand out to the falling spray. Presently the fountains died down, then stopped altogether. Suddenly the villa blazed with light, shining out golden from every window that she could see. The glass cupola, rising up from the undulations of the roof, was filled with flickering golden fire.

There was no sound, only the light. No, it was nothing, the kids had put on every light in the place because they were nervous. Then, just as suddenly, the light altered. There was a dim light upstairs in one of the hexagonal rooms and another immediately below in the dining room. The rest of the house was dark. She went back to the others and reported that the fountains were turned off.

'I told them to handle it,' grinned Jason. 'They try to do their best for their old Dad, don't they, honey?'

Kate sat between Tante Adelheid and Herr Walther and ate her barbecue almost in silence. The lanterns had been lit; Mary said it was a pity the kids had not seen them. The food mellowed everyone more than the wine. Jason praised the barbecue, praised the Limbard salad with cucumber, celeriac and sweet corn that Kate had forced herself to make. Mary talked normally, even a little flirtatiously with Andreas, who was at his most charming. The summer night was full of the scent of red rambler roses from the trellis; the stars came out.

'How is the wood, Franz?' asked Tante Adelheid.

'Too dry,' replied Herr Walther. 'We must send round the loud speaker van here and at the American settlement.'

'Herr Walther,' said Jason, 'what was that phenomenon you mentioned...the phantom fire?'

The forester chuckled.

'Real fires give us more trouble,' he said, 'but I have seen this other. Many strange things have been known to happen at the Villa Florian.'

Andreas was translating for Mary's benefit and she repeated stubbornly, 'I don't believe in anything like that. And isn't our house kind of new to be haunted?'

'Completed in 1912,' said Kate, 'but the site was already old. Wasn't it originally a kind of priory, Andy?'

'It was a priest's house,' he said, 'built in the grounds of the convent. The whole of the Steinberg belonged to the Benedictine Order. Now it has been passed on to the town; we have only a few sisters remaining.'

'Yes!' said Jason eagerly. 'The Sisters! A community of gentlewomen. I must say I have hope of getting a look at their kitchens up there, and their cook-books!'

'They live in seclusion,' said Tante Adelheid. 'Who will have coffee?'

Kate helped clear the table. The guests walked about, stretching their legs. She spoke to the forester when she brought him his decaffeinated coffee.

'Herr Walther, what did you see? I mean the phantom fire.'

He gave her a blank look as if he had not understood her question and walked off without a word. She felt as firmly put off as Jason had been by Tante Adelheid.

Kate was plunged back into a kind of depression that she had not felt for years. She was a stranger in a strange land. Everyone was more or less kind but German speech and German customs were the measure of all things. Even Andy, her dear love, and now especially, Andy, her busy husband, spectacularly failed to understand sometimes. She sat at the trestle alone, drinking her coffee, and Bodo, who had eaten well, gave a groan of well-being at her feet. She patted his head. Mary Limbard came and sat opposite her and Kate saw that Andy and Jason were in animated conversation under the nut tree.

'Well, it certainly has been nice,' said Mary.

'You must come over for coffee in the morning one day soon,' said Kate. 'Or maybe we could go swimming in the lake.'

'I don't get to swim much,' said Mary.

Frau Moor, the black cat, marched boldly out of the house and down the path. Bodo twitched his ears and uttered a sigh. *I must say something,* thought Kate. *I must leave the way open. I must help this woman.*

'It's often difficult in a foreign country,' she said. 'If you ever wanted any help, Mary. Any help about anything, well, you know I'm here.'

'Well, thank you,' said Mary in her thin, flat voice. 'I m-manage quite well.'

She leaned back on the wooden bench so that she could see down the path to the Villa Florian.

'I guess the boys have gotten Liss off to sleep. The light in her room is out. There's just the light in the sitting room... they're watching television.'

'The sitting room?'

'There,' said Mary, 'just beside the front door. I must say the rooms aren't all that *spacious;* the house looks bigger from the outside.'

'Where is the dining room?' asked Kate.

'It opens on to the terrace,' said Mary. 'Jason always has a special dining room, just for us. He doesn't like to eat with the kids.'

She looked Kate in the eye as if daring her to say more, such as 'I could have sworn that was the sitting room' or 'I can't recall how the rooms were arranged'.

'You must take me over the house,' said Kate. '*I'll* pop over for coffee some morning.'

'No!' said Mary Limbard in terror. 'No, I don't mean to be rude but mornings are bad.'

'Afternoons, then,' persisted Kate cruelly.

'I'll call you,' said Mary.

She had flushed and now she turned pale again. Jason was shaking hands with Andreas, with Tante Adelheid, with Herr Walther and with Kate herself. Kate thought sadly: we know Jason Limbard, he looks even better off the screen. Jason grinned at Mary and Kate, 'I remembered the nut tree rhyme for Andreas!'

He was in excellent form, his grey eyes alight with mischief, now he quoted joyously:

'A dog, a woman, a walnut tree,

The harder you beat 'em the better they be!'

'And what did Andreas say to that?' asked Kate, stony-faced.

'I said you wouldn't be liking it too much!' said Andy.

He laughed aloud, with Jason, and Mary joined in.

'Rhymes about beating women and dogs were never my favourite thing,' said Kate. 'Why don't you translate the rhyme for Herr Walther and Tante Adelheid and see what they think?'

She turned and walked into the house, hearing Andreas say, 'You must excuse...'

In the kitchen she poured herself a glass of mineral water and carried it upstairs to the small room Onkel Ernst had used as a study. She put on the desk lamp and watched the Villa Florian through the white net drop between the heavy green curtains. It was a good vantage point. She saw Jason and Mary go in through the left hand gate and take the path to the south lawn. She could see the television screen, a bluish square of light, in the room on the left downstairs... the room that had been a dining room on Monday night, with a table set for dinner and lilac candles.

It was a puzzle. The villa had more than enough rooms for a family of five. Did they use the downstairs front room opposite the television room, for instance, or the lovely room that looked out on the north lawn, the winter room. Wait – perhaps that was the answer, an innocent answer. The Limbards had only been in residence about a week... perhaps they were trying the rooms out, moving the furniture around at Jason's whim. She had seen the dining room and the sitting room interchanged but now they were settled. Jason had taken the pleasanter terrace room – surely it had been the original dining room when the villa was built – for his own special dinners. It figured. And yet, and yet... were there any innocent explanations of Jason and his family?

Did Jason know or suspect that the game was up as far as she was concerned? She had actually seen him behaving like a sadistic monster, terrorising his family; she had heard him curse her as an intruder, and curse his family for letting her into the house. Intruders. The family was in a state of seige: everyone was an intruder. No question even of a neighbour dropping in for coffee in Mary's kitchen, let alone being shown over the house. She rather thought that Jason *didn't* know, in her case. She felt cold at the thought of his knowing. *Don't tell. Don't tell, Mary, ever.* What would he, what would they do if they knew? Well, how about, for openers, they close ranks and change the rooms around so that crazy Kate's story is inaccurate? But still she thought he didn't know... or he would have behaved differently at the barbecue.

She added up all the things she had heard as threats and ironies and *doubles entendres*. It was a cruel game Jason played with Mary and the kids and with the rest of the world, the unknowing, the dummies. It went deeper than that: it was acceptable for a father to refer to his kids as ruffians, savages, little monsters who had to be 'kept on bread and water in the cellar'. It was acceptable for a husband to be mock-threatening to his wife, to order her around, tell her to stop fussing. And the business with the cat. Was that one of Jason's production numbers... the pet cat which dies of strychnine poisoning at the Thanksgiving dinner? It was a sick joke. And Jason reminded his kids of the cat's death as they sat at table.

Andreas came in quietly. 'They've gone.'

'I know.'

He came and stood behind her, massaging her taut neck muscles.

'*Kätchen...Liebste.*'

'What did you think of them?'

'What can I say?'

He drew up a hassock and sat beside her chair. 'They seemed a bit up tight, that's all. Ammies. Jason, old Diet Jason, went out of his way to be nice to me.'

'He is horrible,' said Kate. 'A monster. Making jokes about cruelty, threatening them.'

'Katie,' said Andreas, 'he is giving us his book. I mean Lorbeer Verlag. I'm going to do business with him. Melchior will be pleased, very pleased.'

Kate sighed. 'Just be careful,' she said. 'I'm sure he's unstable.'

'You think about it too much,' said Andreas. 'It's unfair. Five minutes, less, and you judge him *completely*.'

'Andy, would you say Jason Limbard knows or suspects that I saw him acting like a crazy man the other night?'

'No, I'm sure he doesn't. Things he said...his whole attitude. I'm certain he doesn't know.'

'Okay,' said Kate. 'Okay, I'll try to put it out of my mind.'

She felt cowardly. Cowardly yellow-dog Kate. She hardly dared look at the Villa Florian; it knew her fears; it was full of grisly secrets. *Summer is a bad time.*

'Come to bed,' said Andreas.

'Mmm...'

She bent her head and they kissed.

Kate half woke in the night and heard a light tread upon the stairs to the attic. Andreas lay naked on the sheet at her side; a cooler breeze came through the open window. There were no ghosts in the Forsthaus...what was Tante Adelheid doing wandering about in the night? There came the sound of a window being closed, the small gabled window on the landing of the attic stairs. Kate let the cool breeze sweep over her naked body and drifted back into sleep.

She could never sleep very late even on holiday. Next morning she decided not to jog up the Steinberg. When she came out of the bathroom Frau Moor was coming lightly down the attic stairs.

'What's up there?' she asked the cat. 'What is all this attic traffic?'

She went up and peered into the odd-shaped room full of electrical conduits and massive beams. There was a little furniture stored there and a minumum of cobwebs; there had once been as family of owls, Tante Adelheid had said, roosting high overhead. The front window of the attic was small and set high up, with its own tiny grey shutters. Before this window stood a cabin trunk about fifty centimetres high and on the cabin trunk was mounted an old wicker armchair. Tante Adelheid came here even in the dead of night and watched the Villa Florian. In the seat of the chair, on the worn cushion, rested Onkel Ernst's massive pair of field glasses.

II

They had weathered all the storms: the barbecue, the bit with the fountains, the strange time-out bit that Buddy hardly believed, the waiting until Mom and the Old Man came home. The Old Man was in a good mood; he let them see the end of the movie, with John Wayne talking German. They went to bed about half-past eleven with only a cursory bawling out. Buddy was hot and exhausted; he didn't want to talk, just to concentrate on that unbelievable set of frames he had running inside his head. But Roddy was freaking out.

'What *was* it?' he said again. 'What could it be? D'you think anyone else saw it? D'you think the Old Man saw it?'

'Oh, balls!' said Buddy. 'If he thought we set the place on fire or let off a flare or whatever, he'd have killed us stone dead.'

'He saves up some things.'

'Go over it again,' said Buddy wearily. 'When did it start? I was in the bushes fucking about with that damn faucet.'

'I said to Liss "let's run and get the lights on and hide from old Buddy".'

Buddy knew that his brother was always in a rush to get the lights on wherever they went. As he came through the bushes to the steps of the terrace he heard the pair of them, Liss gasping and laughing, as they went into the terrace room, the Old Man's new dining room. He saw the standard lamp go on.

'You went into the dining room and put on the standard lamp,' he said.

'It was nothing to do with the lamp!' Roddy almost sobbed. 'We walked on across the dining room and into the hall and I turned on more lights and we ran on up the stairs. I wanted to get her to bed. I figured we would lean over the bannisters or drum on them a little and shout woo-hoo to you as you came in.'

'Woo-hoo,' said Buddy sourly. 'And then there was this light all over the house.'

How long had it lasted? As much as a minute? Two munutes? Long enough for him to be struck dumb, paralysed on the terrace, then to walk across the terrace, through the dining room and the hall, down to their new sitting room. Where *he* turned on a light because *he* was scared, not only of the mysterious flood of golden light but of the things that only he had seen.

For as he stood there, dumbstruck at the light inside the house, he saw that someone else was on the terrace. Far away in shadow, then coming nearer. Buddy had seen him quite clearly: he was old with a handsome face, snowy white hair and a clipped white moustache. He was sitting in a big chair and wearing a fancy dressing gown. Then he came closer, smoothly, chair and all, and Buddy realised that it was a wheelchair, a big old-fashioned cane or wicker wheelchair. The old man could not see Buddy; the old man made no sound and neither did his chair. In other words this was some kind of show that he was observing, a video with the sound turned down.

The old man was terrifying. Buddy felt himself shifted for an instant into a whole new dimension of terror. The old man's face changed before his eyes, thickening and twisting in a soundless snarl. Then Buddy saw the two dogs loping across the south lawn to the foot of the terrace steps. They were huge, as tall as Bodo, and shaggy grey and rangy, a little like Afghan hounds. They waited and the old man in the chair threw them something which they began tearing apart on the steps. Something... when he thought back Buddy was almost certain that it was a dead rabbit, skinned but with the head left on. He saw the long ears. Maybe it was a hare; they had a lot of hares in Germany. Mom had bought deep frozen hare from the supermarket to cook for the Old Man.

So he stood there being shown these sights and then they were gone. The terrace was empty but the whole of the lawn, the terrace, the house wall with its peeling balcony, was flooded with a suffocating warmth, dry and dangerous. Buddy ran across the terrace into the house feeling that his hair might catch fire.

He ran right into the golden light and it was cool, cool and pleasant. Weird. He stood in the hall under the dome and felt the cool fire all round him and heard Roddy calling from a long way off saying, What was it? Was anything on fire? Then he ran through the light to their miserable too-small sitting room by the front door and turned on the switch. The strange light was gone. No point in scaring Roddy, let alone Liss, by saying anything about the old man, the *other* old man. Buddy wondered if they would have seen the same things he did if they had been on the terrace. Was he singled out, chosen to see such things, like having ESP or Mind Powers? Jesus, that was one faculty he could do without. But they had all seen the light.

'You think he'll take us to this München or Munchkin?' Roddy broke into his thoughts.

'München,' said Buddy. 'He won't take us if he thinks we want to go.'

'I'd sure as hell like to get out of this creepy house for a while,' said Roddy.

Buddy laughed. He had no great hopes of München or anywhere else when the Old Man was along. If he had the choice of a haunted house minus the Old Man, and anywhere else with him, then he'd take the fucking ghosts and boogie men, thank you.

'Bud,' said Roddy, 'Melissa is sick.'

'She's got a cold.'

'No,' said Roddy, 'it's worse than that. She has a bump on her head from last Monday, the day with the teddy bear.'

'Shit, she's been walking around...she was just fine.'

'She should see a doctor. Mom knows.'

'Look, it will be all right,' said Buddy. 'Here no-one knows us. The Old man speaks the lingo real good. He can breeze into some Kraut hospital and tell 'em one about an unfortunate fall. Liss has no record, no fractures.'

Yet he was filled with dread. It made the Old Man worse than ever when he cracked them up. And with Melissa five years old, he would be afraid that she would spill the beans to the Kraut doctors and nurses.

Buddy remembered the time he had spilled the beans himself once, when he was seven, a real dumb kid, and the Old Man broke his collar bone shoving him against a tree. Mom took him across two state lines and put him in hospital under the name Joey Lingard. Pretty smart. Joey for his real name – Joseph, what a drag – and Lingard...close enough so that if he said Limbard it would be just his mushy seven-year-old way of talking. Anyway he went through it all and was enjoying himself. Having ice-cream, and suddenly he told a Pink Lady. She was a voluntary helper who came around with books and cigarettes and candy.

She was old, older than Mom, an ordinary-looking lady with glasses and she knew there was something wrong with him, more than a broken collar bone. She was some kind of a witch. Her name was on a card pinned to her jacket: Ida Hogg. He laughed at her funny name when she had him sound it out. I'd a hog but I sold it for bacon.

Miz Hogg said, 'What is the matter, Joey? I know something is the matter.' So he told her and she knew it was the truth. Her mouth became thin and her eyes dark and spooky behind the thick glasses. She said, 'I don't know if I can help you, kid.'

So he didn't hear anything more, he forgot, he was only a dumb kid, reading comics and kidding around with the others on the ward — the children's ward, of course, with pink and blue furniture and Mother Goose cut-outs. If the doctors or nurses asked how it happened he told the story, same as before, how he fell down a bank and hit a tree. But Ida Hogg had given it a try and the first thing the doctors did was to start asking Mom awkward questions.

He was up and about now, with no temperature or complications. Mom got his clothes from his locker 'to wash'. He put on his jeans over his pyjamas and Mom draped the parka over his cast and they went away through the car park. Miz Lingard and her boy Joey just hit the road and crossed back over the state lines — Mom had been commuting anyway — back home to the Old Man. And Roddy. Liss was not even born. Mom had their other brother in between him and Liss. He was called Danny and he lived two days, he was born with a respiratory problem. In his dreams Buddy saw this brother grown into a little kid and they all lived on a ranch with Mom and Grandpa Hale.

Ever after the hospital in Greenery, West Virginia, he thought of Ida Hogg, the good witch, the Pink Lady, who had just known. Why couldn't more people just know, by looking at them? Ever after that — and he had tough bones or something, tougher than Roddy, poor bastard — he was the Old man's idea of a model patient. 'Yes, sir, playing baseball.' 'Sure, Doc, I'll take more care.'

Roddy told Buddy about this one time *he* had spilled the beans, because it was so hilarious. He was in hospital in South

Carolina with a broken hand and there was an older kid, maybe fifteen, in the next bed with a broken arm and a broken nose, he was plaster up to there. So Roddy told him about his hand – 'My Old man did this' – and the boy said in a real hillbilly voice: 'What the hell you thank happen to *me,* Yank? My Paw can lick yours any day.' Roddy didn't say much more to the boy, whose name was Virgil, except to ask him what would happen, how it would work out?

Virgil knew how things would work out. It had happened to his two elder brothers and it would go the same way with him. One day, when he was seventeen or eighteen, he would hit Paw back, knock him down and leave home.

Buddy knew it couldn't be that simple with the Old man. Who was to say that he was meaner and more psycho than Virgil's Paw? But he had more to lose, they all had more to lose. The money and the show and the houses and the syndicated column with the perfect family, Roddy, the 'Number One Son' and good old good-buddy Buddy and cute Baby Liss and, hovering in the background, My Mary, in a frilled apron.

Buddy stopped remembering and tried to sleep. He put his pyjama top over his head to keep out the brightness of the crazy room with six sides and trees on the wall. It was still hot, a hot night in central Germany, and he wouldn't be seventeen or eighteen for a hundred years.

He slept deeply and knew he couldn't have had more than three hours or he would have been able to wake more quickly. As it was he dragged himself awake when Roddy started to holler. He saw the glow of yellow light and he saw a tall figure and for a moment he was returned to that new dimension of terror. It was the old man ghost from the terrace coming to get them. Then he was awake and it was only the Old Man making a raid. A bad raid, not just an 'I caught you guys talking or jerking off' raid, but a Get Them Up raid.

'Out!' growled the Old man. '*Raus,* you sons of bitches. Time we had some order in this place. Never too late for you two lazy soft-gut cretins to learn to obey...'

He hit Roddy over the head and dragged him on to the floor by his ankles. Buddy struggled up and stood to attention. His father hauled off and punched him in the gut. Buddy rolled on the floor, dying, hurting, trying to get his breath. Jason switched off his torch and turned on the overhead light; he watched his son writhing on the floor and cursed him a little under his breath, stirring him sharply with a hard bare foot. Buddy, gulping air, saw that although it was a hot night his father had come to make his raid in his silk dressing gown.

Chapter 3
Tales of the Villa Florian

Two mornings later when Kate came down at six-thirty, ready to jog, she found Tante Adelheid folding a piece of cooking foil into a small package.

'I have been watching the villa,' she said. 'It is a bad place in summer.'

It was one of those flat, spooky pronouncements that only Tante Adelheid could get away with. The old woman was so matter of fact and so upright that she compelled belief.

'What happens?' demanded Kate. 'And why in summer?'

Tante Adelheid looked at her mildly and poured coffee into the summer beaker, with a flowery meadow before a blue house, a cat in the meadow. She left unfilled Kate's precious winter beaker with a leafless tree before the little house, a robin in the snow.

'You will have coffee at the convent,' she said. 'I would like you to give this package to Mrs Greenwood, Sister Rachel. After breakfast you will hear something of the Villa Florian.'

'I'd better wear jeans,' said Kate, 'not running shorts.'

The convent had no main gate; she went to the gatehouse on the west wall and when she tugged a handle a bell sounded in the distance. The gate was opened by the member of the foundation whom she did not know by sight – the oldest, Kate guessed, a round, medium-sized woman in a navy blue dress and a head covering of the same soft, thick cotton. The impression she gave was one of immense vitality and cheerfulness. Her face was round, smooth and olive-skinned; only her eyes behind thick spectacles were netted with wrinkles.

'*Schwester Claudia,*' she said. '*Grüss Gott!*'

'Kate Reimann.'

They shook hands and Kate stepped into another world. There was a tall brick building ahead, and all about, springing up out of the cropped grass, were ruins in red sandstone, a chapel, an unroofed tower with grass growing inside its walls. There were paths edged with round stones or scallop shells and beds of bright flowers: zinnias, asters, dahlias, salvias, petunias.

Sister Claudia led the way into the kitchen, a large, bleak room, half in sunlight, half in shadow. The long table was covered at one end with a cloth and the sisters were eating toast from a toaster with their breakfast coffee. The kitchen was full of well-worn artifacts still in use although they were very old. Kate saw wooden bowls, a stone mortar and pestle, a set of churns, old shelves upon the wall with glass and pottery containers for herbs. There were racks for knives, hooks for ladles and places for skimmers, bread lifters and warming pans so ancient that she hardly recognised their purpose.

Kate sat down and handed over her package to Sister Rachel Greenwood, a thin dark woman who wore a green dress and did not cover her short cap of dark hair. At the head of the table sat Freifrau von Thal, Sister Florentine, still beautiful, her hair both gold and silver, her features aquiline. She wore a *'Tracht'* or folk costume: a short jacket of green serge over a high-necked frilled white blouse and a skirt of matching green cotton. As she poured Kate's coffee a beam of sunlight caught the cup and saucer with their pattern of mauve orchids and grey leaves; the cup's handle was twig-like. Kate thought of the little ceramic pot around the alpine violet, a modern copy, but *this* was an original. She took the precious thing and held it up to the light; she saw that all the sisters were drinking from these cups.

'Surely,' she said, 'surely the cups and saucers are *Jugendstil?*'

The sisters smiled; Kate realised she had passed a test.

'Yes,' said Sister Florentine, 'they are by a Dutchman, Juriann Kok...a complete tea-set, and of course they come from the Villa Florian. When so much went to Darmstadt after the war we simply kept these cups and saucers.'

They ate quince jelly, home-made of course, with their

toast, and drank the same brand of coffee that Tante Adelheid used. There was a kind of boarding-school jolliness about the breakfast: the Sisters liked to laugh and make little jokes. In fact they were very like nuns, or what Kate had always imagined nuns to be. They were pleased to have a visitor, especially a young visitor, and asked a great many questions about the United States, Germany, Art and Life.

Sister Rachel asked gently, 'Do you plan to have children, Kate?'

'Yes,' said Kate firmly. 'And soon, before I am too old.'

This made all the sisters laugh indulgently; she was young, they were old. *At this moment I may be pregnant*, she thought, she had not taken the pill for a month; they both knew, she and Andreas, that it was now or never.

The sisters were speaking of St Hildegarde of Bingen, that wise woman (or Wise Woman), and of the curious history of their convent.

'No longer dedicated,' said Sister Claudia between sips. 'We sometimes persuade a Father to say mass in our chapel but for him it is no more holy than a living-room.'

'The land and buildings all belong to the town, to Breitbach,' said Sister Florentine. 'They don't bandy this fact about or we would be plagued by speculators.

The sisters kept hens and had a thriving garden; they also supplied herbs to a group of health food stores. Kate recalled her aunt's resigned explanation: they were ekeing out Sister Florentine's personal fortune. Kate asked about the other nuns of the order.

'I am the last one!' said Sister Claudia. 'Elsewhere they had flourishing houses but here I was the only novice. I took my final vows in 1935. We were eight during the war, with seven lay sisters. My, what a time that was. How the breakfast table was crowded.'

'The Abbess, who was very old, died in 1941,' said Sister Florentine, 'and old Sister Elisabeth in the same year. 1944 was our time of sorrow: three nuns and two lay sisters made a journey to Frankfurt and were killed when the city was bombed. In 1945 three lay sisters went to find their families in what is now East Germany; we still send them food parcels at Christmas. Sister Ursula, my girlhood friend from Kassel, died of pneumonia in the winter of 1946. Our oldest inhabitant, Sister Margarethe, died in 1954, aged 93.'

'The order believed for a long time that I had died too,' said Sister Claudia with a trace of complacency. 'I corrected their error but I would not leave this foundation. My petition for release from my vows is gathering dust somewhere. I do not know whether I am a nun or not. It is a mystery. I stay on here.'

'Ah, we are meant to remain,' said Sister Rachel. 'St Hildegarde takes care of her good comrades.'

She unwrapped the silver package from Tante Adelheid and Kate saw that it contained red rose-petals. She seemed to hear her aunt's voice. 'Roses from the Villa Florian.'

'Come, Frau Reimann,' said Sister Florentine. 'It is not my turn for the kitchen. We will go for a walk together.'

They climbed an old staircase, beyond the kitchen, and came to three bedrooms and a sitting room. The disused parts of the convent loomed all around them. To Kate it was oppressively old and echoing, however brightly the sun shone through the windows and unglazed openings in the walls. Sister Florentine led her to the end of a corridor and there were two rattan chairs waiting by a window bay. A bunch of greenery and wildflowers in a blue pottery vase stood on the deep window sill. They sat down together and looked over the wall at the road leading to the Forsthaus and the Villa Florian.

Both houses looked their best from this angle and both could be seen for what they were. The Forsthaus was straight forward, functional, domestic; by comparison with the villa it could very well be described as a cottage. The Villa Florian, with its dome sparkling in the morning sun, the lawns visible and the carriage sweep, had been built on a different scale. It possessed the grandeur of a great house and at the same time the charm of a smaller one. Kate thought of the Petit Trianon.

'The Villa Florian was built for my grandfather in 1912,' said Sister Florentine. 'One of his very few redeeming features was his artistic taste. He was an officer and a gentleman in an age when this meant, very often, a swaggering empty-headed bully. My grandfather, as a young man, was very handsome, intelligent and charming. My grandmother, married at seventeen, must have had reason for hope. As it was her Baron turned out licentious and cruel, no sort of husband. He had a weakness for artistic circles in Paris, London, Vienna...in Brussels he had his own atelier.'

'Did he want to be an artist himself?' asked Kate. 'I mean, with his own studio?'

'No,' said Sister Florentine, 'I don't believe he did. He was always the patron, the connoisseur, the one with money. He collected sparingly but with great acumen: a Monet, a Degas, in London a Turner, a portfolio of Pre-Raphaelite drawings. He had enormous luck...found a Cranach at the flea-market in Frankfurt, a Breughel in a Brussels junk-shop. He owned two Ensors, they hung in the villa, along with work by Walter Crane and Franz von Stück.

'He was much taken by the development of the new decorative style, the New Art, which took in so much. So many objects in common use were designed by artists: the furniture, the china and glassware. He commissioned, at last, his own villa in this style; he worked on the design himself with his own architect, a pupil and assistant of the great Belgian, Victor Horta. This was the young Swede, Magnus Jacobsen. Also working on the project, some said the reason for it, though I doubt that, was a young woman, also an artist. She came from England; her name, probably an artistic pseudonym, was Tamara Paige.'

'She was an illustrator!' said Kate. 'I never knew that she... *Tamara Paige!* Oh, I have a friend in München who would be so interested. Wasn't she very beautiful, dark, modelled for some of the *Jugendstil* artists?'

'That is the young woman. Her name was not spoken... whispered perhaps...in our house, the estate near Kassel. My grandmother, poor woman, felt that Breitbach was still too near for a love-nest. She had three grown children; my father, the eldest son, managed the estate. So my grandfather – they were all very young by our reckoning – went his own way and built on this old site his jewel of the new art.

'The Steinberg is very ancient and humans have always lived here: in the caves around the lake, then in a fort here on the hilltop. It has often seemed to me and to my companions that the site of the Villa Florian was accursed, ages ago. It carries on its ancient evil in a strange seasonal way. Every season has two faces: summer, which seems to smile, can be fierce, hungry, like a wolf; autumn, ripe, misty, can be over-ripe, venomous, drawing off life and vitality. But winter, so much feared, is kind; its ghosts are harmless. Can you accept any of this?'

'I find it hard to believe,' said Kate, wavering. 'Sister Florentine, you know what I saw the other night, Tante Adelheid has told you. A man being horribly cruel to his family. And in the same moment I caught a glimpse of a young girl and a dog...dogs...on the south lawn. Is there some connection between the two experiences?'

'I feel sure that the girl and the dogs were from another age,' said Sister Florentine. 'To put it plainly: ghosts. And according to our theories of the place this cruel man, Limbard, will be encouraged in his cruelty, he will enter into a relationship with the house. Let me tell you more.

'When the old walls of the Priest House on that site were torn down and the cellars rebuilt for the new villa, the bones of two children were found incorporated into a wall. This was an old magical practice to make a building more stable. My grandfather had the bones reinterred, not given a proper burial. He also built the bones of small animals into his new house.

'The house looks to the east and on the east wall there are symbols of spring...'

'Can bad things happen in spring?' asked Kate.

'It is the season of change,' said Sister Florentine, 'and change is not always for the better. My grandfather always favoured the summer aspect, with the south lawn and the terrace. There is a narcissistic reference here to his own name, Baron Wolfgang von Sommer. He completed his beautiful villa and lived there with his English girl and the young architect. He was something of a sportsman still and he had begun to breed his dogs, Irish wolfhounds. His old kennels are on Wolfweg, behind the Forsthaus; now they are used by the German Shepherd Society.

'He entertained a little but the atmosphere in the Villa Florian was never quite what my grandmother and my mother imagined it to be: a bohemian bacchanal, with loose women and drunken artists. The place was full of hatred and tension, there was no love there, not even of the most transient kind. I have this from witnesses: from my father, from servants who came down from Kassel.

'The long summer before the First World War was now at an end. The Baron was forty-five years old in 1914, the year of my birth, a young grandfather but a middle-aged officer. Of course he re-joined his regiment; he was invalided out in 1917, a cripple in a wheelchair. He brought along his batman, a young farm boy by the name of Hans Blümig, a shrewd and brutal character who remained with him and was for long periods the only servant at the Villa Florian.

'The Baron... we must feel some pity for him... cut himself off from the world in his house of art. He was very much alone. The poor young architect, Jacobsen, did not long survive the war; he drowned when a ferry sank off Ostend in 1919. The young English girl left him too, in the early twenties, and he found no other mistress. He lived on with Blümig and his generations of wolf-hounds, enormous and fearsome. When Ernst and Adelheid Kramer were first living in the Forsthaus he was a frightening and unpredictable neighbour.

'My mother brought me to visit the terrible old man once, when I was eighteen years old, in 1932. The Villa Florian had been spring-cleaned for the occasion and so I beheld its last flowering... every room, every object in common use, from the lamps to the spoons, imbued with a living fantasy.

'We arrived at the beginning of summer; the Baron treated us with great charm and courtesy. My mother, who had seen her father-in-law in his cruel mood at Kassel, was distrustful. I wondered what all the fuss had been about. My mother was more and more ill at ease: she confided at last that she believed the Baron had a woman in the house. She had caught glimpses of her in the gardens, in the corridors... the flick of a long skirt or négligée, a scent of musk and roses in the bathroom.

'I was full of curiosity after that and searched a little. I thought the Villa Florian was far too small a place, compared to the rambling country house in Kassel, for any other guest to remain hidden for very long. Of course I never found a lady in déshabille and I was such a matter-of-fact young person that I failed to recognise a certain experience for what it was.

'One warm evening as I came running up the stairs I saw a young man just about to enter the trophy room. It was a room not much used any more because the Baron could not hunt and the sight of his trophies made him irritable. I can still see the young man as he stood there, half turned away from me, wearing a blue jacket and dark trousers. His hair was silky and golden, hanging untidily over his collar, fine hair, the sort that is difficult to manage. He went into the room and shut the door after him.

'I was too shy to follow him at once. I went to the bedroom first, collected the book I had been sent to fetch, and looked at myself in the mirror. When I did look into the trophy room it was empty and it stank like the slaughterhouse yard in our village. I felt sure that some of my grandfather's trophies of the chase had been badly prepared.'

'But who was it?' asked Kate. 'I mean, if it was a ghost?'

'Why, it was Jacobsen,' said Sister Florentine. 'I am sure that it was Magnus Jacobsen, the young Swedish architect. I asked that oaf, Blümig, about the young man and described him. Blümig, a big, strapping bully, the sort of man who always seemed to be bulging out of his coat, went soft and pale. He entreated me not to tell the Baron what I had seen.

'I pressed my advantage and made him tell me more. He produced a photograph and at last a newspaper clipping of the ferry disaster. Herr Jacobsen had been travelling to England in search of a commission. The Baron had not wished him to go but he relented at the last and let Blümig drive him to the train with his luggage. The Baron was deeply distressed by the loss of Herr Jacobsen and the thought of his ghost walking would make him... unmanageable.

'I could scarcely imagine my grandfather being distressed about anything but *I* was certainly distressed by the story. I could not pass the trophy room again without a feeling of deep sadness. Perhaps I was half in love with my first and only ghost, a man dead for more than ten years. I believed that Blümig was not telling all of the truth, that the Baron had quarrelled with Magnus Jacobsen and driven him away.

'My grandfather could certainly become unmanageable. In the middle of June there was trouble with a party of young people who had camped down by the lake. They were *Wandervogel* who tramped about seeking strength through joy. The Baron had an unreasoning hatred of them. When two young women came to ask if they could take photographs he set the dogs on them.'

'Wolf-hounds?'

'Two wolf-hounds, César and Attila, both full-grown. His last dogs, as it turned out. My mother and I saw nothing of this; we were dressing for dinner in the beautiful cool bedroom on the north side, overlooking the *tannenbaum* upon the lawn. Then we heard the sounds.'

Sister Florentine's voice shook. She lifted a fine hand to the holy medal at her throat.

'We stole into the corridor and listened: the dogs were attacking their victims. We were afraid and hung back; when we rushed down at last there was nothing to be seen. The Baron, our docile and sentimental companion of the past weeks, was gloating in his wheel chair. The dogs were trembling with excitement; their muzzles were blood-stained.'

'Were they hurt?' asked Kate. 'Were the girls badly hurt? Were they killed?'

'One was badly hurt,' said Sister Florentine, 'but my grandfather was never brought to justice. Conflicting stories were told... it seemed that the girls had simply trespassed and been attacked by two watch dogs. No-one had the courage to suggest that the dogs be put down. My mother and I experienced little of this. That same night we fled from the Villa Florian. We came to this convent, here on the top of the hill... one of the novices had been at school with me. My mother was a delicate and sensitive person; she was almost in a state of collapse when I got her out of the villa.

'I loved the convent of St Hildegarde from the first. It impressed me as an abode of peace and of a special wisdom. A place – this will sound very mediaeval to you, Katherine – where a woman could be independent. My poor husband, Anton von Thal, was a pilot. When I was widowed in 1941 after seven years of marriage, I returned to this foundation. There seemed to be no hope for Germany or for the world; we were plunged into barbarism. My grandfather was dead. He died in 1936 of rabies...hydrophobia, as we used to call it, contracted of course from one of the dogs. This time the poor brutes *were* shot.

'The Villa Florian now belonged to my father; there was no place in his life for art treasures. Hans Blümig, who remained as caretaker, was on good terms with the new régime, a party member from the first. Pretty soon the house was requisitioned for the use of the local Nazi hierarchy, an order my father could not refuse. A local official and his wife settled into the house. In spite of the war and the repressive power of the state nothing bad was reported from the Villa Florian for a short time.

'When I first arrived in 1941 the house was untenanted; even Blümig was at the front. Ernst Kramer, our estate manager, was on active service, we had only our old priest, Father Helm, to assist us. Together with dear Adelheid we stripped the Villa Florian of its treasures and brought them here for safekeeping. Oh, it was a sight for the angels... six, eight women, in winter, with a farm cart and Father Helm driving his ancient auto. Some of the pieces were too heavy for us to attempt. We concentrated on the paintings, china, glassware and the lighter pieces of furniture. All these things remained in our cellars until the war was over, then my brother had them presented to the Landesmuseum in Darmstadt, where there is a fine collection of *Jugendstil* art.

'The Villa Florian was put into use again at the beginning of 1943; it became a rest home for a select company of soldiers unfit for active service. The medical officer in charge was a certain Dr Wilhelm Ranke, an alienist who specialised in cases of battle-fatigue, what used to be called shell shock. Still, I must not digress; that story belongs to Sister Rachel. I must recall another summer.

'The summer everyone remembers best was in 1945 when the madness began slowly to come to an end. There was never such a summer: blazing hot over the ruined cities and the countryside, the armies and the fugitives. Fields of corn tangled with poppies and cornflowers, trees laden with summer fruits, the woods and lakes and streams unspoiled then and burgeoning. We prayed that the Villa Florian would remain empty – the last of the disturbed veterans had been taken away – so that we could use it as some kind of emergency shelter.

'Then Adelheid, still waiting for Ernst Kramer to return from the Russian front, reported that Hans Blümig was back. With him in the house was a gang of boys, young soldiers turned into scavengers. They were armed and ferocious; they prowled about after food. They terrorised Frau Kramer and the people she had in the Forsthaus even though she had given them all the precious food she could spare. Frau Kramer and two other young women there had to keep watch and drove the boys off with a firehose. There was no way to help the poor creatures or to stop their raids.'

Kate remembered the nickname common to the last remnants of Hitler's army. 'Werewolves,' said Kate. 'The boys were werewolves.'

'It was a word we did not hear at the time,' said Sister Florentine. 'Those wolvish boys were really not fighting a last ditch stand. They were hungry, diseased and homeless; they were living in a nightmare. The vile Blümig had become a lieutenant in the SS. Now he burned his uniform. He mastered the boys with food and wine; he whipped and sodomised them for his pleasure. There were seven boys. Six of them decided to murder him, and one of those seven unfortunates made his escape! He came to us, to this convent on the hill.

'I remember it very well: a boy, fourteen or fifteen years old, filthy, scarred from head to foot, hardly able to speak except to beg for help. It was not only physical help he wanted but to be free from the nightmare. He told us, he confessed to us, bit by bit, a story not only of brutality and terror but of haunting. Blümig saw his old master, the Baron; all the boys at one time or another saw the dogs, the wolf-hounds. At times the whole house burned with a strange golden light.'

'I saw it!' said Kate in a whisper. 'I saw it on the night of the grill-party! What is it, Sister Florentine? Has it any meaning?'

'We have always taken it as a warning of danger,' said Sister Florentine. 'Sometimes it means death. Franz understood it as a warning.'

'Franz?'

'Didn't I say? The boy who came to us was Franz Walther, the forester.'

'He is still here!' said Kate. 'He never went home.'

'No,' said Sister Florentine. 'His father was dead at the front, his mother and a younger sister had died in the bombing of Mainz. Some years later he made contact with his cousins in Bavaria; he still visits them on his holidays. He had walked south as the war ended with another *Luftwaffenhilfer* and they came together with members of a youth battalion. They hid from everyone...the older soldiers walking home, the Americans who would have put them in a camp. Blümig, the SS officer in hiding, caught them in a wood. He gave them food and weapons and brought them back to the Steinberg and the Villa Florian.'

'What happened with the kids and that terrible Blümig?' asked Kate.

'There was no civil authority we could ask for help,' said Sister Florentine. 'It had to be the Americans. Old Father Helm had to be our liaison, although he was very frail and not always in his right wits, poor old man. He did very well. One day we came down the hill to the crossroads and met Father Helm and a pair of military policemen in a jeep. We were three women: Frau Kramer, Sister Claudia and myself. We did not dare bring Sister Rachel, her papers were not in order, she might have been sent to a camp. We did not dare to bring Franz, the eye-witness of conditions at the villa: he would surely have been taken away. Even the family from Silesia who were sheltering in the Forsthaus were afraid that they would be moved on by the Americans so they laid low.

'These were our first Americans... big men, one young, one about forty, armed of course. They had strict orders not to fraternise because all Germans were their enemies, all Germans were National Socialists. They distrusted us even more because we were clean, healthy and respectable; I was thirty-one years old, your Tante Adelheid only a year or two older. Father Helm tried to make something of the fact that the Villa Florian belonged to my family.

'The sergeant spoke German. He shouted questions at us. When I came nearer to hand over our papers he held me off at gunpoint. "Get back, get back!" he said. He was suspicious because Frau Kramer had a husband at the front, she did not know where he was. He could see that Sister Claudia was a nun, in a full black habit...he ordered her to remove her coif, showing her short hair. He held us at gunpoint and had the young corporal search us for weapons. When Father Helm protested, he gave the old man a push. The young soldier, embarrassed, patted us up and down, the way one sees in films. At last the Sergeant understood what we wanted but he believed it might be a trap. We begged him not to hurt the boys;

we had no such scruples regarding Blümig.

'There had been no fighting of any kind in and around Breitbach. The citizens welcomed the Americans or were at least resigned to their presence. The little town contained no soldiers, no able-bodied men, only old men, a few wounded veterans and very young boys. But one SS man and a handful of boy soldiers could open fire and make a pocket of resistance. Frau Kramer assured the sergeant that there had been no movement in the villa for a whole day. He asked angrily why we were wasting his time, why we didn't just go in. I said: "We are afraid."

'In the end the two men drove to the back gate, after I had told them the lay-out of the villa. They went in across the north lawn; we stood at the front gates and heard them shouting to one another and shouting to Blümig to surrender. Presently the young man came to the front door and called us in.

'It was the end of August, a burning hot day in late summer. The villa was cool, its walls are thick; the light from the dome made a great circle on the carpet. I saw how beautiful the house was, unmarked by war and suffering. The young corporal looked sick. The sergeant came thudding down the staircase, making the whole house ring. He was pale too, a tall cowboy of a man, pale under his tan.

'Show them!' he ordered the corporal.

A spasm passed over the old woman's face. 'Oh, Katherine,' she whispered, leaning forward to press Kate's hand. 'You have been spared. Pray God that sights like these never come your way.'

'What was it?' whispered Kate.

Sister Florentine drew herself up and went on with the story.

'We stood at the door of the room that opened on to the terrace, the one my grandfather built as a dining room, with a connecting door to the kitchen. The room stank of excrement and death. I saw a boy lying with his head on the table, another had fallen backwards with his chair; he had one hand up, stiffly clawing the air. Father Helm and Sister Claudia began to pray.

'I went, with Adelheid, to a third boy who lay near the kitchen door; he was face downwards on the carpet in a running atitude, one leg bent, elbows out. This boy and the others were all very young, no more than sixteen; they wore uniform still, their hair was cropped. As I bent down a little to touch the identity disc that the boy was wearing, a stink of almonds came to me from his gaping mouth.

'Adelheid said to the sergeant: "They are poisoned!" The sergeant shook his head from side to side like a dog. He said: "Jesus, Jesus..."

'We looked at the table; its cloth was damask, stained and filthy. The boys had been drinking port wine out of china cups; there was the bottle, vintage tawny port from Portugal, with an English label. I bent over and the reek of cyanide came from the bottle.

'"We found this Blümig," said the sergeant. "You'd better identify him, girls."

'We followed him through the kitchen, which was also disordered from this last occupation of the villa. He led us down the cellar stairs, the inside stairway, off the kitchen. Blümig was in his old room, the basement flat, the *souterrain*.

'It was a cosy nest, furnished with pieces from the Baron's collection. Some we had missed when we cleared the house, some not... there were so many beautiful things. The Samurai swords hung on the wall above a suit of lacquered armour; on another wall was a large poster by Alphons Mucha of a young woman in filmy draperies, a soft and pretty example of the Art Nouveau.

'Blümig was in a sitting position in one of the French chairs from the dining room. He wore a pair of grandfather's silk pyjamas, dark blue with scarlet frogging. He was about forty-five years old with blunt features but now he looked like my grandfather. Or rather it looked as if the Baron had turned into a hideous bloated corpse.'

Sister Florentine shuddered and almost involuntarily her hand moved first to her forehead. She made the sign of the cross.

'Blümig was in an obscene attitude,' she said stiffly, 'his clothes disarranged, his legs spread, a cushion on the ground as if a boy had knelt before him. He was held to the chair by a thick brown silk cord that had caught him across the biceps...it was an old bellrope from one of the upstairs rooms. A thinner rope had caught him around the throat. It was as if he had grown into the chair, caught by the tendrils and arabesques of the chair's design. He had been stabbed many times, in the groin, in the belly, in the throat; his clothes were stiff and dark with blood.

'Adelheid and I both uttered some sound, not as loud as a scream, and turned our faces away. Adelheid cried out to the American sergeant: "Yes, yes, it is Hans Blümig, Lieutenant Hans Blümig. Why do you torment us this way! Why do you do this to Frau von Thal!"

"All right, all right," said the sergeant, not as fiercely as before. "Come away."

He turned aside from the door of the dreadful room and we made to follow him upstairs again. Then something arose in the cellars, some power was released. This was the worst—I was dreadfully afraid. We heard sounds and felt a kind of shock wave. Doors opened and shut, the outside staircase rang. In the death room ornaments fell to the ground and shattered, the corpse of Blümig shifted in its chair, there was a clattering from the Samurai armour. We heard a sound that was indescribably horrible, a thick growling and panting; we saw nothing. We all fled up the inside staircase again and out of the back door, out of the villa into the sunlight. We walked towards the terrace, all three of us entering into a kind of conspiracy to deny the experience, although no word was spoken. If someone had asked why we suddenly rushed from the cellar we might have said, reasonably enough, that the sight of Blümig was horrible, that we felt sick and stifled.

'From the terrace there came a single shot. The sergeant drew his hand gun again, made us take cover against the back porch and ran round to the south lawn with a shout. He began to curse and motioned us to come after him. We found Father Helm and Sister Claudia kneeling on the terrace, they had been still at their prayers. The young corporal had fired the shot at a dog he saw prowling in the shrubbery.'

Sister Florentine sighed and relaxed a little. Her hands were unsteady in her lap.

'The sergeant acted with discretion,' she said. 'A few American personnel came to the Villa Florian, made their examinations and had the bodies taken away. The three boys and Blümig were buried in the Breitbach cemetery. Two boys carried identification and word was sent to their families; I don't know what they were told, possibly that the boys had died of wounds. The third boy was never identified; he was buried as Klaus, the name he had tattooed on his fingers. Three other boys had been at the villa in Blümig's gang of scavengers but they were never seen again.

'Supplies of weapons were not found at the villa, only a certain amount of food and drink. We dumped all the wine but the ham and the canned vegetables were too precious to waste in those days.'

'But the poison,' said Kate queasily, 'Where did the poison...?'

'The problem of the poisoned wine was never solved. Was the bottle laced with deadly cyanide by Blümig and kept in the locked pantry with other food and drink? Did he intend to use it as a booby trap, against the Americans perhaps? Or had the bottle been poisoned years earlier by someone else, even by my grandfather himself? The villa had been used as a clinic for disturbed soldiers... could the wine have been poisoned by a patient, by a doctor? It was at that time, 1945, that prominent Nazis took poison, bit on cyanide capsules, but it did not seem likely that the boys had committed suicide. They were celebrating their release from Blümig, whom they had killed or helped to kill.'

The old woman shook her head sadly.

'The whole hideous episode made me deeply ashamed for my poor country and filled me with despair. I mourned for those lost desperate brutes of boys. We prayed for them, they are never out of our prayers. We could not escape the feeling that they had all met together in a most dangerous place in that zero summer.

'Franz Walther remained in hiding at the convent and regained his health. When Ernst Kramer, our estate manager, came home after only four years as a prisoner of the Russians, Franz went to live in the Forsthaus as an apprentice. His papers were put in order. He has remained, as you see, a shy person, something of a solitary. I am sure he enjoys his family holidays in Bayern but his favorite place is the wood. He spends long periods in the little *waldhaus* beyond the lake. Now the woods of the Steinberg no longer belong to the convent and he is a forester employed by the state, a civil servant. He is a good man, I am sure, and he saved himself from the evil influences at the Villa Florian.

'We went to work straightaway, in that summer of 1945, to clean and purify the place. As soon as the bodies were removed. I do not know how many hours we spent singing to keep up our courage and scrubbing and cleaning in that house. We said prayers, we read from St Hildegarde, we made our own exorcism. We did not dare recommend that the villa be used to house refugees; it stood clean, at least, but empty.

'My father died in 1947 and my brother Felix, together with his trustees, had a plan to turn the Villa Florian into a small local museum... a *Heimat* museum. No-one in Breitbach liked the idea of tearing down such a beautiful house. A couple moved in as caretakers, Herr and Frau Knopf. I am sure you have heard Adelheid and Andreas speak of them, Friedrich and Leni Knopf. Herr Knopf had a wooden leg from the Russian front. He was an old army comrade of your uncle, Ernst Kramer. The Knopfs lived there for eight years or more, their two teenage daughters grew up there, and the house remained peaceful. The Knopfs accepted that it was a little bit uncanny. They talked of a poltergeist, a noisy spirit that rattled, drummed on the staircase, occasionally turned on a tap or made the fountains play.

'The house never did become a museum but during the sixties, a properous time, it was used for art exhibitions and displays. Renovations were made: the kitchen was built in and the second bathroom put in downstairs, in place of the old walk-in pantry and a servants' bedroom. During those summers when the building was going on Franz Walther acted as a watchman; he would never sleep in the villa, he used the garden house.

'At the convent we were busy, we went on our travels, but we could not ignore the mounting toll of summer accidents. A fall from the roof; a smell of decay that would not leave; several alarms for the fire brigade when passersby saw the golden light. The art exhibitions came to an end six years ago: the Villa Florian got into the newspapers. During a private view of acquarelles and engravings drinks were served and a businessman, a company director from Frankfurt, ran amok and attacked his wife. He chased her on to the south lawn, armed with a broken bottle, and inflicted terrible injuries on the poor woman before he could be restrained. The fountains began to play during his murderous attack.

'My brother and the trustees waited until this sad case had been forgotten a little and then began to let the house to summer visitors. Mainly Americans but there was also a group of music lovers from Japan and a Yugoslavian diplomat with his family.

'I am not close to Felix, he does what he wants to do, but I have tried to get him to push for the museum plan. We believe here at this foundation that the house might be better when it is *not* lived in. On the other hand some families have had no bad experiences, even in summer. So it was with the very first tenants, the Saxon family; they stayed for six months, from June to December, and were very happy in the place. They rented the house again for one summer, after two years.'

'They recommended the house to Jason Limbard,' said Kate. 'He served in the Air Force with Major Jeff Saxon. I guess the major has no idea that Limbard mistreats his family.'

'Perhaps he has *some* idea,' said Sister Florentine. 'It is easy to put a man's life into separate compartments, to know only one aspect of him.'

'Sister Florentine,' said Kate out of the blue, 'did you and the other sisters know about the concentration camps? Did you know about the massacre of the Jews?'

'Yes,' said Sister Florentine, 'we knew from the very beginning. Before the war ended we had spoken to several eye-witnesses. We seriously considered...'

'What?'

'Making a pilgrimage to Rome to appeal against this holocaust. Oh, Frau Reimann, Katherine, how young we were then! I want you to promise me something...whatever you believe.'

'Yes,' said Kate. 'What shall I promise?'

'Do not go into the Villa Florian, even into the grounds, until this summer is over and the Limbard family have gone home.'

'I promise,' said Kate.

II

Melissa was sick. She lay in bed with a high fever, her head ached, she couldn't walk properly. One time Mom put her in a bath of cool water to get the fever down. Roddy was out of his mind with worry and the pair of them were not allowed to go near Liss in case it was something infectious. It would have been a relief if she had turned out to have measles or mumps or something, a childish disease.

In the end the Old Man called old Jeff Saxon and got an address. He took Melissa to the St Lukas Privat Klinik not far away, in a suburb of Frankfurt called Neu Isenburg. Not pronounced New Eysenburg but Noy Eezenboorrrg. Oh, what a terrible misfortune for the poor kiddie to get so sick on holiday. Buddy was never sure whether the bump on the head had anything to do with this meningitis that was eating up poor Liss.

Mom lived for the visits that she made to the Klinik. The Old Man was in a vile mood and he was always hanging fire about whether to take her to the Klinik or not. Twice he let Mom go alone on the bus. She was shy, not knowing any German, but she would have done anything to visit Liss, her poor baby. Sometimes the old Man went alone to visit Melissa, or said he had gone, but they didn't know whether to believe him.

Wherever he went it was a relief to have him out of the way. When he was out they hacked around in the garden and went exploring. What d'you know? Roddy found a genuine all-American baseball in the shrubbery. They guessed it was a legacy from dumb old Junior Saxon. They went looking for something to use as a baseball bat and down in the cellar they found a trunk full of old clothes.

Roddy tangled through the things and went off, searching for a bat, but Buddy still knelt by the open trunk. He was left alone in a stifling stone room under the front of the house. He started to tidy up the things; they were horrid to touch, hot and dry. He saw that they were arranged in layers, going back in time.

On top was a kid's T-shirt with Smokey the Bear, another legacy from the Saxons. Had Miz Saxon, old Cindy, packed this trunk? There were some girls' stiff petticoats and flowery skirts, shades of the fifties. Must have been teenagers in the house then. Next came the thing he liked best because it would even fit him. A dark blue overall like a flying suit, buttoned from collar to crotch. The material was a real tough denim, there were lots of pockets. It had been washed and smelled of moth-balls like everything else in the trunk.

Buddy pushed it aside and went on down. Pairs of old washed-out pyjamas. White jackets and a long starched overall or pinafore. Hospital stuff for nurses and doctors. He felt in a few pockets, hoping for treasure, but found none. How far back was he now? As far as the war? Hey! A bunch of armbands, some plain black but one had a genuine swastika, red, white and black. He knew Roddy would like this to swap with the guys at his fucking Academy, old Macarthur, but he was damned if he would steal the lousy thing.

He was nearly at the bottom of the trunk. Buddy was suddenly very much aware of the room he was in, hot and old. Something, hardly a sound, came at him from the floor and the walls. Ah, it was nothing, his imagination, a truck going past on the road. There in the trunk lay a waistcoat, striped black and white, then a bunch of curtains: white net, thick blue plush. Then there was a long scarf, pale green, transparent, with a design of white roses. Now he was right down. The last item in the trunk was a long jagged piece of golden stuff, pressed into folds.

Buddy was overwhelmed with fear and sorrow. Something was there, lurking in the cellar, even in the middle of the day. Something black and spongy, ready to smother him like the Blob. He shoved everything back into place as best he could and Roddy shouted from the furnace room. Buddy ran out and found him waving their baseball bat. It was a table leg of old turned wood.

'Should do the trick!' said Roddy, giving a swing.

'Great!' said Buddy thickly. 'Let's go get a drink from Mom.'

He didn't want Roddy to know that he was afraid, that he thought the cellar was full of bad vibrations.

They were all affected by the Villa Florian; it was about this time that the Old man took to sitting around on the terrace seeing things, seeing dogs. Buddy remembered thinking it would serve the Old Man right if he was spooked. Actually it made him crazier than ever, as if the old guy with the wolf-hounds — that's what they were, wolf-hounds, he knew it now — had taken him over.

There were a lot of night raids with the Old Man taking them down to watch for dogs. There was something the Old Man called a vigil, where they took turns watching all night long. Of course Roddy didn't see anything and he tried to lie but he was not good enough. Mom never saw anything either but she had bad feelings about the Villa Florian. This 'exclusive turn-of-the-century residence in the style made popular by Lewis Comfort Tiffany, now fully modernised, in its own lovely grounds' scared her a lot. She kept saying she didn't believe, she couldn't believe. . . .

One evening, when the Old Man was watching on the terrace, Buddy came around the side of the house and heard him gasp. Then he saw the dogs on the lawn: they came through the trees just in front of the garden shed. The Old Man gasped, choked, as if he was dying. Buddy walked softly on to the terrace and came to his father's side.

The dogs were fearsome, they were so damned big and restless, but their ghostliness, the gleams of dark light on their rough grey-black fur and the metal studs of their collars, made them harmless. They were not there. They were doing their own dog thing in the garden on some long-ago summer evening. For a long moment the fear and wonder that they felt changed Buddy and his Old Man into different people. Buddy was out of time with someone, a human being, whose fear was greater than his own. . . another kid perhaps, or a real father. He put his hand on the Old Man's shoulder and said in a low voice:

'It's okay. . . those are ghost dogs.'

So they watched together. But something else was abroad in the gathering dusk. None of this good feeling, however brief, was permitted at this time, in this place. There was a crash on the balcony; the doors of the unused room next to Mom's and Dad's bedroom blew open. Buddy felt his father's whole body stiffen. He stepped away and the Old Man shot up out of his chair and cried out a single word. It sounded like 'Stay' but Buddy couldn't get it. Was it a German word? Then the dogs were gone; he missed the moment of their going and did not know whether they simply vanished or ran off into the shrubbery. The Old man was himself again, madder than ever.

'You saw them!' he shouted at Buddy. 'Pair of damned, dangerous, savage, rabid, filthy Kraut dogs, terrorising the neighbourhood!'

'Dad,' said Buddy, keeping out of reach, 'what's up in that room?'

The Old Man was suddenly in a good mood again, smiling, almost boyish.

'Hey! That's the trophy room!'

He led the way upstairs, shouting for Roddy who came from the sitting room. The key was in the door of the trophy room; the Old man had forbidden the boys to go around unlocking doors and they had obeyed. There was no overhead light but the feeble bulbs in the four wall sconces were working so the room was well-lit.

It was the strangest room in the house, it even beat the two hexagons. The walls were papered with dark, velvety patterned wallpaper in green and gold and dark red, a design of trees and leaves. The wooden tree-trunk strips were there and the swirling wooden branches, just below the ceiling. The wall lamps were bronze: an eagle, a stag, a horse, a pair of fish. On the walls, among the trees, were pale patches with holes for nails. A lot of trophy-heads had hung there, pretty big by the look of the patches: deer with big antlers maybe, wild boar... were there still bears to hunt in Europe? A few small trophies were still there – wooden shields with horns mounted on them, not heads, just the horns of small antelope or goat.

The room smelt musty. The square window next to the french doors was tightly shut. The Old Man hooked back the doors so that the room could air. There was no furniture in the room but it had a plain green carpet and there was a place to sit, an alcove, with a high step. A gun rack had been left in the back of the alcove, dark against a pale, unpapered wall. It was a big shallow cupboard in black wood inlaid with bronze; inside the glass doors were the empty racks for the guns to stand upright. The Old Man opened two little drawers – for bullets? – under the doors.

Buddy went on to the balcony and looked down at the empty garden. Roddy gave a yelp. He had found something. Roddy was the one who always found things. He found money, he found good stuff like the baseball, he found lost watches, lost exercise books. He also lost things, as many as he found, and all bound to get him in trouble with the Old Man. This time he was a finder and no mistake.

Another drawer lay behind the shallow drawers at the front of the gun rack. It was quite a trick: both front drawers had to be open, then a knob pressed on the left side of the rack. Then the secret drawer came swinging out with the two smaller drawers attached to its edge; it brought with it a reek of dust and hot oil. A bundle wrapped in green silk lay in the deep drawer. Roddy snatched it up, it was *his* treasure, but Buddy shuddered at the thought of that old green silk lying in dust and darkness for years, like the things in the trunk.

The silk was stained with thick grease and very tightly wrapped. The Old Man saw or sensed what was in the bundle. He took it away from Roddy and unwrapped the silk and the layer of cotton wadding underneath. Buddy saw the dark gleam of metal, the unique murderous shape of the thing. A sleeping beauty, the Old Man said, working the action and examining the two extra clips. It was a Luger.

Buddy felt a burning, penetrating fear when he saw the Old Man handling the gun. The Old Man knew about guns: he knew a lot about everything in the world, it seemed to Buddy, everything except how to be a regular human being. Yet the Old Man was not a gun-fancier, he only kept an old twenty-two in their house in Pennsylvania. If he *had* been a gun-fancier, Buddy reasoned, they would all be dead. Now the devilish house had given him a gun in full working order.

For the moment though things had never been better. Roddy was in good with the Old Man. They were like kids with a new toy, rushing down to show it to Mom. Of course they wanted to try it out but that was not going to be so easy. The Old Man and Roddy were going to get up very early in the morning and walk right over the back of the Steinberg past the convent, and see if they could find a place.

Buddy looked at the secret drawer, left hanging open, and saw that it was lined with yellowed paper. He peeled it up, looking for more treasure, and found that it was a drawing in black India ink. It was stained in places with oil from the package with the gun and it showed, in a frame of twisted branches, a man standing in a garden with three dogs. The same sort of dogs he had seen on the lawn, only here they looked more friendly. Only one, the mother dog, he figured, was full grown, then one was half grown and the other just a puppy. And the man was the same, only before he was lamed and had to use a wheelchair. It was a very good drawing done by a real artist; there was no signature but a device of a little open book with the letters TP on the pages.

The drawer was empty now except for two pieces of thin card, two photographs. The first one he looked at showed a young man sitting in a chair wearing a long cotton coat, a sort of duster, and a straw hat with a soft brim. He had a lot of whiskers and a surprised look. On the back was his name 'Magnus, 1913'. The other photograph was the model from which the picture had been drawn. There stood the older man down on the south lawn of the Villa Florian with his dogs. The writing on the back was in English, in India ink: 'Wolfgang and the first wolf-hounds in his kennels. Champion Killarney Mavourneen and her offspring, June 1914.'

Wolf-hounds were pretty neat dogs even if they did grow so darned big. Must have cost the earth to feed, keep them in raw hares or whatever. And now Mavourneen and her offspring and her offspring's offspring were all dead. There was no saying which of the wolf-hounds kept appearing on the lawns.

And the old guy, this Wolfgang, was dead too, and poor old Magnus in his hat, and the person... was it a lady?... who had drawn the drawing and written on the photographs. They were all dead, but in that fantastic room, plagued by fear, Buddy spoke to them aloud.

'Please,' he said. 'Please keep away. Don't hurt us!'

He considered taking the evidence and trying to convince the Old Man that he had been seeing ghosts. It was too difficult and he was too chicken. He laid the photographs and the drawing back in place and shut the secret drawer.

Chapter 4
Never The Same Again

It was the hottest summer for a hundred years, burning over the central plain from the Alps and sweet alpine valleys to the rugged salty islands and raw beaches of the North Sea. Their inexpensive summer holiday jogged along; they made two trips to the *Landesmuseum* in Darmstadt for Kate's critical article on *Jugendstil* glassware. Then Nicki turned up, after a midnight phone call from München. There he was at Frankfurt Airport bidding farewell to a quite-well-known television starlet whom he had just happened to sit next to on the plane.

Kate liked to see Nicki and Andreas, the two school friends, together: specimens of German manhood. Nicki was dark-haired, compact, with an actor's bounce in his step, while Andy was more classically handsome, taller, golden-haired. They specialised in silly greetings.

'Nicki, *alte Pappnase!*'

Nicki, not in the least put out by being called 'Old Papier-Maché Nose', gave her a big hug. There was always an air of bustle and excitement when Nicholas Lenz stepped on the stage. But she realised that, for all his fun and games, she marked him out as one of their friends who was truly grown-up. Perhaps it was the same with Ruth, her dear always tired Ruth, doing her medical finals and coping with three-year old twin girls.

Nicki was on his way to Mainz for an appearance in 'Cabaret at Nine' with the ZDF. They repaired to a Chinese restaurant in the airport and ate Peking duck.

'How is your health food man?' asked Nicki. 'The one renting the villa?'

'Well on the way to becoming *my author*' said Andreas, with a warning glance at Kate.

Kate made a face at him. She had not been about to blurt out the worst about Jason Limbard.

'Nicki,' she said, 'what do you know about an artist called Tamara Paige?'

'Not much,' he said. '*La belle Anglaise*... She drew posters, illustrated books. Worked mainly in line and wash.'

'She lived at the Villa Florian for several years.'

'Marvellous!' he said. 'Kate, you must write something about her. She was a great beauty of course... painted by von Stück among others.'

'I might start collecting material,' said Kate.

'She died in München,' said Nicki. 'Some sad tale. I must check.'

They drove him to Mainz over the *autobahn* and sat in the studio audience for the taping of 'Cabaret at Nine'. Nicki's two numbers went well: a bitter-sweet song about a summer love affair, and his hilarious Kafka parody 'The Hunting Permit'. Afterwards, in a cheerful group, they crossed the confluence of the Main and the Rhine to Wiesbaden and had a flutter at the casino. They saw Nicki off on his plane to München and drove home to Breitbach in the dawn, like strayed revellers.

'He will have to decide,' said Andreas earnestly, 'whether to be a performer or a man who decorates houses and fleeces the rich in a smart antique shop.'

'He can do both,' said Kate, 'in Europe at any rate.'

'German cabaret is nearly always a great flop in America.'

'Something Nicki said reminded me of Jason Limbard.'

'I wish you wouldn't harp on this thing, Kate!'

She fell silent and tried to remember Nicki's exact words. Yes, they had been talking about the Nazis. Nicki had refused to handle 'Militaria' – Nazi uniforms and other relics – in his shop. 'We can examine the lives of these men in great detail but in the end we always ask the same question. How could they have done it? Cruelty is a kind of mystery.'

Now, a few days later, Kate remembered these words all over again. It was hot, hot, sweltering hot at nine in the morning, in the Forsthaus kitchen with doors and windows open. Andreas was in sleeping shorts, Kate in running shorts, running shoes and a T-shirt. She had taken the low road, circled the base of the hill and run past the back gate of the Villa Florian to the lake for an early swim. Her hair was already drying.

'*You* must do it, Andreas,' said Tante Adelheid, 'you are the one he trusts.'

'Oh God, Oh God,' grumbled Andreas.

He slapped cheese, sausage and pickled cucumber on to his buttered roll.

'I've spoken on the phone to Diet Jason about business,' he said, 'but you see how they are, *Tantchen*. They're not sociable. They keep to a narrow family circle. They haven't even attempted to repay the barbecue with an invitation.'

'He doesn't want people in the house,' said Kate.

'Well, he could take us to a restaurant,' said Andreas reasonably. 'A foursome without the kids.'

Kate was surprised that Andreas had noticed so much. She had tried to turn her attention away from the Villa Florian and what might be going on in that strange house. Now Tante Adelheid was going to make her blood run cold again.

'Ask about your book business,' said Tante Adelheid to Andreas, 'Tell him you are driving to München tomorrow.'

'And then?'

'Ask about the child, Melissa.'

Kate was cold indeed.

'What about her?' asked Andreas with his mouth full.

'Is her grippe improved?' asked Tante Adelheid.

'Didn't seem very sick when she was here,' said Andreas.

'I have not seen her for ten days,' said Tante Adelheid. 'I have kept careful watch. I believe that she has not left the house.'

Andreas demanded: 'Kate! *You've* seen her?'

'No,' said Kate. 'I haven't been watching very hard but I haven't seen Melissa. I have seen everyone else... I spoke to Jason last week when he was taking the boys round the supermarket. I've seen Mary in the distance.'

'You must ask, Andreas,' said Tante Adelheid. 'Ask on my behalf – I am your old aunt. I fuss.'

'Suppose she *is* lying there with 'flu or some childish disease?' asked Andreas. 'What then?'

'I would like to know,' said Tante Adelheid. 'Ten days in summer is a long time. Never once to appear on the lawn or the terrace.'

'Good God,' said Andreas, 'what are you suggesting? That Jason has killed her in a fit of rage and buried her in the cellar?'

'Andreas, you shit!' shouted Kate. 'How can you say such a thing!'

He held up his hands in a gesture of surrender.

'I'm sorry. And don't shout. You're becoming very nervous, Katherine.'

He rose with dignity and padded out of the kitchen, saying: 'I'll get dressed and keep an eye open for our neighbour.'

Kate twisted about in her chair. 'I am nervous. If Mary Limbard were left alone in the house, I might go and see her.'

'No, child,' said Tante Adelheid. 'It is dangerous.'

'I'm not sure I believe all that stuff about the place being cursed,' said Kate, 'but some bad things *have* happened.'

Andy clattered down the stairs calling 'Ha-la-lee', some German equivalent of Tallyho.

'Here comes Limbard!' he said. 'I'll tackle him!'

The two women took to the stairs and hurried into the study. They stood like fates behind the curtain and watched Jason Limbard come to the gate of his house. He collected his mail, unlocking the large metal letterbox attached to the extreme northern pillar of the gates. He stood frowning and sorting out the junk-mail and the flyers that overflowed the letter-box. Kate and Andreas called these local examples of junk-mail 'buy-mores'. Germans bought more and were exhorted to do so on every hand. The usual avalanche of glossy throwaways from furniture stores, supermarkets and department stores, jostled with expensively printed brochures for jewellery, wine, leather goods, art objects and gourmet gingerbread. Jason Limbard opened the side gate and came out on to the road to pick up some fallen advertising matter that was blowing against the gatepost. The watchers saw Andreas pounce; he hailed Jason and went towards him, hand outstretched.

The two men stood talking animatedly in the sunshine for some minutes then both of them went inside the gates. Tante Adelheid touched Kate's shoulder as if to say 'See that'. On the drive Jason stood still and shouted for his sons, the names came in at the window of the Forsthaus. The boys ran up from nowhere and were given the waste paper to throw away. Roddy came out and patrolled the gates, picking up more scraps. Jason and Andreas had gone into the villa through the front door; Kate suffered a twinge of anxiety.

'Will he be all right?' she whispered.

'Andreas is proof against the powers of darkness,' said Tante Adelheid wryly. 'Come.'

They arrived back in the kitchen just as Frau Moor came in from the garden carrying a field mouse which she set down under the table, stiff and stark.

'No,' said Tante Adelheid, 'Moora, my dear, you know it is not allowed.'

Kate picked up the small corpse by the tail and flung it into the bushes at the side of the back lawn. The cat remained aloof and went to eat crunchy cat food from her dish.

'Tcha,' said Tante Adelheid, 'I have remembered a significant dream. It was of Franz, our poor Franz Walther. I hope nothing has happened on his little trip.'

The forester was at a two-day meeting, a kind of Foresters' Convention, at Cranichstein, a large well-preserved hunting lodge on the road to Darmstadt.

'What was the dream?' asked Kate.

'Nothing,' said Tante Adelheid. 'He stood in a courtyard and looked full of despair.'

Kate carried a last cup of coffee into the leaf-shadowed living room where she could watch for Andreas but she began to read her Tiffany biography and missed his return. He put his head in the door and said: 'Do you want to hear?'

'What is it?'

When he was sprawled in his chair in the warm kitchen again, he said, 'Hospital. Melissa is in hospital with suspected meningitis. She has been there for five days. Jason took her at night to the St Lukas Klinik in Neu Isenburg.'

'That's awful,' said Kate.

'I am glad she is out of that house,' said Tante Adelheid.

'What did you do?' asked Kate. 'Fraternise? Have a drink?'

'Had a blackcurrant juice on the terrace,' said Andreas. 'Jason was in good form, considering. Mary looked a bit drawn. Anyway, the München trip is on for Jason and the boys...Sunday. Mary will stay because of Melissa.'

'We will send fruit and maybe a picturebook. Later, when the poor child is getting better.' said Tante Adelheid.

She went out of the back door on the way to the laundry in the cellar. Andreas said warily: 'You remember the rooms you were in...'

'They've been re-arranged,' said Kate. 'Mary told me.'

'The dining-room opens on to the terrace.'

'Now it does.'

'Did Mary *say* that the rooms had been re-arranged?'

'No,' said Kate, trying not to be defensive. 'But at the barbecue the other night she took care to tell me that the dining room opened on the terrace and the television room was at the front of the house. I had seen it the other way around.'

'There couldn't be a possibility that *you* made a mistake?' asked Andreas. 'That *you* are capable of error?'

'Sure I am,' said Kate. 'I picked a damned distrustful husband. I saw the dining room at the front and I had a cool drink of ginger beer in the family room off the terrace. And left my cotton bag there. And went back for it. Why in the name of God would I go back to the dining room, all set for Daddy Jason's fancy ritual dinner?'

'Going back was one of the dumbest things you ever did!' said Andreas.

'You may be right,' said Kate. 'It seemed like a good idea at the time.'

'You *thought* you left the bag in the terrace room,' said Andreas stubbornly, 'yet it was hanging on the gate next morning.'

'One of the Limbards put it there,' said Kate.

She went and sat opposite Andreas, knee to knee, and took both of his hands in hers.

'When you were there just now,' she said, 'was there anything extraordinary or uncanny or unusual about the family, or about the villa? Please, Andy.'

'This is Tante Adelheid's nonsense,' he grumbled.

'Please...'

'Nothing,' he said. 'None of your spooks. The place is very sad for you and for me too, Kate, because it is so badly treated. The bareness, the awful junk-shop furniture. It should be redone by an expert. Think of how well Nicki could restore the Villa Florian.'

'He would be the one to do it,' sighed Kate.

She knew that Nicki appreciated the *Jugendstil*. Why, he owned a Klimt, the picture of a tall, angular red-haired woman in a peacock gown and a gold pectoral. She wished she could speak to Nicki about her experiences at the Villa Florian. How much would he understand?

'There was *something,*' said Andreas awkwardly.

'Tell me.'

'The whole family were over-sensitive about dogs,' he said. 'First Jason gave a bit of a tirade about dog-owners who let their beasts roam about and tear up the lawn. Then I excused myself for a moment and went to the downstairs bathroom opposite the kitchen. I was determined to see as much of the house as possible so after I had been to the toilet I drifted into the kitchen, another depressing hole, and found Mary looking out through the glass panel at the top of the back door. She was staring into the orchard. I said: 'Did you see a stray dog?' I thought the woman would faint. She turned chalk white and said, *insisted,* that dogs couldn't get into the garden at all. I went back to the terrace. She really is a bit mad, *Kätchen.*'

'That poor little girl,' said Kate. 'Did they say much about the meningitis? Is it catching?'

'Some complication of the grippe,' said Andreas.

Some complication of a fall or a blow on the head, thought Kate. 'Doctor, she fell down the stairs, she had a nasty fall.' It made her own head ache to think of it.

'I wish someone could save the Villa Florian,' she said. 'I wish Nicki could redecorate it. I wish I could win the lottery and buy the place.'

'Oh, they'd let it go for a song: half a million marks.'

Tante Adelheid seemed to have given up her watch on the Villa Florian. Next day, Thursday, Andreas set off for München in high spirits which he tried to hide in case Kate should feel jealous... at least this was Kate's interpretation. She wondered idly if he was having an affair with someone at the office. It couldn't be very torrid; he had been content for more than a month at the Forsthaus. But perhaps his secret lady was on holiday, rushing obsessively to Spain, Italy, Tunisia, Greece...

Friday was fiery hot, stifling from morning to night. Soon after one o'clock, thirteen hours, Kate saw Jason Limbard drive away alone in his rented Mercedes. He was not long gone when a van with a loud-speaker crawled up and down and round the Steinberg. A loud harsh voice cried: *'Achtung! Achtung!'*

The announcement that followed was pretty garbled but Kate knew what it was about anyway. No-one was allowed into the woods because of fire danger. It had always struck her as a difficult thing to police but Germans were notably obedient so perhaps it helped. The van droned past again with its scary *'Achtung! Achtung!'* and in answer to Kate's silent wishes Tante Adelheid decided to splash herself with cool water and lie down in the spare room upstairs with the windows open.

Kate carried the telephone into the sitting room and called the Villa Florian. It was listed under its owner's name in the Breitbach phone book: Sommer, Felix, Baron v. Steinberg 5. She couldn't remember seeing a telephone at the villa. Was it a real antique or perhaps a fake, offered by the post office? Or was it a plain standard grey? Mary Limbard answered.

'I was sorry to hear that Melissa is so ill,' said Kate, after they had exchanged names. 'I hope she's getting better.'

'Yes,' said Mary, 'yes, she's doing very well.'

'I hear Jason and the boys are going to München.'

'Yes, on Sunday morning.'

It was still very heavy weather. Suddenly Mary said: 'Oh, Kate...Buddy reminded me. What was that with the loud speaker just now?'

Kate laughed and told her. Mary laughed shakily.

'We couldn't understand,' she said. 'Roddy said, "Maybe it's the Third World War."'

'On Sunday,' said Kate, 'when you've got the travellers off, I could drive you to visit Melissa.'

'Oh,' said Mary. 'Oh, well, yes...that would be very kind. I took the bus a couple of times for practice, but a car...'

'Just the old van, I'm afraid,' said Kate.

She arranged to come to the back gate at about two and they ended the call. Kate felt that the ice was broken. She sat and watched until Jason returned, carrying a bag of groceries. He was in shorts, very tanned and fit, and to her eyes madder than before. He drove the car into the grounds then shouted for the boys and gave them packages to carry in. When Roddy dropped an apple his father seized him by the arm and shook him. Then he cast a glance around, stared at the Forsthaus and the hot empty street.

On Friday night, towards midnight, a thunderstorm crashed down on the Steinberg. The thunder had growled in the distance all day, now it was right overhead. As the lightning flashed Tante Adelheid, shutting windows, lamented aloud: 'The woods! The woods! It will start a fire!'

Again the thunder came, incredibly loud and followed by snaps and cracklings, then by rain, heavy drops that grew into a dark torrent. Kate peered at the Villa Florian and saw a faint light in one of the hexagons. Who slept there? The rain went on and so did the thunder and lightning, hardly drawing away as if reluctant to leave the Steinberg. Tante Adelheid made fresh tea and with it the two of them drank raspberry schnapps.

On Saturday morning the world was washed clean, it steamed in the sunlight. Kate woke up to the sound of voices talking urgently in broad Hessian. She looked out of her bedroom window and saw Herr Walther, the forester, standing in the roadway. He was distraught, his clothes were soaked through. He waved his hands, took off his hat, ran his fingers through his hair and put on the hat again. Tante Adelheid seemed to be begging him to come inside, to drink coffee, to get warmed up. In the end he went away, almost running uphill towards the convent.

'What is it?' cried Kate, coming on the landing.

'Bodo is lost!' said Tante Adelheid, returning to High German. 'Poor Bodo ran off from Cranichstein on Thursday afternoon. Franz has been searching ever since, all along the Darmstadter Landstrasse.'

'He might have come back here,' said Kate. 'He could make it in a day, a dog like that.'

'Exactly!' said Tante Adelheid. 'Unless something bad has happened to him, a road accident. Oh God, oh God, the poor man... to lose his closest companion!'

'I'm sure he'll come back,' said Kate. 'I'm sure Bodo will

come back. We must look out for him.'

When Andreas called on Saturday afternoon she was listless and depressed with the heat. It was finally getting to her; she could barely communicate. Bodo was lost, nothing else had happened; there had been a thunderstorm. Andreas on the other hand was full of high spirits. There was music playing in the background. He reported that the apartment was in good shape, the plants had not died. Melchior, his immediate superior, was laid up with a broken ankle, sustained on the Côte d'Azur. Probably slipped in a puddle of suntan oil. *Schadenfreude* all round.

'Katie,' said Andreas, 'are you all right? You sound strange.'

'*You* sound high!'

'It's Brigitte's birthday. Did I say that before? Listen, here's someone to speak to you.'

It was Nicki. His voice, deep and theatrical, made Kate suddenly homesick for München, for someone to talk to.

'Nicki... *Altes Haus!*'

'Katie... *Alte Frauenzimmer!*'

And if it was strange to greet a pal as Old House it was equally odd for a 'wench' or 'common woman' to be a Women's Room.

'I envy you living right on top of the Villa Florian,' said Nicki. 'Funny thing, I was looking through some old photographs of rooms for an exhibition and there was the trophy room. Haus von Sommer, near Darmstadt...that's it, isn't it?'

'Yes. I can't remember seeing the trophy room.'

'Seems to have french windows and a lot of light,' he said. 'A most macabre affair. Heads, you know, antlered heads, worked into a woodland frieze. *Jugendstil* gun-racks, if you can imagine such a thing.'

'Baron von Sommer was not very nice,' said Kate.

'Does the name Maria Paget Robinson mean anything to you?' asked Nicki.

Kate laughed. 'Of course,' she said. 'That was her real name. The first two names are almost an anagram of Tamara Paige.'

'She died here in München,' said Nicki.

'How did she die?'

'She drowned herself in the English Garden,' he said. 'It *is* a sad tale.'

'The Villa Florian is a sad place too, these days,' said Kate. 'Nicki, I must go. It was wonderful to hear your voice.'

'Be happy, Katherine. Shall I call Andreas?'

'No. Bye-bye. See what the boys in the backroom will have.'

He chuckled, they both hung up. Kate went back to her art books and looked at all the works of Tamara Paige over again. A suicide. And in the English Garden. She tried to work but gave it up because of the heat. Tante Adelheid called her attention to Herr Walther; he was in the grounds of the Villa Florian, strolling about sadly with Jason Limbard and the elder boy, Roddy. In the course of the evening he came by again, standing in the roadway and blowing his inaudible silver whistle.

On Sunday she was up early, watching like a hawk. Everything would go well, she was certain. No slip-ups. Tante Adelheid would be out all day: Sister Claudia picked her up in the convent's dark blue Opel and off they went to visit the sick, just as Kate planned to do. Still she watched and promptly at nine o'clock Jason Limbard came storming out with Roddy and Buddy; they piled into the Merc. Mary peeped from the front door and waved. The big car churned off slowly down the hill. Kate relaxed. She had plenty of time to spare.

II

Buddy was in blackest despair. He could feel tears in his throat all the time; he knew that his eyes were puffy from crying. His face, his whole head ached and throbbed; his hands were blistered. Roddy had sore hands too; he was joking and laughing and playing up to the Old Man.

'Where the Munchkins come from, eh Dad?'

'Ha-ha, Roddy-boy, that's a good 'un... where the Munchkins come from!'

The Old Man was on a knife edge, so crazy that Buddy wondered how he could drive. He had had very little sleep since Friday. Maybe on the *autobahn* they would overturn and that would be that; a bunch of lousy cowards and murderers would have paid the price.

This was the worst, the pits, the most terrible thing the Old Man had ever gotten them into. He knew now that he had never believed that his father had had anything to do with the death of Miz Hart, RAPE SLAYING IN THE DUNES. That was just a terrible coincidence. No, this stupid, wicked thing was the Old Man's masterpiece. It made Buddy want to die, to tell the whole story to someone who spoke English and then die, curl up and die, sink in the waters of the lake. This was as bad as Samantha; this was a judgement on them for not telling on the Old Man long ago.

It began with the thunderstorm; it was one of the loudest they had ever heard. Old Thor with his hammer was beating hell out of their crazy house and the woods. You would expect the glass dome to go any minute, even with its tall conductor. He was the one who had to close the window, Roddy was out of his mind. He had always hated thunderstorms, the Old Man had called him a 'gun-shy cur' more than once. Buddy could take them or leave them alone.

This thunderstorm was really a doozie. They couldn't sleep, just sat up in bed listening to the rain and counting between the lightning and the thunder to see how many miles away the storm was. Namely no miles. The thunder came smack overhead on a count of four, how about that? Then it edged away a little, count of seven, count of nine. The rain was pouring down now, it was colder; the wind had not let up and the Villa Florian rattled and resounded like a one man band. Buddy put on the top of his pyjamas because he was cool; he had just got it over his head when the Old Man came in and turned on the light.

He stood there, drenched to the skin, fully dressed in his slacks and T-shirt and the crazy dressing gown. The Luger was stuck in the waistband of his slacks. Roddy sat up; even he had tumbled to the occasion. *This was not a raid.*

'Something has happened,' said the Old Man, medium fierce. 'A family emergency. Get dressed, put on raincoats. I'll be down in the hall.'

He thrust something into Buddy's hand, one of the two flashlights.

'Use this coming down,' he said. 'Some of the lights are out and we don't want too much light anyway.'

They were more scared by this mildness than by his ferocity. Jesus Christ, what had gone wrong?

'A shot, we wouldn't have heard a shot,' croaked Roddy.

They crawled into their clothes double quick and went along the dark hall to the stairs. The storm raged overhead and the house still rattled and sang. The stairs rang as they went down. Roddy went first; he had wrenched the flashlight away from Buddy. When they saw Mom standing at the foot of the stairs, wet and bedraggled in her nightgown, he gave a sob and went to her. Buddy was astonished at what his brother had been thinking.

Mom was crying, tears were mixed with rain on her cheeks. She said something like, 'It is such a terrible thing... a terrible mistake...' She embraced Roddy, then took Buddy by the shoulders and pushed back the hair from his face.

'Oh, Buddy,' was all she could say. 'My poor little Buddy.'

Then the Old Man came through the dining room with the ground sheet of the tent over his arm and told them to get a move on. They followed him on to the terrace and stood there stupidly in the driving rain. The thunder and lightning came again, moving off a little; they saw the lightning strike right down to earth beyond the end of the lawn, towards the base of the Steinberg. Roddy threw up a hand before his face.

'Lights!' growled the Old man.

He turned on the other flashlight and followed him down the steps, both flashlights wavering as they squelched across the lawn to the right, in the direction of the garden house. Buddy felt a shock coming up from the soles of his feet, as if the whole stinking thing had been telegraphed to him. This was the place on the lawn where the dogs were seen. Then the Old Man shone his torch. Buddy heard someone give a groaning cry... he was doing it, it was his voice crying out. He staggered away over the lawn, falling on his knees in the midst of the storm and the darkness.

The great dog Bodo lay at the edge of the lawn, his fur soaked almost black. One shot had hit him in the body, the other two or three had blown away half of his head. Red blood shone out in the torchlight. Buddy felt himself go berserk. He came back and looked a second time, then he cursed the Old Man. He shouted aloud and called him a murderer, a bloody murderer, he said he was crazy. When the Old Man hauled off and knocked him to the wet ground he bounced up again and stood back, opening his arms.

'Shoot me!' he yelled. 'Shoot me, you fucking bastard! You dirty cruel stupid shit. Shoot me the way you shot Bodo! Shoot me or I'll tell the world what you did! I'll tell old Walther what you did to his dog, you dirty murderer! Why don't you write this one up in your shit column, you bloody monster!'

The Old Man came and caught him round the body, slapped his face open-handed, then deliberately hit him on the jaw and knocked him out cold.

He came to in a mist of pain with Roddy and the Old Man half dragging him to the terrace. He tried to find his feet. Mom took him and he tried to walk so as not to be too heavy on her. They weaved and staggered through the dining room and along the hall and he lay on the couch in the living room. Mom took his rain coat and sneakers and wiped his face. There was blood on the washcloth from his bleeding nose, where the Old Man had slapped him. He didn't know if his jaw was broken. Mom fed him pills dissolved in juice. It took a long time but he got them all down. She tucked him up in a blanket; they heard the thunder far away. He wondered what the Old Man and Roddy were doing with poor old Bodo.

Mom left him to sleep and Buddy passed into a dreamy state, half sleeping, half waking. There was a girl arranging red and yellow tulips in a tall glass vase. Her skirt rustled as she walked; he saw her face for an instant and she was Snow White. Her hair was black as night, her skin was white as snow and her lips were red as blood. She said to someone in a very English voice, a real Limey accent: '*Please make sure that I am quite dead.*'

Buddy saw a face reflected in the mirror behind the lady's head: a young man with a high balding forehead and silky blond sideburns. He was afraid of the lady and the sight of the young man filled him with a dreadful sorrow. He tried to cry out and the pain woke him up. Then the dream was gone and he drifted off to sleep again.

He slept until morning and when he woke the Old Man was in the room. Not far away there were voices talking German;

his father listened at the window. Then he came purposefully to Buddy and examined his jaw. It worked all right; it was not broken. It still hurt. In fact, Buddy ached all over. His father was not so much angry as preoccupied, he hardly looked Buddy in the eye. He led him upstairs, made him take a hot shower and put on clean pyjamas, then he led him to the trophy room, where Buddy's folding bed had been made up.

'I will outline the plan,' said the Old Man stiffly, 'and you will go along with it.'

Buddy was in no shape to argue; all the fight had gone out of him.

'The dog is in the cellar,' said the Old Man. 'Walther is looking for it. I'll make sure he sees round these grounds today. Tonight we'll bury the body. You'll rest here all day. You better not try anything. Tomorrow we go to München.'

He went out and locked the door. Buddy saw why he was in the trophy room: it made a good prison. The shutters on the window and the heavy wooden jalousie on the glass doors could be made secure from outside, on the long balcony. The Old Man was taking no chances. Buddy tried to sleep. He mourned for Bodo. He felt the black despair, the hopelessness, welling up in him like a dark spring from the bottom of the lake. He had been brave for half a minute, and look where it had got him.

Mom brought him scrambled egg and chocolate milk; Roddy had sent along the transistor. He thought of asking for one of his exercise books so that he could make a start on his essay 'My Holiday in Germany', but he was too sick and sore. He lay and listened to the AFN.

The thunderstorm had played hell with the Rhine-Main Airbase. The Roanoke Players were casting 'Guys and Dolls'. There were classes available in Judo, woodwork, recognition of personal goals, child care and data processing. There were real neat trips to München, Paris, London and Oberammergau. The German Phrase of the Day was 'Where is the nearest Police Station?' *Wo ist die nachste Polizei Dienststelle?* There were peppy little spots about overcoming shyness, keeping fit, getting help for alcohol and drug problems, stepping up the vocational ladder, preparing for parenthood, returning to God. Burl Ives sang 'I had a dog and his name was Blue'. Buddy turned the darned thing off and wept. Partly for Bodo and partly for himself because he hadn't any dog and he hated his life.

He went to the bathroom once and had an enamel bucket in his room. Mom brought him a whole bunch of stuff for lunch, fed him more pills and said he should get some sleep. It was hot and stifling in the trophy room. He staggered up and opened the window and the glass doors so that air could come in through the shutters and the jalousie. When he turned and looked at the room again it frightened him.

Buddy told himself it was only the afternoon, for crissake, it was broad daylight. Yet it was never broad daylight in that weird room with the shadows of hunting trophies on the green wildwood wallpaper. He pressed back against the wall between the doors and the window. There was a muffled sound, a thump, the room shook. He stared at the white alcove, with a step, like a stage. The black gun rack on the white wall blurred before his eyes, the alcove was full of moving shadows. Wrestling, falling, a blue coat... Buddy gasped, blinked, conjured the house and its inhabitants: Get away! Stay away from me!

He managed to get back to his bed against the wall, under the stag lamp. He lay there in the heat, zonked out from the pills, in a dreamy state that lowered his resistance to any tricks the room might play. Thick gasping sounds from the two men fighting in the alcove. He shut his eyes tight and saw red light shot with green and turquoise. When he opened his eyes again the red remained, flooding the room; red was spilling over the step, not blood but cloth, thick red cloth, a tablecloth, something larger, a curtain. A thick dark red plush curtain and the man in the blue coat lay upon it like a heap of old clothes. He shut his eyes again and felt a wave of sadness wash over him. A voice was bringing out a few words, one by one, as if the chest hurt. Nothing he could understand. The man was young and he knew he was dying, there was no hope for him. Buddy faded right away. Rent with sadness he sank in the dark waters of the lake. He went deep down and slept.

When he awoke again the room was dark; he saw a little gleam of light at the door and was instantly afraid. He tried to draw all his limbs together, to roll into a ball, but he couldn't move. She came into the room silently, her feet were bare, very thin white feet. She was wrapped in a kind of cloak, stiff papery folds of gold patterned silk. Her hair, black as ebony, hung down over the cloak.

She made her own light. Buddy saw her kneel on the red plush curtain beside the dead man. He could not see what she did but there were sounds of effort. Something took a lot of doing and it was horrible, beyond everything horrible, and he must see it because she would turn towards him. He could not shut his eyes.

She rose up and he saw that she was naked under the golden cloak. Her lips were pale now but long streams of blood ran down over her pale flesh into the dark hair at her groin and over her thighs. She shifted the heavy burden cradled against her breasts and more blood came from it. She held it like a baby, like a child along her arm, and he caught a glimpse of fine, blond hair. In her right hand, thick with blood, she held a huge knife. She went awkwardly towards the door, gathering the folds of the cloak about her with the hand that held the knife.

Buddy began to scream; it was forced out of him like a last breath. Then he was hurtling upward out of his drugged sleep and the scream was a feeble whimper that hurt his jaw. He was awake, it was dark, and before he could get his breath Roddy came in and turned on the lights. Buddy could get up and go down to the sitting room.

He had no time to think about his crazy nightmare: he went straight from one nightmare to another. The Old Man was up tight; the emergency was continuing; it was time for a spot of dog-burying.

Roddy didn't wait for him. He made sure he put his bed back in the hexagon before he went down. He found Mom alone with the flickering TV, waiting with his thick shake and pizza. She told him to take his time; it turned out that he had slept nine hours. Buddy asked after Melissa. Mom said she was fine, getting better, and she liked her new bear. The thought of the new bear, Melissa and her new bear, in a Kraut hospital, made him want to cry.

Buddy looked at his mother and knew that she was the most mysterious person of them all. He and Roddy were kids, still stupid kids, and Melissa was still a baby, but Mom was grown up and she was the one who should be able to get away. Living with the Old Man, living a double life with the semi-great Jason Limbard, had turned her into his accomplice, a sort of zombie.

He did what he had to do. He told Mom she must go, take Melissa and go, get away, first chance she got, without telling him and Roddy. Mom whispered, hardly moving her lips: 'I'll try.'

So now it was Sunday and they were driving to München; he was all better except for a headache and blistered hands from digging the grave. The Old Man had made him join in and dig: it was the firing squad principle, it spread the guilt. The Old Man had been worrying away at the garden shed, once more of a summerhouse. It was a wooden building with an open trellis on five of its six sides and a pointed roof like a Chinese temple. The steps were in one piece. They moved these away a little, took up a couple of floorboards and dug the grave under the summerhouse. Then they brought Bodo up the outside steps from the cellar. He weighed a ton. They buried him with his head wrapped in an old net curtain from the trunk. Buddy was sick and frightened, remembering his nightmare; he waited to feel better, to feel some relief, but he was too far down.

They drove to the Frankfurter Kreuz with Roddy navigating from the Shell Tour Guide; the Old Man sat alone in the front...he preferred to have the seat beside him empty. He was in good shape, considering. Buddy thought his father looked just fine, for an oldie, with his brown well-shaven face and his muscles bulging the leisure shirt. Someone looking into the car would think: *Hey, the old guy is in good shape, but how about those two ugly kids, those losers, in the back seat?* He was fat with a swollen face, Roddy was thin with pimples and thick specs.

Now they were on the *autobahn,* going south, in the fast lane. The flat summer fields and tracts of woodland zipped past. Buddy had that indefinable feeling of being in a foreign country. The Old Man loved driving on the *autobahn* because there was no speed limit. Then he cursed because there was the beginning of a jam up ahead; they just managed to take an outlet road. They squeezed off the *autobahn* and drove down the *landstrasse* to a filling station with a big restaurant. And disaster struck even before they went in and tried the rolls and weenies.

Roddy had lost his passport. He had been in possession of the damn thing for all of three-quarters of an hour and now he had mislaid it. The Old Man kept all the passports and doled them out before they went on trips. He had given Roddy and Buddy theirs in the hall of the villa: Buddy still had his, of course, in the zipper pocket of his jeans. Roddy was turning red now and going through and through all his stuff, even his rucksack and Buddy's rucksack and especially the back seat of the Mercedes. The Old Man was doing a slow boil and telling Roddy what he would do to him. Roddy bolted for the toilet.

As they waited Buddy said to the Old Man: 'Will Roddy need it? I mean, will we be stopped or anything?'

'Of course he'll need it, you moron,' snapped the Old Man. 'You can't go anywhere in Europe without identification.'

'What if a passport is lost?'

'Then you report it to those sons-of-bitches at the consulate. I guess they give you some kind of travel document.'

Roddy came back looking as if he had thrown up. They searched some more. The Old Man moved the car until it was between a big truck and a brick wall.

'I'll call your mother,' he said. 'She can send the passport on if it's there. Get out, Roddy, and just come in the front seat here with me. I guess you need another lesson in discipline.'

Buddy felt his stomach contract painfully at the thought of seeing his brother beaten up another time. Roddy was pale as death; he took off his glasses and tried to polish them.

'No sir,' he begged. 'I helped you. I never said any bad stuff to you like Buddy. I found the Luger for you!'

'Quit it, you slobbering coward!' said the Old Man.

'I know something!' cried Roddy. 'I know some things you should know, Dad. Please, Dad!'

'If it's some more of your damned tale-telling about Buddy, I don't want to hear it,' said the Old Man. 'Are you coming in this front seat or do I have to drag you, yellow belly?'

Roddy began to cry. In a voice choked with tears he said: '*Kate Reimann knows! Kate Reimann is a spy!* She was watching you! And she was talking to Mom on the phone!'

The Old Man looked at his watch. It was ten past ten, a fine day in central Germany. He turned back the way they had come, driving north on the *landstrasse,* trying to find a way back on to the *autobahn.*

III

Kate took a shower but she was still not cool. She looked about in the kitchen and took from a high shelf a doll dressed in a dirndl that Andreas had won at the Apple-Wine Festival. A present for Melissa. Things for kids piled up in their apartment and in this house because there was no-one to have them, no-one to grab for the stickers on the margarine tub or the plastic figures in the cereal. She thought of Ruth and the twins and heard her say: 'That could change, kiddo.'

She drove out of the garage and sat contemplating the Villa Florian. Summer would end and the poor Limbards would go back home to Pennsylvania. The fine, spirited house would be left to its own devices. She drove quickly down and round, circling the wall of soft red sandstone, less weathered than the convent wall, and drawing up at the back gate, an old wooden gate with five bars.

She sat there peering through the thick green of the orchard towards the west wall of the house. It was after two. She must go in and fetch Mary. It was rude to honk the horn, and in any case she might not hear it. It occurred to Kate that what she really wanted to do was look at the house some more; she remembered her promise to Sister Florentine and broke it without a second thought.

The gate creaked. The tall grass among the trees was twisted with poppies and cornflowers. There was an old kitchen garden, untended, beyond the orchard to her left; the apples were ripening and there was a tree laden with yellow plums. The path was of red and white irregular blocks of stone, heavily mossed: halfway down it she stooped to pick up a blue candy wrapper. She crunched it up in her hand and slipped it into her shoulder bag. She saw to her right the ribbed and pointed roof of the summer house where Franz Walther had slept, as watchman. Had Bodo been with him then?

She paused at the orchard's end to admire the west wall, the autumn aspect of the Villa Florian. Tamara Paige had stood where she was standing, perhaps, to draw the villa; she had leaned out like the blessed damozel from the balconies looking into the orchard. A great beauty, Nicki had said. Kate sighed, feeling herself angular and tall and passably attractive in her green trousers and blouse of raw silk.

As she came towards the house there was a call: 'Hello there!'

Mary Limbard was standing in sunlight by the cellar steps. She was well turned out in a summery two-piece of pink linen and white sandals.

'Come on to the terrace,' she said. 'We have time for coffee.'

When the cat's away, thought Kate. She walked boldly on to the south lawn and stole a glance at the Villa Florian in bright sunshine. She yielded to its attraction, spread out her arms to the house, to the dark gleam of the iron roses, the sinuous designs on the long balcony. Mary was waiting at the table under a tilted sun umbrella of old, soft red, trimmed with gold fringes.

'This side of the house always get me,' said Kate.

'Just right for summer,' said Mary.

She was excited, with a pretty flush in her pale cheeks. She served coffee in red and white cups, quite nice, an English line, like willow pattern.

Kate said, 'The Sisters have a whole tea-service from the villa.'

'What, the nuns up the hill?' asked Mary.

'They're not really nuns,' said Kate. 'They are lay sisters.'

Mary laughed.

'Yes, it is a dumb name.' said Kate.

The coffee was strong and good; she ate a piece of supermarket cake, refused cream. Mary filled her cup.

'Sister Florentine told me a lot about the history of this place.'

'You really are interested,' said Mary. 'You study this place every chance you get!'

Kate was too hot under the umbrella, drinking the steaming coffee. She longed for a breeze. She felt her cheeks burning hot, sweat dripping beneath her arms and running down her ribs. She began to search for her sunglasses in her shoulder bag. She found the doll and was about to draw it out but it slipped away from her. She came up with the candy wrapper. Mary was saying: '...responding to treatment...'

'I'm so pleased to hear that!' said Kate. She took the doll from her bag and held it up. 'Something for Melissa.'

Mary took no notice of the doll. 'Kate,' she said, 'I want to ask you something very important.'

'Fire ahead,' said Kate.

Mary was sitting on the edge of her chair, looking keyed up, bright and alert. Kate on the other hand was feeling heavy and sick. She half turned to get a breeze from the corner of the house. *Kate.* The words sprang up at her. *Kate, stay.*

'Why did you think I might need help, Kate,' asked Mary gently. 'Was it something you saw?'

'Yes!' said Kate too loudly.

'You came back,' said Mary, 'you came back for that cloth bag. You carried medicine in it from the drug store, and the little pot-plant.'

Kate nodded. She fought a wave of hot faintness and nausea that struck up at her from the marbled tiles of the terrace.

'Yes,' she said, 'I couldn't help seeing...'

'What exactly?' prompted Mary.

'I don't like to say,' said Kate childishly.

She spread the candy wrapper out on her knee and read the message in red ballpoint. 'Kate stay away. Dad is back.' She folded the wrapper and stowed it away in her bag. She sprang to her feet. The darkening sunlight pressed down upon her, pressed her back down into her chair.

'I feel awful all of a sudden,' she said. 'I'd better go home. I saw Jason beating up you and the kids. I know it's none of my business but you're a woman, I guess you and the kids are in some kind of a difficult situation.'

'Yes,' said Mary Limbard. 'And I'll tell you who's to blame, you damned meddling bitch!'

Kate dragged herself upright in her chair and blinked at Mary. She could not speak. Her last long utterance had made her mouth dry, her lips thick. Her limbs were heavy. She was growing into the old rattan chair. It was binding her with reeds, tendrils of vine were at her throat.

'Spy!' said Mary, leaning across the table, her face rosy pink under the red umbrella. 'Filthy interfering spy. Now I will never see her. Now he can keep me from ever visiting her in hospital again. Do you understand what that means?'

'Let me go,' mumbled Kate.

She heard her voice coming from a long way off. She peered into the summer garden and saw the two dogs frolicking among the silver spray of the fountains. A girl in a white dress was twisting this way and that, holding a stick for the dogs, her dress swirling and her long black hair swinging out like a curtain.

'Let me go!' Kate cried. 'Help me!'

She tried to stand. At her elbow was the Baron's chair, a tall bath chair; he stared at her and through her with an expression of frightful malevolence. Jason Limbard walked briskly out of the house, and laughed and said: 'She didn't taste a thing!'

'Go then!' shouted Mary.

She pushed the table at Kate so that she slithered out of her chair and came down on her knees. Jason came right through the Baron's chair and prodded her with his foot. His face was a thickening mask, lips drawn back in a grimace of excitement. He took a step and was astride her back, his legs pressing against her ribs. Kate moaned and rolled; she went down the shallow steps of the terrace on to the warm grass. Mary bent over her, talking angry gibberish.

Kate gathered all her failing strength and heaved up her long body from the ground. She ran drunkenly for the trees, for the beckoning dark girl, a great beauty, smiling and holding out her hands.

She felt the blow on the side of her head. It cracked her skull and made her brain rebound in its bony cage, and it stopped time. She spun round with exquisite slowness and beheld, as she sank to earth, the unmarred summer beauty of the Villa Florian. She saw the awnings, the iron roses among their thorns and the relief upon the long balcony: of a man turning into a wolf.

Buddy had never worked so hard in his life. He sat for hours in the room opposite their sitting room, furnished with an old table and a wicker chair from the terrace. The room was a help, it was wise to his little game, it warned him when anyone was coming. There was a creak and a shudder of the window panes and he had time to hide the extra exercise book.

He knew that he was insane, worse than Roddy. Roddy was 'Number One Son,' good as gold. He cleaned the car; he helped Mom around the house; he went to visit Liss in the Klinik. He said to Buddy, 'There, you see. That stupid Kate – she freaked right out back there in the woods. She never even came near this place. One whiff from that old van should have done the trick but she couldn't make a go of it...'

One reason Buddy started his writing jag was to get away from Roddy and his whistling in the dark.

Buddy couldn't sleep well. He lay awake or tossed and turned with guilty knowledge boiling in his head and in his gut. One night he got up, Wednesday night or early Thursday morning, and went downstairs. He was near the kitchen when he heard voices. Mom and the Old Man were still up, they were spooked bad. Mom was sick with it. He heard her say: 'I pray to God, Jay, I pray to God...'

And the Old Man answered, 'Pray that the crazy bitch never wakes out of her coma.'

Mom began crying again. The Old Man chuckled.

'No, no, she won't remember. Trust me baby. It was just bad luck with the fire alarm. We might have been home free.'

Buddy, standing barefoot in the light of dawn, experienced a great crisis of disgust and hatred and despair. He shivered from head to foot. His stomach and his bowels were full of cramps. He knew that if he had had the Luger in his hand that minute he could have killed the Old Man.

Yet it was not his nature; maybe he was a dove, not a hawk. He thought of Kate Reimann, the little trickle of blood behind her ear, the clumsy soft way she came down upon the stony ground. God, God, if there is a God, let her not die!

'Stop this goddamned blubbering,' said the Old Man. 'She will die, I tell you! She won't remember! The gas had time to eat into her brain... You saw how Andy bought the whole set-up? He has her measure.'

Buddy stiffened as he heard the Old Man moving about in the kitchen; a tap was turned on.

'No place in my life,' said the Old Man, 'for a weak link. A woman who never stops crying.'

So Buddy got himself together and padded softly away to his writing room in the morning light. What he was doing was the right thing. Even for Mom. He made a cryptic list on the inside back cover of the orange exercise book: trunk, passport, headstone, upstairs. He began to work, finishing up the book report for Roddy to copy out. His own essay, 'My Holiday in Germany', didn't matter so much. Thursday, Friday. One night they would give him the chance, he knew it. Tonight, tomorrow night. Forgive me Mom, pray to God for me, cry, cry all you want to and *he will let you go!* He is afraid to keep you around after what happened with Kate.

He saw the old lady come to the Forsthaus gate and get her newspaper. The black cat purred around her legs. He stared at her, thinking of all he knew, and he could not even wish another life for himself. He was a ghost, looking out of the house of the dead. Maybe his mood would change, he would have another good dream or another nightmare. Right now he was a ghost with no past and no future. All that he could see in his mind's eye was the path that led down to the cold waters of the lake.

PART TWO

Autumn

Chapter 5
Reconstruction

Kate and her friend Ruth Hiller were walking in the English Garden, one of the most beautiful parks in the world. An autumn wind flicked the first leaves from the trees, blood-red and gold, and drove them along the shaded paths. They walked beside the swift-flowing little river... it was too cold for the swimmers and the naked sunbathers but there were always people about. Joggers passed them, dogs were walked; the spaces of the lovely park attracted odd and lonely folk. An old man with white moustachios talked to himself, striking at the piled leaves with his cane. A timid woman fed the birds and took flight when anyone approached her bench.

There was a photographic session in progress near the park's most famous landmark, a tall Chinese pagoda. Kate led Ruth to a sheltered garden seat and they read the brass plate. There was an engraved lily and the words: 'To the memory of our young friend Tamara Paige'.

'So that's it,' said Ruth. 'You have quite a file on this girl. Who were her friends?'

'Artists. Franz von Stück and the other old guys from the Münchner Secession. They had a little trouble with this plaque because she was a suicide.'

'Why on earth...?' began Ruth. 'Oh, sure. This is Catholic Bavaria.'

They sat down on the seat. Ruth, who was small and dark and a little bit foreshortened in her mink jacket, looked at Kate, lounging in her long brown cloth coat.

'You look great,' she said wistfully. 'You have good bones.'

'You'll turn my head, Doc,' said Kate. 'Did Dr Geraldus

give me a clean bill of mental health?'

'Kate, if he was younger he'd marry you! You are his most successful patient ever. He took me back into the waiting room to admire your painting of a tree. He showed me an article he published over your case. You are sound as a dollar... so sane, I think, that he'd like you to develop a few more symptoms and come back.'

'He's a nice man,' said Kate, 'and I did all that he said. What the doctor ordered.' She looked at her watch. 'We have half an hour before Andreas arrives. Do you want to make a start on the questionnaire?'

'Ready when you are.'

Ruth took out a notebook, flipped through pages of her tiny speed-writing. Kate looked at the trees and the pale sky.

'Some time has passed since your accident, Ms Reimann,' said Ruth. 'What is the extent of your amnesia?'

'Two months,' said Kate,' nearly three. The whole of one summer, six years ago.'

'How is your memory at the present time?'

'Great!' said Kate fiercely. 'I'm never going to lose another day, if I can help it!'

'You had a head injury, you were in pain... did the amnesia itself distress you much?'

'I can hardly separate the two experiences,' said Kate. 'It was the deepest, most terrible nightmare.'

She shut her eyes, remembering how the light caused great pain. Movement in the void, lifting and carrying. Was it a war? Injured in war...

'Take it easy,' said Ruth.

'I'm fine,' said Kate, opening her eyes. 'There was a continual search for an explanation. I thought of a war. I registered head injury, hospital, and thought of a traffic accident. Had I hit a pedestrian or a dog? Then I thought someone had hit me.'

'Did you have difficulty remembering your own name?'

'Yes and no,' said Kate. 'I remember saying "Kate Cameron", then feeling guilty, as if I had somehow said the wrong thing.'

'Were you informed promptly about the cause and extent of your injuries?'

'No, damn it!' said Kate. 'But there were... special circumstances.'

A beautiful golden-haired man sits by her bed as the mists clear. He weeps and has to wipe his glasses. *My* man. *Mein Mann.*

'Andy?'

'You gave us such a terrible fright... Oh Kate, Kate, what happened?'

'*I don't know!*'

And the corollary: You will never know. To this day the poor fellow does not know what hit him. Years and dreams and a whole life long and it will never be resolved.

'Weeks had passed,' said Kate. 'They said that the van went off the road on the upper Steinberg near Tante Adelheid's house in Breitbach, Hessen. Now we were in a clinic in München.'

'Off the record,' said Ruth. 'When *did* you find out?'

'I felt that something was being kept from me,' said Kate. 'I was much better, having visitors. Our special friend Nicki, Nicholas Lenz, came to see me. He did it too... clammed up on some things, told me to ask Andreas. I became very upset. What terrible thing had I done? I begged him to be my friend and tell me the truth.'

'And he did?'

'Poor Nicki! He rushed out of the room. I heard him raising hell on the ward, saying, *"She must be told!"* At last a doctor came. It was the great man himself, Professor Müller-Heinrich. He gave it to me more or less straight. The van *had* gone off the road and smashed against a tree. I was lying on stony ground beside the open door, suffering severe concussion and a hairline fracture of the mastoid process which led to symptoms of compression. There was also a length of hosepipe fastened to the exhaust outlet... it had fallen from the small vent window on the driver's side. That was the worse blow of all... I had made some attempt at suicide.

'The Professor was very good. He pointed out that I had changed my mind, turned off the motor, pushed the hosepipe away. He said, "So you see, Frau Reimann, you have not hurt anybody." But this wasn't true. I had hurt Andy... permanently. I have always believed that suicide was very cruel, a cruel thing to do to the people who are left behind.'

Ruth said gently: 'I've always believed that suicides are not themselves. They're suffering from a mental illness, usually depression.'

'Are there other would-be suicides who blank out completely on the attempt?'

'Sure,' said Ruth, 'it's not unknown. But most of them are more severely depressed or disturbed.'

'You mean they're crazier!'

'Yes,' said Ruth. 'Much worse than you ever were, judging by the completeness of your recovery. When did you discover that you were pregnant?'

'It kind of seeped through,' said Kate. 'I could honestly say that I had known or suspected all along. It was one of the things that came back. I knew that during the summer we were thinking of a child, it was kind of now or never. I remembered thinking I might be pregnant. Everyone at the clinic was pleased, full of congratulations. Andy said he was pleased. I was working with Dr Geraldus by this time.'

'Katherine, you have much to live for. Do not strain to recapture painful memories. Much of the time will return. Write down your dreams. Your great interest is in art... who says that you are not an artist yourself, like the poor English girl in this book? After such a trauma persons have developed extraordinary powers.'

'Next question,' said Ruth. 'How do memories return?'

'Every which way,' said Kate. 'A picture. A sound. A scent. An atmosphere of *déjà vu*. The difficulty is to distinguish between things you genuinely remember yourself, or things you were told and go along with. Like a childhood memory... do you really recall the day you fell down the steps or is it some kind of family legend? The Geraldus treatment had its drawbacks. It meant that I did no research into my own case. Andy extracted some kind of promise from Tante Adelheid not to discuss the... the attempt with me.'

'She is *his* aunt,' said Ruth, 'some kind of ersatz mother when his parents died. Did she come on like a disapproving mother-in-law?'

'Never!' said Kate. 'There were times when I thought crazy Kate must be worth something only because Tante Adelheid stuck to me. She was, she is...true as steel. She has never wavered. But Andy was ashamed of what I had tried to do, and frightened.'

'Guilt feelings.' said Ruth softly, 'on all sides. After all, Andreas was down here in München with his girl-friend Brigitte.'

'I expect I am kidding myself,' said Kate, 'but I never thought that that had bothered me very much. Andy and I got along fine. Maybe the honeymoon was over but I like to think we loved each other that summer.'

'Next question,' said Ruth. 'Here's a laugh. Has your life changed since the accident that caused your amnesia. Positive changes, negative changes?'

'One could say my life had changed,' said Kate ruefully. 'There was a very bad patch, remember, when I left the hospital. I couldn't have a second operation on my head until after Peter was born. I was like a zombie for another four months. I'm sure that put people off. They thought I might never get any better. But I snapped out of it pretty quickly after that.'

'I have your letters from that time,' said Ruth. 'You got to be a great penwoman with your left hand. Can you still work that trick?'

'Sure. Highly ambidextrous, for what it's worth. I tried, Ruthie, I've never tried so hard to cope with life. And it worked. I wrote and painted. The baby was beautiful and good. Only the thing with Andreas got worse. We didn't fight, we "lived past each other", for three years.'

She fell silent. The wind swept through the tops of the trees; somewhere there was music playing. She said: 'Here they come.'

A tall bearded man, just beginning to take on a little weight, led by the hand a blonde boy of five in jeans, a red parka and a small blue rucksack. Even at a distance they were almost comically alike. Andreas gave serious replies while his son, Peter, pulled and jounced and chattered. At last he broke free, ran to Kate and flung himself into her lap. She held him tight for a long moment.

'Now come,' said Andreas. 'Say good-day to Frau Doktor Hiller.'

Peter, still beaming, stood in front of Ruth and gave her a dutiful paw.

'Why, hello there, Peter!' said Ruth.

'How's Italy?' asked Kate.

'Warmer,' said Andreas. 'Did you get the tax information?'

'Yes, thanks.'

'Your name is Ruth!' said Peter, breaking into English. 'You sent me the big Panda Bear!'

'That's right,' said Ruth. 'How's he doing?'

'He's fine. He lives in our apartment in Darmstadt, where Mom teaches school.'

'I'm off to Rome,' announced Andreas. 'For the Limbard wedding. Brigitte and I will be witnesses.'

'Please congratulate Jason for me,' said Kate.

'I must go,' said Andreas. 'Life is full of stress. Peter?'

Andreas picked up his son and gave him a kiss. Kate turned her head and looked at the trees, thinking of this sad little scene being played out in parks and railway stations all over the world. She was guiltily pleased that it was her turn to have Peter.

Andreas said to her: 'I nearly forgot. Have you seen Nicki?'

'Not for years. Is he in München?'

'He's here somewhere, right here in the English Garden helping with some photographic session. I ran into him in the street.'

'Oh, I would like to see him.'

'You'll see him in Breitbach, putting the finishing touches to the Villa Florian,' said Andreas.

'His masterpiece,' said Kate. 'We always knew he was the one to do it!'

She and Andreas laughed together for the first time. Andreas nodded to both women and walked quickly away, hands in the pockets of his leather coat. Peter stood beside his mother and held her hand.

'So Jason Limbard, the diet guy, will get married,' said Ruth. 'Who's the lucky girl?'

'Anja Schönfeld,' said Kate. 'Photographic model. Very pretty. I've never met her.'

'I have,' chipped in Peter. 'She and Diet Jason came to stay at the beach house in Capri.'

Kate and Ruth exchanged glances. Peter sat between them, swinging his legs, pleased to have their attention.

'She's nice. She has black hair. But she doesn't have a little boy.'

'Can't have everything, I guess,' said Ruth.

'I hope things work out for Diet Jason,' said Kate. 'I think you heard about the terrible thing that happened...'

She broke off, looking at Peter.

'Okay,' he said. 'I'll run away and play, but not too near the river.'

He shrugged out of his blue rucksack and raced away.

'Oh God,' said Ruth, 'I could cry just looking at him. A beautiful bi-lingual kid. I think I'll send the twins to that Language Kibbutz in New Mexico.'

'The Limbard family spent that summer at the Villa Florian,' said Kate stiffly.

'What's the matter?'

'Nothing. A goose walked over my grave.'

She got up and walked a few steps towards the river; the boys on skateboards whisked past. Ruth stood beside her.

'Buddy Limbard was drowned, right?' she said. 'You told me in a letter.'

'I had some memory of Buddy,' said Kate. 'Just a fat kid but there was something sympathetic about him.'

'There was no autopsy, no body recovered.'

'Don't get ideas,' said Kate. 'The Waldsee is cold, even in summer, and very deep. There have been three or four drowning accidents in the past thirty years, including one other where the body was never found.'

'He couldn't have been lost in the woods or even run away from his folks?'

'His passport and clothes were found on the bank,' said Kate. 'He couldn't speak German and had no identification. Last person to see him was a Herr Walther, a forester, a very reliable old guy. He saw him sitting by the lake in his bathing trunks and gave him a friendly warning. The police and the family believe he had a cramp or something and drowned.'

'God,' burst out Ruth, 'what kind of bad Karma was building up over that neck of the woods? The little girl... was it meningitis she contracted? Accidents, sickness. Were you all suffering from meningitis? From some kind of environmental poison, for heaven's sake? Cadmium, mercury...I don't know, some medical explanation. Didn't the papers get on to it?'

'They did,' said Kate grimly. 'Sensational headlines in the notorious *Nacht Post*. "American Boy Dead in the Waldsee. Was it suicide? Buddy-Joe Didn't Take Care of His Little Sister." A garbled report about Melissa in hospital...Buddy was supposed to have drowned himself out of guilt.'

'That's ghastly,' said Ruth. 'Can they get away with stuff like that?'

'They didn't get away with it,' said Kate. 'Jason sued and there was a financial settlement. Enough to put a down payment on the Villa Florian.'

'I can't understand his wanting to live near that lake.'

'The Villa Florian is a special case,' said Kate. 'A really beautiful, neglected house. Andy said that the locals sort of rallied round when the Limbard family had all this trouble and Jason wanted to show his gratitude. The Breitbach Council were pleased...they contributed to the restoration. Our pal Nicholas Lenz got the commission to renovate the villa.'

'What are they like, the Limbards?'

'Well, everyone knows Jason,' said Kate. 'He's a real charmer, big handsome guy.'

'I'm not all that susceptible to health nuts,' said Ruth, 'but he isn't *too* way out.'

'His books are fantastically popular in Germany,' said Kate. 'He really struck a nerve. Andy sort of discovered him for Lorbeer Verlag and they were grateful. He took over the job of his former boss, a man named Melchior. Andy has had three runaway bestsellers with Diet Jason.'

'What happened to his first wife?'

'Mary,' said Kate. 'Poor woman. She became very religious. Jason gave her a divorce about a year after their trip to Germany. She lives in Florida with the little girl.'

The afternoon sun was lengthening the shadows of the trees. They walked slowly towards Peter who was galloping round and round a mighty oak.

'There is something here for your amnesia study, Doc,' said Kate. 'The way I remembered...or failed to remember the

Limbards. You really should question *them*. Did Frau Reimann strike you as a different person before and after her unfortunate contretemps? I know that I met them that summer, they came to Tante Adelheid's house for a barbecue and I guess I dropped in to the Villa Florian once or twice. Then they all came to visit me in the clinic in München, just before they flew back to the States. It was the strangest sensation.'

'You'd met them before but couldn't recall where?' suggested Ruth.

'Worse than that,' said Kate. 'I'd met them all before wearing different expressions. As if they were somehow *changed,* and not through grief. As if they were — it sounds terrible — putting on an act.'

'It's usually the other way about,' said Ruth. 'Amnesia victims are constantly accused of putting on an act. It's the you-can't-possibly-have-forgotten-*that* reaction.'

'I wish I had a dollar for every time I saw that particular gleam in someone's eye,' said Kate.

'But getting back to your Limbard meeting,' said Ruth. 'Did you have this strange sensation with all of them, even the two kids?'

'No,' said Kate. 'Melissa, the little girl, was there. Very shy, didn't utter a word. Just stood there clutching her new teddybear. And I thought . . . no, I *knew* . . . this was how I had seen her before. Weird.'

She tossed her hair back over her shoulders as if to drive away troubling thoughts.

'Enough!' she said. 'I haven't dragged all these skeletons out of the cupboard for years, literally years.'

Peter came up, stood between Kate and Ruth, taking a hand on either side.

'*Sei liebe,*' he said. 'Be nice. Let's eat at MacDonalds!'

'We'll get you a Big Mac to eat at the hotel,' said Kate with a sigh. 'Ruth didn't come all the way to Germany to eat American food.'

'Junk food,' said Peter happily.

They walked towards the nearest park gate, admiring a clump of statuary and the carousel in the distance. Kate saw a tram passing in the street and thought of Tamara Paige. Had she used this gate up ahead, early one morning? She came back to München and worked hard at her line and wash drawings, she worked right up until the last day. That was the day she took the tram to the English Garden, carrying a bust of the mystic philosopher Emanuel Swedenborg in a leather satchel. She slung the heavy satchel across her body before stepping into the water...

'*Kate!*'

Had she been called or was it the wind?

'Did you hear...?' she said, looking about.

'You're being called,' said Ruth, 'and by a good-looking man. Right there.'

He stood on a side path about fifty metres away, a strongly built dark man, of medium height. His broad shoulders made him look a little stocky. He had black hair, fashionably tousled, and a rather pale, mobile actor's face.

'*Nicki!*'

She ran forward and when they met he lifted her right up and spun around.

'Katie! You're looking marvellous!'

'Nicki! *Altes Haus!* Oh, it's great to see you again. Andy said you were here in the park.'

'Is Andreas around?'

Peter held Kate's coat sleeve possessively and said: 'He only came to give me back to my mother.'

'Peter,' said Nicki. 'May I say how you've grown?'

They shook hands. Ruth was introduced. Suddenly Peter burst out: 'I *saw* you. I saw Nicki!'

'What, on television?' asked Nicki.

'In the movies. In *Vienna Blood!*'

'Of course!' cried Ruth. 'I saw it too. You were the waiter, what was his name? The sinister Austrian waiter with the moustache. Oh, that was great! Kate, you must have seen it.'

'Twice,' said Kate. 'It's one of Peter's favourite movies. Rudi the waiter.'

'Was that a real moustache?' demanded Peter.

'Yes,' said Nicki. 'I grew it especially for the part then shaved it off.'

'Can you really skate like that? How did they work the part where you were shot?'

'In the Vienna Woods,' teased Kate, 'while a thousand

violins played guess what on the sound track.'

She hummed the waltz. Nicki gave a sort of groan. He spread his hands in a gesture that she remembered. The cameo part in the lavish Hollywood spy thriller was the sort of thing many European actors or cabarettists would dine out on for the rest of their lives...but she remembered another thing about Nicki. He was a truly modest man, the last person in the world to have his head turned.

'I have a good idea,' he said. 'Let me take you all out to dinner at Carlo's.'

'Oh, yes! Yes!' cried Peter. 'Please Mom! It's much *healthier* than a cheeseburger!'

'Can't argue with that!' laughed Ruth.

'Okay, fine,' said Kate. 'Nicki, will you be doing more films?'

'Who knows? he said. 'I'm still not sure whether *Vienna Blood* was a good thing or a disastrous mistake. At least everyone has seen it.'

'But you were so good,' said Kate. 'I mean it.'

Nicki beamed at this scrap of praise. He reached up and brushed away a rust-coloured autumn leaf that had settled on the shoulder of her coat.

'I'm glad to see you looking so well,' he said.

He turned away, embarrassed, and said to Peter in the accents of Rudi, the sinister double agent:'*Servus, mein Herr!* We must go to the secret meeting place.'

Peter whooped with delight. Ruth and Kate walked behind the pair of them out into the street.

Late at night in Ruth's hotel room the two friends sat together and drank mineral water. Peter slept in a cot in Kate's room. They had had a long, silly, delightful evening at Carlo's restaurant.

'What a terrific end to my holiday,' said Ruth. 'Dinner with Nick Lenz. And he also renovates houses.'

'He's an *Innen Architekt,*' said Kate. 'That's his profession. An interior decorator, more or less. It is kind of different in Europe.'

'Interior decorator suggests someone gay,' said Ruth, 'but I guess that's not Nicki!'

'Of course not,' said Kate. 'He was married to a journalist, Magda. I bet he cut a swathe through the girls in America.'

'He was very pleased to see you again.'

'Yes,' said Kate. 'He was such a good friend, years ago.'

Ruth sighed and cast her eyes up to heaven. 'You are in perfect health, kiddo,' she said, 'but your antennae are not working.'

'*Nicki?*' said Kate. 'Oh, go along with you.'

'He'll be in Breitbach putting the finishing touches to the Limbard house.'

Kate felt a nerve twitch on the right side of her face. Inexplicably she did not want it to be 'the Limbard house'.

'Haus von Sommer,' she said. 'The Villa Florian.'

There were two dreams. One was very bad, a nightmare, and it was always the same; the other was an anxiety dream with many variations. She seldom had both dreams on the same night. Now they came upon her without warning. The bad dream was hard to put into words, she had tried to write it down several times. It had an aura — like the strange feelings that preceded a migraine, perhaps, or an epileptic seizure.

In her sleep she was aware of a torturing unrest in her head. It was almost a sound, like a distant buzz saw or the murmur of voices. It went on and on, spreading over her skull, spreading into her limbs, making them heavy. She talked, in her dream, to drive away this sensation. She walked or tried to jog and to run. Then she was out of doors, it was night, the dream had begun.

She was filled with a cosmic terror. She was delivered over to darkness and pain and to sights which she must see which could not be borne. There was grass under her bare feet, trees brushed her face. She tried to cry out but only a faint mewling sound like a kitten squeezed from her dry throat. Like a yellow moon rising she saw a square of light through the trees and for the first time all the fear and loathing in the dream concentrated on a presence, a dreadful half-human creature.

She tried to escape from the yellow light and the tree leaves rattled, giving her away, for they were of thin bronze. A dark shadow rose up on the surface of the yellow light and she ran at last, conscious that her fear had been too great. It had killed her, stolen her soul, the evil could never be undone. She ran, panting, hearing a louder breath that followed, and as she dived into a thicket the creature leaped upon her back and she awoke in a last convulsion of fear...

For a few seconds she was disoriented, uncertain of the room she was in. She turned over, still breathless from her nightmare as if to take comfort from someone next to her. Then she was wide awake in the hotel room. Peter slept in his folding bed. Kate sat up and hugged her knees, her fear from the dream turning into a dull anger.

No, it would not do to take a tablet or run to Ruth or to seek out Dr Geraldus again. She had puzzled and tried free association over the nightmare for years. Geraldus had been very good and they came up with a bad scene that Kate had not thought of for a long time. Back in high school in Lessing PA a man had grabbed her as she walked home through the park. Tall Kate had fought him off and screamed and been rescued by Father McAndrew and his track squad, out for a training run. The man was never caught, he ran off through the trees. And she had been running and jogging ever since, she had married a man whose name was related to that of her rescuer ... wow, how corny could her unconsious mind get.

'There is something else there,' opined Dr Geraldus, 'something to do with your present crisis. Keep working on it Katherine, don't push too hard...'

Kate gave a sigh. The lights from an automobile climbing steeply out of the underground parking lot washed over the wall of her hotel room and she almost cried out with terror. The yellow light... *the television screen.* It was exactly the right shape, a square but with rounded corners. She lay back with a feeling of discovery. She fell asleep again thinking of horror movies. How cosy they seemed by contrast with her nightmare.

Towards morning she had her second recurring dream. It began with a party in their old apartment in München with overtones of the Forsthaus. Brigitte was there, and Nicki and Ruth and Thomas who taught the art class in Darmstadt, plus a gaggle of colourfully dressed strangers. Things began to go wrong in the kitchen. Her shoes were muddy, her hair was not combed, she could not get the supper ready. Andreas burst into the kitchen and accused her of breaking the headlamp of the new auto. She denied and denied. She had done no such thing, it was unfair, a monstrous injustice that would never be put right. She protested and wept in her dream but Andreas sneered, saying she was a cheat. She awoke with real tears in her eyes and felt warm with relief because she had come out of her tormenting dream.

Chapter 6
Old Friends

Kate slept in the spare room of the Forsthaus which had turned into her holiday studio. She could look out on the tops of the trees and the old stable. In fact, she had hardly had time to look out; the whole week she had been preparing for an art show: Three Women Artists, in the Old Mill Gallery, Breitbach. The opening of the show, the vernissage – how grand it sounded – was only four days away. Along with Gisela and Marlene, and with Thomas Brand who had arranged the whole thing with the gallery proprietors, she had been packing, unpacking, setting up the exhibits. She had painted three large display screens eggshell blue and mended one of the Forsthaus trestle tables for Marlene's pottery. There had been a great coming and going with a small truck and a station wagon.

Tante Adelheid took it all in good part; she would call up the stairs to Kate: 'Here comes poor Thomas again.'

Poor Thomas. He was a wiry sun-tanned man, a little younger than Kate, and he had what she and Ruth would have called 'a bad case'. Nearly two years ago she had gone with him on a painting trip to the South of France and tried for a carefree summer affair with a man she liked very much. She continued to like him, no more than that, but the relationship dragged on for a year or more because poor Thomas would not give up. There was a benign conspiracy among the three women artists to introduce Thomas to as many Kate-substitutes as possible in the hope that he would fall in love with someone else.

Feeling bad about poor Thomas, at seven o'clock in the morning Kate set out to jog. The weather was warmer than it had been in the south but the trees were as beautiful as those in the English Garden. She looked into the big bedroom, a child's room now. Had she and Andreas been children when they slept there in those childless holiday summers? Peter was up and about on his own excursions.

A particular harsh ringing and crashing was louder in the bedroom and she realised that it had been going on for some time. She slipped into Onkel Ernst's study and saw that they were taking down the scaffolding that obscured the façade of the Villa Florian. The pipes rang and clattered as the workmen flung them into a large flatbed truck; Kate felt the sound go through her head and gave an involuntary shudder. She ran downstairs, out of the house, and took what she called 'the low road', turning to her left outside the gate.

A modern villa had been built below the Forsthaus, a dark low building, crouched behind a wall of concrete lattice and guarded by two Dobermanns. It belonged to a banker and his family and was rumoured to contain an indoor swimming pool with a wave machine and a billiard room. There had been a good deal of building activity on the Steinberg since that lost summer. The road over the brow of the hill had been up-graded and led directly on to the *landstrasse*. Kate ran on, skirting the south lawn of the Villa Florian with its towering autumn trees and coming into the misty silence of the back lane. The road was not steep but she began to pant. She did not dare turn her head to look up at the curves of the roof and the dome, touched by the morning sun. The wall had been repaired, topped with two strands of wire, hidden in places by the trees. Jason Limbard had had an elaborate security system built in; his home was his castle.

Kate leaned against a tall pine some distance from the new security gate of dark wire mesh and looked at the orchard trees. There were roses, red and pink, blooming beside the red and white tiled path.

What was this? She was all better, the star patient of Dr Geraldus.

I am afraid, she thought. *I am afraid of the Villa Florian. If I admit it, perhaps I can do something about it.*

She thought of a woman standing among the roses – yes, Tamara in her artist's smock, sketching the western aspect of the villa.

Slowly she raised her eyes; the scaffolding had been taken down and the autumn wall was creamy white, a warm colour. She saw the vineleaves upon the balconies, the wrought iron leaves and fruit, and the long relief, in subdued autumn colours, brown, dark green, gold. *It is beautiful*, she thought. *I can't be afraid, I must go in one day soon and admire Nicki's work, take a present to the Limbards when they arrive.*

A dark figure loomed up so close that Kate jumped. He came out of the woods very quietly, all dressed up to save Rotkäppchen from the wolf or to cast silver bullets with the devil: the forester in his loden jacket with silver buttons. He stepped up to the back gate of the Villa Florian and turned the handle, testing the security.

'Good morning, Herr Walther!'

He gave a start then favoured Kate with one of his rare smiles.

'Frau Reimann, how well you are looking!'

They shook hands. She felt better with someone at her side; they admired the autumn aspect. Kate wondered aloud if Herr Lenz was about and decided not to use the electric buzzer.

'I expect he's very busy,' she said.

'I think he has some last-minute jobs for us, for the boys,' said Franz Walther.

His two young cousins had come up from the farmyard in deepest Bavaria. She had seen them in the distance working on the villa or roaring past in an old Volkswagen. They were jobbing, a sign of the times. Even an apprenticeship was hard to find.

'I must finish my run,' she said.

A cyclist idled past them exercising a large *Schäferhund*, a German Shepherd.

'You never thought,' she asked gently, 'of getting another dog?'

He shook his head, unsmiling, and glanced at the villa again. He asked, in his grumbling bass, when Jason was arriving. His voice came out reserved, even hostile.

'*Wann kommt der Haus-Herr?*'

Didn't he approve of the villa coming into the hands of an American?

'In a few days, I think,' she said. 'Herr Limbard has married again.'

The forester's dour look turned to something like alarm. Kate pressed on. 'He has married a German girl.'

Herr Walther shook his head sadly. Kate saw that a long spray of rambling red roses hung down from the wall. She picked them and said, 'I think I might run down to the Waldsee. I haven't been there for years.'

'You will see the boys down there,' he said. 'I'm glad to see you looking so well, Frau Reimann.'

They shook hands and she went on steadily to the place where a dirt road ran down through the trees to the banks of the lake. The Waldsee was dusty and hot in summer. The gaiety of the swimmers, the laden picnic tables and bright awnings on the kiosk, did not really suit the place. In autumn it was sombre: the grey rocks, the trees in autumn foliage and the dark conifers reflected in the steely waters of the lake. Some of the conifers had a rusty look...the woods and forests of Germany were dying. Kate sat at a weathered picnic table and thought of this slow and dreadful catastrophe, trying to translate it into other terms. The Great Lakes are drying up. The White Cliffs of Dover are turning black and crumbling into the sea. The valley of the Loire is turning into a desert. The world is coming, slowly, to an end.

She could not think of Buddy Limbard. In hospital, years ago, she had tried to conjure up the scene...the summer evening, the choking grip of the dark water. Here it was too frightening. She looked round shyly and walked to the very edge of the lake with her spray of red roses. There was an old green Volkswagen parked further round the shore to her left, and there on the other side of the lake were the two young guys painting the kiosk rust red. They had not seen her, they were kidding around...suddenly a burst of sound echoed over the lake and climbed high into the trees. One of the boys was yodelling. Kate had to grin. How folksy could you get! *Typisch Bayern.* Then they spotted her and were quiet. She looked at the grey water, lapping the rocks, and saw another bunch of flowers, white chrysanthemums, floating. Had someone else remembered Buddy...or one of the others who drowned in the Waldsee? She dropped the roses into the water and ran off.

From morning to evening, without even the traditional two-hour break for lunch, the Villa Florian was the scene of hectic activity. The scaffolding came down and went away; trucks tangled with a last stream of delivery vans. A device with a steel basket on a mobile arm was brought through the gates to the north lawn in order to clean the roof and the dome. Kate dragged Peter inside twice and ordered him to watch from behind the garden gate. More than once a vehicle threatened to ram the poplar tree; Tante Adelheid opened the window and leaned out. When her newly planted cypress were in danger, Frau Thurnheim, the banker's wife, ran shrieking into the street and threatened to let loose the dogs.

'My God,' said Tante Adelheid, 'so much bed-linen! Another leather couch! And look, the refrigerator van with deep-frozen food, the wine merchant...'

'Poor Nicki!' said Kate.

Once or twice they caught sight of him, gesticulating wildly or making notations on his clip-board. Kate sat in the study with a small pile of printed invitations to the vernissage which had arrived late. Poor Thomas had parked his car at the corner and toiled up the Steinberg to deliver them. He had to be rewarded with a cup of coffee.

'Do you think Jason Limbard and his wife might be persuaded to come to the show?' he asked.

'Well, I can give them an invitation,' said Kate. 'And I'm sure Nicholas Lenz will come. More in his line, really.'

'You know so many fine people,' said Thomas sadly.

'Thomas, that's not true.'

Now she sat at the study desk thinking how few, how lamentably few people she could invite. The Limbards, the Sisters from the convent, Herr and Frau Thurnheim, the banker and his wife, Nicki, the lady from the bookshop in Breitbach. Of course she was not a resident, more of a holiday visitor. She had been at the Forsthaus with Peter once or twice a year; for three years the Villa Florian had been in the throes of redecoration. She thought back to the summer of the divorce, three years ago, when the villa was just beginning its face-lift. Had it frightened her then? Certainly she had never so much as entered the grounds, except to chase out three-year-old Peter.

She had never seen Nicki working on the villa; in fact she had wondered if he were avoiding her. In the summer of the divorce she did not see him... he arrived when the shift changed, when Andreas and Brigitte came to stay and have their time with Peter while she fled to her new apartment, her new job in Darmstadt. Nothing much had been said over the years but it transpired that Andreas − or perhaps Brigitte? − no longer cared for holidays at the Forsthaus. It was too old-fashioned, too cramped. She saw the day fast approaching when Andreas and Brigitte would stay with the Limbards across the road in the Villa Florian. Yet she loved the Forsthaus and so did Peter.

It was five o'clock, the autumn day was drawing in. The last van had gone on its way but Jacobsen's absurd gates were still wide open. Kate looked up as the last rays of the setting sun turned the dome of the Villa Florian to gold. *The dome full of golden light, every window, then suddenly the light is gone. Only a faint glow remains, upstairs in one of the hexagon rooms and in the left-hand front room underneath.* A memory? It felt like a memory but it was nonsense. Was it a dream she had had or a picture she had seen?

Sometimes her precious new-found memories had told lies or played tricks on her. For a long time she could not get it out of her head that Nicki had driven with them to the Forsthaus, they had been having an important discussion. Andreas pointed out that this was a distorted memory of a brief meeting at Frankfurt airport and in Mainz...they hadn't discussed anything in particular. Kate shut her eyes and rubbed her forehead. To be so *fixated* on the past. To play it cool with the whole world, even with Ruth, and to come back and back to that little span of lost time.

There was a warm light inside the Villa Florian now. She combed her hair, as a tribute to Nicki's masterpiece and to Haus von Sommer. Downstairs she said to Tante Adelheid: 'I'll see if Nicki can tear himself away for a short time.'

'Tell him I am cooking roast pork,' said Tante Adelheid.

Kate glanced into the sitting room where Peter was watching 'The Rockford Files,' dubbed of course. '*Himmel, Herr Gott Nochmal!*' shouted James Garner. She went out of the front door and strode across the road. The carriage sweep was empty except for a big brown Ford. The magnificent trees absorbed the last of the light, leaving the world to semi-darkness and to Kate, alone, prowling up to the front porch of the Villa

Florian. Nicki was surely in the back of the house with whoever it was, the foreman or the wine merchant or his trusty helpers from Möbel De Vries.

She engaged in a long double-take, deciding to go round to the back door, cut through the trees on to the south lawn. As she passed the steps of the terrace, suddenly she was almost paralysed with fear; she began to shiver and to sweat, all at once. She could not run, she could scarcely put one foot in front of another. It was not quite dark and there was light shining out of the new glass doors. She stood transfixed, hearing a little trickle of sound, a buzzing like a large insect. Was it in the air or in her own head? Was it an animal sound, the growling of a dog?

Kate was able to move again and she dived around the corner of the house, clinging to the rail above the area steps that led to the basement apartment. Warm light streamed out of the new kitchen windows. One was open, she could hear the murmur of Nicki's voice, low and resonant, inside the kitchen. She denied herself the relief of a loud shout for Nicki and tried to walk normally towards the little hooded porch. An inimitable American voice floated out upon the evening air.

'...started an *epidemic* of suicides,' said Cindy Saxon. 'Maybe she triggered off poor old Buddy...'

Kate felt her blood run cold. She stood stock still, heard the murmur of Nicki's voice replying.

'You're a very loyal friend, Nick!' said Cindy.

Embarrassment had wiped out Kate's fear. She backed up a little then clumped along the path, calling idiotically: 'Hello, Nicki? Anyone home?'

There was a satisfying yelp of astonishment from Cindy. As she came up to the back door, Nicki flung it open.

'Kate!'

He drew her into the kitchen. Cindy Saxon stood at the new sink, gathering up a heap of fallen petals and flower stalks. Kate realised that she had aged perceptibly since their last meeting, whenever that had been. Perhaps she had aged in the last few seconds. In a situation where almost any word she uttered would sound insincere, Cindy fought a good rearguard action.

'Why, Kate,' she said, 'I didn't hear the bell.'

'I didn't ring,' said Kate. 'The gates were open.'

'Must get them shut,' said Nicki.

'We were just talking about the new housekeeper,' said Cindy.

'A housekeeper?' said Kate, warily.

'Yes! The bride isn't going to cook and clean, at least not on her honeymoon,' said Cindy. 'I guess Jay can afford it these days.'

She wiped her hands on a wad of paper towels.

'I'll be on my way, Nick.'

'The flowers are wonderful,' said Nicki, 'I'm sure the newly-weds will appreciate them.'

'A woman's touch,' said Cindy. 'It helps in a new house. Even one as beautifully refurbished as this one.'

She slipped into her reefer jacket. Nicki took keys from his pocket.

'I'll show you out,' he said, 'and see to the gates.'

He gave Kate a questioning look.

'I'll admire the kitchen,' she said.

She sat in the new upholstered eating alcove and looked around. It was a marvellous kitchen, functional and comfortable. The colours were those of autumn; the vineleaf cupboards had returned in a roomy modern edition. The pottery clock on the wall was a *Jugendstil* original, decorated with lilies and field flowers. The lights were unfussy orange moons, with extra strip lights concealed over the work areas.

As she looked up at the ceiling Kate thought of... remembered?... a terrible circle of neon. Yes, and the kitchen door had made a loud creaking sound. When was that? Why surely the time when Tante Adelheid took her over the Villa Florian, cold, deserted, stripped of all its treasures. They had stared at the lone *tannen* in the snow, upon the north lawn. *No,* she said to the house, *no, I saw the kitchen light, heard the door on a hot night, a hot summer evening. Who else was here?*

She rose to her feet and followed her instinct. She looked into the hall and saw a golden flower shape, the light of the dome, warmed by the new carpet. Which way to the summer room, the terrace room? 'You can use this door or the one in the passage,' a woman had said. She wandered down the hall, stood in the very centre of the golden shape and shivered. Summer was gone.

She went on slowly, looking up the stairs, following the breaking wave. Someone might be sitting there, on the stairs, a child... She went on deliberately. It was as if she passed from one season or one age to another. The house was beautiful again, marvellously restored. She had passed the door to the terrace room, now she stood between the two front rooms. She shut her eyes and was carried away on a wave of warmth and perfume. Roses, roses... the impressions or memories were surely not her own. The small sitting room in autumn, a vase of roses and bright leaves... *'Turn your head, don't get up from the chair, he is sleeping.'* She opened her eyes as Nicki came in at the front door. The fresh flowers on the telephone table were chrysanthemums.

'Well, what do you think?' he said eagerly.

'Out of this world,' she said. 'You must show me around.'

'Do you remember any photographs of this hall?' he asked. 'Franz Walther had some story of a hanging lamp that fell down.'

They both stared at the ceiling, bumped dizzily against each other and laughed.

'There was some sort of a lamp,' said Kate. 'Brass, vaguely eastern, with chains. I think it was French: Guimard or "School of Guimard'. When did it fall down?"

Nicki grimaced.

'In 1919.'

'Come on already!' said Kate. 'Franz Walther wasn't even *born* then. He must have heard it from someone else.'

They glanced into the library which housed Jason Limbard's collection of cook-books. As they strolled into the small sitting room Kate saw that an archway had been opened into the dining room. Nicki explained the concept, his own, and as far as he could judge, that of Jacobsen.

'Poor Jacobsen,' sighed Kate.

'When he did all this,' said Nicki, 'he was full of enthusiasm. The villa was built for the new century, the new art... the poor devil was hopeful when he built it!'

'Is there no decent picture of him?' asked Kate. 'Only that misty old shot enlarged from the group in the Brussels café?'

'I've never come across another,' said Nicki. 'Silky whiskers. Shy. Scandinavian. An Ibsen...no, a *Strindberg* character!'

'Ah, but she must have drawn his portrait!' said Kate. 'They were here together, with the Baron.'

'...*turn your head again, don't get up from the chair...*'

'The Baron,' said Nicki, 'was a monster.'

'You admired him,' said Kate. 'Thought he was a hell of a fellow.'

'When we took out the wall for the archway...'

He broke off short, looking at Kate with concern.

'Nicki,' she said, 'I don't need to be cossetted for the rest of my life!'

'We found four mummified squirrels, in a cage,' he said. 'Walled up. The Polish workmen walked off the job, making the sign of the cross.'

'Ugh,' shuddered Kate. 'I suppose that must have been the Baron. Did Jacobsen know, I wonder?'

Nicki shook his head, went on with his commentary on the new dining room. Practical colours and materials, kiddie-proof yet keeping the style intact. A hint of a soaring line at the archway, the Baron's tree-trunks. Kate walked back and forth from room to room.

'Morris wallpaper,' she said. 'Original?'

'Brought down at enormous expense from the trophy room.'

They walked across the hall, went behind the staircase and came to the family room, with its new north terrace. It was comfortable, frankly luxurious with two leather couches and a tiled stove, red-brown, perfectly in style. There had never been any open fireplaces at the Villa Florian, Kate remembered, only the elegant tiled stoves and then central heating, installed in the late twenties. She sighed and flung herself down into an enveloping chair.

'I guess you can renovate my mansion, Herr Lenz,' she said. 'You have a magic touch.'

'One day I will build you a house,' grinned Nicki.

He went to the long windows and adjusted the heavy gold curtains.

'Bad security,' he said. 'People shouldn't be able to look in and see the goodies.'

'Listen,' said Kate, 'I came to ask you to take pot luck. Tante Adelheid is cooking roast pork.'

His face fell.

'Oh, Kate, I don't think I can,' he said. 'I'm alone here tonight. The watchman and his wife from Security Services have moved out. And I'm half expecting Limbard to phone. I'll take a raincheck.'

He sat near her in the corner of a leather couch, and Kate began to talk of the art show, four days away. Nicki gave her a strained look and rubbed tired eyes. She felt a rush of compassion.

'You must be utterly bushed,' she said softly. 'This has been such a day.'

'Everything under control,' he said. 'You haven't seen the upper floor... or the basement.'

'Another time,' she said. 'What will you be eating?'

'Steak,' he said. 'Microwave oven. The place is groaning with food and drink, naturally. Limbard has shares in a firm called Food Enterprises.'

They sat in silence for a moment, staring at the empty screen of the huge television set.

'There's a monitor in the library,' said Nicki.

Kate was suddenly moved to speak.

'I'm getting some strange vibrations at the Villa Florian,' she said. 'Mainly out of doors. Here with you it's just fine but I wouldn't like to stay alone in the place.'

'Don't you start.' He grinned wearily. 'Old Walther said the same thing.'

'I'll let myself out,' said Kate. 'Is there a side gate open?'

'I'll come to the door,' he said, springing up. 'I have to switch on the juice.'

'Will you organise the garden, too?' she asked.

'No, Limbard will get that done himself, in the spring. I'll have Armin and Sepp Walther in to tidy the grounds. *Die Holzhacker Buam* ... The Wood-chopping Boys.'

Kate laughed aloud. The old folksy musical number was just right as a name for a pair of Bavarian originals. She patted Nicki's arm in farewell and sprinted for one of the side gates without looking back at the Villa Florian.

II

Nicki leaned against the front door and peered through an amber leaf in one of the glass panes at Kate's flying figure in the dusk. Was she really all better at last? She was teaching, painting... God, what if she was painting badly, amateurishly. What if he did not like her work?

Oh, Kate, Kate my beautiful Klimt girl, hair the colour of autumn leaves. Did she have any idea how he felt? Was it just old pals, the three musketeers, minus Andreas? For a long time he had thought of himself not only as a friend but as a false friend, Nicki whose gags and snappy patter ran out. Who could not bear to see beauty destroyed, who could not bear to see her laden with the child of Andreas. The friendship had cooled for what seemed to be the usual reasons. Commitments overseas, his own sobering American adventure. Stress. A year or so of Christmas cards. 'I knew them well.' 'At one time we were close friends.' He knew better. He had deliberately quarrelled with Andreas. He had distanced himself from the Reimanns to save himself pain.

He was more bushed than he had thought; a heavy pall of exhaustion settled upon him. Steak, he thought, without enthusiasm. He looked at the control box, artfully concealed beside the front door, and hoped that the windows were all shut. He might have to make a round before bed. He threw the switch for the perimeter.

There was a light sound in the sitting room, no more than a squirrel jump. He walked briskly into the softly lit room, shut the window and saw that one of the bronze fish on the wall lamp had inexplicably shed its tail. He bent down absently, picked up the piece of jointed metal and tried to fix it back in place. One of the hooklets had sheered off, it would have to soldered. He gritted his teeth at the small imperfection, slipped the broken piece into his jacket pocket.

There was a strange odour in the room, a dry and dusty smell that he had not noticed anywhere else. He saw a black dot on the carpet directly under the archway, where the wall had been removed. He bent down, still inhaling the dusty reek, and picked up a small object about the size of a fingernail. It could best be described as a kind of bead, a small cylinder wound over and over with fine dark thread, firm and silky. A fine plait of thread was attached to this smooth bead or knob, about five centimetres, a finger length, broken off short.

'Very interesting,' he said silently to the room, to the crowding phantoms of the *Jugendstil,* 'but where from?'

He stood holding the little windfall and stared up at the archway. Nothing marred the smooth grey-green wallpaper. When he stepped through into the dining room it was difficult to see the place where the arch blended into the ceiling. The arch was framed on this side with the trunks and branches, a modern copy of those in the other rooms. Nicki stepped further into the room and switched on more lights. This was all new work, he had seen it done himself. The Villa Florian was not some mouldering palazzo where the ceiling showered plaster or mystery beads upon the client.

It struck him that the ceiling just beyond the arch was a shade uneven. Perhaps a fold in the paper? A shadow, tree shadow, shadow of the window pelmet, hindered his view. He felt a stab of vocational terror. Structural defect. The ceiling *bulged.* Jesus Maria! No! He must be imagining it. He sat on a chair staring until his eyes watered, not daring to fetch the step ladder, trying to recall the exact cross-section of the house at this point. He shut his tired eyes to see the plans: the wall of the trophy room, low dais emerging from the alcove, gun-rack, writing desk...

Nicki jumped as the buzzer sounded at the back gate. He had an idea who it might be. He went out quickly, switching on outside lights so that the garden path sprang up, red and white. Franz Walther gave a solemn wave from the back gate and Sepp, the tall blond cousin, who sported a silky, youthful beard and moustache, called out a greeting.

'Sorry I can't open up,' said Nicki, 'but the damned fence is switched on.'

'No worries,' said Franz Walther. 'Do you have anything for these two layabouts?'

'Strong and willing,' grinned Sepp, in his thick Bavarian. 'We also yodel and dance the *Schuh-plattler.*'

'Hola, Herr Lenz!'

Armin, who was stocky and dark, came trotting up from the Volkswagen.

'Hands off the gate,' warned Sepp.

'What?' said Armin, 'you mean the alarm goes off if I fling myself against the wire.'

'No! No!' shouted Nicki and Franz Walther both at once.

The boys fell about, laughing.

'Come tomorrow about nine,' said Nicki, 'and do some cleaning up in this garden. The lawns were mowed the day before yesterday. Just rake the leaves, pick up twigs, you know. And no yodelling – it scares the birds.'

They talked briefly about payment, the whereabouts of the garden tools. The young men thanked him and wandered off back to their auto. Franz Walther hung back to thank him again.

'Who told you about that hanging lamp?' asked Nicki. 'the one that fell down in 1919?'

'Ach, it was the Lieutenant,' said the forester. 'Hans Blümig. That was the worst brute who ever lived in this house.'

'Worse than the Baron?'

'Good question,' said Walther earnestly. 'Sister Florentine, his own granddaughter, might not agree. But von Sommer had a heavy burden.'

'What was that?'

'Why, to come home to his lady-friend a cripple.'

They said good-night. Nicki watched the Volkswagen drive away. He turned back to the house, and just as the lights of the little car swept over the autumn aspect of the villa, his heart thumped. Some trick of the light. He thought he saw a figure standing in the upstairs bathroom, a woman. He forced himself to stare at the window, faintly lit from the hall lights coming up the stairwell. Nothing. A fold of the curtains. The cool night air was full of the scent of the late roses blooming beside the path.

Inside again he admitted that he was really very tired indeed; he wouldn't need any rocking. The steak gave him just enough energy to check the doors, the taps, the windows on the ground floor and in the basement. He spent some time in front of the security switchboard beside the front door. He switched on everything except the upstairs west...he needed open windows in the back bedroom, where he meant to sleep, and the bathroom. Fine, nothing blared out, windows all tight. The villa was under security.

He imagined a commando troop of masked men in stocking caps and dark track suits swarming over the building. A deafening clangour of sirens and bells would ring out and the floodlights would go on. Lights would flash on this board, showing which areas of the security net had been breached. After this there followed a period of anti-climax. The burglars were frightened away, the inhabitants of the villa and their neighbours up to half a kilometre away rang the police. There was no direct connection with a police station: the villa was just a little too far out of town. When the owners were absent something could be arranged – a nightly patrol of the Steinberg by the local police or by the guards from Security Services.

Nicki sighed. What would the burglars be looking for? The posters, original paintings and genuine *Jugendstil* pieces did not constitute a rich haul. They couldn't be sold readily. Of course there were smaller pickings: the canteens of cutlery, the silver clock and candlesticks. The basement could yield wine and frozen food, usually stolen at Christmas, but there were few Persian carpets, the German thief's favourite booty. This left a small fortune in stereo equipment, television, video, kitchen appliances, exercise machines...

In the old days, he reflected, the Baron had lived among priceless treasures. The Breughel, which he did not hang, fetched thirty thousand pounds at Christie's in the fifties. He had protected his house with various wolf-hounds and a brace of shotguns. Times had changed. Nicki stumbled over a piece of information from the very early days with Limbard when he was submitting plans. Didn't Limbard have some kind of a hand gun? Andreas – yes, Andreas said that Diet Jason had a gun but the old boy became enigmatic when Nicki had mentioned weapons.

He fetched his heavy overnight bag from the library and went upstairs. The shot of Limbard's whisky that he had taken was having an effect. As he came to the top of the stair he saw himself reflected dimly in the blue door of the trophy room. He flung it open for another despairing look. It was a hopeless maverick of a room, too precious to change completely into, for instance, a dressing room or bathroom for the large bedroom on the summer side of the house. There was a writing desk now, on the dais, and the beautiful ebony gunrack still in place. Jay Limbard talked of a collection of memorabilia of the villa itself — photographs of Haus von Sommer, prints of the Baron's pictures, as if this odd room could hold the essence of the Villa Florian.

Nicki though of the archway underneath. The floor of the trophy room looked solid as a rock. He spared a thought, as he always did, for Jacobsen. This was all his work. Nicki himself had done no more than a renovation.

All the same he had fulfilled his contract very well. He shut the door of the trophy room and went on his way, admiring the upper floor. Limbard must be pleased. For years now, he reflected, Jason Limbard had had no home, no family at his beck and call to fill his family room or move into his fine house. He had been spending his time in Germany in a tiny apartment in an exclusive München hotel. The Aurora House was smart, anonymous, with a macabre reputation for suicides, who crashed screaming on to the lower terraces and put the tenants off their breakfasts. Now Jason was leaving this doubtful environment, starting all over again with his dark beauty, Anja.

Nicki staggered on to the back bedroom, a soothing place with pale turquoise and gold wallpaper. The imitation Tiffany lamp showed an autumn tree, shedding its leaves. There were two pictures: an original by Ludwig von Hofmann called 'the Grove', in its own silver frame, set with onyx and lapis-lasuli. The other was a print...the wrong print. What an extraordinary thing! This was the von Stück portrait of Tamara Paige, full-sized, 95x80, framed in black lacquered wood, and it should hang in the library. Why, he had been in and out of the library and not noticed the switch. The print for *this* room was a Grasset, the enlargement of a 'callender girl' for September in a formal garden. Something much more lighthearted and suitable for a guest room.

She stood, Tamara Paige, on the banks of a stream, wrapped in a golden cloak of silk taffeta. She leaned against a birch tree, its black and silver bark echoing the blackness of her hair, the pallor of her skin. For years he had avoided pictures and mementos of this pale tubercular creature from another age because they reminded him too cruelly of friendship with

Kate Reimann. Now he found that Kate had gone on collecting. She had several of the rare Rosebush Press editions, books of poetry, usually English, illustrated by Tamara Paige. The references to her life and work were sparse. Fragments. Autumn leaves. One could only guess how *la belle Anglaise* had lived in the studios of Europe.

Should the print be changed back? He would think about it tomorrow. He refused to sit down in the beckoning armchair or to fling himself down on the rattan bed with its inviting blue featherbed. He found his spongebag and bathrobe and tottered across to the bathroom.

The perfume hit him in a warm wave. Roses, roses, fields of roses to make a few drachms, *attar of roses,* a little green phial in the depths of his mother's dressing table... The big warm room was steamy and damp; someone had just taken a bath. One would expect to find traces of bubble-bath in the new built-in tub with its original dolphin taps, damp footprints on the dark blue mat of fluffy synthetic, the padded bench pushed back from the discreetly lit vanity bar of golden procelain, perhaps a damp towel on the heated rail or a négligée on the curling hooks of the tall rattan stand beside the potted palm.

It was an illusion of course; the bathmat was bone dry. Nicki turned off the heater and swung the window out at the top. He put his clothes on the stool and adjusted the hot water carefully in the new shower cabinet. He would personally have chosen curtains but the client had preferred a cabinet with sliding doors. The new dolphin taps on the shower and on the hand basin were a half shade too bright, and reminded him of a hotel room.

He was never happy under a shower – he couldn't hear things with the water running. He soaped and sang an operatic air; it turned out to be from *Il Trovatore,* the romance sung by the troubadour in the moonlit garden, telling of love and loneliness. The acoustics of the bathroom were fine, his hearty baritone rang out above the sound of the shower. He heard his breathing alter as the song died in his throat, then gamely started up again like a gramophone rewound.

Nicki, thinking of the western wall of the villa, had half turned to see the window. Someone stood at the window. Right there with him in the bathroom. A figure seen through the bubble glass of the shower cabinet, gold, green, black – a woman, he could see a woman! His attempt to keep on singing failed. He was hot and cold with terror; he was unprotected, ridiculous, wet, hearing the shrieking violins of the ultimate shower scene.

He twisted his head about but the figure would not vanish, would not turn into anything else. It moved. *She* moved, made that single unthreatening movement... had he seen it before when the lights struck the window pane? A downsweep of the hand, perfectly distinctive: she brushed her long hair. Nicki gave a confused roaring sob of terror and resentment and wrenched open the sliding door.

Nothing. The window curtain had hooked itself over one curling projection of the tall stand so that there was a curious shadow. The bubble glass did the rest. He turned off the shower, listened hard, stepped out. He was not game to try again, shut himself into the glass booth and recreate his apparition. He was ashamed and jittery, waiting for some third party to appear and witness his distress. 'What were you shouting about, Herr Lenz?' He dressed himself quickly, struggling into his sleeping shorts and bathrobe.

In the bedroom he faced up the portrait of the English girl, long dead, and marvelled at the workings of his own mind. He looked at the print sternly. There she stood on the banks of a rushing stream, sensualised, perhaps, by von Stück, her flesh like pearl, her red lips parted. The stiff folds of the golden cloak hardly concealed her slender nakedness. She did not stare hypnotically out of the frame, her gaze was intense but aloof, she seemed to be staring over the viewer's left shoulder. The title of the picture was simply 'Tamara'.

She had been regarded very often as an artists' model rather than an artist in her own right. Not by Franz von Stück, however, who commissioned some of the Rosebush editions and kept several of her posters in his vast villa.

Nicki stared hard then reached for his leather blouson and fumbled in the pocket. A bracelet on the right wrist, the arm bent lightly across her body. A loose plait of something like... yes, surely, a hair bracelet, with two cylindrical beads hanging from it. He found the black bead again and tucked it into the frame of the print. *Unheimlich*. No, no, he was damned if it was *unheimlich*. All far too subjective. He might go so far as a 'sense of presence', quite a different thing from a haunting. Almost against his will he allowed her one tribute before he settled down to his letters and accounts. This was his nightly ritual; he was becoming a creature of habit.

Now he raised his eyes to the portrait and said aloud: 'Maria!' The Anglo-Saxon pronunciation was harsh, as in Black Maria. 'Maria Paget Robinson!'

Last name uncertain, it could have been Robson. Perhaps he and Kate could go to London one day and find out. An autumn wind rattled the balcony while he pored over his two loose-leaf files. He soon slithered his books off the bed, switched off the blue glass bedside lamp and fell asleep.

He lay in the dark room in a dreamy state; all his limbs were heavy. She came to him in his dream and stood at his bedside. The golden cloak fell rustling to her knees, her hair swung free over breasts and shoulders. He was aroused, yet gently, warmly, as it was in dreams. He felt the rush of cold air against his naked body as she flung back the bedclothes. He could not see her face, then the shadow receded a little and he saw her mouth and chin, as if she wore a half mask. The cold increased. He was cold from head to foot and could not move a muscle. He saw her hand, thick with blood, as she laid it upon his upper arm. Then she let her body rest its cold length against his and still he could not move or speak. He lay half fainting, filled with an unspeakable sensation, compounded of revulsion and desire.

The dream would not end. He was, for a moment, freed from his paralysis, lying in his bed feeling the cold imprint of her body. Through half-closed eyes he saw the light of dawn and he heard a sound. It was a loud ominous creaking; timber snapped, plaster crumbled, the structure could not hold. The Villa Florian was breaking to pieces. He stood in the corridor before a tulip window and heard the dreadful sound again. He heard a man's voice which said distinctly: '*Oh, Emmanuel! Oh, Prophet Emmanuel...*' A door slammed so that walls shook; heavy boots made the staircase ring. The upper floor was full of moving shadows and *she* came towards him, creeping along against the wall, wrapped in the golden cloak. She entered the trophy room.

The creaking sound came again, the whole house shook, the dome would shatter. Elsewhere there was a tinkling of glass. He felt the shocks in his own body; he felt waves of shrieking terror wash over him. He tried to run, to shout, to wake the dead, but he was utterly powerless. He was whirled about in chaos like an autumn leaf. Then all was still and a cold, sweet voice spoke of death.

Nicki sat up, gasping and choking. He was awake, really awake, in broad daylight; the nightmare had gone. The down quilt had fallen off his bed and he was chilly. He staggered out to the bathroom, seeing the very landscape of his dream. The last words escaped him. Death...his death...unnatural death. . . . Oh God, God! He ran back and huddled under his quilt with a shuddering that went on deep inside him and would not stop.

He mastered his fear and rejected the dream. *Come, Lenz! None of this morbid imagining.* He sprang up, flung on clothes and began packing away his things. He removed every trace of his presence from the back bedroom except for the featherbed placed on the windowsill to air. He went downstairs, lusting for coffee, lugging his possessions which he dumped in the library.

As he finished shaving in the downstairs bathroom, the bell rang at the front gate. Nicki grimaced at himself in the glass; it was going to be another one of those days.

He watched her come towards the house then ran out to meet her. A little woman, middle-aged, in a grey suède jacket, a pleated skirt and tiny grey boots. She carried a grey suitcase which she set down on the gravel.

'Bauer!'

The little woman rapped out her name and stuck out her hand, unsmiling, a strong hand with a firm grip.

'Lenz,' said Nicki. 'Come into the house, Frau Bauer.'

He picked up her suitcase and led the way.

'No news of the Limbards,' he said. 'they should arrive...'

'Three o'clock this afternoon,' said Frau Bauer. 'Frankfurt Airport. Spoke to her on the phone last night.'

She went past him into the house after wiping her little boots on the mat. Her suède jacket was new but the boots were old,

Nicki decided, old and comfortable, although they did not look it. He found her hard to place and wondered if the whole world was becoming strange to him. Frau Bauer was in her fifties; the hair under her grey knitted hat was grizzled dark brown, tightly waved. She had wide cheekbones, dark eyes, a holiday tan that made her skin leathery and showed up the wrinkles around her eyes. Housekeeper? She was staring, sizing up the place as she stripped off her leather gloves.

'I'll make some coffee,' said Nicki.

Frau Bauer emitted a long sigh that came right up from her little boots.

'The Villa Florian!' she said.

She fingered the chrysanthemums upon the telephone table.

'Who did the flowers?'

'Mrs Saxon, a friend of the family.'

'The American woman,' sneered Frau Bauer, showing her teeth. 'The one who answered the phone.'

'Before I forget,' she said, 'two invitations, hand-delivered. From an elderly lady across the road.'

'That must be Frau Kramer.'

She laid the two envelopes on the telephone table. Then she strutted ahead of him, paused under the dome, looked up and veered off behind the stairs towards the family room. Nicki opened the door and she stared in silence. At last she said: 'Tiled stove.'

She went on into the room, fingered the curtains, the two sofas, the carpet. She peered out on to the terrace.

'A fortune,' she said. 'Cost a fortune, eh?'

'Well, yes,' said Nicki. 'Didn't come cheap.'

She turned to Nicki and asked her next question.

'*Is* he a millionaire?'

Nicki thought it over.

'In Deutsch Marks, yes, I think he is.'

She led off again to the kitchen. While Nicki made coffee she went methodically through the cupboards and examined the appliances. She took off her hat and coat at last and hung them in the porch. She wore a pink hand-knitted sweater with a frilled collar, and a pink stone on a gold chain.

'Sit down, sit down,' she said. 'I'll pour.'

She poured, found a jug for the cream.

'You come from Frankfurt?' he asked.

The accent under the high German seemed to be Hessian.

'Frankfurt/Sachsenhausen,' she said, squeezing out a half smile. 'This place reminds me of the old patrician houses on the river. Big places, really big.'

'The Villa Florian isn't very big,' said Nicki, 'not for the time it was built.'

'Still too big for one person to manage,' she said. 'Need other help.'

'Such as?'

Nicki was becoming laconic himself.

'Some foreign woman to do the cleaning,' she said. 'The Yugoslavs are best. In the spring the whole place could do with a Cleaning Brigade... windows, the lot.'

'What will Frau Limbard do in the house?'

'She could just manage with a daily cleaning woman. While I'm here she'll do the flowers, bit of cooking, shopping.'

'How did you come to get the job?'

Frau Bauer poured herself another cup.

'Her uncle,' she said carefully, 'was a former employer of mine. She thought I might oblige.'

'Did he live in a patrician villa in Sachsenhausen?'

Frau Bauer gave a short bark of laughter.

'No, for God's sake! He ran the Hotel Schönfeld in Baden-Baden soon after the war.'

Nicki believed he had placed her at last: the hotel trade. The kitchen clock gave its delicate chime, quarter to nine, and the buzzer rang for the back gate. Nicki explained and went out to start off the Wood-chopping Boys in the garden. He gave out Limbard's estimated time of arrival; Sepp and Armin, subdued, began to rake leaves. When he returned to the kitchen Frau Bauer said: 'All right, I'll see what you've got to offer in the basement.'

The basement pleased Nicki very much. He took pride in the souterrain with its café curtains and Lautrec posters but her pretty apartment left Frau Bauer quite unmellowed. Yes, said Nicki, the colour TV was connected to the house antenna. They went on to examine the new laundry, the utility room with the oil furnace, the sauna. It was no trick, he thought, to make Jacobsen's salons up above harmonious and pleasing...

but a furnace room? A laundry? At the door of the sauna Frau Bauer raised her head and sniffed the air.

'What is it?' he asked.

'Iodine!' she said. 'Can't you smell it? Place reeks of disinfectant, like a hospital.'

He could smell paint, old house, a whiff of oil from the furnace. The tour continued: sauna, wine-cellar, at last the games room, his production number. Warm light reflected from a dozen shiny surfaces: the slot machines, the exercise machines, the beautiful clockwork carousel. Limbard shared Nicki's enthusiasm for musical boxes. There were more posters, including several originals under glass; the room was dominated by a large mural with motifs from Eugene Grasset. Young ladies of the *Jugendstil* in modish, fantastic costumes disported themselves against a background of woodland and formal gardens. Frau Bauer was pleased and impressed. She chuckled.

'Like something out of a kino-film.'

Nicki went behind the bar, switched on the lights around the mirrors and wound up the little Hong Kong Harlequin who danced to the music of the can-can.

'Too early for a schnapps?' he asked.

'No.'

He selected a bottle of *Kirschwasser*. While he reached for the glasses Frau Bauer operated quickly and brutally on the foil cap.

'*Prosit!*'

She perched on a stool and asked abruptly: 'Limbard's not a drinking man?'

'No,' he said. 'Never touches spirits. Drinks a little white wine.'

They had another. Frau Bauer put away the bottle, washed the two glasses, wiped down the bar in a series of swift movements. Nicki was standing before his favourite poster, advertising a display in the Vienna Workshop. A young woman in black and cobalt blue accepted with a backward glance a rose from a gentleman. She held a book with the device TP. *Unheimlich* 'Will you admit it?' mocked the poster girl. She wore a loosely woven hair bracelet with two cylindrical beads. Threads of narcissism ran through all her work...the bracelet of her own hair, the self-portraits. He thought of one in the Rosebush Edition of *The Rime of The Ancient Mariner:* Tamara Paige, her hair brazen yellow...

'The nightmare Life-in-death is she,
Who thicks man's blood with cold...'

Frau Bauer was pummelling the two day beds. Her next question caught him unawares.

'Is he Jewish?'

'What?'

'Limbard,' she said impatiently. 'Hard to tell with some Americans. Is he Jewish?'

'No,' said Nicki, remembering a scrap of information. 'His great-grandfather came from the Tyrol.'

'Ha!' she was satisfied. 'Must get on with it. They'll have people in this afternoon: champagne, coffee, apple-cake, and savouries from one of his books.'

'I must drive down to Breitbach,' he said.

Nicki was becoming depressed. Outside the games room the light was grey and cold. The ceiling seemed to press down upon them. Frau Bauer shivered, put a hand to her throat. Something happened very quickly. For ten seconds, less, time lagged or changed. There were footsteps pacing on a stone floor and a voice, high and light but a man's voice, wavering, crying out: *'Transport...'*

Frau Bauer cleared her throat:

'You hear something?'

'Outside,' said Nicki. 'Voices come in from outside. The lads in the garden.'

The lie was second nature to him. He could not accept these experiences and there was no-one to share them with. Kate, could he tell Kate? She complained of strange vibrations last night. Jason had thrown out a few joking remarks about the house being haunted. The *Haus Herr* was a great kidder, he liked to scare his listeners a little. As they went up the stairs Nicki began searching for something Andreas had said years ago, then never said again.

In the kitchen he heard a hollow grating and rumbling. Nicki reacted with alarm. He was flung back into his nightmare. Then he recognised the sound and started to head for the open air.

'Won't be away long,' he said to Frau Bauer. 'You can hold the fort? Screen visitors?'

She was setting out stainless steel saucepans on the work counter.

'No worries.' she said. 'No-one can get past Beata Bauer!'

Nicki believed her. He rushed out of the house gratefully and spoke to Sepp and Armin who were wheeling the heavy barrow down the path from the garage.

Chapter 7
Starting Again

Kate had been standing at the living-room window when the little woman stepped out of her taxi. She called Tante Adelheid from the kitchen.

'I think that must be the new housekeeper.'

'I hope Herr Limbard pays her well,' said Tante Adelheid, 'and that she has good nerves!''

Before the woman in grey could ring the bell at the gate, Peter came into the picture, tootling along with a rollicking small boy's gait. He had been playing postman with Kate's invitations... up the hill to the convent, now to the villa. He held the two invitations firmly and marched up to the letter-box in the right hand gatepost. He spoke to the woman, nodded politely, and stood on tip-toe to reach the slot. The woman dumped her suitcase down, stood over the child and tried to snatch the envelopes. Peter backed away, holding the envelopes behind his back. The woman held out her hand, demanding.

'Wow!' said Kate.

'Ach!' said Tante Adelheid.

She turned and swept out of the house; Kate heard her calling to the woman from the front gate. Peter had turned tail and disappeared towards the Forsthaus. Now Tante Adelheid appeared, holding the envelopes, a tall white-haired old woman in a sleeveless floral *kittel* over her decent blue dress. The two women spoke, then shook hands. Tante Adelheid spoke, indicating the Forsthaus, then the Villa Florian. She held up the envelopes and the housekeeper graciously accepted them. She rang the bell.

Peter had come into the house. He cuddled up to Kate at the window and she put an arm around him.

'A little lady at the gate,' he said. 'She wouldn't let me put them in the box.'

'Never mind,' said Kate. 'Tante Adelheid has taken care of it.'

'Kind of a cross lady,' said Peter. '*Kinderfeindlich.*'

Kate looked down into her son's face and wondered what it was to be '*kinderfeindlich*', hostile to children. They both stood watching Nicki carry the woman's suitcase into the villa. The black cat landed on the window sill without a sound and Kate let her in. Frau Moor, a sleek, solid eight-year old, jumped down into the room with a 'prrp' of acknowledgement. When Tante Adelheid returned she sent Peter to the kitchen to get himself a glass of his favourite chocolate milk.

'Frau Bauer,' she said thoughtfully to Kate. 'She comes from Frankfurt.'

'And she doesn't like little boys?'

'A harsh manner,' said Tante Adelheid. 'Rather a rough person.'

Kate was surprised. It was almost the first reference she had heard Tante Adelheid make to anyone's social class.

'She didn't look...' said Kate.

'Oh, no' said Tante Adelheid. 'Her clothes were quite expensive.'

For the rest of the morning Kate tidied the studio then sat in the study composing a letter to Ruth. She spent too much time gazing out of the window at the Villa Florian. Tante Adelheid called her down to admire the well-grown hibiscus which they had prepared for the Limbards, Jason and his new bride. Quite a suitable present for people-who-had-everything. The plant came from those flourishing on the Forsthaus balcony; Kate had picked out a handsome *cachepot* down in Breitbach. Nothing more personal or inspired was called for.

Kate saw and did not see the two young men tidying up the garden. Leaves were raked, dead branches piled into an old wheelbarrow which ground along the paths. She saw them standing, heads together, beside the naked lilac trees. They slapped hands like a pair of soul brothers then the fair boy – was his name Sepp? – went to the south and Armin to the north. Minutes later there was some kind of disturbance on the north side. Was it Frau Bauer, the housekeeper, scolding at the top of her voice?

The disturbance continued in a fashion that brought Kate to her feet, dry-mouthed, her heart pounding. Something moved on the front lawn, there ... and there on either side of the cariage sweep. Two spreading columns of water rose up, rust-coloured in the autumn sunlight. Down below in the Forsthaus Tante Adelheid cried out, and a child screamed with excitement. Peter dashed across the road and stood before the gates.

'Peter!'

Kate shouted aloud, not knowing why. The fountains had played before, more than once. *Rising from cups of stone on the south and east lawns*... The fountains played and the dome glowed with a golden light. When was that? When? Was it on a hot summer night?

Frau Bauer, scolding indeed, rushed about in front of the house, crouching to avoid the spray. The Wood-chopping Boys both appeared, pulled their forelocks to her, more or less. They went into the trees at the south-east corner of the Villa Florian; the fountains stopped. Peter ran back across the road, to home base.

Downstairs Kate found Tante Adelheid sitting bolt upright at the kitchen table.

'What was it?' she whispered.

Adelheid Kramer shook her head.

'No good will come of it,' she said. 'Oh, Katherine, have I done the right thing?'

Kate controlled her panic. The old woman, her tower of strength, was sick, overtired, mortal. She suggested foolish, practical things: a cup of herb tea, a rest.

'Forgive me,' said Tante Adelheid. 'I'm quite well. I keep forgetting that it is autumn already. The fountains...'

'I've seen them before,' said Kate, 'years ago. Is there something I should remember?'

Peter came crashing into the kitchen, full of unholy glee.

'The little lady kept saying "*Scheiss! Scheiss*!"' he cried. 'All the time those water-spouts were playing!'

'Well, no need for you to say it, Buster!' grinned Kate. 'I think it's time to wash your hands for lunch.'

'Aw, Mom!'

As they finished their *Würstchen* and potato salad Kate took a phone call.

'Kate!'

'Nicki! Is everything all right over yonder?'

'More or less.' He sounded mildly distraught. 'Prayers to Saint Florian are in order. I hope the place will hold together.'

'Any news of the Limbards?'

'We roll out the red carpet this afternoon. You and Frau Kramer will come over?'

'Yes, of course.'

'The Saxons are meeting the plane,' said Nicki. 'Bound to be a few reporters. Estimated time of arrival three o'clock at Frankfurt Airport.'

Frankfurt Airport was grey and cold and echoing. Travellers, sitting all day in artificial light, soon turned into refugees, bloodless and weary. They sat about on the long rows of chairs, guarding their luggage. It made no difference whether they were Germans in holiday gear, bound for Gran Canaria, or Americans with kit-bags, waiting for space available: after a while they all began to look like extras from *The Night of The Living Dead*. In autumn the airport was sometimes fog-bound, day long, and the suffering travellers or refugees might be transported by bus to Dusseldorf.

He kept moving, watching the arrival slots. He looked into shop windows at cameras, men's wear, souvenirs. In a florist's shop he purchased two long-stemmed roses, one red, one pink. When the plane had been down twenty minutes he took an escalator to the grey nowhere place with more plastic chairs ranged outside the swinging doors and turnstiles.

There was a corridor where he could look through the glass panels at baggage retrieval. Not too busy. He drew back behind a broken pane of glass mended with plastic sheeting. On target. The man and especially the woman. The Old Man still looking good, a little greyer at the temples, sporting a heavy continental tan. He was dressed in a full length leather coat, grey-green, and a soft tweed hat. He went forward impatiently to the carousel, seized pieces of luggage and dumped them on the ground.

The woman stood back holding a trolley, half smiling, marking time, trit-trot, in her pretty bronze pumps; her coat was gabardine, lined with brown and white fur. A white felt hat with a curved brim, a Garbo. Now she took off her hat, shook out her short dark hair. He could see her face.

Yes, she was really high-class, smooth and pale and perfect, like a film star. People looked at her. Men looked her over but she had eyes only for the Old Man. She was his German whore; she had married him for his money. Maybe he would even give her some of his fucking money. He'd already shelled out plenty for the terrible Kraut house when Mom and the Kid were still scraping along.

The voice of reason said to him in a brotherly fashion: 'She is some kind of model, from that München. One of those good-looking girls he was always seeing in the street. She's quite old, not so old as Mom but maybe thirty-five.' He could still work the trick so that he actually heard the voice. But the years had passed and he had changed, he knew more, he had gone through a lot. He didn't need to hear the voice any more, he had taken his brother into himself, along with all the other shadowy creatures who lurked inside his head. Now he knew that the main thing was to survive. To survive by telling the man what he wanted to hear, by acting the way he wanted you to act.

So he would go along with the Old Man even now in this newest scheme. The proof-that-he-had-changed, tied up with the not so subtle threat to Mom. Or else. Well, sure, he would go along. Old Man in a generous mood, money to burn, easy pickings, maybe, at the villa, all done out by some faggot fairy from München. How was the time bomb in that precious villa, was it still ticking away? Oh my Lord, a real time bomb, big hunk of plastique, how would that be? You sit on a hill in the vicinity and know that when the Old Man sits down to eat or lies down with ... seconds ticking away.

He wandered away behind a pillar, unbuttoned his raincoat and hung it over his arm. He slicked back his hair, put on his cap and stood to attention. Then he slowly approached the group, carrying his two long-stemmed roses. There they were all right – welcoming, embracing, talking too loud. There was even a photographer flashing at the bride and groom. At the sight of his father he felt hatred rise up in his throat like black bile and he spoke to his brother, long dead. *Cowards hate worse, Buddy-boy, because they are cowards and they're weak. They can't hit back, they do it by stealth.*

Now Cindy Saxon and Old Jefferson Airplane had seen him.

'Roddy! Hey, look who's here! Roddy!'

The Major returned his salute. He gave Cindy a peck on the cheek. A red rose for her and a pale pink one for the wicked stepmother. When he saw her close up she was even prettier but tired, droopy, as if she had been sick on the plane. She smiled and kind of cooed at him.

'Such a cavalier.'

Then she whispered to the Old Man, a fine son, a son to be proud of, some of that bullshit. The Old Man clapped him too hard on the biceps and got off a good 'un.

'Home training!' he said. 'Discipline! Firm but fair, eh Roddy-boy?'

'Yes sir!'

Then this Anja started to walk away a little and the Old Man reached out automatically and caught her by the wrist. Roddy had seen him do it to Mom a thousand times.

'Where you off to, my girl?'

He thought to himself: *Anja, baby, you are going to wish you had never been born* .

Five cars wound up the Steinberg and turned in at the open gates. The afternoon sun came through the edge of a cloud and blazed down upon the Villa Florian. The scene was overlit, with the automobiles and the people struggling out of them casting odd heavy shadows. Tante Adelheid, Kate and Peter, looking angelic in his best Italian T-shirt, stood on the edge of the lawn in a rather feudal group. *The Lord of the Manor takes possession*, thought Kate, *the Patroon enters into his estate upon the Hudson*. At least Nicki had taken the pot plant inside.

The Saxons climbed out of their big Ford, and a prosperous looking youngish man helped his wife from the BMW. She wore a silk suit. From the Breitbach City Council, probably. A late arrival swished up in a Porsche and parked under the poplar tree; Kate caught a glimpse of a tweed jacket. There were the reporters scrambling out of two smaller autos: the chubby girl in a raincoat had her own photographer, the shy blonde person in jeans took her own pictures. Nicki, on the steps, looked nervous, Kate's heart went out to him; she began to feel nervous too on his behalf. Under the porch stood Frau Bauer, every inch the housekeeper in a short grey nylon jacket over her skirt and blouse.

The big Mercedes ground to a halt and Jason Limbard sprang out of the driver's seat. He glanced around quickly and gave a hearty shout of 'Hello there!' before opening the rear door. Apparently he had chauffeured his wife; now she stepped out with practised grace, turning to gather up her bouquets. All the spectators moved closer. Jason gripped the arm of his bride who swayed delicately across the gravel and mounted the steps. The cameras flashed and whirred.

The bride's bouquet was of hothouse roses, white, apricot, salmon pink, starred with jasmine. Kate saw that she had a lovely heart-shaped face, framed by dark hair, brownish-black, feathery and soft. The ripe mouth, painted with a very delicate, brownish-pink lipstick, was not quite under control. She gasped as she dazzled the photographers with a smile, and caught at her underlip with her teeth. Jason looked splendid; the touch of grey at his temples suited him. Kate, watching the pair of them, was carried away on a wave of hope. She had lost sight of Jason... her accident, the divorce... but now she could meet him again in her own right, so to speak, and really make friends. She could help Anja settle in. Why, she would surely be interested in the *Jugendstil* and in the past glories of Haus von Sommer.

Nicki allowed himself to be drawn into the group. He stood next to Jason and handed over a set of keys. Cindy Saxon and the Major, to his uniform, stood beside their auto and applauded.

'We'll take a break!' cried Jason. 'Hold it, boys and girls!'

Anja turned away, prettily confused, and went to embrace the housekeeper. Kate heard her soft cry: 'Beata!' Jason came down the steps, greeted the Councillor and his wife, then made a beeline for the group from the Forsthaus.

'Hi, there, Pete!'

He cuffed Peter playfully on the back of the head.

'Frau Kramer,' he said, 'this is an honour!'

He stood still and took both of Kate's hands in a firm grip.

'Kate!' he said. 'You can't imagine how it feels to see you again! How's your health? How's the treatment?'

'I'm fine,' said Kate. 'Jason, I wish you all the happiness in the world.'

Tante Adelheid chimed in with her good wishes.

'*Spätes Glück* !' exclaimed Jason, 'Late happiness ... wonderful German expression! Starting all over again.'

He cast a glance at the villa, the guests, the photographers.

'You'll both come in,' he said, 'and meet my wife. No... no, Frau Kramer, I won't let you off. This young man can come in, too, for a piece of apple-cake, eh Pete?'

'But no Coke!' said Peter.

Jason roared with laughter.'

'See? He knows his Uncle Jay!'

He veered off suddenly and spoke to the reporters. For them, apparently, the honeymoon was over. The chubby girl and her photographer climbed into their battered Renault and drove away. The blonde girl hung about beside her VW and neatly intercepted the party from the Forsthaus as they went into the villa. She was from the little local paper. Would Jason Limbard be coming outside again? Were they neighbours? She would so like another photograph. Kate took pity on young Frau Schumacher.

'There's just a chance,' she said, 'that Herr and Frau Limbard will be coming to a vernissage... the art show that opens on Thursday evening in the Old Mill Gallery. Nick Lenz will certainly be there.'

Frau Schumacher made a note and went away, thrilled. Kate followed Peter and Tante Adelheid into the Villa Florian.

The house had suddenly come alive: lights blazed, there were delicious odours – coffee, apple-cake – and a babble of hearty voices in the dining room. Jefferson Saxon beamed down at Tante Adelheid and Kate, eyes twinkling behind his rimless glasses.

'Nick has certainly done a mighty job of refurbishment!' he said. 'I guess the little lady will be pleased.'

'Oh, it was so beautiful at the airport,' said Cindy. 'Roddy came along!'

'He's here?' asked Kate, looking around.

'No, he just stopped by. Gave me a red rose, and a pink one to Anja. Isn't he a thoughtful kid?'

Tante Adelheid took charge of Peter and proceeded to extricate the boy and herself from the cheery gathering as quickly and politely as possible. She wiped Peter's fingers, led him up to the bride, who gave him a kiss. After a brief exchange with Anja they were gone. Jason Limbard stood at the head of the dining-room table and rapped on a glass with a spoon.

'Here he is,' he announced, 'the master magician, Nicholas Lenz! Your health, Nicki!'

Nicki found a glass and acknowledged the toast. Kate saw that he was on his mettle, looking about at the distinguished company. The Saxons, Anja, Jason, were all good-looking, well-dressed; Frau Bauer went about, efficient and unobstrusive, a waitress at the Officers' Club.

'Thank you, Jay,' said Nicki. 'I'd like to give credit to another man... his work made it all possible. To Magnus Jacobsen, architect of the Villa Florian.'

There was a warm response from the guests. Kate felt that the house responded too, the name echoed through its splendid rooms. She headed for Anja, to pay her respects, and found herself with Nicki.

'What's the matter?' she asked.

She followed his anxious gaze. Sunlight, slanting in from the south-west, through the new glass doors, showed thick sun motes dancing under the archway.

'Nothing,' he said without conviction. 'A fall of dust...'

Before Kate could meet Anja, Jason took his bride by the hand and led her away through the house. Kate was surprised by a kind of sweet envy. The place was *theirs*, it belonged to them, to Anja and Jason. The moment was theirs too.

'All's well that ends well,' said Nicki.

He refilled her glass. The small reception had become quite noisy and cheerful.

'Who on earth is that man in the tweed jacket,' Kate said, 'and why is he walking round in circles on the south lawn?'

Nicki looked and began to laugh.

'Why not go and find out?' he said. 'Take him a drink.'

Kate was in the right mood to take a dare. She set out with two glasses of champagne: the autumn day was still warm, the terrace absolutely unfrightening. The man in the tweed jacket saw that he was being brought a drink and gave a quick, shy smile. He was more than sixty years old but well-preserved and handsome. His eyes were very blue in a tanned face. Kate knew who he was at once: he bore a strong family resemblance not only to his sister but to his grandfather.

'Is that for me?' said Baron Felix von Sommer. 'Thanks, thanks...'

He took a gulp and peered at the lawn again.

'Can't find the little devils ... the fountains.'

'They're further back, I think,' said Kate. 'Level with the oak.'

Sure enough, she stretched out the toe of her boot and touched a cup of stone. The Baron found the other.

'You know the place,' he said. 'You must be Florentine's art expert.'

Kate was flattered. She gave her name; they shook hands.

'A great day for me!' said the Baron. 'The nasty little jewel box has gone out of our family at last. Sold to a rich American. I've been dreaming of him for thirty years. Now tell me, Frau Reimann, what do *you* see in that mural, yonder?'

There was a cool, even light on the south lawn; the summer colours of the large relief panel were almost garish, too bright. Green leaves, twisted branches of bright yellow-brown. A figure lay full-length among the convolutions of foliage, bright flowers and huge black thorns.

'I can't be sure,' said Kate. 'A male figure... a man...'

'Mythical beast?'

'A satyr or a silene,' suggested Kate. 'But his hand... is that his hand?'

It had become a grey, furred claw. Kate felt a curious discomfort stealing over her, an aura of unrest.

'A wolf,' said the Baron. 'And you see, don't you, that he is trapped in the thicket. A werewolf.'

He tossed off his champagne.

'Who... who designed the panel?' asked Kate.

'Who indeed?' said the Baron. 'I detest the *Jugendstil*. Mass-produced, mannerist kitsch, the lot of it.'

He smiled his quick charming smile again.

'Come,' he said. 'Let us look at the orchard. I can show you something.'

He set off briskly across the lawn and around the side of the house. They stood on the flagged path and looked at the autumn aspect of the villa.

'Once I caught a glimpse... ' said the Baron. 'There, the back bedroom. Where the young soldier died. Have you heard *that* sad tale yet?'

'You're trying to frighten me!' said Kate. 'What did you see, Baron von Sommer?'

'Nothing,' he said. 'Trick of the light. A woman.'

The three upper windows were quite empty. A cold wind whirled through the orchard trees and lifted the dead leaves in rustling spirals.

'I must go in,' said Kate.

'I'll slip away,' said the Baron. 'Make my excuses to the new man and his bride. Florentine was very much against the sale, you know.'

Kate was mildly surprised but she felt that she ought to know the reason. It was something else that she had forgotten.

'Was there some plan for a museum?' she suggested.

'No, it wasn't that,' he said, watching her very closely. 'She disapproved of the purchaser. Thought the house would have a bad influence on him. And vice-versa.'

Kate could only shake her head. When he had slipped away she ran up the steps into the kitchen and nodded to Frau Bauer who was washing glasses. She placed the two champagne flutes on the draining board and ignored the housekeeper's disapproving look. She stood alone in the hall and heard Jason's soft laugh in the family room. She went towards the sound.

On the shadowy threshold she was drawn up short by a woman's voice, Anja speaking urgently in German.

'*Es tut weh. Liebling, ich bitte dich...*'

Kate was consumed by embarrassment again. What on earth were they up to? Her shadow had given her away.

'Who is it?' called Jason cheerfully.

'*Oh nein*!' said Anja.

There was nothing for it. Kate went into the room and found Anja on all fours on the carpet in her bronze silk dress. Her little bronze pumps were side by side near the big tiled stove. Jason was sprawled at his ease in a leather sofa.

'Oh, this is terrible!' said Anja. 'I have broken my pearls and he will not help me collect them.'

'Shame on me!' said Jason Limbard. 'This is Kate ... Kate, the lady on the carpet is my wife, Anja.'

Kate bent down quickly and they found the rest of the beads still on a piece of broken thread. Her embarrassment did not quite go away, although Anja was trying her best to make things right. There was something about the little scene which bothered her. Anja's quick greeting, her kind remarks about Peter did not square with what she had overheard. *'It hurts! Please, darling...'* Come on, she told her self firmly. They were necking, they're honey-mooners.

'And thank your aunt too,' said Anja, quite restored, 'for the most lovely gift!'

A few wedding presents were displayed upon the large teak coffee table: a set of antique goblets from the Saxons, a tall vase of golden glass from the Breitbach Council. In the midst stood the hibiscus, glowing with rich red flowers.

'I must take a look!' said Jason.

'There!' cried Anja. 'Now he stands up!'

She ran up to Jason, gave him a quick kiss on the cheek and moved away as if eluding his grasp.

'I'm going to fetch us all some new drinks!'

She was gone with a pretty flounce. Side by side Kate and Jason admired the presents. Jason took up each card. She heard his sharp intake of breath.

'Why, Kate,' he said softly, 'have you been holding out on us?'

'In what way?'

He reached out, fingered a crimson petal.

'What would you call that — a flowerpot?'

'*Ein Übertopf,*' said Kate. 'It's only a Jugendstil copy, of course, but I thought...'

It was a very large straight-sided pot of creamy ceramic, bearing the motif of a brown tree with swirling branches which formed the handles on either side of the vessel. She had bought it at the large florist's shop on the Lutherplatz. It was one of a popular line by a local potter; they had displayed the same *cachepots* in that shop as long as she could remember.

'Oh Kate, Kate,' said Jason Limbard, as if gently scolding a wayward child. 'Andy said you remembered nothing... nothing at all of that long, hot summer.'

'Things keep coming back,' she said defensively, 'but I don't understand exactly what...'

For a few seconds he pressed his hand on her shoulder very hard. She could feel his strong fingers through the silk of her jacket.

'*I* remember very well,' he said. 'Great memory for details ... the design of the *Übertopf* is a remarkable coincidence.'

Kate stared at the swirling tree design.

'No,' she said, 'it has no associations for me.'

Even as she said it, she was lying. The *cachepot* seemed to shrink before her eyes, as if she saw it through the wrong end of a telescope. She felt terror, raw uncontrollable fear, welling up inside her. She was in her nightmare, among the rattling leaves of bronze, with a dark, monstrous shape ready to spring upon her. *This had to do with Jason*? No, it was all nonsense. She was crazier than she had imagined. She took a step backward and forced herself to look at Jason Limbard. She was surprised by an extraordinary expression on his handsome face, a thickening and splaying of all his features. It passed instantly and he said, smiling: 'You don't remember? Well, it's all down in your unconscious, I guess.'

Anja came into the room with Nicki, followed by Frau Bauer with a tray of long drinks which she set down on a side table. The tough little woman beamed at her employer and asked the *gnädige Herr* how many there would be for dinner.

Jason gathered Anja up again and nuzzled her neck.

'We've eaten too well already,' he said. 'The dinner can wait until tomorrow. My wife is tired – eh baby? Forty-eight hours married to an old ruffian like me.'

Nicki took this as a hint.

'I must be getting down to Breitbach to see about my hotel room. In the morning, Jay, we can make a start on the accounts.'

'What, you're leaving, Nicki?' said Jason.

'Wouldn't dream of disturbing your honeymoon!'

'Not at all!' said Jason heartily. 'This is a decent-sized house, you must stay. Anja...'

'Of course, Nicki,' said Anja smiling and laying a hand on his arm. 'You must stay, really.'

She sounded quite sincere, Kate thought, but both men were making an effort. Jason didn't really want anyone in his house and even Nicki gave a nervous jerk of the head as if he were reluctant to stay.

'Well, if you're sure,' he said. 'I'll just bunk down in the corner room, through here.'

Kate was shaky and sick. She wanted to escape and cast a glance at Nicki as Jason struck again.

'Dinner tomorrow,' he said, 'and Kate must come... make it a foursome. Right?'

'Oh, that would be so nice!' said Anja. 'Oh please, Kate, you must come!'

Nicki moved to Kate's side, trying to take the pressure off her. He murmured 'How will it fit in with the last minute work on the art show?'

Kate gave way. Good God, what was there to worry about? Nicki would be there and she could persuade the Limbards to come to the vernissage.

'That would be very nice,' she said.

'All settled,' said Jason. 'Dinner for four tomorrow night, Frau Bauer. We can go over the menu later tonight.'

Frau Bauer took herself off. Jason relaxed, drawing Anja down beside him on the couch. Kate and Nicki slipped away; the guests were leaving.

'He's a strange man,' said Kate. 'I wish I could remember what he was like before...'

'Andy said something once.'

Nicki began and then stopped.

'What was it?' asked Kate. 'Was it about that summer?'

She looked up, dizzily, at the dome of many-coloured glsass and found that the sky was dark overhead.

'Rain coming.' said Nicki, changing the subject. 'I hope all the luggage is inside.'

They stood under the porch and met Jeff Saxon coming in from the Mercedes with two last pieces of luggage. Nicki turned to lend a hand; Kate went back to the Forsthaus as the first drops of rain began to fall.

In the cosy sitting room Tante Adelheid and Peter, in pyjamas, rosy from his bath, were watching an early evening serial. A commercial artist had married a charming divorcee with three children. Kate waved to them and went on up the stairs to the spare room, her studio.

She went directly to a large shallow basket which contained odds and ends that might be used in a collage. There were pieces of coloured glass and china, stones, wood shavings, dried leaves and flowers. She found the piece she wanted and sat staring at it under the bright studio lamp. A scrap of brown and white ceramic, piece of a jigsaw puzzle. Yes, it was the handle of a very much smaller version of the *cachepot* she had bought for Jason Limbard and his new wife. She had no memory of ever buying such a thing. Did she receive it as a present? Jason behaved as if she must know. There was a memory there, vague and frightening. The little pot glowing with red – no, with pink, with cyclamen flowers. Kate caught her breath... a cyclamen, an alpine violet... **Where? Where and when**?

The guests had gone. Nicki helped Frau Bauer clear the dining-room table. Jason and Anja came drifting into the kitchen.

'Where are you off to, sweetheart?' asked the new wed lord.

'I must freshen up,' said Anja.

'Not before you've seen the basement,' he grinned.

He shepherded her down the cellar stairs. Frau Bauer took an ice-cold bottle of schnapps from the refrigerator, planted herself on a kitchen chair and tossed off two glasses. Her gaze flicked over Nicki, unseeing. The music of the carousel floated up from below.

'He couldn't wait!' said Frau Bauer. 'Poor girl. Still, you make your bed and you must lie on it.'

'You think they...'

'*Na, was wohl?*'

What else? Now that she had put the idea into his head, he couldn't think of anything else that the honeymooners might be doing. Pah! What an incredibly vulgar woman, this Frau Bauer. Where did they find her? He wandered away, thinking of private lives. The sound of the carousel was sweet and penetrating, right under his feet as he paced the corridor. Well, since Limbard would be occupied... Nicki ran quickly up the stairs and into the trophy room.

The room was softly lit by the remaining stag lamp. The

window curtains were swept back but not much daylight came in; outside it was rainy and overcast. Deep shadows remained on either side of the dais extending from the alcove. The idea he had was shadowy too, half-formed. It had to do with the position marked for the stoves in Jacobsen's plan: one on an inner wall of the hexagon bedroom, and a corresponding stove in this room which had never been installed. Instead there was the alcove and its platform, a miniature stage. Suppose the flooring was incomplete or jerry-built because of the alteration of the plan? He deliberately took up a stance between the platform and the window then jumped up and down as hard as he could.

The amount of tremor surprised him. The flooring moved beneath his feet, loose and soggy. There was a sound, not the crack of doom from his nightmare, but enough to make him shudder inwardly. He heard a shifting and grating. He wanted to run downstairs and see if plaster had fallen in the dining room. Instead he strode about and tested the flooring in other parts of the room. Solid as a rock everywhere – except the sides of the platform.

Nicki sat on a thronelike oriental chair and cursed aloud. He leant down and felt the green carpet: tough pre-war quality, in excellent condition. All that had been done in this room was to add two persian rugs with hunting scenes.

He believed he knew what the original purpose of the alcove had been. Von Sommer's plan for an African safari came to nothing. He brought home no 'big game' for his trophy room. He did not set up a tableau with, for instance, an entire lion or a wildebeest among potted palms. Instead the Baron went to war and returned a cripple.

Nicki went rather gingerly up the two steps on to the dais. It felt solid enough even if it were poised over some abyss. Outside the daylight had faded. He was feeling for his pocket-knife with the idea of tackling the platform itself, peering under it, when he looked at the window.

The room was reflected perfectly, flung back at him as if framed in leaves from the wallpaper. He took it all in as a *Gestalt*: the four bronze lamps, the antlered heads, the large stonemarten climbing with its mate on a tree-stump in the alcove, the eagle erupting from a dim corner with its wings outspread, the laden gun-rack.

He had thought of palms and in fact he saw green foliage all along the sides of the platform. He saw – and this at last terrified him – the man on the dais. A thin streak of a man poised in his own attitude, head half-turned. A high, balding forehead, light eyes, silky whiskers, fine wisps of blonde hair standing out behind and around the head like an aureole. he wore a blue coat of odd cut; one long-fingered hand, with a strong bony wrist, clasped a lapel.

Nicki moved involuntarily and for an awful moment he saw his own head superimposed upon the head of that other. Then in a flash the vision faded and the dark glass gave back the room as it was, stripped of its trophies and greenery. He leaped down from the platform and drew the curtains. His hands were shaking.

He heard sounds coming closer and was tense with fear. Running footsteps, laughter... he relaxed again. Limbard and his new young wife were running up the stairs. A hearty bass note then her sweet gasping laughter as she ran ahead. The door of the master bedroom slammed. Nicki left the trophy room and went silently downstairs.

He thought of something that Andreas had said years ago, then never said again. He had not repeated it to Kate, this afternoon. Jason Limbard was a macho type who had the family very much under his thumb, the *Haus-Herr* was a *Haus-Tyran*. Not the thing to say about one's most successful author. Not even the thing to say about an excellent client who wanted a family home. On the bottom step he found a long scrap of bronze silk torn from Anja's dress. Fun and games...

Chapter 8
Surprises

Drinks before dinner were served in the games room.

'Our sporting club, Kate,' said Jason, behind the bar. 'Nick wanted you to see it.'

'It's gorgeous!' said Kate. 'You and Anja have a great exercise programme going.'

She had seen the honeymooners jogging vigorously in the grounds, and steam issuing from the lower regions of the villa. In fact, she found the games room a little too opulent for the basement. It was like a film set that could not quite conceal the rough contours of the stone room, a bordello or a gambling den that had to be hidden away, underground. She saw that Nicki loved the room and was very proud of it; she filed away her criticism under 'never to be said,' then wondered if this was wrong. She had often done it with Andreas but with Nicki she had always argued and discussed.

'Look!' cried Anja, pointing to the mural. 'The girl with the opera glasses is Kate!'

The girl stood on a balcony before a lighted room, resting her opera glasses on the parapet. She was certainly tall and red-haired and she wore, like Kate, a cream blouse and a long black skirt.

'Is it an interval at the theatre?' asked Kate. 'What am I doing?'

'Spying,' said Jason. 'Watch out! You'll be caught!'

'I'd make a rotten spy,' said Kate. 'More in Nicki's line.'

'*Küss die Hand, Madame*,' said Nicki obediently. 'I think that is Anja in pale blue.'

The dark-haired beauty in floating pale blue draperies was

reaching up into the branches of a tree. Anja wore a silky blue-grey kaftan, her fatigue had gone, she was even prettier than the Grasset model. She played up to her husband with grave concentration, her eyes hardly leaving his face. Her smiles came and went, reflecting his mood. She sipped, with him, a 'health cocktail' while Kate and Nicki were allowed martinis.

Kate yielded to the charm of the *pièce de résistance* , the clockwork carousel. It was a marvellous construction of enamelled tin and polished brass, fifty centimetres square at the base and more than sixty from the base to the gaily striped pennant over the yellow roof. It belonged in the open air, on a fairground, among the orchestrions, the baroque organs and the laughing clowns. There were four horses on the carousel: the white and the bay had no riders but on the brown horse a saucy minx perched sideways. Perhaps she was a nursemaid in her ribboned hat and frilled apron. A soldier in a red coat rode the black charger and there were two children, a girl with golden curls riding on a goose and a boy in a sailor suit mounted on a pink pig.

'How do I turn it on?' asked Kate.

'Slide the leaver,' said Nicki. 'It will play the first selection.'

The carousel played a rousing waltz song from *The Gypsy Baron*. The painted figures swung out with airy grace; Nicki took Kate in his arms and they danced a Viennese waltz. Nicki was an expert dancer. He made any partner seem good, Kate thought.

'Am I too tall?' she asked.

'Of course not,' said Nicki. 'Do you remember a painting by Klimt? The woman is kneeling... obviously taller than the man.'

'Nicki!'

Kate remembered the painting very well and blushed. The man did rather look like Nicki from the back. The Limbards were waltzing expertly together.

'I can't breathe,' laughed Anja.

In the tiny interval when the music changed to 'Roses from the South' Jason ordered: 'Change partners!'

Nicki and Anja whirled away, executing some fancy footwork around the exercise machines. Kate, dancing with Jason Limbard, was distressed at once. He held her far too tightly and she hated his closeness. She concentrated on the music and on waltzing, turning... she was a clockwork figure, she smiled into her partner's face. She sensed that Jason was making a great and deliberate effort, he was bringing the force of his personality to bear on her for some reason that she was unable to understand. The pressure of his hand between her shoulder blades, his fixed grin, his grip on her raised hand, were a provocation, the expression of some bad feeling.

The music changed again: 'Tales from Vienna Woods'.

'Playing your song, Nicki!' cried Jason.

'Shall we?'

Nicki, thank goodness, changed partners again.

'Wait! Wait!' said Anja loudly, clinging to Jason's arm. 'I *heard* something!'

'Can I turn if off?' said Kate.

She slid the lever back. The music stopped, the figures on the carousel swung out one last time.

'I heard a noise,' said Anja. 'Truly, Jay. What's through this wall?'

'Wine cellar,' said Nicki. 'Hope nothing has fallen down.'

They listened. Kate half-remembered some very uncomfortable tale she had heard long ago. 'Something arose in the cellar...' said Sister Florentine quietly, fearfully, inside her head.

'Check the wine cellar if you like, Nick,' grined Jason, 'but I think Anja heard one of the resident ghosts!'

'Oh, Jay, please!'

'Perhaps Frau Bauer is coming to fetch us?' said Kate.

'She'll use the intercom,' said Nicki.

At that moment the intercom crackled into life; Frau Bauer called for Herr Limbard. There were hoots of relief all round.

'Thank you, Frau Bauer,' said Jason. 'No, kiddies, stay here. Dinner in five minutes. I'm going to fix the sauce for the appetiser.'

They listened to his steps receding. Anja went behind the bar, refilled all their glasses and spiked her own drink with vodka.

'This room reminds me of a bar on Sylt,' she said wistfully. 'Do you know the island, Kate?'

'Andreas and I went there once,' said Kate, 'seven years ago.'

She had not thought of the chic North Sea resort for years. They had been able to afford it once only, the summer before the lost summer.

'Nicki has been to Sylt lots of time,' she said.

Kate was almost certain then that *she* heard a bump in the corridor. She turned aside, pretending to examine the Tamara Paige poster, then turned back as Anja dropped a name.

'Franco Tirelli...'

'What, the racing driver?' said Nicki. 'He used to give those famous parties in a converted barn.'

'Yes,' said Anja flatly. 'I was engaged to Franco when he crashed at Le Mans.'

'I'm sorry to hear that.'

Kate made some sympathetic noise too. Anja smiled and shook her head.

'It was eleven years ago. Were you at those parties Nicki?'

'I went along twice,' he said. 'Perhaps you remember Magda, a blonde girl.'

'Dark-blonde,' said Anja, 'Some kind of journalist. Was she your friend?'

'My wife,' said Nicki, 'my ex-wife.'

Kate thought of Magda, petite, clever, whom she had known briefly. Magda had had a trick of making Kate feel stupid at a time when she was struggling to improve her German. Now, see how the carousel had turned. She was here, so was Nicki; Andreas and Magda had moved on or melted away. The intercom crackled. Jason announced dinner. Kate looked back at the glittering playroom as Nicki held the door and felt that it was wearing a smirk.

They were four people at a table for six. Kate could find no fault with the menu – Frau Bauer was obviously an excellent cook – but Jason maintained a sober, critical attitude, testing and tasting every dish, once going to the kitchen to improve the sauce for the ducklings. Over the seafood cocktail, Anja said with a sad little laugh: 'A coincidence, Jay. I've met Nicki's wife, years ago, on Sylt.'

'God, we've all been through the mill,' said Jason fiercely. 'Death, divorce... *Kate*...'

His look was almost stern. *Death, divorce, suicide*, thought

Kate. Was *that* bothering Jason? He took more wine, presently he smiled.

Spätes Glück!' he said, raising his glass. 'Late happiness. I'm working on it, Nicki. Getting together the ingredients. Comfortable house, lovely wife...'

'What more do you need?' Nicki said gallantly, raising his glass to Anja, who sat next to him on Jason's left.

'Privacy is important,' said Jason. 'I need a home world. I'm hard to live with but Anja will soon come to dig my little ways, won't you, baby?'

'Yes, Jay,' she gave him an adoring look.

'I want to salvage a little from the past,' contininued Jason.

'Do you mean... by keeping up the Villa Florian?' asked Kate.

'Partly,' said Jason. 'The past is very close to us in this house. I've seen glimpses of another age...'

'I don't like this talk about haunting and ghosts,' said Anja, 'Please, Jay.'

Kate thought, inexplicably, *he always picks wives who say that.* Jason rang his silver bell and they were occupied with the main course, but he did not change the subject.

'Admit it, Nicki,' he said, 'this place is *unheimlich*.'

To Kate's surprise Nicki said: 'Yes, a little. What do you think, Kate?'

'I'll pass,' she said. 'But do ghosts have to be frightening? I mean, Tamara Paige – a beautiful woman, an artist?'

'Or Jacobsen,' said Nicki. 'Sad to think of poor Jacobsen.'

Jason made his foray to the kitchen to improve the sauce and Anja said timidly, 'I have a kind of anti-ghost story from Sylt. There were some very weird types who celebrated a black mass in the dunes on Midsummer Eve.'

'Oh God,' said Nicki grinning, 'I think I heard something.'

'It was very dark,' she said, fighting hysterical giggles, 'and we were all kneeling there, not wearing ... many clothes, while some fat woman in a black robe droned on. And suddenly Gunter-Peter – the one who wore earrings – fired off a gun!'

'Fired a gun?' echoed Kate.

'A big revolver, a forty-five... he fired it into the air. Oh God, you never heard such screams! People were crawling about, burrowing in the sand. It was like the end of the world!'

They all laughed uneasily. Jason swept back in.

'Now then, we'll all try the improved sauce. A sliver more meat? Another half?'

He watched them eating and said: 'I'll salvage my own past. I have a surprise or two coming up, honey.'

'A surprise for me?' Anja said obediently. 'Oh please, give me just a hint?'

'Not a word. That sauce is just right now, I think?'

Kate assured him it was perfect. Presently Jason rang the bell again and they sat in silence while Frau Bauer cleared away and set out the magnificent Limbard salad for Jason to complete. He stood up again and went to work in his shirt-sleeves, mixing and measuring. The bowl was a collector's piece of Jugendstil glassware twined with green leaves. Jason held forth about the vitality content of radicchio, endive and capsicum. Kate remembered that Diet Jason, who would have made an excellent TV cook, had turned down offers. The role was beneath his dignity.

She admired the dining room; the way the drapes fell; the overhead lamp, unlit. She thought, *Something will happen*, and dismissed the thought quickly. Tempting fate. She saw Nicki staring anxiously at the archway as he had done the day before at the reception. What was he afraid of?

Suddenly there was a frightful metallic clatter from the kitchen. Everyone jumped and Anja gave a loud scream. Frau Bauer appeared in the doorway and apologised. She had dropped a tray. Nothing was broken. They munched their delicious salad and finished up the moselle.

'You are nervous, sweetheart,' said Jason slyly. 'Did you think it was the poltergeist?'

'Oh, Jay, no...'

She was laughing and shaking.

'What does it take to frighten Kate?' said Jason.

'Things that I can't remember,' said Kate, looking him in the eye. 'Uncertainty.'

'Enough!' said Nicki, coming to her aid. 'Jason, think of our digestion.'

Frau Bauer came in again, subdued. Coffee and cheesecake would be served in the family room but first... if Herr Lenz would be so kind as to look at the drapes over there. They seemed to have caught in the terrace door. Nicki sprang up and excused himself.

'My step ladder number,' he said.

They dawdled a little, giving Nicki time to unhook the new drapes in the family room, then slowly rose from table.

'I remember,' said Jason. 'There were dogs. Ghost dogs, baby. Wolf-hounds!'

He threw back his head and howled as they walked into the hallway. Anja put her hands over her ears.

'Oh, stop,' said Kate, 'she really is frightened,'

Jason chuckled.

'You can't tell a man how to behave towards his wife, Kate!'

He drew Anja's hands down and whispered loudly into her ear, 'And what about the Baron? The Old Man himself.'

They went down the hall and as they passed under the dome they were caught and held, all three. Music held them. The sharp lilting sound from the clockwork carousel: it played a Paul Lincke melody, *Luftschlösser*, 'Castles in the Air'.

'Is someone down there?' whispered Anja.

'No!' said Jason. 'Which would you rather have, baby? A prowler or a ghost?'

Kate could see the silken edge of Anja's sleeve trembling against her brown arm.

'I switched if off in the middle of a waltz,' she said. 'Maybe that makes it leap ahead somehow, turn itself on.'

'Someone,' said Jason, 'had better switch the darn thing off.'

'Sure,' said Kate. 'No problem!'

She walked off briskly. She found Frau Bauer stock still beside the laden desert trolley, staring at the door to the basement.

'*Scheisse*!' she whispered.

Kate went on down the grey carpeted stairs, ran her hand down the elegant iron railing. The music was louder in the basement. The English words of the song rang in her head.

> 'Castles in the air above you
> Ever vanish as you roam,
> Here on earth are hearts to love you,
> Happiness is here at home!'

The corridor was well-lit, unshadowed, all the doors were shut. Kate jumped a litle when the music changed with a little flourish. Then she had an hysterical urge to laugh, to tiptoe along in time to the next song in the medley:

'Shine little glow-worm,
Glimmer, glimmer...'

Past the utility room on her left, the sauna on her right, its round window like an eye, staring. She reached the door to the games room, hit the light switches, which were in the corridor, and went in boldly. She looked quickly around, her courage holding. A games room, a rumpus room, what could be nicer, more harmless? The carousel went around and around; the painted figures rocked gently, the music played. Kate watched and waited but she turned her head nervously and missed the change again. The final number was a jaunty march celebrating the air, the carefree atmosphere of Lincke's vanished city. This one was untranslatable:

'*Das is die Berliner Luft ... Luft! Luft!*'

Kate bent closer to the carousel and saw a red switch marked in English 'Emergency Stop'. She switched off the carousel and watched the toy riders settle, quivering, into stillness. She wanted to get out of the games room as quickly as she could. There was a short wooden-sounding bump quite close by, through the wall. She took a deep breath and went out into the corridor as briskly as she had entered.

A shadow cleft the air behind her. She ducked instinctively and was pushed aside. The lights went out. Footsteps went on, running, with an odd little sliver of light bobbing ahead. Kate had half fallen. She dragged herself upright and saw a dark figure with a pencil flashlight swallowed up by the door to the souterrain apartment. She began to cry out, to shout for help, for Nicki ... She swung across the corridor in the darkness, groping for the light switches. The lights came on before she found them; Jason Limbard had come down the stairs.

Kate ran towards him as he strode down the corridor. Her feet tangled in her skirt and she leant against him. He caught her lightly under the elbows.

'A man!' she babbled. 'A man... he got away! He was hiding!'

'You're crazy!' snapped Jason.

His face was splayed with anger and disgust. He stepped backwards and let her fall to the ground.

'Jason!'

Kate tried to call him, to call him back, although he still stood towering over her. She stood up, shaking.

'A man was hiding in the basement,' she said. 'He went out through the souterrain.'

Jason did not turn his head.

'You're brain-damaged!' he said in a low, terrible voice. 'You're a ghost, Kate. *Hysterical*!'

He hit her in the face with his open hand. Kate was filled with terror and it gave her strength. She bent low, gripping her skirt, and ran under his arm. She ran up the stairs and into the hallway, stumbling and gasping. Nicki was there at last; he caught her in his arms.

'A man,' repeated Kate doggedly, 'hiding in the basement. Nicki, truly!'

Frau Bauer and Anja were clustered about.

'Heard something outside,' said Frau Bauer.

'He went out through the souterrain,' said Kate.

'Come in here,' said Nicki.

It was the small sitting room beside the front door. Kate sank on to the nearest chair.

'Jay!' said Anja in alarm. 'I hope Jay doesn't go after him.'

'I think we should call the Breitbach police,' said Nicki 'One man, Katie? Did he hit you?'

'P-pushed me,' said Kate, 'as he went past.'

Jason came quietly through the archway from the dining room.

'Now Kate,' he said, full of concern. 'No more moselle wine and ghost stories for you. How's the head?'

'Jason,' said Kate. 'There was a man hiding in the basement.'

Jason chuckled and shook his head. He caught Nicki's eye and made a small grimace of disbelief. Nicki and the two women looked at Kate, flushed and dishevelled, and at Jason, the benign head of the house.

'Kate,' said Nicki, 'tell us what happened.'

'I went down to turn off the carousel,' she said. 'It was playing away, I guess it had switched itself on. I turned it off using the Emergency Stop. I heard a kind of wooden-sounding bump, somewhere in the basement. I walked straight out of the games room, turning off the lights. A man ran past me. He pushed me aside and hit the corridor lights.'

'This is all nonsense, I'm afraid,' said Jason. 'Kate could have fumbled those wall switches herself. How could she see this guy in the dark?'

'He had a flashlight,' said Kate. 'Why don't you believe what I'm telling you?'

Jason raised his hands in a gesture of surrender.

'Kate, you're overwrought. Remember your... trouble.'

At that moment a monotonous ringing sound began outside the house and did not stop.

'The fence!' said Nicki, working at the security board. 'The alarm for the perimeter... south-west.'

'Someone got in!' said Anja.

'No,' said Nicki, 'I would say he got out. This is Kate's intruder.'

Jason marched into the hall his face dark with rage. He burst out: '*In my house! Some thief! Some spying bastard!*'

He was ready to storm away but Nicki checked him.

'He's gone. We'll put the house under security. We should call the Breitbach police.'

'No police!' snapped Jason. 'I don't want them in this house again.'

With a great effort he calmed himself and came towards Kate. She shrank back in her chair; he knelt at her feet.

'Kate,' he said, 'forgive me. I doubted you, I never dreamed ... No-one would believe how badly I behaved.'

It sounded like a fancy apology but it was the truth. A demon lurked in his eyes and at the corner of his mouth.

'Okay,' she whispered. 'Okay, Jason.'

'Can you describe this guy?'

It was a miserably vague description. A man, taller than Kate herself, wearing a dark tracksuit and a dark 'balaclava' woollen cap. He carried a pencil flashlight. He didn't speak, had no distinctive odour...

Jason sprang up again and began giving orders to Nicki and to Frau Bauer. Doors were slammed. Then everything became distant and grey in a way that Kate remembered only too well. She lay back half-fainting in her chair and was revived by Anja holding a glass to her lips.

'Careful, it's brandy.'

Kate sipped gratefully.

'You want to put your head down?'

'No,' she said. 'I'm better. In a moment I'll go home.'

The room was warm and pleasant, there was a bowl of red roses on a side table. Kate felt that there was a third person in there with them. If she could turn her head without breaking the spell another woman would be standing close to them. They heard Jason's voice raised in the distance. Anja said confidingly, 'Did I ever tell you how I first met Jason?'

'No,' said Kate.

This is the man's wife, she thought, *his pretty, nervous new wife*.

'In the elevator of the Aurora House,' said Anja. 'It was very romantic. I never did... keep my appointment that afternoon.'

The others were coming back. Anja gave Kate a warning glance as if she had been telling secrets. Frau Bauer wheeled the dessert trolley into the small sitting room and began to serve coffee. Jason was unable to sit down. He tossed off his own decaffeinated brew and prowled with a cup in his hand. Nicki sat beside Kate and murmured, 'Drink your coffee and I'll take you home.'

'Those types sweeping leaves,' announced Frau Bauer. 'They tried to get into the house.'

'What, the Walther boys?' said Jason. 'I wouldn't have thought...'

'Of course not, said Nicki.

'The tall one came to wash his hands,' said Frau Bauer stolidly, 'then I heard a noise and the dark boy, Armin, was in the family room, said he was looking for you, Herr Lenz.'

'Oh God, poor devils, I know what it was,' said Nicki. 'They needed their pay.'

Kate stood in the hall and Nicki put her black shawl around her shoulders. There was a loud peal from the electric bell:

someone at the front gate. Nicki cursed. The neighbours had heard the alarm for the fence. The caller identified himself through the intercom in a bass voice.

'*Walther.*'

'Speak of the devil,' said Jason, coming into the hall. Nicki operated various switches and opened the front door. They heard heavy boots crunching over the gravel and the forester stood before them in the doorway, all in loden green with silver buttons.

'The fence?' he enquired, removing his hat. 'Do you have a problem?'

Kate thought it was obvious that they did. She was pale, the two men were nervous, each in his own way.

'Come in Herr Walther... Franz,' said Jason.

The forester stepped in shyly and looked about him. Kate recalled that he knew the Villa Florian better then any of them and did not trust it. Jason rapped out the story of the intruder and Herr Walther, taking Kate's hand, enquired gravely after her health. Was she hurt? Did she need a doctor? Kate was touched by his concern; she told him she felt fine. The forester persisted: had the police been called?

When Jason said that they had not been called Herr Walther nodded sadly. He bowed to Anja and to Frau Bauer through the doorway of the sitting room. Jason made the half-hearted offer of a schnapps but he shook his head.

'I'm keeping you. You'll be wanting to lock up.'

'I'll see Kate home,' said Nicki.

She murmured her thanks, intent on getting out of the house. She stood on the front steps breathing in the cool air while Nicki spoke to Herr Walther.

'The boys will be glad of this,' he said, pocketing money. 'They went to Gross Gerau, chopping down trees.'

The three of them walked slowly to the front gates. They looked to right and left at the lawns, the shrubbery, the noble trees, all silvered by the moon, and the inky blackness of the shadows. The forester sighed and muttered.

He turned to confront the Villa Florian and he was, for an instant, a figure older than the house itself... that creature from German legend, the forester. Franz Walther made a curious gesture as if he began to shake his fist at the house, then opened his palm, turning the curse into a blessing.

'This house!' he said. 'My God, this house! So much pain ... for those long dead... for those here and now, our friends. I've spent the worst times in my life at the Villa Florian. I pray that it will all have an end.'

It was one of the longest speeches Kate had ever heard him utter. Walther pulled his hat down and shook hands with them both.

'I'm sure there is nothing to fear from that intruder,' he said.

He went out of the gate and mounted his mo-ped. He called: 'Some letters in your box, Herr Lenz!'

Away he went up the hill with a popping sound from the small engine.

'More bills!' said Nicki, collecting the letters. 'They're sent to me at this address.'

'Oh God!' said Kate. 'I never had a chance to mention the Art Show.'

'I'll see what I can do,' said Nicki.

She felt foolish and dishonest. She never wanted to be near Jason Limbard again but she must compromise.

'Come in for a minute,' she said. 'Nicki, I have to talk to you.'

'Take it easy,' he said. 'You've had a terrible night.'

Her luck was holding. Tante Adelheid was asleep, she must have missed the excitement with the alarm ringing. They stole into the warm sitting room where the standard lamp was alight to show Kate the way home.

'In the basement,' said Kate, 'Jason was pretty unbelievable. He really over-reacted.'

'He was very upset by the break-in,' said Nicki. '*If* it was a break-in.'

'Jason has it in for me some way,' said Kate. 'I've no idea why but I think it has to do with that bad time... that summer.'

'What did he say?' asked Nicki. 'I hadn't noticed anything.'

'I don't want to tell tales,' said Kate. 'Seems kind of childish.'

She was overcome by a wave of *déjà vu* ; she *had* told some embarrassing tale, right here in this room, before...

'Just sound him out, if you can,' she said. 'See how he reacts when you remind him of the Art Show.'

'Perhaps it was this thing Andreas mentioned, years ago.'
'Andreas?'

Andreas in summer, striding up and down in this room. And now there was Nicki, looking at her with great concern.

'He said that Jason Limbard was a kind of home devil, very hard on his wife and children,' said Nicki seriously. 'Could that be the missing link?'

'How do you mean?'

'Did you and Jason have words, maybe, at a party or something? Quarrel about women's rights, male chauvinism?'

'Could be.' she said. 'I don't remember. I must have been very depressed, under a strain...'

'Perhaps Tante Adelheid...?'

'No!' said Kate. 'I can't ask her. She... she's a little frail, sometimes. I can't bother her with this.'

He kissed her cheek and said:

'Get some sleep, Katie dear. Are you feeling any better?'

'Yes,' she lied. 'What did you mean just now... *if* it was a break-in. What else could it have been?'

'A burglary isn't one man hiding in the cellar,' said Nicki, 'it's three men with a truck. That's why I think we should have called the police.'

'How about an amateur? A sneak-thief?' said Kate.

'Well, I hope we scared him off,' said Nicki. 'I wonder how Frau Bauer feels about sleeping in her souterrain?'

'She seems a pretty tough customer.'

When he had gone Kate realised that they had said nothing at all about ghosts. *Did the carousel warn us*? she thought. It played in an empty room and there was a real intruder in the basement. A touch of the Sylt effect: a gun, a real danger, that sent the naked thrill-seekers screaming and scattering.

The corner room had a single long window with a climbing plant in stained glass. Nicki put aside his account books and thought of human personality, the mask and the face. Kate. Jason. Anja. Frau Bauer, who had returned to her apartment without a murmur. When the lamp was turned out the colours of the stained glass leaves and bell flowers were still visible in the moonlight. Tomorrow he must face up to the rest of the accounts with Jason. He must tackle the problem of the trophy room.

He woke or half woke several times in the night and knew that Jason prowled about his villa with a heavy tread. It occured to Nicki, half asleep, that the intruder in the Villa Florian had triggered off some mad reaction in Jason Limbard. He heard the low thrumming note of the staircase and a sharp cry, further off. Anja? The squeak of a ghost? Then it was morning and he was wide awake trying to remember a thought from the edge of sleep. Franco Tirelli, Anja's lost love... something Magda had included in a Sylt expose...

II

She said: 'Let's case the joint a little.'

He paid off the cab at the foot of the hill and they walked up slowly. Roddy felt bad, his head ached, he hoped things would work out. Too much depended upon him and he was a weak link, always had been. The Kid – he looked at her stumping along with her pink nylon zipper bag – acted plenty grown-up but that was all it was: play-acting. Who could tell how much she knew, how much she understood, let alone how much she remembered?

'That wasn't there before,' he said.

The new house had a flat roof and was set back behind a concrete fence. Two dogs began to bark; they could see the sleek dark shapes racing back and forth in a kind of run behind the fence. Dobermanns. Killer dogs.

'Bodo was a whole lot bigger than that,' said Melissa. 'He was the biggest dog in the whole world!'

'Well, shut up about him!'

He had told her about Bodo. They stared at the other house, the Forsthaus, with the afternoon sun on its roof, then they came right up and stood before the gates of the Villa Florian. The sun was on the dome so that it glowed pure gold.

'Wow!' said Melissa. 'Welcome to the Overlook Hotel.'

'Quit that!' snapped Roddy. 'Just you quit that kind of talk!'

Melissa dumped her bag then and held him tight by the arm, staring at the house while the sun moved over its roof. A wind sprang up and ranged through the garden, scattering the dead leaves.

'Tell me,' she said. 'Tell me, God's truth, did you ever see or hear anything ghostly in this place?'

'No,' he said. 'No, I was pretty scared but I never saw anything except once: the light. You were with me, we both saw it. I told you before.'

'I can't remember it at all.'

'Mom never saw anything either. But Buddy definitely saw ... people. People who lived in the house before. And the Old Man saw things too... dogs, ghost dogs.'

'Has he changed? Has he really... you know... seen the light?'

'Sure he's changed,' said Roddy. 'He has people in the house. To visit. I guess we will all eat at the same table with him. I know for certain he has bought you some fancy presents.'

'Spending his money,' she said. 'Spending all that money, trying to buy this house.'

'He bought it already. It belongs to him.'

'Uh-uh,' she said. 'This is a hex place.'

'What's that supposed to mean?'

Where did she get stuff like that? Hanging around with poor unsuitable people in the inland from Lauderdale. The Old Man had condemned them to that cheap life-style. But now, look at the Kid, she was upwardly mobile, she would do better than any of them.

'There are some places,' said Melissa, 'that don't belong to anyone.'

There was a burst of laughter, right behind them. A little kid was galloping down the path of the Forsthaus and a tall redhaired woman strolled after him. Melissa said urgently: 'Is that the lady called Kate?'

'I guess so,' said Roddy warily.

'It is,' she said. 'It's the lady called Kate Reimann and her baby boy. I *have* to speak to them.'

'Aw, come on, Liss.'

He wondered if they were being watched from the Villa Florian. Was the Old Man looking out?

'I made a sacred promise to Mom,' said Melissa. 'I have to check on her!'

She marched boldly across the street and Roddy followed.

'*Hello there*!'

For a moment Kate was dazzled by the afternoon sun. Peter turned shy and hung back behind the hedge. She saw the tall young man in army uniform . . . good-looking, well-built, still wearing glasses . . . the son, Roderick Limbard. She saw the young girl who had hailed her and knew that she was seeing someone who had changed out of recognition. This was a tall sturdily built girl, the sort of American child for whom the categories 'sub-teen' or 'pre-teen' were invented. She was pretty, a tomboy with freckles and a head of short golden curls. She wore pink bib overalls, sneakers, a faded blue sweatshirt.

'Ms Reimann?' she said smiling. 'Kate? I guess you don't remember me!'

'*Melissa* !'

They smiled at each other. They had both come through, thought Kate. Melissa, the silent child with the teddy bear, the only one of the Limbards who was not shamming. Kate, the poor, brain-damaged suicide in the hospital bed.

'What a wonderful surprise!' said Kate. 'You just got here? Hello there, Roddy!'

'Hello there, Ma'am!'

Jason's big surprise, Kate realised. She wondered what Anja and Frau Bauer would make of it.

'Mom said I should be sure and ask after Frau Kramer. . . your Auntie, I guess,' said Melissa dutifully.

'Frau Kramer is fine,' said Kate.

'And I should ask how you were doing. Last she heard you had a baby boy.'

Peter gave a hoot of protest and Kate dragged him into view.

'This is Peter.'

'I grew!' he said.

'You sure did,' said Melissa.

She gave him a stick of gum.

'I remember this place,' she said. 'There was this cat . . .'

'The cat is doing fine,' said Kate.

'We better check in,' said Roddy. 'It was great to see you Miz Reimann.'

Melissa said, quite unembarrassed: 'Mom sends her love. We always remember you in our prayers.'

She watched them cross the road again and ring the bell at

the Villa Florian. Peter ran back into the Forsthaus and when Kate went into the kitchen he was giving Tante Adelheid a glowing description of 'Diet Jason's big girl'.

'Good Heavens!' said Tante Adelheid in a shocked voice. 'This is Melissa? The mother has sent her poor little child...'

'Melissa isn't a poor little child,' said Kate firmly. 'And the eldest son is there too, Roderick.'

Tante Adelheid looked unconvinced. It was the moment to take her aside and ask questions. What was it? Something from the lost summer? Something to do with the Limbard children? But Kate remained silent and the moment passed.

Chapter 9
Tales of the Villa Florian II

The Old Mill Gallery in Breitbach was housed in a massive half-timbered building on a corner site. The old mill had brick barns, some very old, looming to left and right, and a flourishing vegetable garden. There was a good turn out, Nicki was pleased to see, as he slipped in among the guests in coats of fur and leather. He cocked a weather eye for Kate because he wanted to scan her work before they met.

He was thrown up against a table of attractive figurines and met the sculptor, a cheerful woman in her forties. Then across the open spaces he was drawn by a picture of a tree in a meadow. It was a big uncompromising oil, more post-impressionist than anything else, full of light. Nothing but the plum tree, full of blossom, and the grass entwined with flowers. He drank it in; it was worth the trip. Nicki was taken out of himself. Then he saw the signature: K.C.R. Kate Cameron Reimann. Good God!

It was too late for him to back-pedal, to pull the art critic or connoisseur bit. He raced to her next picture of a stream and a bridge. He was examining four smaller still life pictures, each of a different season, when Kate hove alongside. She carried a reviving glass of *Sekt*, or German champagne, and some excellent hot savouries. Nicki wolfed the food, still peering and changing his distance.

'Mmmm?' said Kate.
'Mm!' he replied.
He wiped his fingers and stared, not at the paintings but at Kate herself, looking very beautiful in a trouser suit of turquoise silk and a heavy gold chain.

'You've become a painter!' he said reproachfully.

'Have I?'

There was a gleam in her eye which he recognised: the stubborn pride of the creative artist. Inwardly he sighed and melted and wished he could bend her proud head down and give her a kiss. *It was all going to be very difficult*, he thought, *but in the end*...

'How much are you asking for the plum tree?' he asked sternly.

'I knew you from the first,' said Kate. 'You're an art dealer.'

She put down her tray and they walked around, haggling gently. He found some of the aquarelles by the third artist accomplished and interesting. Quite a number of items then that he would try and take to München from this provincial nest. Some he would purchase, some he would try to sell on commission. It must all be worked out.

There followed one of those diversions that Nicki felt he should enjoy more than he did. Thomas Brand, who had organised the exhibition, turned up with a pretty blonde girl ... of course, Eva Schumacher, the local reporter. As Nicki was photographed with Kate, Gisela and Marlene, the three artists, a voice came out of the crowd. 'My God *he was the waiter* !' Was the wretched thing turning into a cult film? A bunch of art students in gorgeous raiment began to sing 'Vienna Blood' while Nicki signed several autographs.

Kate laughed at his side. The sculptor, Marlene, had said: 'Katie, I think it worked at last!'

'Have I missed something?' he asked.

'Thomas has found a friend,' she said innocently.

Herr Brand was steering the blonde reporter eagerly through the gallery and explaining the finer points.

'How is the family reunion at the Villa Florian?' asked Kate.

'A reason for Jason and Anja to stay at home,' he said, smiling.

'I didn't really expect them,' said Kate. 'How are the children?'

'Melissa is a lot of fun,' he said. 'Has a running battle with Frau Bauer. Anja tries to keep the peace. Roddy, the son, acts a bit hangdog.'

'And Jason?'

'Edgy,' said Nicki. 'Pleased to have the kids in the house but he comes on rather strong at times. Quite an atmosphere at the dinner table.'

He was playing things down. Jason's veiled threats of reprisal over the salads were less worrying to him than the man's night wanderings and sudden alarms. He felt that Jason Limbard was, mysteriously, cracking up.

At the same time Nicki told himself this was a personal reaction. He wanted to be done with the Villa Florian and its owner. It was a feeling that he experienced at the end of every big assignment. In months or a year he would take out his designs and photographs and assess what he had done. The Villa Florian remained a special case: it would always tease him out of thought.

'Do something for me?' asked Kate.

'Anything!'

'I can't get away,' she said. 'We must have our dinner and post-mortem another time.'

'And now?'

'You must chauffeur some ladies.'

Two ladies, it seemed, and the term was not used loosely. Frau von Thal, an aristocrat in a tailored folk-lore costume. Mrs Greenwood... was she English?... in tweeds. It was not until Sister Claudia bustled up in a modified navy-blue habit that he realised who they were.

'Herr Lenz!' said Sister Florentine. 'We have heard so much about your work!'

He felt their mild eyes upon him and knew that his curiosity could be satisfied – at a price. They knew a great deal about the Villa Florian but he would have to travel their way. He would have to tell them his own secrets; he must become some kind of initiate.

They lingered for a while in the brightly lit white rooms of the gallery, then set out. The sisters were impressed with the BMW, though they still spoke affectionately of their veteran Opel which had recently given up the ghost. It had grown dark and the stars were just visible under a thin net of cloud as they drove through Breitbach. The conversation was sprightly; he accepted an invitation to supper at the convent.

Past the ruined tower, through the autumn fields... they

purred on up the Steinberg. They passed the Forsthaus where Frau Kramer was baby-sitting with Peter. They looked in silence at the Villa Florian.

'Where do the children sleep?' asked Mrs Greenwood, softly.

'In the two hexagon bedrooms,' said Nicki. 'The light is on in Melissa's room.'

Once inside the covent grounds they took a path to the kitchen, a vast room crudely lit by strong globes with old white-enamelled shades.

'How was the convent heated?' asked Nicki.

'Inadequately,' rejoined Sister Florentine. 'We suffered from chilblains in winter.'

'There were stoves in the common rooms,' said Sister Rachel, 'but no heating at all in the bedrooms or the chapel. We made do with hot bricks, warming pans, extra clothing.'

'This room with the big coal range was always warmer,' said Sister Claudia, who had put on a large white apron. 'Now we have central heating in this small section, our living quarters.'

'Come upstairs, Herr Lenz,' said Sister Rachel, 'We will have our goulash soup in the sitting room.'

He found the sitting room plain and comfortless. There was a sentimental nineteenth-century print of St Hildegarde under which Sister Florentine lit a candle in a porcelain candlestick. On the south wall, near a window, there was a small picture of a madonna and child in a lofty medieval stable with ox and ass. Nicki peered at it for sometime and exclaimed: 'Good heavens!'

'Yes,' said Sister Florentine. 'It is my grandfather's Cranach, the one he found at the flea market in Frankfurt. My father left it to me in his will.'

They spoke a little of the von Sommer family over the excellent goulash soup. It had arrived in a rattling 'dumb waiter', hauled up by Sister Rachel, while Sister Claudia climbed the stairs unencumbered. The dishes were piled in this contraption after the meal and the cupboard shut. There as an air of expectation at the small round table; Sister Claudia served everyone a glass of sweet but rather medicinal liqueur.

'*Also, zur Sache*!' said Sister Florentine. 'All right, let's get to the point!'

The sisters gazed at him earnestly, their old shapely hands resting lightly upon the table cloth. Nicki thought of a séance, a magical ceremony – time for someone to fire off a gun.

'Herr Lenz,' said Sister Florentine briskly, 'are you convinced that Katherine Reimann tried to take her own life?'

Nicki could not speak. He looked from one woman to another and finally stammered: 'But she was found... I mean...'

He pulled himself together with an effort.

'It was hard for us all to believe,' he said, 'but was there ever any doubt? Andreas accepted it and so did Kate herself. What else could have happened?

'Our friend Adelheid Kramer could *not* believe that Katherine would do such a thing,' said Sister Rachel. 'She knew her well, spent the summer with her, left her alone on the very day of the accident in a healthy well-balanced state.'

'It happened years ago,' said Nicki. 'Kate has recovered. Surely the time to ask questions was back there when it happened?'

'When Kate came out of hospital in München, Andreas exacted a promise from his aunt,' said Sister Claudia. 'She agreed never to discuss her doubts with Kate or to make them public. *We* made no such promise.'

'Andreas believed,' said Nicki. 'He was tremendously sad ... ashamed...'

'There was a certain tension and resentment in this marriage as in any other,' said Sister Florentine. 'Andreas was not a perfect husband... he was not faithful to his wife.'

'No,' said Nicki. 'It wasn't that. I never believed it was that. I thought that Kate was mentally disturbed and had hidden it from us all. That she was suffering from depression. We spoke about it, Andreas and I, and we recalled several friends and acquaintances who had done just that: unexpectedly committed suicide. There was even a school friend, a young boy in our high-school class, who hung himself at the age of fifteen. I hate to talk about this business.'

'Please, Herr Lenz, bear with us,' said Sister Claudia. 'You spoke to her on the telephone?'

'Yes.'

'Yes,' said Sister Rachel eagerly. 'You were one of the last people to speak to her before the accident. What was your impression?'

Nicki put his head in his hands, overcome by the memory of that summer day. The Reimann's flat in München, the quiet place in the hall by the telephone, the music... and Kate's voice, far away in Breitbach.

'She seemed... she *was*... perfectly normal,' he said. 'We made jokes. We had a special way of talking. It was quite a short conversation. I mentioned the Villa Florian, some photographs I had seen. We talked about Tamara Paige, the young English artist, who had lived in the villa. And I... I said something like "She died right here in München ... drowned herself in the English garden." Kate didn't reply directly to this. She said, "The Villa Florian is a sad place these days." That was all. We signed off. Andreas had phoned her in the midst of a sort of party in the München apartment. I asked if she wanted to speak to him again, and she said, "No. Bye-bye... *See what the boys in the back room will have...*"'

He heard his voice tremble. The sisters made no sound.

'The song,' he explained. 'The Marlene Dietrich song goes on *"And tell them I died of the same!"* I thought of that later. At the time it seemed quite normal and harmless. When the news came about Kate I wrote down our conversation... it was fresh in my mind. There were two references to suicide in those few minutes.'

'What did you think Kate meant,' enquired Sister Florentine gently, 'when she said that the Villa Florian was a sad place?'

'Andreas had told me that the house was very run down, stripped of its Jugendstil furnishing.'

'Of course,' she nodded, 'but do you know that Kate witnessed a very disturbing scene in that house a few weeks earlier?'

'What?' he said. 'What scene? I've heard nothing.'

'She saw Jason Limbard beating and terrorising his wife and children,' said Sister Florentine.

Nicki looked at the three women, feeling his jaw drop.

'*She saw...*'

'We have it third-hand, from Adelheid Kramer,' said Sister Rachel. 'Kate went back to collect something she had left behind after a first meeting with the family, one evening. What she saw was very frightening... it seemed to be part of a secret, sadistic ritual. The family were being punished for allowing a stranger... Kate... into the house. Minutes before Herr Limbard had greeted her warmly and accepted an invitation to a barbecue at the Forsthaus. Now he cursed and raged. He knocked the child Melissa to the ground, he almost broke the elder boy's arm, he made sexual demands on his wife.'

'This is ghastly,' said Nicki. 'Kate remembers nothing about this dreadful thing.'

He realised that this was not quite true. She had a feeling that something had occurred that summer, in the Villa Florian. She felt threatened by Jason, who had behaved 'unbelievably' in the basement. Nicki was plagued by unbelief himself. He remembered how Andreas had played down the incident... for the very good reasons he had though of earlier.

'This is too much for me to take in,' he said. 'It involves the integrity, the sanity, of several people I've known well or worked with for years.'

'It involves belief,' said Sister Florentine. 'Adelheid believed Kate completely. Andreas not so completely. The situation was complicated by the house itself... things are to be seen in and around that place which come from another age.'

'You mean ghosts?' asked Nicki abruptly.

'Kate received impressions of a young girl in the garden,' said Sister Florentine. 'A young girl and a dog, or dogs.'

'I can understand how that shook Andreas,' said Nicki, grasping at straws. 'This thing, this dreadful thing with Jason ... perhaps it triggered off Kate's depression. But she doesn't remember it in detail any more than she remembers the day she was... injured.'

'However that happened,' said Sister Rachel. 'Suicide attempt? Accident?'

'We believe the Villa Florian is a dangerous house, particularly in summer,' said Sister Claudia.

'Herr Lenz,' said Sister Florentine, 'we are coming into a place where you may not be able to follow, but please bear with us.'

'A violent man might draw spiritual sustenance from the stored evil and bloodshed of centuries,' said Sister Rachel.

'We believe that Kate ignored a warning I had given,' said Sister Florentine, 'and went to the Villa Florian on the day her accident took place.'

'You think Jason Limbard attacked Kate, monkeyed with her van and tried to fake a suicide?' said Nicki loudly. 'You think *that*? No! It's too far-fetched! There must be evidence!'

'Hush,' said Sister Claudia. 'We have no idea what happened. It may have come to a confrontation. She was at the villa and for a specific purpose.'

'How do you know? What purpose?'

'The Limbard family moved out three weeks later, following the death of their son,' said Sister Florentine, 'and Adelheid Kramer searched the house and grounds. I went with her. We found evidence. Nothing in the house but in a flower bed just beside the steps to the terrace we found this.'

She nodded to Sister Claudia who produced from a capacious pocket a small paper package which she unwrapped on the table. It was a doll, a doll in a peasant costume, with blonde braids and a striped skirt, now stained and faded. Nicki stared.

'What does it mean?'

'This doll came from the Forsthaus kitchen,' said Sister Florentine. 'Kate took it as a present for a child in hospital: Melissa Limbard. She meant to drive Mary Limbard to visit her daughter. We are guessing. We do not know for certain.'

'I don't like to speculate about this,' said Nicki. 'There's no end to it. What about the Limbard boy, Buddy? He died, drowned. Kate at least survived and started a new life. Do you think Buddy Limbard committed suicide?'

'We have prayed for him and for enlightenment, but we do not know,' said Sister Florentine. 'We have in his case some very strange readings. Herr Lenz, we are tapping about in the dark. We are afraid. We fear for your safety and for the safety of all those in the Villa Florian.'

'It is not only violence that we are afraid of,' said Sister Rachel. 'There are other possibilities. A haunting that saps the will... a kind of possession...'

He could not protest. Sister Rachel rose up from the table and walked to a cupboard. She returned with a taper which she had lighted at the candle under St Hildegarde's picture. She set down in the middle of the table a seven-branched silver candlestick, a menorah, and began to speak as she slowly set alight its candles.

'I must tell you, Herr Lenz, how I came to the sanctuary of this place and I prefer to do it in the presence of my dear sisters. I will connect my story with the Villa Florian but first I must tell you that I am Jewish... my family came from Lithuania and settled in London after the First World War. My father anglicised his name from Grünwald to Greenwood. By the early thirties he was the owner of a prosperous tailoring business.

'I grew up in Hampstead. I had an older and a younger brother. When my mother died the warmth went out of our family life. I quarrelled with my father because I wished to train as a nurse, but in the end I had my way.

'When I had finished my training I married a young doctor who had also studied in London. My father was rather doubtful about the match although the young man was my own cousin, Jonas Grünwald. He took me back to the old homeland, Lithuania, in 1936, and I saw a way of life that has now gone forever. We lived in Memel, a German town which had become a Lithuanian protectorate after the First War. We had no doubt that a bad time was coming for all Jews in or near Nazi Germany.

'We planned to return to England. You must remember that we thought of ourselves as very modern and enlightened, distanced from the life of the Jewish communities with their synagogues and scholars. My husband's parents were dead but it was still difficult for him to break away from his family. Their last request, before we set out, was that he should visit his poor Aunt Soshe. She was married to Hiram Meyer and lived in the town of Breitbach, near Frankfurt-Am-Main. We should persuade the Meyers to emigrate, with the help of the Jewish community in Frankfurt.

'It was not quite so foolhardy as it now seems for us to travel through Germany in 1938. My husband was blonde and blue-eyed; he had a Lithuanian passport and I a British one. English people were not unpopular in Germany at the time of the Munich agreement. So we "bade farewell to the forests", as Jonas put it, and set out on our journey. We went by ship from Memel to Hamburg; we made believe it was a pleasure trip. We were young, we had money... In Hamburg, I remember, I shopped for clothes and we sunbathed beside a lake. We bought a small car, a second-hand Adler, and motored down to Frankfurt, going out of our way to drive on a new *autobahn*.

'We saw things that others did not see or did not wish to see, and when we arrived in Breitbach the horrible reality was brought home to us: how Jews must live in Germany. Our uncle by marriage, Hiram Meyer, sixty years old, a veteran of the First World War, had long been stripped of his civil rights. He had run a bakery in the town. He was forced to sell his business and he made an arrangement with a former apprentice, Herr Krauser. The new owner allowed his former employer to continue living in the flat over the shop, provided the blinds were kept down in the front room overlooking the street.

'Few peole knew that the Meyers were still there. Aunt Soshe hated to go out wearing her *Judenstern*. She went down for fresh air into the little garden at the back of the bakery. Uncle Hiram had a particular reason for staying in the flat: the bakery was next to the little old brick synagogue and he had always taken care of the building. I do not know to this day how many Jewish families were living in Breitbach when the National Socialists came to power... I would guess about two hundred souls. By 1938 many of them had left town. Hiram's two sons had emigrated to America in the early thirties.

'So we came to the darkened rooms where the elderly couple lived under a sort of house arrest, creeping out to buy food from those who would still serve them. We hardly had time to catch up on the family gossip. Our timing was fatally bad. We arrived in autumn, November the 8th, and on November the 9th I went out before supper to post a letter to my brother in London.

'I was glad to get out of the house with its smells of bread from the bakery and Aunt Shoshe's cooking. I wandered down the back lane and I remember thinking that the streets were rather busy. Trucks full of uniformed men roared past. I knew the way to a letter box in a quiet old square with a well. I was away perhaps twenty minutes; as I went back I took a different way, down the street that led to the front of the shop.

'A fire engine went past me, then it stopped and I caught up with it. The driver was arguing with a pair of young brown-shirts. I went on and found the street full of people; I saw that the synagogue was burning, smoke rose up in a black column. I was seized with terror. As I pushed through the crowd I heard the sound of glass breaking. There was a murmuring from the crowd and the sound of raised voices, shouts and cries.

'The bakery had had its windows smashed and Herr Krauser was angrily protesting his aryan origin. It was no use... this shop had been "the Jewish bakery" for too long. A lorry load of SA men, mostly very young, were in charge of the action. I saw flames spring out of the windows of the apartment. The crowd parted and the old couple were dragged into the street, then my husband Jonas, struggling with three or four men. He was very strong.

'Uncle Hiram, frail and white-haired, was beaten to the ground and kicked. My Aunt Shoshe, her hair streaming, flung herself upon his body. Jonas saw me in the crowd. He shouted in English and in Lithuanian: "*Get away! Save yourself!*" A rifle butt caught him on the side of the head. As he fell I would have rushed forward but my arm was caught in a firm grip.

'I turned and found that it was a woman of my own age, one of the few people I had met in Breitbach. Adelheid Kramer and her husband regularly brought presents of game to my aunt and uncle. Now she forced me to draw back. She whispered "Come away! You must come away!" She pulled me back through the crowd and we walked quickly down another alley. I was sobbing now, and half fainting. Adelheid wiped my face and made me walk. We walked for miles, it seemed, out of the town, with Adelheid wheeling her bicycle. We climbed up the Steinberg and came to the Forsthaus. The Kramers cared for me that night.

'Very early the next morning I was brought up the hill to this convent. The Forsthaus was not safe enough. The beautiful Art Nouveau house opposite, the Villa Florian, was occupied now by Professor Tankred Röhr, a local *Kreisdirektor* of the Labour Front, who passed as a party intellectual.

'I was deeply shocked, I was sick... in fact I suffered a miscarriage. I lay here in the convent for several weeks before I was able to think about my situation. I had my passport and the clothes I stood up in. All the rest of our belongings had been burnt, confiscated or even looted. The automobile had simply disappeared from the back lane. Ernst Kramer, who had gone down into Breitbach the next morning, brought word that my husband and my aunt and uncle had been taken to Weidenau, Willowfield, a local camp where "anti-social elements" were collected: a true example of a "concentration camp". In fact Herr Kramer knew that my Uncle Hiram was already dead when he was carried away.

'At last I managed to get to Frankfurt and contact the Jewish community. I was told to wait for news: Aunt Shoshe and my husband might be held for a short period, then released. I might still have returned to England but I was determined to wait. I sent word to my father through the Jewish community but I never revealed my hiding place... the convent... to anyone. I came and went very carefully. I travelled on buses and trams, I walked... sometimes I walked through the woods for miles to return here.

'I spoke twice to an English diplomatic official in a hotel, the Frankfurter Hof. He deplored the *Reichskristallnacht*, the night of the broken glass, but he was suspicious of my story. A Jewish doctor? From Memel? He asked if my husband was by any chance a Communist. The question of Memel and its territories was tricky: Hitler had just demanded their return.

'Although I often thought that I was followed through the dark streets that winter, it became increasingly clear that no German officials knew of my existence. There were no enquiries for a Frau Grünwald; the baker, Herr Krauser, confided to Ernst Kramer that he believed the Englishwoman had driven away in her car. Word arrived in March, through unofficial channels, that Aunt Shoshe was in KZ Ravensbrüch, a camp for women, far away in Mecklenburg. She died there in 1944.

'No word came of my husband; we feared that he was in the hands of the Gestapo. The truth, when it came out, was so cruel that it almost destroyed me. Jonas had never recovered from the injuries he received on the night of the broken glass. He lay in the prison lazaret at Weidenau for six weeks and died without regaining consciousness. I had waited in vain.

'I dragged myself back to the convent after I heard this news and collapsed completely. My journeying back and forth in the cold and wet brought on pneumonia. Everything for which I had lived had been taken from me. I was nursed here at the convent and I stayed on to nurse others. There was no longer any question of my going back to England; the war was upon us.

'I was always conscious of my great debt to the sisters of St Hildegarde and knew that I was a great danger to them. I had to be hidden away, for instance, when Frau Professor Röhr, a pretty, harmless-seeming little woman, came up the hill to collect for the Winter Aid Programme, the great national charity.

'I learned more about the Villa Florian when my dear friend Florentine arrived at the convent in 1941, also a young widow. Nothing was taken for granted in those days... I remember how the sisters gently questioned Florentine about her feelings over the persecution of the Jews and then led me forth from hiding. When the Röhr family were transferred there followed our famous expedition to rescue the treasures of the Jugendstil: I was allowed to help, dressed in a nun's habit. I felt a strange mixture of fascination and uneasiness inside that house. I could believe that it was here Florentine had seen a ghost, here that the old Baron sat by the hour, soothing his loneliness with Debussy on the gramophone.

'The villa was given over to its ghosts for a short time, then in late 1942 it was renovated and we heard that it would become a clinic, the Ranke Clinic for War Victims. At this foundation the news was received with... apprehension.'

'Doctors,' sighed Sister Florentine. 'Doctors and the Third Reich. What associations does this topic have for you, Herr Lenz?'

Nicki felt apprehensive himself.

'Nothing good,' he said. 'The medical experiments... euthanasia. But did you know any of this in 1943?'

'The worst things, the experiments brought out at the Doctors' Trial, were known years later,' said Sister Rachel, 'but the convent was informed about other programmes.'

'We visited the sick and did charity work,' said Sister Claudia. 'We were asked to send in lists of those with "damaged heredity" so that they could be sterilised.'

'Well, those who asked knew our views,' said Sister

Florentine. 'And our views on euthanasia. Now that the Abbess had passed on the convent was in charge of Sister Felicitas, the Director of Studies. She was a woman of noble principle, the daughter of a landowner from South-west Africa. She made this foundation a centre of quiet but stubborn resistance to the regime.'

'And you got away with it?' asked Nicki.

'I am the living proof,' said Sister Rachel. 'There was a good deal of incompetence in the bureaucracy... obfuscation, lying, playing off one official against another, these were the weapons that were used.'

'God forgive us,' said Sister Claudia. 'God forgive us all. I was one of those who worked in the new clinic, in the kitchen. Poor Dr Ranke had this chronic lack of staff: one senior nurse, Sister Marlies, and the two medical orderlies, Heinz and Teddy.'

'Teddy?' asked Nicki, bemused.

'Oh heavens, Teddy!' said Sister Rachel. 'When I think of him. His real name was Thaddeus but the shortening suited him... a round fat little man with curly hair. He was far too excitable to make a good nurse. He was a Pole, a Polish prisoner of war, a corporal, that the Doctor had dragged out of a bombed lazaret.

'But I am racing ahead. It was plain from the first that Dr Wilhelm Ranke was no friend of *Rassenkunde*, the pseudo-science of racism which had spread like a blight through his profession. Sister Claudia and the other nuns and lay sisters who helped in the clinic reported favourably on him. He was not a stickler for the bureaucracy or for any of the shabby heroics of the Nazi cult. When he appealed for a Night Nurse to care for a special case, we judged that the time was right.

'One afternoon in September I went down the hill wearing a long grey dress, a white apron, a grey veil edged with white. I was the lay sister Rosa Grün. I came into the Doctor's study at the front of the house and saw this large sallow untidy man seated at his cluttered desk. He asked for my papers. I told him I had none, they had been lost in an air-raid when I visited my family in Cologne. I had applied for their replacement. My accent was strange. He asked where I came from. I told him that my mother, now dead, had been English. He had heard that I had some nursing experience and asked where I had done my training. I told him the truth: Guys Hospital. This aroused his interest. He paused but only for a moment.

'"You are a rare bird, Sister!" he said. "Come with me."

'An important feature of his treatment was peace and quiet: loud noises and raised voices must be avoided wherever possible. Sometimes, driven to desperation, he broke his own rule and shouted for "Himmlischer Ruhe", heavenly peace, at the top of his lungs. Most of the time the house was very quiet, as hushed and still as a battlefield when the fighting was over. Doctor Ranke could treat only ten or twelve patients at a time. Only one or two of the young men... they were all young men ... had suffered physical injuries. Yet the sight of them, shaken, mute, blank-faced or trembling with fear, was terrible.

'Great emphasis was laid on sleep, on regular periods of sleep following a long period of induced sleep as soon as possible after the trauma that made the soldier unfit for duty. So they slept, were forced to sleep, with barbiturates or with other preparations... bromide, baldrian. The notion of leading a man back through his experiences, which the Doctor did very skilfully, was not exactly new. I believe that in certain circles at that time in Germany it could not be used because it smacked too much of psycho-analysis, the method developed by Sigmund Freud, a Jew.

'I have strong impressions of the Villa Florian in its hospital incarnation but I am not too clear about the layout. Sister Claudia will remember more than I do. There was a sitting room on each floor. Who knows where the staff found a place to sleep? Sister Marlies, a gaunt old woman from the Charitén Berlin, slept in a tiny little room at the back of the house, the corner room. The nights were never completely quiet: the patients suffered nightmares, they cried out and murmured in their sleep. One morning, very early, I found Teddy sitting on the bottom step of the staircase.

'"Did you see him?" he asked. "Did you see him, Sister Rosa?"'

'I was afraid that a patient had run away but Teddy was speaking of an old man, an old man in a wheelchair. He said "Not to worry! These spooks can't hurt me! I have a medal of

St Florian, you see? He is the patron saint of my beloved Krakow!"

'On this first afternoon the Doctor led me upstairs to a sitting room; a large room overlooking the terrace, perhaps it was originally a bedroom. Heinz, the orderly, was there, and a young man, a patient, in pyjamas and dressing-gown. He was thin and dark with blue eyes. When he was in good health he must have been very handsome but now he was drawn and haggard. His right arm was awkwardly bent at the elbow and held across his chest; the hand was a stiff claw.

'The young man was introduced to me simply as Tankred. Only first names were used for the patients and only the familiar "du" was supposed to be used at all times. This broke down only with the Doctor himself, it was difficult for us to call him anything but the formal "Sie". This particular name "Tankred" had only one association for me and it was the correct one. This poor fellow was the very foundation on which the clinic was built: Tankred Röhr, the eldest son of that successful party intellectual Professor Röhr and his charitable little wife.

'Tankred could not speak. Though he looked pale and sick he was in his right mind; he had just beaten Heinz, the orderly, at chess. He gave me a polite nod and mouthed a silent greeting. Doctor Ranke examined the young man's paralysed arm, for my benefit, and mentioned that Tankred had been serving in the East. He had just recovered from an attack of typhus. He spoke to Tankred with easy confidence, encouraging the young man to move his lips in reply. Then he led me away to complete my tour of the upper floor.

'I had seen what he wished me to see. The paralysis was functional... it bore no relation to anatomical rules... and Tankred was also hysterically mute. His condition would not yield to treatment; he had the greatest difficulty in sleeping and was unusually resistant to drugs. The Doctor feared psychosis: there had been an incident in which Tankred had tried to steal a safety razor-blade. He was never left alone; he must be carefully watched. It was impossible to separate the fate of this young man from the fate of the clinic itself. Tankred had been slightly wounded during the invasion of Poland and his parents had gone to great lengths to protect him afterwards;

they had pulled strings to get him a non-combatant post. Now they had moved heaven and earth to obtain treatment for his war neurosis. He must not be lost.

'I remember passing through the upper rooms seeing the colours of autumn in the trees and hearing Dr Ranke's deep voice. He practised suggestion on me, just as he did on the patients, to give me courage. That evening, for the first time, Tankred was settled into the back bedroom overlooking the orchard and I became his night nurse.

'At first all went well. The days or nights had a distinct atmosphere which I can never forget. Every afternoon, just as the light was beginning to fade I came down the hill and took the road to the back gate of the Villa Florian. I had my own key. I walked through the orchard, and the scent of the roses that grew beside the path seemed to cling around me as I came into the house and went upstairs.

'Sometimes, as I looked up at the western aspect of the villa, I saw shadowy figures moving about in the rooms overhead. The weather was becoming cooler so I wore a long dark cloak borrowed from the convent. Once or twice I saw in the corridor up above, or in the bedroom, a figure in a similar cloak. I accepted this... it must be one of the sisters, Claudia perhaps, or Ursula or Barbara, who were acting as Nurse Aides. I even played with the idea that the figure looked like myself. I was in two places at once like saints or holy persons.

'Tankred ate his supper in his room. He did not like the other patients to see him eating awkwardly with his left hand. I walked with him round the upper floor or else he spent time in the sitting room. No-one could beat him at chess except Teddy and the Doctor, and they often allowed him to win. Hot water was far too precious for daily baths, there was a strict rota, but Tankred was permitted two baths a week. He was put to bed at ten o'clock; I saw to it that he took his sleeping medicine which was measured and varied by Dr Ranke.

'The back bedroom was a pleasant room which retained its Art Nouveau atmosphere. There was a walnut wardrobe with an oblong mirror framed by carved roses on long ornamental stems. The bed had a matching headpiece with an inlaid central panel of two hands holding a rose. The rest of the furniture was plain: there was a comfortable wicker chair, a locker and a lamp with a white shade. Overhead, unlit, hung the last Tiffany shade in the Villa Florian. It was large and shallow with a pattern of autumn leaves in every colour from deep red to palest gold.

'I read to my patient a little. He chose from the Doctor's library a book of German lyrics and, in translation, a dog story, *Michael* by Jack London. It did not occur to either of us that this author was on the Nazi index as a socialist... his books had been burnt. Tankred had a strong personality. Even in his weakened state I sensed the alert, slightly overbearing manner of the young officer, and at the same time he was sensitive, sentimental, moved to tears by certain lyrics and by the misfortunes of the poor performing dog, Michael.

'One evening when Tankred was playing chess I came along the corridor with some towels and saw the flick of a woman's dress entering the back bedroom. I was sure it was the lay sister, Emma, who brought up the supper trays. Yet when I looked into the room, calling her name, it was empty. I was upset and thought someone was playing a joke. I even thought that one of the patients might be behaving strangely, hiding away from me; what I had taken for a dress might have been a dressing gown. I looked into the wardrobe but all I found was Tankred's dress uniform in fine black gabardine, custom tailored of course, with the insignia of a skull. The non-combatant post found for the Röhr's son was that of a guard in a concentration camp. He belonged to one of the *Totenkopf* regiments of the SS.

'All through the night my patient lay trying to sleep; he became restless; he moved his lips as if in prayer. His paralysed arm was sometimes painful and I put cold compresses on it. Towards morning he did sleep, always; he suddenly dropped off from sheer weariness. I waited for this short sleep period and saw the paralysis in his arm lessen. His hand was no longer a twisted claw, it lay across his chest quite normally. He even began to vocalise in his sleep, to groan, to whisper. He slept sometimes as long as three hours. I would wait until he woke up even if my relief, the day orderly, had arrived. Then at last I made my way down through the clinic as it stirred into life. Sometimes I drank tea with one of the sisters in the kitchen before walking back up the hill in the morning mist.

'Gradually Tankred's sleep periods lengthened. I believed, and so did the Doctor, reading my reports, that his condition was improving. There were one or two warmer days and nights, a kind of Indian Summer, and I found myself dozing off in my chair. Through the open window came the scent of roses ...

'Then all at once, on a certain night, I awakened and heard a voice. Tankred had cried out in his sleep and he had drawn himself up so that he cowered against the head of the bed. I soothed him and he woke up, terrified by what had passed in his dream. For the first time, although it was forbidden, I urged him to speak, to tell me what the matter was. He answered me, choking out a few words before a visible spasm seized his throat and he was mute again. He said distinctly: "*Judith! She is Judith!*"

'It was a puzzle. I wondered, for instance, if I had misheard, if he had said "*Judish*", Jewish, but I knew this was not so. I wrote the name "Judith" upon the little writing block which lay on the locker. Very occasionally Tankred wrote requests with his left hand but he did it so badly, he was so very right-handed, that he seldom used pencil and paper. I showed him the word and he nodded, frowning. He lay trembling with fear for the rest of the night and he made signs for more light. I switched on the overhead light; the beautiful Tiffany shade filled the room with colour. Naturally I wrote this incident into my report the following afternoon, after I had slept myself in my convent room.

'When I came on duty the following evening I found Tankred nursing a book, a new book from the Doctor's study. It was a volume of a history of European Art; he had marked a place. The picture he wished me to see was from the German Renaissance, I cannot recall the artist's name. The woman, luxuriously dressed, with a tight low-cut bodice and a plumed hat, was armed with a huge curved sword. In the folds of her gown she carried a man's severed head; her fingers were entwined in his hair. The title was, of course, "Judith with the Head of Holofernes". This was the figure that haunted the young man's dreams.

'At this point I should have called in Dr Ranke but I knew that he was asleep, after two days and nights handling a violent patient, a yong man from the Italian front. I soothed Tankred, gave him his prescribed medicine, and suggested to him that the dream image would help him to recover. I was by no means as skilful as the Doctor but I tried to suggest that he would wake up at once and speak to me if this or any other frightening figure appeared in his dreams. So the long night took its course, with reading, drinks of barley water... Tankred was quieter, not so restless. I believed that the crisis had passed and wished that the Doctor had been there to handle it.

'At last Tankred fell asleep but I was wide awake. I watched for any sign of a recurring nightmare. About four o'clock, before dawn, my little lamp suddenly went out. In the darkness I heard Tankred moving in his bed, huddling up, cringing away from his nightmare as he had done before. I sprang up and went to switch on the overhead light and as I did so I was aware of a strange, an indescribably strange sensation. It was as if I had walked through a patch of very thick fog, chill and clammy, full of semi-solid particles that stung my face with cold. The light of the Tiffany lamp showed Tankred awake, staring, and he had the power of speech. I knelt down beside his bed and seized his hands. He said: "Sister, I have committed a great crime!"

'I was shocked. This speech was a cliché of mental illness, almost a definitive symptom of melancholia. I soothed him, told him it was not so, but as I tried to break away he, in turn, took my hands strongly in both of his.

'"No," he said, "I am not mad. Let me tell you, Sister. You are a good Christian woman. My mother, my poor mother, is very pious, how can she be told all this! Hear me ... nothing went quickly enough. Shooting uses up too much ammunition, they twitch and roll in the pit, in the mass grave, they can be heard crying, far, far down under layers of corpses. Then there were the vans that used exhaust gas... ridiculous! The women began to shriek as soon as the motor was switched on, as soon as the doors were shut. Once they broke open the floor of a lorry with their bare hands and were dragged along the road in their eagerness to escape!"

'He breathed deeply and went on. "Now the problem has been solved. At peak efficiency they can process six thousand a day. I stood in the midst of the excrement watching the men with hooks tearing the flesh of the dead. I ran into an outer room where they left their clothes and the corporal had found a live child that the mother had left hidden under the clothes when she went into the gas chamber. I ran out into the sunshine and the girls, the young girls, were playing a Viennese waltz, "Roses from the South". I looked up to heaven and saw the smoke from the crematoria. It turned into a great black cloud that fell down upon me. I knew that we were all damned for what we were doing in that dreadful place. Nothing else counted any more. The stain will never be wiped out. I fell down. I would have liked to burrow into the earth to hide from the sight of God. I was taken to the infirmary; it turned out that I was suffering from typhus. I knew that I had experienced a great revelation."

'He was weeping, tears poured down his cheeks. I was appalled by the story he was telling but still, even at this point, I held some of it for his fantasy. I did not know who these prisoners were; I thought of Russians, partisans.

'"Tankred," I asked, "Who are these people?"

'"Why, didn't I say that?" he answered. "They are the Jews."

'"The Jews are being killed?" I repeated.

'"They are being systematically killed off, every day several thousand. The end sum will reach into millions. Some other poor folk, the Gypsies, but mainly the Jews. Every day."

'"Where is this happening?"

'"In the east; Poland. In the Destruction Camps."

'It was the first time I had heard the words *Vernichtungs Lager*.

'"There are several camps for this purpose," he said. "I was at the most advanced. It is called Auschwitz."

'He lay back exhausted. I could not speak. I could say nothing to comfort him. Presently he said: "I have lost faith in him. I have lost my faith. I can see it no other way. It is a crime. A great sin. None of us can ever hope for forgiveness."

'I was like one turned to stone. I thought of my father and mother, of Jonas and of his family in Lithuania, of Aunt Shoshe in the hands of the destroyers. Under the gaze of all these people I saw myself as a creature chosen by God, just as Tankred had been chosen by God. I said: "Tankred, you *are* forgiven. I truly believe that you are forgiven. Do not lose your faith."

'Then he shuddered from head to foot, turned on his side without speaking and fell asleep. I did not doubt that his symptons... the arm, the loss of his voice... were healed. As I thought over what he had said and his words about a loss of faith I realised that he had not meant "faith in God" but faith in *his* God. In the Führer, Adolf Hitler.

'It was still dark outside; I switched off the light so that Tankred would not be disturbed. I was in a state of shock. I lay in my chair feeling as if all the life was draining from my body. A fatal weakness and passivity came over me and left me open to the presence that existed in that room, in that autumn season. I performed a whole series of actions over which I had no control and for which I had no proper explanation.

'I remember standing before the mirror, and what I saw there in the very first light of dawn was the figure from the young man's nightmare. A woman, young and beautiful, but very pale, with long black hair falling over her shoulders. I could feel the weight of that hair, I could feel a vague stirring of triumph, I felt in my right hand the haft of her knife. For she carried a knife and she was grossly contaminated with blood from head to foot. It had smeared her garment, a long stiff gown or dressing-gown, perhaps an evening coat, of deep yellow taffeta. She was naked underneath this robe and she carried against her breasts, cradled in her left arm, a human head. The head of a blonde young man. She spoke to her reflection in the glass and her voice was my voice, at least an English voice, speaking English.

'She or I, the woman I had half become, went about briskly cleaning up. I went into the bathroom and took a bath. I remember lying in the tub and seeing the water red with blood. There was long periods when I knew nothing but acted with a blind automatism. The morning mist was cold on my face; I carried a heavy burden in a leather satchel; my dark cloak was an officer's cloak with braid and a silk lining. At last, in the bright light of the rising sun, just shining through the trees, I came to myself standing at the edge of the Waldsee. One step more and I would have been in the lake!

'My first thought was that I had deserted my post. I had left

Tankred alone. I ran back to the Villa Florian and rang the bell at the back gate. Heinz, the big orderly, came to let me in; I told him that I had left behind my keys. Nothing was amiss, no-one had noticed my going or the strange state in which I had been. Tankred was still asleep and Teddy, on duty upstairs, had already seen that he was much better.

'I waited downstairs in the small front parlour until Dr Ranke was awake and ready to see me. I gave a report of all that Tankred had said and of his nightmares. I was distraught, I wept, but I could not tell him of the strange experience that had followed Tankred's confession. Anything that drew attention from the horrors that he had spoken of, the *Vernichtungs Lager*, anything that destroyed my own credibility as a witness and as a nurse, I had to avoid. So the woman in Tankred's nightmares was simply Judith, a personification of Jewish vengeance; I could not suggest that she had ever had any independent reality.

'Dr Ranke received my report with a kind of sceptical resignation that shocked me bitterly. *He* had heard, certainly, of massacres and mass graves; he knew there were camps in the east where terrible things were done. He had treated a few other men whose duties in these camps had brought them to the verge of madness.

'The feeling of his technique of soothing suggestion being used upon me in this case was more than I could bear. I was brought to the very edge of the abyss. I could very well have explained my deep emotion to him by revealing my true identity. Again I drew back. The danger to my dear sisters at the convent who had hidden me for so long was too great. I could not risk *their* lives if the Doctor reacted unfavourably to a Jewish nurse. His civil duty was to turn me over to the authorities at once, not only as a Jew, but as an enemy alien.

'Wilhelm Ranke was a good Doctor and something of an independent thinker, but in this dark hour he spoke of hysteria. He asked, very reasonably, if all that Tankred had said were true... what could be done about it? At any rate he took over the case at once and prescribed three days rest for Sister Rosa Grün. I remember how I dragged myself up the hill to the convent at last. It was nearly midday, a beautiful autumn day on the Steinberg, but a cloud had settled on my mind and spirit and to this day it has never completely lifted.'

Nicki did not know how long he and the sisters sat there without speaking but at last he broke the silence himself.

'No,' he said, 'no, the cloud has never lifted. I can't understand those who say that it has. I can't understand those ... involved, those who never experienced Tankred's revelation. It sounds very little, Sister Rachel, very little to offer you and all the others, the Jews, but I identify with them. I suffer with them.'

'In the end,' said Sister Claudia, laying her hand on his, 'in the end, Nicholas, it is all that we can do.'

'But Tankred,' he asked, 'what became of him? Could he be *sent back*?'

Sister Rachel gave a sigh.

'I never saw Tankred Röhr again,' she said. 'He had made a complete recovery. He had several sessions with the Doctor, slept the clock around, moved all his limbs and spoke freely. On the third morning Teddy left him sleeping and went down to breakfast. Tankred woke up, climbed on a chair, smashed the overhead lamp to pieces and cut his throat with a piece of the glass.'

'*His* suicide can be explained,' said Sister Florentine, 'as a failure of the vile indoctrination he had undergone. We pray for him still.'

'Think of this,' said Sister Rachel earnestly. 'What if I had taken another step on that autumn morning, plunged into the Waldsee and drowned? Who would have known the part played in my death by the spirits of that place, the Villa Florian?'

'You are suggesting that Kate was acting under some compulsion?' he asked.

'It is a possibility,' said Sister Florentine.

'The woman who appears in those rooms is Tamara Paige,' he said bluntly. 'I saw her too. First as a figure seen from the orchard, then again in the bathrom. They were quick glimpses. The first did not frighten me, the second very much so. I spent one night in that back bedroom... I took a sleeping pill on top of a glass of whisky and slept very heavily. I saw her in a long, vivid dream. She wears the same golden robe in the von Stück portrait; there is a large print of this portrait in the back bedroom, her room. In my dream experience I saw that she was stained with blood... she went into the trophy room. I wish I could remember her words... death, unnatural death...'

'Yes,' said Sister Rachel. 'Something like that. I recall the words: *"You cannot say..."* You cannot say he is dead? I have often tried to remember the words.'

'The severed head is... must be... her fantasy,' said Nicki. 'It is Jacobsen's head, I think, but there is no suggestion that she actually cut off Jacobsen's head. She had a macabre imagination and she posed for von Stück who painted both a "Judith" and a "Salome". Perhaps he posed her in these roles and in her mind it became the head of Magnus Jacobsen that she carried.'

'He drowned, alas,' said Sister Florentine. 'I believe I saw him in the villa. It is my own small ghost story.'

'All we can do, Nicholas, is to tell you to take care,' said Sister Claudia. 'The more you know of the house the less it can hurt you. You are forewarned.'

'I must put in a word for the house,' said Nicki. 'It is a beautiful house... Jacobsen's work, the Baron's concept. Without getting into art for art's sake, I must say that I can't blame a building for anything. A house should carry within it the spirit of the age in which it was built, it should be a responsive place with its own atmosphere.'

'Perhaps you are right,' said Sister Florentine. 'I was very much against Jason Limbard's purchase of the villa. I quarrelled with my brother Felix and the Trustees. Has Jason Limbard changed? He has a new young wife. He was deeply moved by his son's death. Would he ever tell us what happened to Kate on that day?'

'One can work with a man,' said Nicki, 'admire some of his qualities and disapprove of others. He *is* a dominant personality but I can't quite picture him behaving like a monster. I could never get close enough to him for any serious discussion.'

'The little girl is there, so Kate tells me,' said Sister Claudia.

'If Jason Limbard was such a dreadful father,' said Nicki 'how could the mother allow Melissa to visit him?'

'I believe that pressure must have been put on Mary Limbard,' said Sister Rachel. 'Money. Custody. I'm sure

Melissa and her mother are poor while the father is well off.'

'Surely the presence of the brother is important,' said Sister Florentine. 'He is taking care of Melissa.'

'Yes!' said Nicki. 'Yes, he is. The atmosphere is... rather strange at times.'

'Oh, please take care, Nicki!' said Sister Claudia.

'Melissa herself is a bright, out-going kid,' said Nicki. 'I'm sure she is a power for good in that house.'

'It is sorely needed,' said Sister Florentine.

When he emerged from the convent it felt like two in the morning but was in fact only a quarter to twelve. There was no moon, the sky was overcast now with a smell of rain in the air. Dead leaves blew against his legs as he opened the gates of the Villa Florian. The BMW was obedient and quiet as he drove in and the house, when he slipped inside, was the same.

Yet no-one except Melissa was asleep. A tiny chitter of sound from the television crept out of the family room. When he looked in to say good-night he found Jason and his son slumped in their chairs watching an old western – in the original of course. The set had a receiver for the American Forces programmes. What could be more harmless? A dark and grainy film world of men, dead men, badlands, the mystique of the quick draw and the Indians, whose mouths were stopped with dust.

In the kitchen it was warmer; the room had a fragrance of spices. Anja, in a drifting négligée, and Frau Bauer, in a woolly dressing gown, sat huddled together in the alcove. As Nicki paused at the kitchen door he heard Anja say almost conversationally '... completely insane, we are dancing on a tight-rope...' and Frau Bauer answered: 'Hush, drink your tea. This was a chance you had to take.'

When he went in to get himself a drink of mineral water, the two women stared at him wearily; his cheerful greeting was barely acknowledged.

In the corner room he thought of the two women with pity and with curiosity. Franco Tirelli, the dashing racing driver, had been involved in dealings with drugs and more especially with girls. He began to wonder how Jason Limbard had met Anja. Even the Aurora House had a bit of a reputation. It made him feel a prig and a non-sophisticate, but he had to admit that he didn't have much experience of such things. Could Anja fit the picture of a high-class call girl?

Frau Bauer certainly fitted the picture of a motherly old friend from the 'milieu': a retired madame. Hotel trade indeed! He found himself grinning and the grin became fixed when he asked himself another question. How much did Jason Limbard know about all this? It might be another unpleasant family intrigue and he wanted no part of it. This was his last night in the Villa Florian, he swore it.

Chapter 10
At Breaking Point

Melissa was wide awake at once and she lay in her bed, under the new sheet and the big plumped-up feather bed, with its new cotton cover. Another day in Daddy's house in West Germany. She was beginning a letter to Mom in her head.

'Dear Mom, hope you got my card, you must not worry, Roddy is taking care of me and Daddy is not getting out of line. This place has been all done over, you wouldn't know it again, it looks like a million bucks, my room is quite nice.

Mom, I meant to say I saw Kate Reimann first thing when we got here. She is just fine and her little boy is called Peter. And the old lady is okay and so is the cat, still there, over the road. I don't know how Kate feels about being divorced from Andy but she seems to be doing all right moneywise. She teaches school and paints pictures on the side, so Nicki says, but Daddy would not go to her art show down in the town.

Melissa crossed out half a line in her head. Daddy had been rude about Kate once Nick was out of the way. He said she was crazy, and no, Anja couldn't go see her pictures.

There was going to be a lot she couldn't say in the letter. She didn't want Mom to feel bad, they had tried so hard to make ends meet. This trip was part of a whole new deal with Daddy where he paid up half a year in advance. This was about the prettiest room she had ever been in. It had six sides, crazy, and brown tree branches and a special wallpaper between the trees, beginning with flowers and grass, way down by the thick, soft, pinky brown carpet. There was a dressing table in pale shining wood, with the drawer handles shaped like birds, and three mirrors, like a star's dressing room. The drapes matched the wallpaper; there were carved birds on the head of her bed. It was all too much.

On the little armchair sat one of Daddy's presents, a Nostalgia doll with a china head and real hair, long and brown. She was dressed in silk and velvet and she had her own parasol that really worked. Next to the doll sat Bear, wearing his sun glasses. He was old and scuffed, she had had him for years now, she didn't even remember when she had got him. It was the time when she was sick.

She remembered the room she had slept in as white and glaring sometimes, and other times too dark. She could hardly believe that this was the same room. Her memory played tricks. It was like wandering through a wood, a kind of Disney forest, with little April showers and a bright clearing where she remembered everything, then a patch of darkness with spooky trees clutching at her hair. Take the time she was sick. The only thing she really remembered about the St Luke's Clinic was when she was nearly better. Daddy came with Mom, together, and Roddy. Mom began to cry and they told her Buddy was dead.

Buddy. She stretched her eyes wide open and clenched her teeth so as not to cry. Stupid, after so long! Mom had never stopped crying in the night. She reckoned Mom had cried every night for years and still had a weep now and then. Sad movies made them both cry and the tears became tears for Buddy, for Grandpa Hale, for Samantha the cat, for their house up in Penn, but mostly for Buddy.

Funny how she remembered about him. She came out of her dark wood into a sunlit clearing and there were Roddy and Buddy, her two big brothers. Roddy took care of her, sure, but Buddy was something else, she and Roddy both knew it. He was wonderfully clever and brave. He grumbled and cussed and was fat but he knew the score better than any of them.

For a long time she hadn't believed that Buddy was dead. She still had dreams about him coming back, tall and fat and jolly, like Meatloaf, the rock singer, cleaned up of course, or like a young Hoss Cartwright. But Roddy swore he was dead, lying dead down there, all the long years. He knew something he wasn't telling but he did tell her about *the stone*. Down by the lake...

She had hardly ever been to the lake, couldn't remember it at all. It haunted her, that dark lake that she couldn't remember. Down by the lake there had been a big stone, a round stone about the size of, well, a large head. Buddy called it the headstone, joke, like the headstone in a graveyard. And when Rod went down that night he found the clothes and the passport next to a hollow in the ground. The headstone was gone. He tried to tell it to the police, the young Kraut policemen in green uniforms who were swarming all over the place, but he had to tell it through Daddy, because of the language difficulty. Daddy was too freaked out to pass it on.

Melissa had a sudden vision of Daddy and the way he used to be. Roddy always said she had missed the worst, she had escaped after only five years. This made her feel like a quitter. She couldn't remember much that he had actually done but the feeling was very strong. Everyone miserably afraid like they were walking on tip-toe, waiting for a monster to wake up. She remembered waking in the night, hearing an angry voice and the dull, awful sound of her brothers being hit, punched. Yeah, that must have been him, the bad guy, non-Daddy, the one he turned into if you weren't careful. She shut her eyes again and said a prayer: *Dear Jesus, Son of God, don't let him try anything, help him to be good, help me to get through this visit and come home safely to Mom, in Florida. Amen.*

She got out of bed and checked her new digital watch on the dressing table. It was twenty past six. She put on her new terry-cloth robe that Mom had sewed on Mrs Garcia's machine. She took her spongebag and a cake of the beautiful lily of the valley soap that Anja had given her. *Dear Mom, she is quite good-looking and can talk English. Roddy calls her 'The wicked stepmother' but she is friendly and trying to make us feel at home. I'll tell you who is just terrible, it is the HOUSEKEEPER. Think of Mrs Danvers as some kind of Nazi and you have the picture...*

The bathroom was at the end of the hall; at first she had the idea that it was occupied but then she tried the door and it was empty. She quickly took her shower and tidied up, didn't leave puddles, put her wet towel on the heated rail. It was a beautiful bathroom, old-fashioned but lush like everything in the house.

Hey, Mom, the guy who did this house out for Daddy, Nick

Lenz, is a MOVIE-STAR! He played Rudi the waiter in 'Vienna Blood'. You know, the black-haired waiter in the café who passed messages under his tray and turned up in the forest and got shot? He has shaved off his moustache in real life. Roddy says he is gay but I am not so sure. Anyway Rev. Sam says we are all God's children and Nicki is a real nice guy, very cute-looking but shorter than Daddy.

Melissa pulled on her bathrobe again and stood looking out of the window. Would it be okay to eat the apples? Should she offer to sweep leaves? Maybe they could have a bonfire. She drew back a little; there was someone down there staring right up at the window. An old guy was planted among the rose bushes; he wore brown and blended in with the scenery. Must be some kind of gardener leaning on his spade. Boy, could he stare! He was old, really old, his moustache was white. She took a step back from the window. *Go away, Buster, don't you know it's rude to stare? Get lost, Gramps, I've got as much right to be here as anyone* . When she looked again he had taken a step, hanging on to his stick and a branch of the apple tree. He was lame, he was a handicapped person. She didn't look any more and felt bad about telling him to scram, even in her head.

As she came past the stairwell and stopped to look up at the beautiful glass dome there were creaks and rustlings as if people were moving about, waking up the house. She went back to her room and dressed in her best jeans and a new pale blue Fruit of the Loom sweatshirt from Daddy. A holiday. A holiday in Germany with her father and his new wife. Don't make things worse than they are, kiddo. Thousands of kids, millions, had parents who split up and married again.

She looked at her watch again... ten to seven... and wondered how much it would fetch. Not so much as popular items like deep sea rods and diving gear. They couldn't take it, *Mom* couldn't take a custody battle: lawyers, doctors, dentists. The cheques that never, never came on time. Taking care with clothes and food and shoes and postage stamps...

A door slammed, then another... the bathroom?... and heavy footsteps came around the stairwell, almost running. As if a wind had sprung up. Storm warning.

'*Anja?*'

Melissa charged out because she didn't want him charging in. Daddy was at the head of the stairs in his track suit, calling for Anja.

'Hi baby!' he said. 'Sleep well? Anja! Where are you hiding?'

He had a look in his eye and a tilt to his head that she didn't like. He talked too fast and his smile came and went like a blinker light.

'She must be jogging!' said Melissa, following him down the stairs. 'I'll find her, Daddy. Shall I run around and find Anja?'

He chuckled then and put an arm around her shoulders, squeezing too tightly like he always did. Every time he laid a hand on a person, even for an instant, Daddy seemed to leave a mark.

'That's my big girl!' he said. 'You go ahead and do that!'

She peeled off and went towards the family room and watched to make sure Daddy went into the kitchen. She heard him talking German to Frau Bauer, the housekeeper, and her knife-sharp voice replying. The family room was empty, the doors were open for it to air. She went out on to the north lawn, looking for Anja, jogging, but the grounds were empty as well. A misty silence hung over the tall trees and the thick underbrush. She reckoned the old gardener didn't do a very good job because he was so lame. She came past the kitchen garden near the orchard and bent low, running under the kitchen windows right to the outside steps. No-one on the south lawn; the summer house was a sagging grey shape among the trees. Poor Bodo. She wished she could put flowers on the steps for him.

A light morning rain had begun to fall. Melissa went down the area steps and stood on a stone coping to look over the short net curtains, which were patterned with windmills. The basement apartment was small and cute; she just knew that that was a colour TV. She thought of the two of them, her and Mom, sitting there, snug, on stormy nights, watching the colour TV.

Melissa held her breath. There was the couch, still unfolded into a bed, and there was Anja. She lay there in her fancy pink joggers sound asleep under the blue featherbed. Snow White in the dwarfs' house. Melissa knew something was wrong ... there was no question of her shouting out 'Hey Daddy, I found her!' She opened the door at the foot of the stone steps and went inside, very quietly.

Anja didn't wake up. She had a bandage on her wrist; on the low table was a first aid box. Melissa was very frightened for a second, until she saw that Anja had no bandage on the other wrist. Anyway it was an elastic bandage; Anja had some kind of sports injury, a sprained wrist.

Melissa tip-toed across the room to the inside door, opened it and looked into the empty corridor. She whispered, 'Anja!' Up above there were heavy footsteps, she couldn't tell exactly where, and Daddy echoed her timid whisper with another shout of '*Anja*!' Melissa was frightened even more, not only of Daddy and the edge in his voice. There was a kind of tingling unpleasant stillness all around her, in the little bed-sitting room, in the basement, in the entire house, rearing up high over her head. The dome would shatter and break and they would all be cut by flying glass.

'Anja!' she said. 'Wake up! Please, you've got to wake up! Daddy will be mad!'

Anja did wake up. Her eyes flew open, she sat up stiffly like a great doll. She even said in a small fluting voice: 'Mama?'

'Ssh...' soothed Melissa, 'Daddy is *calling* you.'

Then Frau Bauer came in through the outside door. She bustled over to Anja, sat beside her on the bed and put an arm around her shoulders. She looked at Melissa with so much hatred that it made her flinch away. She bared her teeth and uttered a word that even Melissa understood.

'*Raus*!'

Melissa stood her ground and summoned up all her courage but she was losing the battle — she was going to cry, to burst into tears like a baby. Because, seeing these two women, one young, one old, both staring at her with eyes wide-spaced and dark, she suddenly wanted her own mother very much.

'I'm supposed to find Anja!' she said. 'Daddy will be mad... please... I won't...'

Frau Bauer leaped up and came at her, hissing a furious stream of German and a few scraps of English.

'*Out! You get out*!'

Melissa whisked through the door into the basement and ran for the games room, blinded by tears. The terrible woman didn't come after her. She flung herself on a couch and hugged a cushion and cried for her Mom. She knew no-one would hear her; she could only just hear the people moving about overhead. Roddy? He would worry. He should come and find her. She wiped her face on a fluffy towel. Outside the rain had stopped and now the light changed in the room. One of the exercise machines gave a muffled click. Melissa sat up slowly; she had been found.

Nothing bad, exactly. She bet there were a lot of people who could sit in the room alone and not realise there was anything going on. She looked around and saw what a very *noisy* room Daddy and Nick Lenz had set up down here. Her favourite, the merry-go-round, and the big square lift-the-lid musical box that played 'The Bluebells of Scotland', and the little dancing clown on the bar. The fruit machines could let rip with bells and flashing lights and the rattle of coins, and maybe the exercise machines would give off a rhythmical panting and straining, like people working out. Yeah, and there was the burglar alarm at night. If you so much as opened a window for some air, all hell broke loose. Daddy had explained it all.

She saw herself at the centre of a whirlwind of sound, conducting the noises like a band leader, bringing in the snares and the trumpets. She saw super-charged Melissa moving from one noise-maker to another in speeded up action like the roadrunner, setting everything going so quickly that no-one could believe she had done it all by herself. Maybe the room or the power that lived in the room would help her. The levers would move, the keys turn just before her fingers touched them or even when she pointed at them...

The force was with her. *She* couldn't possibly be scared by all these noises, but other people? They would be very frightened. First a little tune, a waltz on the merry-go-round, and then a whump-creak from the rowing machine. Someone might be *caught* in the middle of the room, not able to move while the noise became louder and louder, tinkling, creaking, crashing... The housekeeper, that mean old Bauer, serve her right if she was *caught* and she couldn't take it. The sounds would get louder and louder until she fell down, terrified, holding her head and screaming. And maybe things would start flying around, hard things, sharp things, broken bottles, the darts from the dart board, all raining down on anyone who was *caught*, here in the room, at her mercy...

Melissa sprang up from the couch and cried out: 'No! That's all mean and cruel, and you won't get me doing anything like that!'

So there! And the Force, whatever it was, was *still* with her. It had chosen her and it tried to please her. See how quiet and innocent the room was now, with the pretty model girls smirking on the wall-painting and little golden haired Melissa, mounted on her goose, rocking gently on the merry-go-round. She marched out of the games room and headed for the kitchen stairs. The lure of breakfast was very strong even if she had to get past Frau Bauer and tell Daddy some fib about not finding Anja.

Nicki was shaving in the downstairs bathroom when Jason began calling loudly for his wife again. He had heard some vague commotion a little earlier and supposed that by now a jogging party was underway. Perhaps the shower of rain had caused a delay. He stared critically at the room reflected in the mirror over the handbasin, and wondered if the octagonal tub with jacuzzi had been a mistake. The chequered floor, black and white with tan rugs, was a little obvious, but comfortable. The acoustics of the villa were unpredictable: here he felt encapsulated, cut off. A whiff of perfume from the rain-wet roses came in at the window.

There was another distorted cry and the sound of heavy footsteps directly overhead. Nicki found that he had done the impossible, cut himself with a disposable razor. Blood fell on a white square as he groped for a tissue. Jason in the old bathroom? He ran out, cursing.

He found Melissa in the corridor, hanging back. At the foot of the stairs Anja and Frau Bauer stood gazing upward. Roderick Limbard came padding barefoot halfway down the stairs. He was tousled, without his glasses, zipping up a worn pair of jeans.

'Melissa?' he croaked.

She waved to him, standing close to Nicki. Frau Bauer gave an audible hiss.

'Is something wrong?' asked Nicki.

'My Dad,' said Roddy. 'He saw... thought he saw *her*... Anja...'

'I'm *here*!' said Anja desperately. 'I'm here!'

'Thought he saw her... going into the bathroom,' said Roddy.

Nicki felt his stomach tighten into a knot. He set his foot on the stairs and thought of Teddy, the Polish orderly, protected by his medal of St Florian. '*These spooks can't hurt me.*' The silence overhead was broken by a dreadful cry.

Nicki ran up the stairs and Roderick went ahead of him to the landing. Behind them Anja cried out: 'Jay, Jay honey, it's me!'

Nicki and the young man stared at each other wildly. Roddy was very pale. He jogged nervously on the spot.

'What did he see?' demanded Nicki.

'Her,' said Roddy, 'a woman. He came by, shouting, chewed me out a little.'

Nicki rushed past, heading for the bathroom, pursued by Roddy's voice.

'I wouldn't go in there.'

He tried to react quickly, without thinking, but he could not erase from his mind all his own ghosts and all the horrid tales he had heard. He opened the door and stepped in, expecting the same steamy warmth, rich with attar of roses. This time the room was cold, icy cold, and dark.

The heavy blue curtain was half drawn; Nicki edged past the rattan stand to the window and flung the curtain back. He saw Jason Limbard half lying on the tiled floor, his hands clasped around the pedestal of the marble basin. His gasping breath filled the room. A voice said hoarsely: '*Teufel's Weib*!'

Devil woman. Nicki felt a choking fear which did not lessen when he realised that it was in fact Jason who had spoken. The voice was distorted with fear and hatred. Worse still, it was the wrong voice.

'*Teufel's Weib*!' it said again.

And on a rising note of anguish: '*What have you done*?'

Heavily accented English, a bad, theatrical 'German' accent, and even in that tortured cry the harsh timbre of the parade ground. An officer's voice. Nicki was overcome by fear and yet he sensed the opportunity slipping by. If only he dared question: '*Herr Baron...*?'

In the cold light of the autumn morning Nicki saw that the bath-tub was filled with blood-stained water. Jason, or that other, dragged himself painfully erect, his head elaborately turned aside towards the window. Not looking. Not looking at what Nicki glimpsed between his arm and his body, in the marble handbasin. Face upwards and at a hideous angle, showing the great severed vessels, the features flattened and drained, the spikey peaks of hair.

Nicki had stepped backwards like a cat and his groping hand reached the light switch. He found his voice.

'What is it?'

In that instant it was nothing. The bath-tub was empty, and the basin. Jason was himself again, and in an ugly mood.

'Slipped!' he said. 'Could break your neck on these bloody tiles!'

'Come out!' said Nicki, 'Can you walk?'

'Fine! I'm fine!'

He brushed aside Nicki's outstretched hand and blundered into the corridor. Nicki came out, leaving the door wide open, and found Limbard backed up against the wall, taking in gulps of air. He stood watching the big man slowly gather himself together. Anja's voice came up the stairs.

'Jay, are you all right?'

Jason Limbard flashed Nicki a grin and called: 'Just coming, baby!' His smile broadened, ruthless and cruel. 'Time to get this family in shape.'

He strode off, favouring his left leg a little. As his father reached the stairs Roderick came out of his room fully dressed.

'Come on down, you slob!' ordered Jason.

As the young man went past him he gave him a slap between the shoulder blades that sent him down two steps. Out of Nicki's sight on the stairs, he could be heard talking to the family... asking Anja where the hell she had been.

'Beata saw to my wrist, honey. I have that sprain.'

'We'll keep to the training programme!' said Jason. 'Twice round each of the lawns... let's get going!'

Melissa's voice rose up.

'Daddy, I'm *starving*!'

'You'll run!' he said evenly. 'Then you'll eat. Frau Bauer is getting together a great breakfast.'

They went crowding out of the front door; it slammed behind them so hard that Nicki gritted his teeth. He was alone ... was it for the last time? ... on the upper floor of the Villa Florian. The sun was coming out, shining through the tulip window in the east. Everyone had gone, the dead and the living; he would never know all the answers to his questions. He was still nervous and full of unbelief.

He walked into the trophy room, took out his pocket knife and went to work on the platform. The tongue and groove flooring under the carpet on the dais was solid work, but on the side nearest the window there were signs that the steps, conveniently in one piece, had been moved aside at some time. He ran the knife blade down the dividing line and encountered no resistance; he gently applied pressure and moved the steps a few centimetres.

He bent down and peered through the crack. The musty reek streamed out: an old, dry, foul smell from an Egyptian tomb. He drew back, choking, and then looked again. Some thread of light came in from the other side of the cavity. Red, he saw red. A trick of the light – no, some kind of packing – was it cloth? He did not like the look of the only patch of plaster he could see. It sagged. His idea was more or less correct: the platform was raised over an unfloored area where the base for the stove should have been laid. Packing or debris of some kind had edged down between the joists on to the plaster. It might hold, it *had* held, for many years, until one day there was a crack...

He was covered, of course. He was in no way responsible. The work that *he* had to do was all agreed upon. But he couldn't walk away. He must inform Limbard, even order the carpenter. It would mean a tiresome repair, a few days of dust sheets and workmen in the house. Better than a nasty surprise as the family sat at table.

Nicki wiped his hands on his jeans, bade farewell to the trophy room. He went lightly down the stairs and went into the kitchen where Frau Bauer was stolidly making wholemeal pancakes. He drank a cup of coffee, standing, and carried off a piece of buttered toast. No, he would not be taking breakfast with the family. He wandered away and packed his overnight bag. *Kate, I'm coming. We'll have dinner in Breitbach. I'll take a hotel room for a few days and ransack the art show of its treasures.*

He opened the long window of the corner room just a crack and saw the runners on the farther side of the north lawn. He shut the window again as they turned and jogged steadily towards the house: Roddy and Melissa in the lead, Anja keeping up well, Jason shepherding them along.

He felt in the pocket of his nylon sports coat before he packed it and came up with an envelope. Another account addressed to himself. Yes, of course, there had been *two* envelopes in the box, the night Kate had seen that guy in the basement. He had missed this one. Loose ends. Damn the loose ends! Just go, get out of the house, leave them to stew in their own juice. He ripped open the envelope angrily, ready to stuff it in a folder.

What he drew out was not an account but a single sheet of typing paper, A4. On one side of the paper there was pasted a photograph on glossy paper, cut from a brochure: a piece of furniture that he recognised at once... the ebony gun rack in the trophy room. The photograph stood alone in the middle of the sheet and there were arrows drawn from it in blue ballpoint.

On the other side of the paper there were ten lines of printing in the same blue ballpoint. Block letters. The language was German.

There is a secret drawer in this piece of furniture in the trophy room of the Villa Florian. The two small drawers must be pulled out and the knob indicated on the left side of the rack must be pressed. Then the secret drawer will swing out. The drawer contains some archive material and an exercise book in a brown envelope. This book must be retrieved from the drawer at once and it is for your eyes alone, Herr Lenz. You are our last hope. Do not let any other occupant of the villa see you take this book. Read the contents and act as you think fit. Please regard this communication as absolutely serious.

Someone, he thought dreamily, *has sent me a secret message.* He slipped the page into a folder and retraced his steps, quickly, lightly, without reflection. He climbed the stairs and went back into the trophy room. He spared a thought for the gun rack before he tackled it. It had been locked away in the basement, with other pieces, old and newly acquired, while the top floor was repainted and renovated during the summer months. Afterwards the villa had been under security...

He stepped carefully on to the platform and did as he had been told. The secret drawer swung out without a sound. The archive material, or part of it, was neatly placed on top of the brown envelope. A photograph of Wolfgang von Sommer and his dogs, dated and inscribed by Tamara Paige. A photograph of Magnus Jacobsen, dated 1913. The envelope itself was unused, with an inscription, and not very thick. Underneath, as lining to the drawer, lay an original drawing by Tamara Paige, done from the Baron's photograph.

The paper was yellow and stained – could anything be done with it? He carried the drawing to the window, then out on to the balcony in search of more light. Below him the joggers were completing their first round, moving steadily down the western edge of the lawn, passing the garden shed. Melissa waved to him; Roddy stumbled and ran against his sister; Jason shouted at his son. Nicki stepped back quickly into the room and fastened the balcony door.

The inscription on the brown envelope was carefully written in black ballpoint, in a cramped cursive hand. The writing of a young person. It reminded him of Kate's handwriting, although hers was more developed. The inscription read: *Please deliver this book to Major Jefferson Saxon, U.S. Air Force, Rhine Main Air Base, West Germany or to the next Polizei Dienstelle.*

Nicki felt sick, foredoomed. He slipped the photographs and the drawing back into the secret drawer and shut it firmly. He almost ran back down to the corner room and sat crouching on the day bed. He drew out of the envelope an orange-covered exercise book, 15×21 centimetres, not much bigger than a notebook. The thin book was half filled with the same cramped English-American script. He read the first sentence and shut the book. Then he gritted his teeth, opened the book again and read it through three times.

II

Roddy jogged miserably and tried to get his head right. He had seen it coming, he knew the Old Man's moods better than anyone in the house. The others were innocent, more or less. Old Nicki probably still thought J. Limbard was a respectable citizen. Had Anja and the housekeeper ever seen him really hog-wild? The Kid couldn't remember too well. But the house knew, the house was lurking, ready to play its tricks on the Old Man. Started before he arrived with some story of a burglar in the basement. Now there was this ghost woman in the bathroom.

He must save the Kid, force the Old Man to stick to the agreement. Shape up or we ship out. Not one day with a crazy man. Blow the bridge! Launch the missiles! Out! *He* carried Melissa's passport and return ticket, he could feel the flat safety wallet slapping aginst his chest as he ran. Pick the area of strategic retreat... little Episcopalian Mission in Frankfurt, run by the couple who met Melissa's plane. Money. Take the bus. This was getting into tactics.

There was an unexpected diversion. He was trying to get a word to the Kid, running at his side. The sun was coming out. The design on the long balcony was all in bright colours now, some kind of a goat-man, maybe. Great God Pan. There was little old tricky Nicki on the balcony. With a sheet of paper. The picture. God almighty, he had checked first thing and nothing was disturbed. Now the time bomb had gone up. He lurched against the Kid as he ran and the Old Man cried out: 'Watch it, you clumsy oaf!'

Too much! They jogged on and on, past the garden shed. Good night Bodo. He thought of Buddy, brave as a lion, telling the Old Man where to stick it. Oh, Buddy, why did you have to die and leave me to handle your last will and testament?

On this last round of the south lawn he began to weaken. He jogged better than anyone, he could have done a marathon, but his plans began to cool off. Maybe it was all a false alarm, with the Old Man's temper, and with Lenz and the secret drawer.

The Old Man told them all to wash and dress, ten minutes to breakfast. He was alone with the Kid downstairs while Anja was dragged off to the master bedroom with its own bathroom. He had no pity to spare for her, not even when the Old Man grabbed her sore wrist and she screamed aloud.

'I'm going to cheat,' said Melissa. 'I'm just going to have a wash up there. I already took a shower.'

He didn't push it by asking if she was afraid of that Roman Bath damn place upstairs. Seemed she wasn't. He made some tactical dispositions. Keep things packed, according to the plan. Bear, presents, clothes always packed in the pink bag, ready for an emergency. She said okay. Who knew how much she trusted the Old Man? He took his own shower in the downstairs bathroom. He was singing the chicken song again.

But one thing he managed to do. He had to fetch a clean T-shirt from his bedroom so he checked, one more time. Dad almost caught him coming out of the trophy room. He felt numb. Oh Buddy, oh Buddy, you son of a gun. Why aren't you here to see the bomb go sky high! The gaff is blown. Did I ever tell you I got an A for that god-damned book report?

So he went through the beginings of breakfast in a kind of trance: Melissa tucking into the pancakes, Anja trying to smile and cover up the pain of her injured wrist. The housekeeper came in and seemed to be saying that Nicki Lenz would not be joining them. Roddy felt the old fear crawl along his spine. The housekeeper went back to the kitchen and for the first time they were alone with the Old Man, at table. His father said: 'This is the moment I've been waiting for!'

He got up from the table, flinging back his chair, and Roddy remembered. This was the way it had been. Five years with only the terror of school and then boot camp and the service had left him out of practice. The Old Man strutted round the table. Four people at a table for six; Anja near the terrace, the Kid opposite her and he was at the end, near the archway.

'Together again,' said the Old Man, 'with Anja. We have to show her how the system works... mmm?'

Then he pounced. He found the weak place. He pressed Anja on the shoulder in passing and he came round the table again, past his own place and stood behind Melissa. He sank a hand into her hair and gripped tight, straining her head back.

'*No, Dad!*'

Roddy was choking with fear.

'Keep your place, Mister,' said the Old Man.

Melissa croaked out: 'Daddy?'

He shook her head about.

'Baby,' he crooned. 'Baby, you've gotten very slack, living with your mother. Over and over again I had to discipline your poor mother...'

Anja began to speak in German. He couldn't tell if it was just hysterical babbling or if she was putting across some line so he would release the Kid.

'*Slut*!' said the Old Man. 'You could go back to the gutter where you belong *any time*!'

Without releasing his hold on Melissa he swiped up a great handful of warm blueberries from a dish and flung them in Anja's face. She gagged and moaned and wiped her face with a napkin. The Old Man was turned on by Anja, gazing at him with big eyes, her face and her fluffy white sweater all filthy with the purple juice. Panting, grinning, he wiped his hand on Melissa's shoulder. He changed his grip. Roddy came around the table, half crouching, and struck out blindly.

'Let her go!'

'Get back!' said the Old Man. 'You are out of line, dogface!'

He caught Roddy on the neck and he hauled on Melissa's hair so that she gave a squeak. Roddy went back.

'Now get that goddamned pouch from around your neck!' ordered the Old Man. 'I know what you've got in there. Her passport and her return ticket come to me. We have to cash in that return, baby. You're never going back to that sick woman in Florida!'

Roddy did as he was told. Some time, if he played along, the Old Man would have to let the Kid go and then he would jump him. He would kill or be killed. He would keep at it until he was pounded into blueberry pulp.

He stood up, not looking at the Kid, and slowly unfastened the thong of the safety wallet. He could see through the archway into their old sitting room where they had had the TV. Oh Buddy, help me. Help me get the bastard. He could look through the front window; he saw movement in the world outside. The BMW revved; Nick Lenz drove slowly out of the front gates. Roddy held up the safety wallet.

'Dad,' he said, 'Nick Lenz is leaving. You should get after him, Dad. He has the goods on you. He knows more of the rotten things you've done than any person alive, except me and Mom. If Kate Reimann was a spy, then Nick Lenz is a superspy!'

'None of your cowardly bullshit!' said the Old Man. 'Put the wallet on the table.'

'Let her go, Dad!' he said. 'A little sample of what he knows. Mom drove the van. She wore a headscarf.'

The Old Man slackened his hold on Melissa's hair. He stood still, his cheeks twitching a little, one hand resting lightly on Melissa's shoulder.

'*You* know,' said the Old Man. 'You were a god-damned spy yourself!'

'Not me,' said Roddy. 'I was too much of a coward. It was Buddy.'

'Leave your brother out of this, you lying bastard!'

Roddy laughed.

'Buddy wrote it all down,' he said. 'Wrote it all down in an exercise book, sitting over there in the library. Remember how hard he was working? He wrote it all down, everything... He wrote a *suicide note*... a suicide *essay*! He left it up in the secret drawer in the trophy room and your fancy decorator found it. Just this minute. You'll see!'

'Let's get this straight,' said the Old Man.

He strolled back to his place and sat down. Melissa was pale as death; she began to shake all over. The room itself was colder; the sweat on his face was turning to ice; far away there was music playing. Melissa clenched her hands on the table top, her lips moved. In the basement the carousel was playing a waltz: 'Roving, free as the breeze...'

'Let's get this straight,' repeated the Old Man, trying to control his voice. 'Buddy wrote this stuff down and showed it to you, huh?'

'Nope,' he said. 'He just left it in the drawer and headed for the lake. He said... he wrote down something about "leaving the book to fate" I found it just before we left this house. I read it and put it back in the drawer. I thought of giving it to Jeff Saxon or the police but I didn't.'

'Any special reason?' snapped his father.

'Because of Mom,' he said, '*You* know...'

'And Lenz found it, out of the blue?' said the Old Man. 'I won't buy that! How come he found it?'

'Why the hell not?' said Roddy. 'Lenz is a furniture freak, all the time hanging around with antiques. Today your luck just ran out, Dad. The time bomb exploded. What d'you suppose he'll do?'

Melissa was weeping. Slow tears were running down her pale cheeks. She wiped her eyes with her fist. The music played in the background, the front door opened and shut. The housekeeper spoke to someone in the hall. Nick Lenz walked into the room.

'I'm off!' he said stiffly. 'I just wanted a word.'

It was obvious to Roddy that Lenz *knew*, that he really had the measure of the great Jason Limbard for the first time. *Roddy*, said the voice in his head, *Roddy, you creep, you've done it again. Trading information. Why in the name of God had the stupid guy come back!*'

'The ceiling of the trophy room has a weak place under the platform,' said Nicki. 'A carpenter should see to it. Chance of a crack in the plaster. I couldn't leave without mentioning it.'

'Fine!' said the Old Man. 'We'll certainly have it seen to!'

He came smoothly out of his chair and followed Nick into the hall. There was no-one to beat the Old Man as a quick-change artist. He could go from monster to your genial host and back again in a word, in the blink of an eye. They all listened and could hear only the music.

'What is that tune?' asked Melissa.

'Strauss,' said Anja flatly. '"Roses from the South". The first one was from *The Gypsy Baron*. The next one is best... Poor Nicki, it is his death song!'

She began to laugh and cry at once. She was having hysterics, not loudly, sitting there at the table with a napkin held to hide the berry stains.

'Out!' he said to the Kid. 'Here, take your passport. Mayday. Go to the Mission, like we worked out.'

'No!' she said. 'We have to stay. What will he do to Nick?'

'Get *away*, Liss!' he said. 'I'll stay. Only get out of this house.'

'I can *work* this house,' she whispered. 'I can go along with it, make it do things... the music...'

A door shut firmly. The library door? Melissa took the safety wallet from the table and fastened it around her neck.

He saw that she was growing up, getting to be a big girl, and he wanted more than anything to keep her out of the Old Man's reach.

'Go somewhere and wait,' he said. 'I'm begging you. Go down to the lake!'

'No, not the lake!' said Melissa. 'I'll go down in the basement. The games room. Okay?'

'Okay, okay,' he said, 'only keep out of his sight. Come through the kitchen, that bitch housekeeper ain't there.'

'You mustn't say that,' said Melissa, nudging him.

Anja wiped her face again and looked at the pair of them.

'Anja is Frau Bauer's little girl,' said Melissa. 'Her daughter.'

Anja stood up.

'Hide yourself, Melissa, like your brother says,' she whispered. 'In the basement. Come. You are a good girl.'

The music changed again and even he knew the tune. 'Tales from the Vienna Woods'. Two things happened, almost together. The staircase rang as someone went upstairs and the BMW started up again out in the sunshine.

'Quickly!' he said. '*Schnell*, for Christ's sake! Nick got away. The Old Man will be back!'

Anja took the kid into the kitchen; he heard the cellar door open and shut. He was alone in the dining room with the music playing Nick's death song. There was a sound up above his head, in the trophy room. The Old Man was checking the secret drawer, maybe, or the flooring. Nick had sold him a bill of goods and escaped. Maybe he simply handed over the envelope. The pair of them made some sort of deal.

The music played itself out. There was a burst of excited German from the kitchen, the housekeeper talking to Anja. Now that was some tough mother! He heard the staircase ring. The Old Man was coming down, cursing. Roddy went quickly through the archway into the sitting room and peeped through the door into the hall. He saw his father meet Frau Bauer far away in the shadows. They exchanged a few quick words and went on towards the family room.

He didn't know what was going on or how to play it. The house was unusually still... watching, waiting. He wondered if he should try for the stairs, haul their things, his and the

Kid's. He drew back when Anja came scuttling out of the downstairs bathroom. She had washed her face and her hair; she was still crying. She ran lightly up the stairs. He jumped when the telephone rang, stabbing into the silence. Frau Bauer came to answer it, almost running; the Old Man came along too and stood at the foot of the stairs.

Frau Bauer spoke German to the caller but ever so distinct and ladylike, so that he got what she was saying, more or less. Herr Lenz is not here. And something about München. He is on the way to München. The Old Man gave a satisfied chuckle when she hung up, then he stuck his head into the dining room and called softly: 'Roddy? Liss?'

He flattened himself against the wall of the sitting room but the Old Man went away, preoccupied. When Roddy looked again the hall was empty. He knew there was something screwy going on, some terrible thing was going to happen. He went into the empty kitchen. He looked through the window over the sink and saw the Old Man come running up the back roadway and in through the open back gate.

On the brown tiled kitchen top beside him lay a pair of gloves, women's gloves. They looked like Frau Bauer's: grey leather gloves that still held the shape of her small, hard hands. He began to understand. If he had a minute he could figure out the whole sequence of events. He thought of running down into the cellar, to the Kid, and going over it with her.

Instead, with trembling hands, he took off his glasses, put them in their case, laid the case carefully on the kitchen top beside the gloves. He was shaking as he saw the Old Man come closer. He rushed out of the kitchen and confronted his father on the path.

'Where's Nick?' he shouted. 'Dad, what have you done with him?'

The Old Man was as bad as he had ever seen him, ready to walk through walls. This was an ice-cold, determined, murderous rage that he was seeing, nothing like the old get-the-kids stuff at the breakfast table.

'*Find the book*!' he said. 'Find the book you left for that asshole Lenz to steal from the drawer! Find the book or you are *dead*, Roddy-boy. Dead as your no-good lying fat slob of a brother. I should have drowned the pair of you at birth!'

And at last Roddy felt his fear and his hatred turn into anger. He stepped up and punched the Old Man in the face. The Old Man swung at him and missed. He knew, as he moved in again, keeping his guard up, that the time had come. He could take the Old Man, he had the stamina and a longer reach. He could beat the Old Man in a fair fight.

Then his father sagged and as Roddy moved in again he felt metal smash against the side of his face. The Old Man had never fought fair. Now he hit him twice with the Luger, gripped flat in his left hand. Roddy died then, he thought he was dying, blinded with blood, lying on the path. His father kicked him. Liss was there, screaming like a banshee, and the daylight was fading. 'Good try!' said Buddy in his poor aching head. 'But you blew it!'

Chapter 11
A Fall of Dust

Kate was sleeping. She had come back weary and slightly let down from the vernissage. It was like the first night of a college play... after all the hard work the feeling of triumph at a successful opening was rather muted.

At the end of her long sleep she began to dream. She was swimming in a beautiful marble pool, surrounded by statues and cypress trees. She was swimming with her lover, a dark man; she felt wonderfully settled and cherished; they were happy. The people beside the pool were happy for them. Then the dream began to change into her anxiety dream. It began with a sense of haste, she couldn't dry her hair or put on her shoes. Then she was alone with Andreas, still beside the marble pool, and the quarrel began. He accused her of leaving on the microwave oven. She swore she had done no such thing but he would not take her word. It was unfair, a terrible injustice. She shouted at Andy: 'This is the last time I'll say it!'

Then she was awake in the pleasant space of the guest room, looking out at the tops of the trees. There was a new picture, begging to be completed. The show had been a success. Kate sat up and grinned. The man in the pool had been Nicki.

She heard the thump of little boy's sneakers on the stairs. Peter slithered across the landing on a rug and burst in, shouting: 'Mom! Mom! Are you awake?'

'I am *now*, Buster!'

'This is for you!' he said, breaking into German. 'It's very important. Nicki says it's very important!'

'Nicki?'

'He gave it to me.'

Kate took the brown envelope and gave Peter a hug.

'Where did he go?' she asked.

'His car is still there. He has to go back into the villa for a minute,' said Peter.

Kate placed the envelope on her drawing board, gathered up some clothes and made a dive for the bathroom. Under the shower she felt like singing. Peter followed her and cried out reproachfully: 'Aren't you going to open your present?'

'Is that what it is?' she teased, sticking her head through the curtains.

'He said it was *important*!'

Peter galloped away again into his own room. Kate put on a track suit, brushed her hair fiercely and went back to the studio and the brown envelope.

She read the words on the envelope and, puzzled, she drew out an orange exercise book. She came back to the horror of that summer six years past. Without warning.

My father, Jason Limbard, is a psychopath, a crazy man, almost a murderer. He has always given us a hard time. He has beaten up my mother and threatened her and forced her to do sex things, he hardly cared if we were out of the way. He has beaten up my brother Roddy and me so often I have lost count. Roddy has been hospitalised five times, always in different towns and states, and I have three times. My father has hit our little sister Melissa, five years old. She is this minute lying in the St Lukas Klinik Neu Isenburg with meningitis, which might have come from a bump on the head.

He has this thing where he makes us kneel before him and he doles out punishment. He comes in our bedroom at night and makes a row and drags us out of bed. My Mom tried to overdose on pills seven years ago, not long after she had a baby and it died.

My father has power over Mom and us kids because if it got out how mean he is, we would lose our support. We have to be careful because Jason Limbard is a big up and coming TV personality and a health writer, that is how he earns our support money. At least this has been the pitch as long as I can remember. The truth is that we are all punch drunk and the victims of a crazy man.

My Mom tried to get away and get divorced more than once. There was one time we escaped to Canada with Grandpa Hale, Mom's father. He was a good guy and he really tried to help us but even he couldn't do it. He tried to turn my father over to the police but Mom was afraid. Dad talked her round and he swore to be better. So we had to leave Lake Miscogan where I was happy, the only time in my life, and Roddy, too, and Liss.

A sample of how bad my father is. We had a dog and a cat at the lake. The dog, Blackie, went to some neighbours, but Dad let us keep Samantha, the cat, and take her back to our house in Gifford, Pennsylvania. She was Mom's cat, three years old, black, and sterilised so she wouldn't have kittens. We went back at the end of the summer and on Thanksgiving Day my father poisoned the cat and made us watch her die.

He fixed up a little dish of turkey in the kitchen and brought it in and gave it to Samantha. We were all sitting at table. It was strychnine poison in the food and it acted right away. My Dad raved on at us while she was dying and he slapped my Mom around when she tried to shut her eyes. He said this was what he would do to us all if we dared to leave him. He threatened to kill us, he said this more than once. He would drive the car over a cliff or lock us in the garage with the motor running or get a handgun and shoot us.

I am writing all this down because it is the end for me. I can't take it any more, I have seen too many terrible things. I feel bad all the time, day and night, and I cannot sleep and I want to die. I will leave this book in a special place, in the secret drawer of the gunrack in the trophy room of the Villa Florian, Steinberg 5, Breitbach West Germany. I am giving this book up to fate. Either it will be found or it won't. Oh sure, Dad could find it himself and so in this case I will say, 'Dad, this is what I think of you. This is what you did to us all. Let Mom and Melissa and Roddy go free and get some treatment for yourself.'

On the other hand I guess this book might lie in the drawer for years, along with other stuff that is there. This place, the Villa Florian, is a haunted house. Bad things, murders and quarrelling and cruelty have gone on in this house. I have seen the following things – two big dogs, which are Irish Wolfhounds; the old man who owned the dogs, name of Wolfgang, in a wheelchair; a girl with black hair and a young guy with fair hair, name of Magnus. There are relics of these people in the secret drawer. The times I saw them are hard to describe and they frightened hell out of me. (I am not so easily scared as my brother Roddy.)

The worst thing that was in the secret drawer was a Luger pistol. Roddy found it. Now my Dad has it. He said it was a war-time souvenir.

I expect Roddy could open the drawer again and find this book so I will say to him, 'Roddy, be brave. Take this book to the police either in Germany or the States or send it to Jeff Saxon. This is the only way, even for Mom. You will be doing a brave thing, braver than me, because I am chickening out fast, leaving the book in the drawer and heading for the lake.

Now I will tell the two worst things that happened, one after the other. This crazy villa was part to blame. Dad had this gun and he also saw the ghost dogs. He kept watch and was paranoid about dogs, and in a big thunderstorm he shot and killed Herr Franz Walther's Deutscher Dogge, Bodo. I loved Bodo, he was a real neat dog, everybody loved him. When I saw what my Dad had done, I went crazy and called him a cruel dirty murderer.

I suppose I should say that Bodo *was* only a dog and it *was* an accident. But it was so stupid and cruel, it showed my Dad was dangerous to everything. He should not be allowed out. Anyway, Bodo is buried under the garden shed.

I should now say that a lady called Kate Reimann lived across the road at the Forsthaus. Her husband Andy is publishing Dad's diet books in Germany. One time I bent the front wheel of my bike on the Steinberg and she helped me back to our house and Mom asked her inside although this was strictly forbidden. Dad came home while she was still visiting with us and we knew we were in for a bad time. Dad had to discipline us when she had gone.

But this night Kate came back to the terrace to pick up some bag she left behind and I guess she saw Dad in action. And Roddy saw *her*, he was on the balcony over the Terrace. I knew that in the end Roddy would get into a tight spot with the Old Man and he would spill the beans about Kate knowing.

This happened when we were driving to München. Roddy lost his passport. Dad was going to beat him again so Roddy traded the information and it worked. The Old Man drove straight back to Breitbach, to this villa and I was afraid all the way for what he might do to Mom and Kate. He was in a very dangerous mood. Roddy had spilled the beans good. He told how Mom was letting Kate drive her to see Melissa in hospital.

I tried to warn Kate. On the way back the Old Man was happy, like he was high, and he even let us go into a Macdonalds and get some stuff for our lunch. I went into the toilet there and wrote a warning on a Milky Way candy wrapper. When we came up to the hill here we never drove round the front, we went to the back gate. Dad had us take our bags in again. It was after twelve o'clock and Mom was very nervous when we trooped back in. Roddy was sweating it out, he knew what he had done, he was afraid for Mom. The Old Man took her in the dining room and it didn't sound too bad, he just bawled her out. She was saying she had no idea Kate was a spy.

Then Dad made us get our trunks and towels and he drove us to the lake to eat our lunch. We weren't supposed to come up again until it was dark. I took a chance, going out last, and dropped the candy wrapper on the path.

We did what he said, ate our lunch, waited for half an hour, then went swimming. But I was getting more and more nervous. I went up the track from the lake and I saw our car, the Mercedes, parked off the road, just above the lake. Dad was hiding it out of sight so Kate wouldn't know he was back. I got dressed and I was very nervous and very mad at Roddy for telling on Kate, though who knows I am no hero where the Old Man is concerned.

I left Roddy there swimming and went back up to the road. It was too late. There was Kate's old van parked at our back gate. I went through the fence at a place we had and hid in the orchard. I heard voices on the terrace and I came right through to the back of the garden shed. I saw Kate Reimann and Mom sitting at the table on the terrace under the red sunshade. My Mom was acting very angry. Kate tried to stand up, she was groggy, like she was drunk. My Mom pushed the table at her and Dad came out of the house. Kate was trying to get away. She was on her hands and knees and she fell down the steps on to the lawn.

This is hard to tell but I will do it. My Mom followed after

Kate and Dad was on the steps and he was excited, like he gets when we have to be disciplined. My Mom picked up a piece of wood, it was the leg of an old chair lying on the steps, a heavy piece of old turned wood that Roddy and I had been using as a baseball bat. As Kate got up and tried to run, Mom hit her on the side of the head. Kate spun around and went down. My Dad laughed a little but he was surprised at how angry Mom was acting. I don't know how he expected things to work out. He came down the steps and they both stood staring down at Kate, and my Dad said something like 'Get her in the van.'

Now I will say this, my Mom was acting under the influence of my father. She was putting on some show for him because he had threatened something – like she couldn't visit Baby Liss. This has been his top threat ever since Liss went into the Klinik. I will say another thing although it is so bad. My Mom deliberately struck down Kate because she was afraid of what Dad might do to another girl victim. He was excited and on the terrace he stood over Kate in a bad way, astride her back. Once Kate was out cold, hurt bad, the situation was changed.

I kind of dug in behind the garden shed in a deep patch of brush. I saw them take Kate into the house. My Mom came out wearing a head scarf and she turned the van around, she must have had Kate's keys. Then my Dad came out with a long bundle wrapped in a rug, you could tell it was a body. I thought Kate would surely die. Dad put her in the back of the van and climbed in after her.

Then Mom drove away, quite slowly, along past the road down to the lake, then turning up towards the convent. It was Sunday afternoon, very quiet and hot, and everyone was *verboten* to go in the woods because of fire danger. I guess no-one saw them.

I waited until they were out of sight and then I followed. I thought it was hopeless, they would just run the van off the road or over a cliff or something. I thought of calling the *Polizei* but I couldn't because of Mom. All I could do was follow because I did have some idea where they might be going. Over the back of the Steinberg where Roddy and the Old Man had done some target practice with the Luger. It is a real lonely place.

At the top of the hill I was nearly caught by Mom and Dad coming back. They had been pretty quick. Now they walked arm in arm down the hill on the other road, past the front gate and the Forsthaus. Mom carried a basket with the rug, just like they had been for a picnic. When they were gone I came out of the woods and ran on up and I found the van.

It was at a steep angle against a tree and there was a long hunk of hosepipe taped in the exhaust and turning in through the side window. The motor was running and Kate was in the driver's seat. First thing I did was to tear away the hosepipe. The doors were locked but the catch on the back doors was no good, I busted right in. I knew there was only a curtain between the front seats and the back of the van. I turned off the engine and opened the door on the passenger side and hauled out Kate. I was terrified she would die, and if I would be caught by anyone what could I tell them?

I ran back up the road and there was a fire alarm on a telegraph pole. I broke the glass and turned the knob and it made a terrible racket. I ran away downhill, past the van and Kate, and kept right on going as far as the lake. When I got to the lakeside, by the kiosk, I heard the fire engine coming, so I hoped Kate would be saved. Roddy was still swimming. We met up again but I just said I had been in the woods.

From that time on I have been feeling terrible and it has only got worse. We went back up to the villa at six o'clock, even though it wasn't dark. The car was gone, the folks were gone, but soon they came back and said they had been visiting Liss. They were spooked pretty bad, especially Mom. She was sick, she had to lie down. Dad said the München trip was postponed. He hung around looking at the Forsthaus and I watched too and saw there was a police car, green and white, going by. Then the old lady, Frau Kramer, came back from wherever she had been and she was driven away again in an old Opel with one of the nuns from the convent. They followed the police car.

Next morning there was Andy Reimann come back from München. He rang our bell and Dad spoke to him. He came back in and told us Kate, that crazy bitch Kate, had freaked right out and tried to kill herself in the woods. No wonder she hadn't turned up to take Mom to the Klinik. So he has given us the official version. I guess he and Mom are still nervous about Kate but Dad has been making points. Namely Kate might still die. Kate will probably not remember much when she wakes out of her coma (I heard him say this to Mom), and also Kate is a crazy person. Who would believe a word she says after this?

So early on Tuesday morning I decided to write all this down and I have been working on it ever since, to set the record straight and ease my mind. I have a good cover for all this writing... I am supposed to be doing my holiday essay, 'My Holiday in Germany', and Roddy's book report on *The Red Badge of Courage*, which I am doing for him. I have been working in the other front room, opposite our sitting room downstairs, where there is an old table. I look out at the Forsthaus and see Andy Reimann and the old lady and her cat and I wish I could just tell them.

Once long ago, when I was a little kid, seven years old, Dad broke my collar bone and I was hospitalised in a place called Greenery, West Virginia, under the name of Joey Lingard. I told on my Dad to a Pink Lady hospital visitor named Ida Hogg. This can be checked.

I hear Mom and Dad and Roddy coming and going in this queer, sick, spooky house and it seems to me that we are all ghosts, like poor Magnus and the dogs and all. I must do something. I must change the situation. I can't go on pretending and going along with my father and his terrible lies. Last night I had a dream that I was climbing in the mountains somewhere and I had changed into a completely different person and I was talking German in my dream. Then I had the old dream of mine about Lake Miscogan which changes into a nightmare with the Old Man coming after me. This dream always ends where I sink in the lake. If I didn't wake up straight after this dream I am sure I would die in my sleep. My heart would just stop and there would be no pain any more.

    End of the report written by
     Joseph J. Limbard (Buddy)

Kate sat very still, gazing at the tops of the trees and the grey ragged streaks of cloud. She became aware that Peter was in the room again, watching. He had spoken to her.

'No,' she said, 'No, it wasn't a present, honey.'

He was off again, pounding down the stairs. Kate began to cry. Perhaps the book was a present after all, the best and strangest gift she had ever received. Was this the explanation of Jason's hostility... and, yes, her nightmare, out of doors at night, the leaves rattling, the awful terror... this might be all that remained of that primal scene where she saw Jason Limbard terrorising his family.

It certainly explained her cruel anxiety dream. She had denied and denied in her dream, had wept and cried out for an injustice that could never be put right. She really had not done it. She had accepted the suicide attempt consciously and in dreams she had denied it. In fact she had just woken from a prophetic dream. It *was* the last time she would have to protest this way, in her dreams.

She dried her tears and thought with burning compassion of Buddy and of his mother, Mary Limbard. She firmly believed in every word that the boy had written but his story had not awoken any memories. Yet perhaps it explained her feelings in hospital, her meeting with the Limbard family, stricken with grief but guilty. She thought of Mary Limbard in a flood of tears at her bedside.

Kate drifted across the landing into Onkel Ernest's study and looked out at the Villa Florain. She thought of Andreas. Yes, the 'suicide' had been a major cause of the divorce. She had felt that he reproached her because she had hurt him too badly. She could shut her eyes and imagine them all together, all three, a family, happy enough. Happy enough. She thought of her painting. She might never have begun to paint. Nicki had said, 'You have become a painter.'

Where *was* Nicki? His car had gone from outside the villa. She badly needed to talk to him. Kate went downstairs, clutching the book, and Tante Adelheid was standing in the kitchen doorway.

'*Aber Kind,*' she said, '*was ist geschehen?*'

'Oh, Tante Adelheid,' said Kate, 'it is the most terrible thing....'

They sat down side by side on the sitting room couch and she translated Buddy's report straight off for Tante Adelheid. The old woman sighed and asked questions.

'God forgive me,' she said. 'I kept silent about what you had seen... and didn't remember. I gave that promise to Andreas.'

'Hush,' Kate said. 'I have recovered.'

They spoke in low voices, the dreadful flood of information weighing upon their spirits.

'Where is Nicholas?' demanded Tante Adelheid. 'I saw his auto.'

'He had to go back inside for something,' said Kate. 'I don't know... perhaps he drove down to Breitbach after that.'

It occurred to her that Nicki was ashamed or shy after reading the report. He had believed in the suicide attempt.

'And if Herr Limbard were to know that he had this book...?'

Kate drew in her breath.

'He came out!' she said quickly. 'Nicki came out and drove away.'

Peter spoke from the doorway. He stood half in half out of the room fiddling with the door handle.

'He didn't.'

'Don't play with the door, honey,' said Kate.

'He didn't drive away,' said the child.

Tante Adelheid turned slowly, catching Kate's eye. They both looked at Peter who swung and rattled at the door handle.

'It was the little lady,' he said. 'I saw her from behind the tree. The little lady who wouldn't let me put the letter in the letter-box. *She* drove Nicki's car away.'

Kate was seized with terror. Her had ached. She reached out for the child and drew him close.

'This is very important,' she said. 'Not a game, Pete.'

'No,' he said. 'I know. I really saw her.'

'The little lady, Frau Bauer, the housekeeper, drove *Nicki's car* away?'

Peter nodded.

'She wore gloves,' he said. 'Little grey gloves.'

'Jesus Maria!' said Tante Adelheid under her breath.

Kate stared out at the Villa Florain, looking for any flash of movement. How long had it been? Twenty minutes? Longer. She said: 'I'll telephone. I'll ask for Nicki!'

'If that man answers?' said Tante Adelheid.

Kate shuddered. She had known nothing for so long; now she knew too much. Tante Adelheid marched boldly out of the room and came back with the telephone on its long lead. She placed it on the coffee table, looked at Peter, sighed and positioned herself on the couch.

'The number has never been changed,' she said, dialling firmly.

They waited and Tante Adelheid said in an altered voice: 'Good day, this is Frau Dornberg calling from München. May I speak to Herr Lenz?' Then, nodding her head: 'Yes, yes, I understand. Thank you very much. *Wiederhören*!'

She replaced the receiver gently.

'Frau Bauer,' she said. 'Herr Lenz is not there. He is driving to München.'

'You said you were someone else!' said Peter.

'I lied,' said Tante Adelheid. 'And so did Frau Bauer. Katherine, we must get help. Something has happened. We know what that man is capable of.'

'Pete,' said Kate, 'go upstairs!'

'Aw, Mom!'

'Go up to the study,' she said. 'Look out at the Villa Florian and tell us if you see anyone, anyone at all, inside or out.'

'Okay!'

He went thumping up the stairs.

'There are a lot of people in that house!' said Kate. 'Anja, poor girl, Roddy and Melissa... how could Jason and Frau Bauer *detain* Nicki?'

'The auto,' said Tante Adelheid. 'It is the proof. We must find his auto.'

'There is a place Buddy mentions in the book,' said Kate with an effort. 'Among the trees, just at the turn-off down to the Waldsee. I could slip around and look.'

'No! You must not go adventuring on your own.'

'At least we would know,' said Kate. 'This could all be nonsense. Maybe Nicki *did* get Frau Bauer to move his car. We must find out one way or the other.'

She looked out of the window, hoping Nicki would appear, knowing he would not. Something *had* happened.

'I will call Franz Walther,' said Tante Adelehid. 'It is an emergency.'

'Perhaps his boys could drive down the back lane,' said Kate. 'The Wood-chopping Boys... Nicki calls them that.'

She laughed unsteadily. She left Tante Adelheid alone to make the call. In the hall she heard Peter's voice.

'I saw the big girl!'

She ran up the stairs and joined him in the study.

'Who was it?'

'The big girl. Melissa.'

'Where did you see her, Pete?'

'She came around to the front and then ran right back around the house, as if she heard something.'

'That's all you saw?'

'She did something to the big gates. I thought she was going to open them up.'

'Ssh!' said Kate.

She reached across Onkel Ernst's desk and opened the window. It was a day of fitful sunshine, the sky was filled with tattered banks of grey cloud. On the Steinberg it was very still. Kate looked at her watch and saw that the time was exactly a quarter to eleven, quarter to eleven on a Saturday morning. The postwoman had been; no delivery vans ground up the hill; no cars went by. The only sound was high and sharp as the cry of a bird.

'Do you think,' said Peter, embarrassed, 'it would help for us to ring up Daddy? He could... he could maybe speak to Diet Jason.'

Kate felt her eyes fill with tears.

'No,' she said. 'It's a good idea, Petey, but Daddy is just too far away.'

She thought of Andreas suning himself on an Italian beach with a rush of the old resentment which was strong as remembered love. Unbelieving beast! She imagined handing him Buddy's book... there, there, read it for yourself! How will you handle your top client after this? And Andreas still did not quite believe, he began making excuses. Who could be sure? Buddy, poor boy, was not reliable. He was disturbed, a suicide, he hated his father...

Then where is Nicki? What has happened to him? Is he driving to München without a word, without saying good-bye? Is there going to be another accident?

'Peter,' said Kate, 'I want you to stay here, in the house. Keep watch, okay? Promise you'll stay here!'

'I promise.'

Downstairs Tante Adelheid was still seated before the telephone.

'Franz and his boys are coming,' she said, 'and I called the Sisters. Help is on the way. Franz Walther said a strange thing.'

'What?'

'He said: "This book may not be as important as it seems. Other evidence could still exist!"'

'Now what is *that* supposed to mean?'

Kate snatched up the orange-covered exercise book; she wanted it to be important. She wanted it to be true, every word, and the only existing record. She knew what she must do but she could not look Tante Adelheid in the face or even say good-bye.

'Just stay here, with Peter. *Please!*'

Kate walked out of the Forsthaus, seeing only the Villa Florian, white and stark among its autumn trees. She crossed the road, rang the right-hand bell long and hard, then planted herself before the double gates, holding the orange book in plain view.

She directed all her will-power at the house and at Jason Limbard. *See what I have for you! Make him look out...* She conjured all the spirits of the dead, pictured them trailing across the lawns. The fountains would play and Tamara Paige, her fellow artist, would stroll about with the Baron's wolf-hounds. *Buddy*, she thought, *old good-buddy, my rescuer, where are you amongst these ghosts*? She peered at all the windows on the façade. *Send me a sign! I won't be afraid.*

A furtive wind made the dead leaves whirl across the gravel, 'like ghosts from an enchanter fleeing'. The double gates moved, one after another, sending a ripple of movement through Jacobsen's springtime girl.

Kate reached up, seized a bar of the right-hand gate and set a foot on the lowest curl of the nymph's draperies. She pushed and the catch, half unfastened, yielded to her weight. She rode inwards, clinging to the iron maiden, and dropped to the ground.

The front door was opened cautiously and Frau Bauer came out. She stood under the pillared porch looking back into the villa and then at Kate, gathering herself together. She came quickly down the steps and they met halfway to the front door.

'What are you after?' demanded Frau Bauer. 'How dare you!'

The stream of traditional protest dies on her lips. She stared up at Kate; she was grey-faced under her tan, her eyes fathomless and dark.

'Nicholas Lenz!' said Kate. 'Where is he?'

'Get away!' said Frau Bauer in a low voice. 'Get away, you silly cow, we've got enough trouble!'

Towering over the little woman, Kate held up the orange book.

'Give it to me!' said Frau Bauer. 'He wants it. For God's sake let me try...'

'*Where is Nicki*?'

'Give me the damned book!'

The little woman snatched for the book tigerishly, clamping a hand on Kate's arm and baring her teeth with effort. Kate, a big girl fighting a little one, pushed her hard in the chest with the flat of her hand and dived for the open door of the Villa Florian.

The hall was still and beautiful. She saw how the golden carpet warmed the cold light from the dome, transformed it into a golden rose. All was new and perfect; the whole house was perfumed with roses. In the shadows high above her head there was a hanging lamp with brass chains and lustres of coloured glass that caught the light. Kate saw that she was not alone in the hall. Far away, separated from her by bars of light and shade, there was a woman in a yellow dress. She reached up, took down a dark cloak from a rack and slung it about her shoulders.

Frau Bauer came in behind Kate and broke the spell. Jason Limbard's voice rang out: 'Who was it, Frau Bauer?'

Kate strolled into the dining room. There was Jason, larger than life, but no longer handsome. He had grown old and mad; a bruise on his jaw was oozing blood; his features were thickened and congested. She thought of Blümig, the Baron's servant, hideous and bloated in death, a caricature of his master, and saw that the damask tablecloth was deeply stained.

There were three persons at a table for six; Anja, very pale, rigid with fear, sat at Jason's left. Opposite her was Melissa, a big girl now, a child who knew far too much. Their eyes met. Melissa blinked and her glance slid away towards the ceiling over Kate's head.

'Why, Kate, take a seat,' said Jason. 'Frau Bauer is bringing more coffee. Are you all better, Kate? What the hell are you doing in my house, Kate?'

Kate perched on the edge of the nearest chair, her back to the archway. She had been holding the book behind her back, like a shy lover with a bunch of roses. Now she brought it out.

'Where is Nicholas Lenz?' she demanded.

At the sight of the book Jason was shaken by a wave of emotion. His face worked, he gagged. When he could speak he said; '*That's my property*!'

Someone else was missing. Where was Roderick Limbard, the other poor devil of a son?

'Quiet, you crazy bitch!' said Jason. 'That book belonged to my dead son. If Nick Lenz gave it to you he had no right. Leave it right there on the table and get out!'

'Not without Nicki!' said Kate. 'Buddy's book is one of a kind. There isn't another copy. We'll make a trade.'

'You've read this thing Buddy wrote'

'Sure,' she said, 'but my memory is not so good.'

'Read me a little,' said Jason. 'Put me in the picture.'

'You won't like it!'

'*Do what I say*!'

He smiled, shook himself a little. His right hand, holding the Luger, came over the table top at last.

'*Read*!' he said.

Kate felt a kind of cold exhilaration. She got a glance at Anja and saw that she was straining back in her chair in terror. Melissa was deathly pale; she moved her lips and pleated the tablecloth between her fingers. *I will get us all killed*, thought Kate. She looked for something to throw at Jason, lined up a heavy jar of maple syrup. She flipped back and forth through the book and began to read aloud from the first paragraph. Buddy laid it on the line pretty well.

'*My father, Jason Limbard, is a psychopath, a crazy man, almost a murderer. He has always given us a hard time. He has beaten up my mother and threatened her and forced her to do sex things, he hardly cared if we were out of the way.*'

'Stop that!' said Jason hoarsely. 'How do I know what he wrote? Give the book to me and get out. Lenz has gone to München. These girls will all say the same. Eh, baby?'

He swerved the long barrel of the gun vaguely in the direction of Anja.

'Yes, Jay,' she said. 'Yes, he drove away early this morning.'

'Melissa?' he asked.

Melissa said faintly: 'Daddy, I can't...'

'Speak up, baby!'

'Daddy, I can't lie!' said Melissa in a loud, ill-controlled voice.

'I wouldn't want you to lie,' soothed Jason. 'Where d'you think Nick has gone?'

'He came back in here,' she said, looking down at her fingers, still pleating the cloth. 'He said there was a crack in the ceiling.'

The room was unnaturally still for a moment. Kate heard a car pass in the back lane, a Volkswagen. She heard a grating sound, directly overhead. Frau Bauer came in from the kitchen with cups of coffee on a tray. She set one down before Jason, ignoring the gun he held, moved closer to Anja, set down another. Then she raised her eyes and cried out.

The grating sound had come again, much louder. Kate looked away from the gun and saw a long fissure open up in the smooth plaster of the ceiling. It ran from the new archway almost to the hanging lamp, which sagged and jolted. Timber began to break and splinter; plaster trickled through the gaping edges of the crevasse. Kate shielded her eyes and leaped away, towards the glass doors.

'Stay where you are!' shouted Jason, coming to his feet.

The disturbance overhead stopped; an eerie stillness settled in the room again. They waited as if for another earthquake shock.

Melissa said: 'That's where he is, Daddy. You locked Nick in the trophy room up there.'

'Throw me the book, Kate,' said Jason. 'I mean it!'

He raised the gun. The room began to shake; a network of cracks ran across the sagging ruin of the ceiling. Kate flung the book at Jason and he caught it in his left hand. There were women's voices in the corridor and the room was invaded. Tante Adelheid and Sister Claudia stood in the archway, Mrs Greenwood at the door.

'What!' cried Sister Florentine, coming in with the rest. 'Will you shoot us all, Herr Limbard?'

Then they all cried out, pressing back against the edges of the room and their voices were drowned. With a dull roar the ceiling split wide open. A heavy mass, dark red, urged itself like a monstrous birth through the broken place. It fell slowly, struck the table with a sharp crack of old bone and slipped to the floor beneath. The room was filled with a choking cloud of evil-smelling dust. Kate saw a skeleton hand, wrapped in parchment brown skin that rattled on the bone, detach itself from the vile mass and land at her feet.

The four old women stooped, then knelt down. Sister Rachel flung back one fold, then another of red plush, dry as dust. They all reached out to complete the unwrapping. Sister Claudia began to pray. Eddies of dust curled in the room. The light had taken on a queer reddish tinge.

On the red cloth there lay the mummified body of a man, its crumbling tissue held together by the clothes, dark trousers and a coat that had once been royal blue. The laced boots had been displaced, taking with them the feet. One hand had disintegrated. Kate bent down, lifted the remaining hand carefully and laid it in place.

'Who is it?'

Kate did not know who asked the question. Perhaps it was Frau Bauer.

'It is Jacobsen,' said Sister Florentine tenderly. 'It is Magnus Jacobsen, the architect.'

'I wonder where...?' said Tante Adelheid.

She was patting about in the remaining folds of the red curtain. Anja uttered a long, soft, echoing cry.

'It is not here,' said Sister Rachel. 'His head is missing. It has been severed at the neck.'

Kate slipped quickly past them without a word and stumbled tnrough the sitting room into the corridor. The whole interior of the Villa Florian was suffused with dark red light. The golden shape upon the carpet turned blood-red before her eyes and cool waves of light, deepest red, washed upward towards the dome. She turned, and through the open front door she saw the dome itself reflected in the windows of the Forsthaus, a huge, crimson rose.

She set her foot upon the stairs, knowing that she must not be afraid. As she climbed up through the waves of unearthly light, Roderick Limbard came down the hall holding a towel to his face. He called out to her but Kate could not stop.

She rattled at the door of the trophy room, purpled by the blood-light. She ran through the summer bedroom out into the daylight on the long balcony. The old wooden jalousie was lowered and fastened on the door and on the window but the fastenings were on the outside. She ran them up and peered into the room but could see nothing.

She looked about and found a doorstop on the balcony, the stone figure of an owl, weighted at the base. She beat and beat at the double glass until it shattered. At last she was able to raise the window and climb in.

The red light was fading away. There was little destruction visible in the trophy room: the floor sloped inward on either side of the dais and the steps had detached themselves from the rest of the platform. Kate crept along the edge of the room and found Nicki lying beside a chair, under the stag lamp.

There was so much blood that she thought he was dead. Most of it had come from a scalp wound and a bleeding nose. There were damp blood-stained towels in a heap on the carpet. She untied his hands and feet, wiped a little of the blood away. She did not dare move him. She looked hoplessly at the locked door and cursed Jason Limbard and cursed the Villa Florian. She wrenched aside the steps and stared down through the gaping hole in the ceiling beneath. She began shouting for help: someone must come with a key: someone must call the ambulance. Then she sat with his poor wounded head in her lap.

Presently Nicki tried to open his swollen eyelids. He said distinctly: '*You cannot say it was a natural death*!'

Then he said 'Kate!' and 'Has he gone?'

It was only at this moment that she realised Jason *had* gone. Roddy had been crying out in the hall 'Where's the Kid?' Jason Limbard had slipped away, taking Melissa with him.

Chapter 12
Strange Readings

She was half dragged through the kitchen, out of the back door and into the orchard. It all went so quickly she hardly had time to catch her breath.

'Daddy, no need to *pull*!' said Melissa. 'I'll go with you.'

Now they were walking slowly along the back road, trying to be normal. He had the gun in his waistband, under his jacket, he carried Buddy's book under one arm. His right hand gripped her wrist but not all the time. She knew they were going down to the lake but still she was not afraid. He gave a dry chuckle.

'Roof fell in!' he said. 'Some crack in the plaster! You suppose Lenz knew how bad it was?'

'No,' she said. 'No-one knew.'

There was a lot she could not explain. It started when she went back down to hide in the games room. She couldn't settle, she was so sad and frightened because Daddy had freaked out. She was worried for Nick Lenz and for Daddy in case he had killed him. She prowled around the games room and said, 'Where is Nick Lenz?'

She was near a framed poster of a lady with a blue rose. Suddenly the room was dark, all going away from her like a dream sequence, and in the glass of the picture she saw Nick lying in the trophy room. Then a redness spread through the scene and instead of Nicki there was another guy, taller and with blonde hair, lying on that awful enormous red curtain. She knew he was dead and what she was seeing was a flashback. Something worse was coming so she switched off. She said 'No more!' and she was obeyed.

She couldn't stand it in the games room for much longer. She sneaked out through old Bauer's apartment again and came up the outside steps, then ran around to the front of the house. She had some idea of getting help, of seeing the old lady with the cat, Frau Kramer, or Kate Reimann. She tried the nearest side gate but it was locked, you had to use a key or the electric buzzer, even to get out. So she was trying to open the big gates when the house called to her. It was like a light going on in her mind.

She ran round to the orchard and found Daddy beating up poor Roddy on the path. He had them all going along with him after that. Roddy had been their only defence and now he was out of action. Anja and her terrible old lady helped to take poor Rod into the downstairs bathrom. Daddy said something about second breakfast being a German custom and ordered more coffee. She hated the idea of sitting at table with him; she was afraid.

When Kate came with the book, Melissa knew what she had to do. The power of the house was with her, stronger than ever, as she pushed and worried at the crack in the ceiling.

'Something came through the ceiling!' she said aloud. 'Did you see?'

Her father glanced in her direction but said nothing. Melissa felt a dull aching sadness – for him, for the house, for the way things had turned out. She saw that someone was ahead of them on the road to the lake. It was a woman in a long black cloak, carrying a leather bag, trudging along the way they were going.

They went on, through the tree-shadows and the cloud-shadows lying over the road. Then they were at the turn-off to the lake and there was a white automobile – Nicki's car? – parked in among the trees. Daddy marched her over to the car. Melissa was suddenly very much afraid; driving away with her father scared her a hundred times more than going down to the lake.

She strained away from him and suddenly he let her go, so that she nearly fell. He went to the hood of the white car and Melissa saw that it was raised, just a little. Daddy threw it back and looked into the engine and he went wild. He cursed and swore, looking around at the woods, and he drew the terrible gun again.

'They're here!' he said, putting his face down to hers and gripping her arm. 'They fixed the car!'

'Who is it?' whispered Melissa.

'God-damned spies. Out to get me. Bastards!'

She looked into his angry face and felt hopeless. They didn't go back to the road. He dragged her around behind the car and they went into the trees. They walked more slowly over the thick carpet of the fallen leaves. The woods closed round them; they were under a spell. The wind sounded in the dark firs and overhead there was a pattern of bare branches and coloured leaves against the sky.

'Daddy!' she said.

He stood still, panting, and stripped off his jacket. There was a fallen tree trunk and he sat down. He was pretty bushed. He took Buddy's book and flipped through it, and she didn't think this was a good idea, it would only make him mad. But the way he handled the book showed that he couldn't read it too well without his glasses. Daddy was long-sighted. He set the book down on his jacket and it slipped into the leaves. Melissa took a step nearer and picked it up.

'Daddy, please listen!'

'What is it?' he growled.

'Whatever bad things have happened,' said Melissa, 'we shouldn't run away.'

'What the hell are you talking about'

'Okay,' said Melissa, catching her breath. 'Whatever bad things *you have done*... like that with Nicki, you hit him, and with Roddy... and that things years ago, with Kate...'

'With Kate?' he said grimly.

'You can't run away,' she said. 'You must *just stop*, like an alcoholic never taking another drink. We wouldn't desert you. God wouldn't desert you. There was a reason you did all these terrible things, maybe it was because of Grandpa Lombardini. Mom told me it all. How he was a cook and made you slave in the kitchens. You could *just stop*, and even if you went to jail it wouldn't be the end of the world!'

He said something very softly and raised the gun until it was pointing at her face. She couldn't imagine being dead. It was impossible. She was going to be a singer, a dancer, a swimmer, a great discovery. High up overhead, in the bare branches, birds flopped about noisily. Daddy grinned and looked up, shading his eyes, then quickly stretched up his arm. The shot made a sharp crack and a big bird, a crow, came hurtling down. It landed with a thud so close to Melissa that she shied away, putting up an arm before her face.

'Keep going!' he ordered.

She didn't look at the dead crow. She had struck out; everything was finished. The woodland sloped gently down towards the lake. She looked down a long tunnel through the trees and saw the woman standing on the lake shore. Swinging the black bag back and forth, back and forth, then letting go. She saw the water come up but heard no splash.

Something moved in the fallen leaves at the base of a tree and Melissa jumped. Her father laughed:

'It's only a squirrel!'

He pointed with the gun and she was afraid he would kill the squirrel.

'Don't, Daddy!'

The squirrel was hurt; she could see it crouching in the roots of the tree. Her father stooped down then cursed, drawing his hand away.

'Little devil bit me!'

The squirrel was gone, burrowing into the leaves. Daddy wrapped his left hand in a handkerchief and she saw the little spot of blood.

She could see the lake coming closer through the trees. Then they were right down on the lake shore and it was a terrible place, bad as her nightmares. The trees only grew down to the water's edge in one place where it was very steep. There were patches of grey stone and the dusty road leading around the shore. The wooden seats and picnic tables looked bare and neglected this time of year.

The lake itself was smaller than she had expected and its water was black. The lake was old as the hills, it had been there forever, black and cold and deep. It was like a tar-pit full of mammoth bones and the puny skeletons of human beings, sucked right down into its depths a thousand years ago – or just six years, what did it matter to the lake?

They had crossed the road now and they stood on the rocks, looking out over the dark water. In the distance there was some kind of horn blaring out: it wouldn't stop but kept on sounding an urgent two-note call. It was the ambulance or the police or even the fire brigade.

'Time to go! said Daddy.

He fastened on to the back of her neck with his left hand, still strong and hard, even if the squirrel had given his a nip. He ran her a few steps forward and then pushed so that she really thought she was going into the water. Then he pulled her back.

An engine started up with a roar and an old green Volkswagen came barrelling down the road through the trees, drove past them and parked. Daddy tucked his shirt in, slicked his hair, arranged his jacket over his arm to hide the gun. The two young German guys were climbing out of the car; one was short and dark, the other tall and fair, with a beard. Not policemen or anything, though they had short haircuts. Just innocent bystanders who were going to get themselves shot if they messed with Daddy.

'Take it easy,' he said. 'I know who these guys are.'

The two men came up to them, smiling. Melissa suddenly had the feeling they were in a hurry. Then it was *'Guten Tag'* and they all shook hands, even with her. Her hand was dirty and sweaty, she was sure of it. Daddy had effortlessly changed over with the jacket and the gun so that *he* could shake hands.

There was something very strung out about the fair guy, Sepp. He said her name and gave her a hard look, as if he was trying to pass a message. Then he fixed his eyes on her father's face. His eyes were grey-blue, he was tanned heavily, like his brother. They both had a kind of rumbling way of speaking German.

Daddy was spinning them a line, she could tell. He looked very sad, pulled down the corners of his mouth. Then he reached out and stroked Melissa's hair. The fair guy nodded, very solemn, and said in English: 'Maybe Melissa should come back to the villa in our car; Herr Limbard?'

He looked at the sky, said something to his brother who agreed. Then in the same thick, creaking voice, Sepp said: 'Going to be a thunderstorm.'

'No need for that,' said Daddy. 'We're making our own special pilgrimage to the lake, eh baby?'

She could not speak. She thought, quite seriously, of doing

her best racing dive into the lake and trying for the other side. Surely these two guys wouldn't let Daddy take a pot-shot at her?

'A pilgrimage?' repeated Sepp.

'There was a tragic drowning accident here,' said Daddy. 'My boy, my son, went into the lake.'

Sepp cut in on Daddy.

'Round the shore a little,' he said. 'There... right about there. You lost your son. Damn near. Or maybe you did lose a son – *Herr Limbard*!'

She couldn't figure out what Sepp was getting at. Something was happening to Daddy, he made a choking sound and every scrap of colour drained out of his face. He tried to speak but couldn't. He reached out, automatically, and pulled Melissa to his side.

There was a sound behind them and a sharp command, in German. Melissa looked back over her shoulder and saw an old guy in a green jacket, with silver buttons. Herr Walther, the forester, with his double-barrelled shot-gun nearly touching her father's back.

'Do what he says!' ordered Sepp. 'Drop the gun and let Liss go free. Or he'll shoot you like a dog!'

Melissa felt a light touch and it was Herr Walther, patting her arm. She walked backwards; Daddy had set her free. She kept on walking away from him. They all walked away from him. Daddy let his jacket with the gun fall on to the rocks and the dark man, Armin, whipped in and gathered it up. Daddy turned right round in a circle. There was no sound except his panting breath. Then, far away, there was a rumble of thunder and running footsteps, getting closer.

Roddy came down the road. He looked terrible, the side of his face all black and swollen. She wanted to cry out and stop him, say it was all over, she was safe. Daddy didn't have a gun any more. But Roddy came on down and he hit Daddy another time. They all stood and watched. It was cruel and horrible. Daddy hit back but Roddy was quicker and stronger. She began to scream again and this time it was for Daddy, the beaten one.

Daddy went back and back and then he turned and went diving into the lake. The water came up in a mighty splash and she shut her eyes as the drops fell on her face. When she opened them her father was swimming strongly for the shore. The water was blacker than ever; the storm was coming and a wind was making waves across the lake. They stood and watched him go, Sepp and Roddy and Melisa. All three of them. Then Roddy fell to his knees. She would have gone to him but Herr Walther slung his shot-gun over his back and said gruffly: '*Komm! Komm, Kind*!'

She felt too sick and weak to do anything else. He walked her up the road.

'The boys take care of him,' he said.

They walked along together and she was still clutching the exercise book, Buddy's book, that all the fuss was about. She felt really weird, light in the head, as if she might faint or something, right there on the road. Was it always this way when a miracle happened?

She whispered 'That man... that boy? What kind of a name is *Sepp?*'

Herr Walther looked at her, and he had a kind, sad face. He seemed to understand what she meant even if his English wasn't so good.

'*Sepp*,' he said, '*Sepp ist Josef.*'

'Joseph,' she said.

The rain began to fall; Herr Walther smiled at her; he grinned. She felt a smile growing on her own face. The storm broke overhead and they ran for the back gate of the Villa Florian.

Roddy knelt on the stones by the lake and strong hands hoisted him up. A voice said: '*Komm, Bruderherz*!'

The pair of them were holding him. They were brothers. They were all brothers. They sat him at one of the crazy picnic tables and gave him a silver flask of schnapps. He tried to push it away but they laughed.

'The Kid,' he said. 'Melissa.'

'She'll be fine. Franz took her back to the house.'

The voice. Rusty, half-German. He thought of a place in the book where it said something about turning into another person. But hadn't that been a dream? He lifted his head and the rain ran down his face like tears.

'Have some Schnapps,' said Buddy. 'You're going to need it!'

II

In the softly-lit hospital room it was easy to lose track of time. Kate held Nicki's unbandaged hand and tried to look him in the face without flinching. It was nearly six o'clock in the evening, Sunday evening; she had hardly left his side.

'He's very tired,' she said, 'perhaps we should wait.'

'I can go on!' croaked Nicki.

'Just clearing up a few points,' murmured Police Commissar Franke.

He was a man of about forty, good-looking, rather flat-faced, with a dashing moustache. He was extremely neat in his pullover and checked sportscoat but wore no tie. Kate had to admit that he didn't look like her idea of a policeman.

'Herr Lenz,' he said, '*why* do you think Jason Limbard ran amok? What triggered off his outburst?'

'He was extremely restless... couldn't sleep,' said Nicki. 'He wandered about in the night ever since the incident with an intruder in the basement.'

'Yes, yes,' said the Commissar.

'He was vaguely threatening towards his wife and children ... spoke of discipline,' Nicki went on, shifting uncomfortably as if his strapped ribs hurt. 'Then he discovered that I had found his son's book.'

'The book,' sighed the Commissar. 'We have not seen the book. May request a transcript.'

Earth-shaking revelations were commonplace. They spoke of Sepp-Joseph-Buddy as if it had been known. Frau Bauer was Anja's mother... she had gone along with Limbard for her daughter's sake. They spoke of Jacobsen... his body had been taken to a police laboratory.

'... solved a mystery,' said Commissar Franke. 'Communication was not so goon in 1919. Jacobsen was done to death in the villa, very probably, and his luggage dispatched to the ferry in Ostend. It happened to sink. If it had *not* sunk...'

'A suicide,' said Kate, 'who slipped over the railing into the channel.'

'Exactly,' said the Commissar. 'At any rate we have the rest of the remains. It appeared during diving operations in the sixties. A young American soldier drowned in the Waldsee — they will drink and then take a swim. The skull that was found has been part of the Breitbach police museum since that time.'

The Commissar showed interest in Nicki's injuries. The nose not broken, ten stitches in the scalp, more in the cheek. Some concern about the bruising of his back, the broken ribs. Franke spoke of a charge of assault... Limbard would be charged with assault when the evidence had been assessed.

'I hope you believe me!' said Nicki, his poor voice faltering.

'Have you any idea what you look like?' said Kate, pressing his hand.

There was a nightmarish quality about the interview. She looked at the Commissar and did not trust him.

'Will Jason Limbard be taken into custody?' she asked.

The Steinberg was under seige, lights burning far into the night, even at the convent. The Limbard children were at the Villa Florian, with Anja and Frau Bauer. Could the security system keep Limbard out? Kate did not like to think of nights at the Forsthaus with Tante Adelheid and Peter — who had bravely called the fire brigade — while Jason roved the countryside, a wolfish fugitive.

'Limbard is dangerous!' said Nicki. 'Commissar, you must protect...'

Commissar Franke looked from Nicki to Kate with a most curious expression.

'A man's house,' he said, 'is his castle. English proverb, mmm? Herr Lenz, have you ever fallen down the stairs at the Villa Florian?'

'No,' said Nicki.

'Frau Reimann, were you treated by a psychiatrist for three years after your accident?'

'Yes,' said Kate. 'I can give you his name.'

The Commissar waved his hand.

'Herr Lenz, have you ever used hashish, heroin or cocaine?'

'No, never!' said Nicki.

'Frau Reimann, did you attempt to blackmail Jason Limbard?'

'*Hey, what is this*?' yelled Kate.

'Quiet!' snapped the Commissar. 'You are in a hospital. Herr Lenz, have you ever been charged with breach of contract by a client?'

'The charge was thrown out of court!'

'That will do!' said the Commissar. He shut his notebook, clicked his ballpoint pen loudly several times and stood up.

'Herr Limbard,' he said, 'was treated at a private clinic in Neu Isenburg for shock, exposure and bruises. His lawyers have outlined *his* side of the story.'

He turned at the door and said cheerfully: 'You should each consult a lawyer!'

'Just a minute!' said Kate. 'Has Limbard been charged with assault?'

'I don't have to answer any questions,' said the Commissar, still smiling.

'Oh, yes, you do!' said Kate.

She sprang up and found she was half a head taller than the Commissar.

'You have to answer to *me*!' she said fiercely. 'Right now, without any fooling around. Because I'm an American citizen, the stranger within your gates, and you stand for German justice. This man, Nicholas Lenz, is the victim of a cruel beating... am I right?'

'*Schön gut*!' Commissar Franke said urgently, making soothing motions with his hands. 'Yes! Yes, of course it does seem... the facts do seem to indicate...'

He slipped out of the door and left them alone.

'*Bastard*!'

She was not sure whether she meant Jason Limbard or the Police Commissar.

'Kate,' said Nicki, 'I love you! I have always loved you.'

'Hush!'

She bent and kissed a patch of skin, visible in the region of his left ear.

'You said so before, on the way here in the ambulance.'

'And so?' he persisted.

She was overwhelmed by a wave of tenderness. Nicki, dear Nicki, her old friend, her new love...

'Yes,' she said, surprised. 'Yes, I... I do love you. When this is all over we'll go away together and work it out.'

She kissed him again and he sank back on his pillows with a twist of his bandages that could have been a happy smile.

'Limbard won't get away with this legal nonsense,' he murmured.

A young chap in whites, his hair in a ponytail, ambled along to take care of the patient. He answered to Wilhelm and was a Civvy, a young man who chose to do civil duty rather than serve in the army. Kate took her way through the hospital corridors feeling bereft and lonely. As she came out of the elevator into the lofty spaces of the entrance lobby, someone called her name.

'Kate! Frau Reimann!'

There he was, a tall bearded young man, completely German in his grey parka, his thick-soled tramping shoes and in his firm, obligatory handshake. Yet she looked into his face and was able to see again the fat, overgrown boy by the roadside. She had helped him; he had saved her life.

'*Oh, Buddy*!'

Kate's eyes filled with tears. What did one say to someone who returned from the dead? They bought paper cups of coffee from a machine and sat down in the lobby. Roddy had been discharged from the hospital after an overnight stay; Armin was driving him back to the Villa Florian.

'I figured you might give me a lift,' grinned Buddy. 'How is Nicki Lenz?'

He had to tell his story to the police and to the American Consulate. One of the first rehearsals of this strange tale was for Kate, as they sat together near a large potted palm, looking out at the traffic passing on the Landstrasse.

'I felt very bad,' he said, 'like I wrote in the report, but there was some play-acting in it too. Hinting at suicide. I really did have some idea of running away, after leaving my passport and clothes and throwing the headstone in the lake. What I *didn't* say in the report was that I had Roddy's passport as well. I found the darn thing when I came in last from the car on our aborted trip to München. It fell to the ground when I opened my door. I was mad at poor old Rod for telling on you, Kate, so I hid it in the drawer of an old dresser in the downstairs bathroom.'

'Maybe the idea of an extra passport put the scheme in my

head... and it was only because the Old Man was so worried about... about your accident, Kate, that he forgot to collect my passport again. Anyway I had seen a bunch of young Americans, back packers, as we came through Frankfurt Airport and I thought I might hang around with people like that, go underground. I'd starve myself thin and get some glasses and use Roddy's passport.'

'You had no clothes!' said Kate. 'You left them.'

'I had an old work overall from a trunk in the cellar of the Villa Florian. It belonged to the boys, the young soldiers who were there with that bad guy, Leutnant Blümig, in 1945. When Franz Walther came by he saw a boy like himself in deep trouble. I started to cry, told him about Bodo. We had a language difficulty but we managed to understand each other. I knew it was a matter of life and death for me. I swore I was never going back to the Old Man. Franz saw what I was doing with the passport and the clothes. He said okay, and we went to the old Foresters' Hut, right deep in the woods. I lived there for a week. There was a hiding place under the floorboards, a kind of dug-out, Franz said it had been used by poachers. I hid there when the police came through one time, searching. When he had some days off we drove down to Bayern, before my family even left the villa.

'Franz brought me to the farm, the *Carmelhof*, owned by his cousin, Max Walther, I called him Onkel Max. He is married to Tante Clara, Armin is their youngest child, the only one left at home out of a family of six. They took me in. They all knew the story, more or less. The *Carmelhof* is out of the way; I stayed there all winter. By the time it was spring I spoke fluent German. I sounded like Armin.'

'The people in the village think I'm Franz's illegitimate son. They have a lot of understanding for extra kids back there on the farms, even if they're very pious, very Catholic. I was just *"der Franzl-Sepp"*, Franz's Josef. Franz took me and Armin climbing in the Alps in summer; I kept on growing and got a tan; I turned into a different person: Sepp Walther.'

'What did you do about identification?' asked Kate.

'There is something illegal about that,' said Buddy. 'Franz might have to get a lawyer. The only shady characters he knew were two guys from the Tyrol who smuggled birds. They caught falcons in the mountains and sold them to Arabian sheiks, for hawking. He sold them Roddy's passport and they got him a genuine identity card, not a passport but a *Personal Ausweis*. I'm down as Josef Walther.'

'I went to school in the village for two years. I guess Herr Bloch, the teacher was in on part of the story. When it was time for me to move on to the high school, it became too difficult with the documents. I dropped out. Herr Bloch coached me in Maths and German. I worked on the farm. I was Onkel Max's apprentice in farm management. We all knew that one day I would have to go back, become Buddy Limbard again.

'The Old Man, my real father, has never gone away. Franz had news of him buying the Villa Florian, he turned up on televison. We knew about the divorce and it made me feel better about Mom and the terrible thing I had done to her, pretending to be dead. If I had changed the situation enough so that she and Liss could get away from my father, then it was worth it. It wasn't just some crazy, selfish thing, running away.'

'Oh, Buddy,' said Kate. 'How will you tell her... your mother?'

'Through her friends, the two Episcopalian missionaries in Frankfurt, Sally and Joe Eberhart. They have called her minister, the Reverend Sam Fox, in Fort Lauderdale. I spoke to him. He's going to break the news.'

'I don't know how to say this,' said Kate, 'but I want you to know that I will do anything to spare your mother pain. I don't want to, well, sue anybody or take any action at all about what happened six years ago. It's over and done with. I wonder what we should do with... your book?'

'At least *I* have it,' he said. 'And you've read it. You know the truth. But I think the old Man will fight tooth and nail, Kate, to prove everyone else crazy. There's stuff in the book about ghosts... *that* would work against me in court. I hardly thought of that book for years... for months at a time I *was* Sepp Walther. Then I was eighteen, I wasnt't a juvenile any more, so I couldn't be sent back to my father. We figured it would be okay for me to come to Breitbach last summer and start looking around. I kept away from people who might recognise me... I look different. But I started thinking about the report poor old Buddy Limbard left behind in the trophy room.

'I thought I could easily get it back while the house was being renovated but that just wasn't possible. The gun rack was locked away in the cellar, then the villa was under security. The report got to be a kind of obsession with me. I knew that with the Old Man and Roddy back in the villa, it would only be a matter of time before *they* found it. Well, you know what happened... first we tried to sneak in past Frau Bauer...'

'And then you managed to hide in the basement!' said Kate.

'Kate, I'm sorry I gave you such a terrible fright. I might have talked to you but everything went so fast. I was out of my mind... that basement is not a good place to hide, believe me. I couldn't face my father, so I made a run for it. Armin was waiting on the other side of the wall. We had to send Franz in to pick up the pieces and leave a letter in the box for Nick. He was our last hope.'

'Buddy,' said Kate, 'what will you do... about Jason?'

'Let him cool off,' he said. 'Then I'll put out peace feelers. I ... I thought I might speak to him in some neutral place... American consulate maybe, or the Saxons' house. We might come to some agreement. I hear he acted pretty sad about losing a son.'

'That would be best,' said Kate.

But she was still afraid.

III

Nicki decided that this was one of the worst times of his life. He spent ten days in hospital and emerged sore and sick, threatened with financial stress and hellish injustice. His hopeful prediction – that Limbard would not get away with his legal nonsense – proved to be another grave misjudgement. Jason Limbard was going to make life uncomfortable for a number of people for a time-span of years. He played the role that he had perfected in public and embellished it with a touch of pathos. Generous, quick-tempered Jason Limbard had been preyed upon by a group of unstable and unscrupulous people. Drink and drugs played a part in the débacle. He second wife, who was now filing suit for divorce, had conspired with the incompetent decorator, Nicholas Lenz. The mad and embittered ex-wife of Jason's publisher had forced her way into his house. Limbard's attempts to discipline his two rebellious sons had failed. The elder son attacked him, the younger son, who had run off under curious circumstances in the company of an older man, had returned to threaten and blackmail his long-suffering father.

Limbard did not trust himself to return to the Villa Florian at this time, so his lawyers explained as they collected his car and clothes. The house held too many painful memories. He generously allowed his wife, Anja, to remain in the place, together with his son Roderick and daughter Melissa. It could only be a temporary arrangement so far as the child Melissa was concerned. She must soon go to a suitable boarding school, until new custody proceedings could be decided. A careful inventory of the Villa Florian was taken and the two damaged rooms were sealed, pending an examination by several independent assessors, hired by Limbard's lawyers and by Frau Vishinsky of Darmstadt, who represented Nicki and Kate.

The substance of Limbard's lying accusations came out piecemeal, from law office to law office, and were dreadfully hard to refute. Of all the persons ranged against Jason Limbard, including his first wife, far away in Florida, only he, Nicholas Lenz, had any money... while Limbard had a great deal. Franz Walther, for instance, stood to lose his pension if the courts took an unfavourable view of his rescue of Buddy Limbard.

Life went on. Nicki helped Kate move back to Darmstadt when her holidays were over. The weather had broken; the storms of autumn swept over the Steinberg. The very sight of the Villa Florian, in which he dare not set foot, on the advice of Frau Vishinsky, filled him with a raging sadness. As Kate drove off with Peter in her Ford Cortina it began to rain heavily. A figure huddled under a raincoat loomed up beside Nicki's car and tapped on the side window. He opened up and Frau Bauer slipped into the passenger seat.

'News from the front!' she said. 'Thought you and Frau Reimann should know.'

The light of battle was in her eye; he was glad that fate had placed Frau Bauer on *his* side after all.

'The police know Limbard is lying,' she said. 'I've got friends on the force who tip me off. He'll have to drop a couple of the really wild charges... kidnapping, for example, against Herr Walther.'

'Good God!'

'He certainly made a job of you,' she said.

She dropped her eyes, twisted her hands in her lap.

'Sorry,' she said. 'Sorry I went along with him. Thought I was doing the best for her, for my daughter. Had no idea he would take you to pieces.'

Nicki nodded, accepting her apology.

'How is Anja?' he asked.

'Ashamed,' she said. 'Marriage goes *kaput* after a week or so... it always looks bad.'

'Did she... love him?'

'Why not?' countered Frau Bauer. 'Her millionaire, her marvellous American. They had been together for six months. Nothing she couldn't put up with until after the knot was tied.'

Nicki felt his eyebrows fly up so that his scalp wound gave a twinge. Frau Bauer laughed grimly.

'Imagining all sorts of things, eh? He tormented her. Night after night. Let's leave it at that.'

'Do you hear anything of the Saxon family?'

'Yes, that's another thing,' said Frau Bauer. 'The Major is running what he calls a Peace Mission. Meeting between Limbard and Buddy, the long-lost son, together with a type from the American Embassy. Might do some good.'

Before she climbed out into the downpour she surveyed his dashboard and said: 'Lovely car. Pleasure to drive. You wouldn't believe it but I've driven in a rally or two.'

In the Darmstadt apartment he slept in Kate's bed... and she slept on the visitors' couch. He played with Peter's Lego castle and began to get well. He took part in a long, three-cornered, incoherent phone conversation with Andreas, calling from Capri. It was impossible to explain what had happened. What had they done to Diet Jason? Andreas wanted to know. Why was there nothing in the papers?

Nothing in the papers. It was a relief and at the same time a part of the black cloud that hung over them. No-one knew or cared about their distress. There was nothing for the respectable papers to report, as yet, and *Nacht Post*, twice shy, had blacklisted Jason Limbard, his family and his house. Not a line appeared concerning the goings on at the Villa Florian. Nicki and Kate looked in vain for the headline 'BACK FROM THE DEAD! Buddy-Joe returns!' in what Mencken had called Second Coming type.

Nicki tore himself away from convalescence in Kate's warm rooms, drove to München and attended to business. The shop, once his joy and care, was flourishing under the management of his two assistants. They looked at him as if *he* had come back from the dead. He had been absent exactly five weeks.

Life in the city soothed his shattered nerves. He enjoyed long foolish telephone conversations with Kate. He was too upset to get in touch with Andreas, who was back at work. He took part in a large charity concert, brushing up the text of two cabaret numbers: 'The Merry Peasant' and 'Capt'n Samstag', the horrible week-end sailor who accompanied himself on the piano accordian. Backstage at this extravaganza he encountered a strange scrap of gossip from one of the electricians: Jason Limbard had smashed a lamp and attacked an actor during the run-through of a quiz show.

The telephone woke him out of a deep sleep. He was still nervous of night alarms; for a moment he was back in the Villa Florian. Cries in the night. Music from the carousel. No! This was his own friendly apartment, smelling of books and coffee. The breathing silence at the end of the line told him that something was wrong. He asked who was there and after a long time there was a hoarse whisper. 'Lenz?' Yes, yes, who was it? What was the matter? 'Lenz... help... help me...'

The voice was dreadful: thick, choked with pain, dragging out every word. Now some German, not coherent, but he knew at last who was speaking. He asked questions. The receiver had not been replaced but the voice said no more. He hung up, and after a brief struggle with his common sense phoned Andreas.

It was an even more difficult call than he had imagined. Two in the morning, what in hell did he want? Andreas was stiff, angry, a stranger. What about Limbard?

'He's sick!' said Nicki. 'For God's sake, he sounded as if he overdosed. Is he at the Aurora House, tell me that?'

Yes, Jason was in his apartment. In fact, he had the flu. Why on earth would he call Nicki, after all that had been going on?

'My number,' said Nicki patiently. 'We've spoken of it before, remember? My number is the easiest thing in the world to remember because of all the threes.'

'I don't know,' said Andreas suspiciously.

'Get it through your head, this is an emergency!' said Nicki. 'Shall I ring the ambulance or will you?'

'We have a key,' said Andreas. 'Brigitte used it to water his herbs.'

'Call me when you've checked!'

'I insist that you come too!' said Andreas. 'How do I know this isn't some of your damned play-acting with Kate?'

Nicki shuddered, feeling his wounds burning. This was what he had feared, what had kept him from his old friend. Andreas believed some story that Jason had told him.

'I'll meet you at the apartment in twenty minutes,' he said, his voice just as cold.

It occured to him that he should not go at all. Frau Vishinsky would advise against it. He thought of the brandy he had had as a night-cap, and of the pain-killing tablets he still must take in order to sleep, then he ordered a cab. He entered the darkly glistening lobby of the Aurora House on the heels of a crowd of revellers, with balloons and streamers, who had been making a good start to the *Oktober Fest*.

The corridors were well-carpeted but square-cut and oppressive. He stepped off the elevator with a noisy group, including several pretty girls, and was relieved when they were swallowed up by the stifling anonymity of the place. Andreas, at the aprartment door, looked alarmed, the whites of his eyes showing in a tanned face.

'The phone is off the hook,' he said, 'and he doesn't answer the bell!'

'Go in, man!' urged Nicki. 'Quickly! I swear it's an emergency!'

Light burned in the tiny hallway and half-illuminated the single large room. The place was too hot and it stank of sickness – sweat and vomit. Nicki reached for the switches; one standard lamp had been overturned but the other showed the telephone hanging off a low table. There was movement on the rumpled sleeping couch. Then came sounds that raised the hair on Nicki's head; hoarse, agonised, inhuman. Every breath seemed to shake the room; a cough rattled in the chest.

'Jesus!' whispered Andreas. 'What is it? Jay! Jay, are you hurt?'

'The phone!' ordered Nicki.

They stumbled across the shadowy room; Andreas gathered up the phone and carried it back into the hall. Nicki stood beside the couch. The sick man was deathly pale and beaded with sweat; the flesh seemed to have fallen away from his cheeks and the strong cords of his neck. Mucus hung in strings from his half open mouth. He lay very straight, arms and legs stretched, quivering. Nicki squeezed past Andreas into the shower room, wet a towel and rushed back.

As he wiped at the dreadful mouth Jason's eyes flew open, wide and sightless. A powerful spasm drove his head back into the pillow, made rigid the muscles of his neck and jaw, then his chest. His whole body arched, creaking like a bow; he rose up, balanced momentarily on head and heels, then toppled side ways, still in the grip of the convulsion. At last it passed off with a weak flailing of all his limbs. His eyes snapped about; he gasped for breath, with nostrils dilating and his mouth opening painfully.

The ambulance was on its way and Andreas had done even better. He had raised a doctor, another tenant of the Aurora House, who was on the board at Lorbeer Verlag. Andreas came closer and spoke gently to Jason Limbard. Nicki could not speak a word, it was as if his head and neck ached in sympathy. He groped about in the disgusting room, set the lamp upright, poured himself a Bourbon from the bottle Jason kept for visitors, and choked getting it down.

Andreas cried out: Jason had gone into another violent convulsion. The doctor, a solid middle-aged man, still wearing his dinner suit, came tapping at the open door of the apartment. He rushed across the room and pushed Andreas aside. When the spasms subsided he bent very close to the patient and began questioning fiercely. At last he gave an injection. There was a silence broken only by the sick man's gasping breath.

'Doctor?' demanded Andreas. 'Doctor, what is it?'

The doctor was behaving strangely. He switched on other lamps and began peering into the corners of the room. He came up to the two younger men with an expression of fear and wonder.

'Is there a dog?' he asked. 'Does Herr Limbard own a dog?'
'No!' said Andreas. 'A dog?'
'Is *that* what you think?' whispered Nicki.
'It looks very much as if...' the doctor was whispering too. 'Of course one must rule out...'

The ambulance arrived with a young doctor who conferred with his colleague. As Jason Limbard was carried away, one of the ambulance men made the sign of the cross. Andreas went with them, leaving Nicki to lock up the apartment. He tip-toed about, reluctant to touch anything, in the grip of an age-old fear. He washed his hands with hot water and soap, dried them with his own handkerchief and fled.

He escaped from the Aurora House and walked the streets until it was light. He came past a florist's shop, just as the shutters were being rolled up, and persuaded the woman to sell him a bunch of red roses. He took a tram ride to the English Garden, misty and chill at this hour. There were joggers about and people walking their dogs. He chose a lonely spot where the river was wide and still and threw the roses one by one into the water. He knew that he was trying to make an end of mystery, ill-fortune, madness, death.

When he got back to his own apartment the phone was ringing. It was Andreas, wanting to know where in hell he had been? Andreas was in tears. The diagnosis had been confirmed. It was rabies. *Tollwut*. Jason Limbard was already in a coma. The phone call to Nicki was his last communication. His situation had been hopeless for days. He had been spared a little by simply not knowing what was the matter with him. Victims of the disease generally suffered great terror, knowing that their fate was sealed.

Jason Limbard died in the evening at 19.00 hours. His contacts in Bayern and in Hessen, beginning with Nicki and Andreas, were all innoculated. It was some time before the source of infection was known but in the end Melissa, the only witness, remembered. Her father, she said, had been bitten by a squirrel in the woods.

Nicki, contemplating this cruel death, felt deeply divided. Limbard was widely mourned; following a hasty private cremation there was a large memorial service organised by Andreas Reimann. Anja Schönfeld Limbard represented the family; she was also Jason's main heir. He had not revoked his will; she had not got very far with the filing of her suit for divorce.

Nicki felt a vile relief spreading through all those whom he regarded as Jason's victims, himself included. The cloud hanging over them had gone. As Frau Bauer put it: '*Der Spuk ist vorbei.*' Nicki refused to believe that Jason Limbard's death had been deserved, or that it had been timely, or that it smacked of 'poetic justice'. He would admit no hint of any cruel design.

Chapter 13
If Winter Comes

On a Saturday morning, two weeks before Christmas, snow began to fall on the Steinberg. The lawns of the Villa Florian were thickly carpeted before midday. Kate and Nicki walked around the dining room and gazed at the new ceiling. His team had made the repair with speed and precision. Anja had demolished an edifice of law-suits, assessors, counter-claims and stopped cheques in order for him to complete the work.

'It's a different room!' said Kate. 'The light... everything is different.'

The new overhead lamp was simpler, the room was more evenly lit.

'The atmosphere has changed,' said Nicki.

The table was extended and set for eight. The room, in fact the whole house, smelled of Christmas cookies. As they went into the kitchen, Frau Bauer was taking another batch out of the oven.

'Hands off!'

'Give us some to take to the children!' begged Nicki.

Frau Bauer, for no reason that anyone could fathom, had taken a liking to Kate. She gave her a twinkly look, slipped her a handful of the warm cookies.

'Spoil their lunch!' she said.

They put on their coats, and at the north-west corner of the house they found a big girl and a small boy, well wrapped-up.

'Look!' said Peter. 'Frau Moor is doing her snow-plough'

'Hey, she's a snow cat!' said Melissa.

The black cat had been set down on the wide untrodden spaces of the south lawn. She placed her two front paws together and skidded around in circles, sending up a cloud of snow. They laughed, munching cookies, and applauded this marvellous performance. As an encore Frau Moor raced up and down with her tail up. Melissa and Peter ran after her. The snow was full of footprints and cat tracks.

'Inside!' called Kate. 'Lunch is nearly ready. Time to come and wash!'

She slipped her arm through Nicki's and they strolled along to the north lawn. They admired the *tannen*, the north wall of the villa with its hooded figure, the starry balconies. They saw a ghost: Buddy Limbard, alias Sepp Walther, standing alone looking up into the branches of the tree.

Kate often asked what would happen to Buddy and to Roddy? She and Nicki talked it over in bed, in the Darmstadt apartment or in the Forsthaus guestroom, during the long loving hours of the night. What would happen to them? What happened to children or young people who suffered, who had dangerous adventures? Where were the boy soldiers, the orphans, the children whose lives had been disarranged? Jason Limbard had been driven and mishandled as a boy, so had Franz Walther. There was no end to it.

Now, walking around the north lawn in the snow, Nicki thought he had a glimpse of truth and tried to explain it to Kate. Play-acting. Long sustained games of hide and seek. Buddy's long masquerade. More than a hint of childishness even in the person who had helped him most Franz Walther. Jason Limbard's insane bullying and his struggle to hide it from the world. Was this what happened to children who had a bad time?

Buddy hailed them in flawless back-country Bavarian.

'Where are the boys?' asked Kate.

'We've got something going,' he grinned. 'A surprise. Roddy and Armin are working on it in the garage.'

A beautiful lady appeared on one of the starry balconies and announced that lunch was ready. Anja wore a black and white patterned sweater. She allowed herself half mourning: black and white, sometimes purple or grey. Kate saw how things would go with the *châtelaine* of the Villa Floria. She would lead a busy, cultivated social life. Already she went to coffee with the banker's wife in the new villa. She would re-marry. As Frau

Bauer had pointed out, the first millionaire is the most difficult. She admired the understanding and tact that Anja showed towards her three step-children... and she would have the opportunity to show more.

On the afternoon of that same day Anja drove off in her new Polo to Frankfurt Airport, with Roddy and Melissa. They waited, Tante Adelheid, Kate and Nicki, in the snug living room of the Forsthaus and passed the time sorting the decorations for the tree. Peter played with his cars then hung about downstairs, awed by the stillness of the adults.

'Too much has happened,' opined Tante Adelheid. 'Oh, Katherine, when I think... '

'There they are!' said Nicki.

Kate had made her decision.

'We must all go! You too, Pete!'

So they hurried across the road as the outside lights came on at the Villa Florian. Roderick Limbard was on the steps, and in the lighted hallway Kate saw a woman who had subtly changed. Mary Limbard was still pretty and youthful but somehow more solid. Her fragile nervous manner had gone. There was silence as Kate came into the hall, and there was only one thing for her to do. She embraced Mary; they held each other tight and wept. Peter let himself be kissed by Melissa's mother. Anja said softly: 'Come.'

She led Mary towards the family room and they all trailed after the two women. Kate saw that the doors to the new terrace were wide open; she held Nicki's hand tightly. Roddy stood at the doorway and called: 'Okay? Can you see us?'

'Okay,' said a voice from the darkness.

Then the switch was pressed and white lights flowered from top to bottom of the *tannenbaum*. Mary Limbard went forward stiffly and saw who was standing beside the tree. She gave a cry and ran out over the snow and Buddy took her in his arms.

So the winter season when the ghosts were kind came to the Steinberg. On their snowy walks Kate confided to Nicki that she had never completely trusted Christmas; it promised more than it could deliver. The celebrations developing that year in the Villa Florian and in the Forsthaus were warm but muted.

Tante Adelheid said that it felt like a war-time Christmas. There were reunions and farewells. The Saxon family came to call. Franz Walther and Armin drove off down to Bayern, to the *Carmelhof*.

In the Villa Florain there was really nothing more for Nicki to do. He found himself making work, straightening picture frames, altering the position of the objects d'art. He was listening, feeling for the least trace of those lost ones but finding nothing.

More than once he sat alone in the restored trophy room. The dais had been removed. On the writing desk Anja had placed a silver vase of hothouse roses beside the photograph of Magnus Jacobsen in its silver frame. He considered the circumstances surrounding the architect's strange death. These meditations were nothing like glimpses he and others had had of the savage past.

The pathologists had determined that Jacobsen had had a weak heart: he had died of a massive heart attack following a fight or a beating. Nicki supposed that a mummified corpse sixty years old was at least as easy to examine as the mummy of an Egyptian pharoah. He believed he saw traces of ill-health in the new-found photograph of the young man.

He thought he knew some of the facts now and they were shocking enough. The Baron quarrelled with his architect and did not want him to leave the villa. Blümig used his fists, it came to a fight and Magnus Jacobsen's weak heart gave out. Tamara Paige put an end to any plans there might have been for calling this an accident or a death from natural causes. Blümig and his master, Wolfgang von Sommer, were left with a headless body which was thrust out of sight. '*You cannot say it was a natural death...*'

The heart of the mystery remained untouched. How could she have done such a thing? What aroused the beautiful young English girl to such a perverse and ferocious act, an act which shocked even that hardened old sinner, the Baron? What did TP feel for Jacobsen? What did the Baron feel for his two gifted young protégés? What part did the house itself, or the power that lived in the house, play in their dance of death?

Now all of them were gone. The artists' colony in München had provided a modest grave for Tamara Paige in the

Protestant corner of a large suburban cemetery. The Baron's ashes, enclosed in a basalt urn, were in the family vault at Kassel. Jacobsen had been laid to rest in the cemetery at Breitbach; the Sisters and Tante Adelheid stood at his grave, as did Nicki and Kate. An old man, summoned by Sister Florentine, gave a reading from the works of the mystic, Emmanuel Swedenborg.

Nicki had no time for cemeteries. He did not join Kate and the four old women as they visited the graves of Blümig and of the three boys who had died at the Villa Florian in the summer of '45. The cemetery was beautifully kept with winding paths, old trees and many flowers. Nicki was parked outside a handsome old white house, a kindergargen, decorated for Advent, with visitors streaming in to a Christmas bazaar. Between these two bright places there was a wilderness, untended, overgrown, its monuments fallen, its iron gates chained and locked to keep out vandals: the Jewish cemetery. Ghosts walked everywhere; there was no hallowed ground. One could only remember the dead and beg them to lie still.

On the twentieth of December Kate was sweeping snow away from the Forsthaus gate. The weather continued unseasonably cold and snowy. Breitbach was known for disappointing greenish Decembers but this year Christmas would definitely be white. She was so absorbed in her work that she jumped when Nicki loomed up and laid a hand on her arm.

'You're freezing,' he said. 'Come inside.'

'I was thinking about a painting,' she admitted.

They were alone in the warm kitchen of the Forsthaus; he thawed her out with cognac, put the kettle on for tea.

'Did you hear the phone?' he asked.

'No,' said Kate. 'What was it? Has something happened?'

'It was for me. From Miriam. From my agent in Hollywood.'

'Nicki! That's marvellous! A part?'

A featured role. The very thing that Miriam, at any rate, had been waiting for. The director wanted *him*, yes, quite definitely, and the accent would be Hungarian this time. Leader of a gypsy orchestra who helps the hero to escape and loses the girl. Goodbye Rudi. Hello Lazlo.

'I might have had to fake it with a violin.' he said, 'but she was thrilled when I admitted to the piano accordian.'

He took Kate's cold hand and laid it against his warm cheek.

'You will come, won't you, Kate? You and Pete?' he asked anxiously. 'We have to be there on January 7th.'

'Yes,' said Kate. 'Yes, we'll come!'

They talked things over very coolly, everything that would have to be done. There would be no problem with Peter or Andreas. In fact things would work out well... Andreas was going to be in the United States in the summer and the boy could spend time with his father.

'It's warm on the west coast,' Kate said wistfully.

'Hot!' cried ;Nicki. 'Hot, baking hot. You have to swim to get cool. Petey can swim in the pool.'

'Where will we live?'

'In a movie mansion,' he said. 'How do you feel about Art Deco?'

They sat hand in hand, staring blindly at the warm German kitchen, and gave themselves over to thoughts of the New World.

There was still time for one more revenant. As Kate and Nicki returned from an afternoon walk on the twenty-third of December, they passed a man trudging up towards the convent. He was getting on in years but fresh-faced, dressed in a thick, shabby overcoat and a fur hat with its ear flaps tied up. He gave them a cheerful *'Grüss Gott!'*

At the gates of the Villa Florian they found Frau Bauer waiting with Melissa and Peter, an unusual combination, all moved by curiosity.

'See that man?' said Melissa. 'He wanted to see over the house.'

'A Pole. Probably looking for a job of work,' said Frau Bauer. 'Spoke good German. Told some tale of being stationed here during the war.'

'Did you show him over?' asked Kate.

'Told him to come back in the spring if he was interested in a bit of gardening,' said Frau Bauer. 'He asked for the Sisters so we sent him up the hill.'

'His name,' announced Peter, 'was Thaddeus Boronovski.'

Nicki ran out into the roadway and looked up the long snowy slope.

'*Teddy*!' he cried. 'By God, it was Teddy!'

The man was out of sight. The Sisters would be delighted to see him again.

'He knew this place all right,' said Melissa. 'He gave me a holy medal to hang in the house.'

'*Um die Gespenster fernzuhalten*,' said Peter and translated helpfully. 'To keep away the ghosts.'

The grown-ups exchanged glances. They bent to examine the small silver medal stamped with the image of a young man dressed as a roman soldier: St Florian, the patron saint of the city of Krakow.